DATE DUE		
8-20-00			

Daughter of Zion, A

The Zion Chronicles #2

Thoene, Bodie

Books by Brock and Bodie Thoene

THE ZION COVENANT

Vienna Prelude
Prague Counterpoint
Munich Signature
Jerusalem Interlude
Danzig Passage
Warsaw Requiem

THE ZION CHRONICLES

The Gates of Zion
A Daughter of Zion
The Return to Zion
A Light in Zion
The Key to Zion

THE SHILOH LEGACY

In My Father's House
A Thousand Shall Fall
Say to This Mountain

SAGA OF THE SIERRAS

The Man From Shadow Ridge
Riders of the Silver Rim
Gold Rush Prodigal
Sequoia Scout
Cannons of the Comstock
The Year of the Grizzly
Shooting Star

NON-FICTION

Writer to Writer

THE ZION CHRONICLES/BOOK TWO

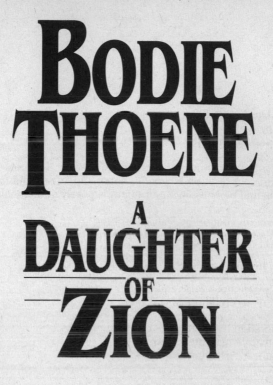

BODIE THOENE

A DAUGHTER OF ZION

BETHANY HOUSE PUBLISHERS
MINNEAPOLIS, MINNESOTA 55438

A Daughter of Zion
Copyright © 1987
Bodie Thoene

Cover illustration by Dan Thornberg,
Bethany House Publishers staff artist.

Published by Bethany House Publishers
A Ministry of Bethany Fellowship International
11300 Hampshire Avenue South
Minneapolis, Minnesota 55438

Printed in the United States of America by
Bethany Press International
Minneapolis, Minnesota 55438

Library of Congress Cataloging-in-Publication Data

Thoene, Bodie, 1951–
   A daughter of Zion.

   (The Zion chronicles ; bk. 2)
     1. Israel—History—1948–1949—Fiction.
I. Title. II. Series: Thoene, Bodie, 1951–   Zion
chronicles ; bk. 2.
PS3570.H46D3   1987   813'.54   87–8064
ISBN 0–87123–940–X (pbk.)
ISBN 0–7642–2108–6 (mass market)

For Brock,
my Moshe.

Pass through, pass through the gate!
Prepare the way for the people.
Build up, build up the highway!
Remove the stones.
Raise a banner for the nations.

The Lord has made proclamation
to the ends of the earth:
"Say to the Daughter of Zion,
'See, your Savior comes!'"

Isaiah 62:10, 11a

BODIE THOENE (Tay-nee) began her writing career as a teen journalist for her local newspaper. Eventually her byline appeared in prestigous periodicals such as *U.S. News and World Report*, *The American West*, and *The Saturday Evening Post*. After leaving an established career as a writer and researcher for John Wayne, she began work on her first historical fiction series, THE ZION CHRONICLES. From the beginning her husband, BROCK, has been deeply involved in the development of each book. His degrees in history and education have added a vital dimension to the accuracy, authenticity, and plot structure of the Zion books. The Thoenes' unusual but very effective writing collaboration has also produced three other major historical fiction series with Bethany House Publishers.

Acknowledgment

With much love, I wish to thank my three oldest children, Rachel Thoene, Jacob Thoene, and Luke Thoene, for their faithful help and loving support as work continues on The Zion Chronicles. They have shouldered responsibilities without complaint and have spent a lifetime of sharing parents with a plot line. Together we celebrate the completion of every project with joy. Only their love and enthusiasm make it possible for this work to be done. They have made my work their own, and without them there would be no story.

Contents

Part Three: The Passage, Late January 1948

Prologue

The drumming of the battering rams had not ceased for three days and nights. Those few who remained alive within the walls of the Temple were half mad with the thunder that echoed from the stones.

Elizabeth clutched the sleeping boy closer to her at the thought of what would come when the gates finally collapsed. Her eyes lingered on his tousled head. Gently she touched his forehead, then his ear, and stroked his cheek with the tips of her fingers. What hopes she had had for him on the day of his birth! He, a firstborn son of the house of Levi, would serve the Lord in His holy temple in Jerusalem. But now she knew that it was not destined to be. Aaron, her son, the only child of her womb, was to die with her. With them died the hopes of her people.

Her hand clutched the mezuzah Enoch had given her on their wedding day. The delicate gold tube glistened as it caught the moonlight. Carved on it in tiny letters was the promise she and Enoch had chosen together to mark the path of their life: "I have loved you with an everlasting love   ." But all was trampled now under the feet of the conquerors. And the love of her heart lay sleeping in her arms, soon to wake no more.

The child stirred and gazed at his mother silently as she stared in sleepless heartache at the scene before her. Finally he spoke, "Mama, I am thirsty. May we not have water now?"

She nodded and helped him stand on spindly legs. The last of the food had gone days ago, but still there was water in abundance in the Temple. Aqueducts and cisterns crisscrossed below the courtyard, carrying water from the springs in the Kidron Valley. They might die of hunger, but the ancient kings of Israel had made certain the people of Jerusalem would not die of thirst.

She picked Aaron up and stepped carefully around those who slept on the stones in the Court of Women. The thunder of the rams boomed a deadly cadence to their fitful sleep. Tears filled Elizabeth's eyes as she cradled Aaron's head and hugged him even closer to her.

"Where is Papa?" he asked.

"Gone, son. Hush now. Just a moment more and there will be water." She choked back a sob at the thought of her brave and wonderful Enoch. One week before, he had slipped beyond the walls of the city in search of roots. He had not returned. The next morning a priest had told her. Enoch was one of the hundreds who hung, crucified, beside the road that led to Mount Zion. She had climbed the walls herself, refusing to believe that one so brave and strong and good could have been taken to die such a death. She had to see it for herself. And as her eyes followed the outstretched arm of the priest, pointing to where Enoch hung, her heart had died within her. Had it not been for Aaron, she would have flung herself from the wall onto the rocks below. Instead, she had chosen to live one more hour, one more day, for the hope of their son's life.

"Is Papa coming back soon?" the boy asked.

"Hush now, Aaron. There is water here."

She approached the dark forms of four young zealots who stood beside the uncovered cistern. They peered down into its black depths. "It's here. I have found it," a hollow cry echoed up from beneath the ledge.

"But the water. How deep is the water?" a man called from the side of the cistern.

"Only above my knee. The way is narrow. If we were well fed, we could never make it. But here is the way out."

The men had not seen her; they were too filled with hope that they might escape from the prison of their own making.

She spoke suddenly and too loudly, causing them to start and turn menacingly toward her and the boy. "Have you found the way of escape?" she asked incredulously.

"Where did you come from?" A young scarecrow of a man took a step toward her.

"We came for water," she answered, holding Aaron even closer.

"Well, now everyone in the courtyard will know, and the people will run screaming from the pool until every Roman in the camp will find the route of escape." The big zealot's voice was filled with disgust.

"You can take us with you." Elizabeth spoke in a rush.

"Or kill you where you stand," said another man, moving a step nearer her. The blade of his sword glinted in the moonlight. "It would save her from being raped by the Romans, eh?" he said menacingly.

"No, wait." The scarecrow stepped between them. "She has a child to care for." He reached a hand out and placed it on Aaron's tiny back. "I had a son." Then he demanded. "Who are you, daughter of Zion?"

"I am Elizabeth. Wife of Enoch the Levite who was crucified."

He nodded, then stood silently for a moment.

"Come on!" the man in the cistern whispered hoarsely. "You waste precious moments."

"Kill her!" snarled the big man.

"Will the child cry out if we take you with us?"

"You will not cry, will you, Aaron?" she pleaded with the boy.

"No, Mama. I will be brave like Papa."

"Then come on, woman," the scarecrow took her arm and helped her into the cool water of the cistern. As she slipped over the rough ledge of stone, the leather thong that held her gold mezuzah caught and broke, sending the gift of Enoch plunging to the depths of the cistern.

"My charm!" she cried, tearing at the water.

"Come on, woman. Leave it! Leave it!"

"But it is all I have left from my husband!"

"Do you want to die, you fool?" The scarecrow took her roughly by the arm. "You have a child. You have the son of your husband's body to think of. Follow me!" he commanded. The torch inside the narrow aqueduct licked the ceiling and reflected off the water and walls, which were so narrow and twisting that they pressed their bodies sideways to pass through.

Elizabeth cupped her hand and dipped water, then put it to the thirsty lips of Aaron. He slurped noisily and asked for more as the zealots pressed on ahead of them.

Elizabeth rushed after them, the water weighing down her robes and holding her back.

"Where are we going, Mama?" Aaron asked as the light bobbed away down the long tunnel.

"To freedom!" Elizabeth gasped. "To life."

PART 1

The Journey
January 1, 1948

"We have one treasure left—the daring after despair."

Yitzhak Lamden

1 Jerusalem

The tiny lamb roast looked pitiful and forlorn in the center of the large black roasting pan. Rachel wiped her hands on her apron and frowned as she studied the chunks of lamb she had skewered together. Then she pursed her lips and squeezed the garlic press, counting tiny drops as they fell on the meat. "There is not much left of this little lamb," Rachel winked and smiled down at Yacov, who watched her with rapt attention. "However small it is we must treat it with respect, eh? When Ellie drives me to the bus station, you must remember to remind the good Professor Moniger to baste it, or it will shrivel up like shoe leather!"

Yacov wrinkled his face in disgust at the thought, and adjusted his eye patch. "At least you are staying long enough to season the meat!" he sighed. "Good and kosher, like Grandfather likes it. Such a meal! But I do wish you could stay and eat it with us. Lamb and cabbage rolls and good white challah bread to eat! This Gentile New Year is a very nice holiday, I think. And David has promised an American radio program later on, too. Can you not stay with us for this evening and go into the Old City later?"

Rachel took Yacov's chin in her hand. It did indeed seem strange to her that she would be called to such an important and dangerous task when all she truly wanted to do was putter around in the kitchen and care for Yacov and live in peace at last. Often she gazed wistfully at Moshe when he was not looking, and her heart had softened and filled with dreams of what her life could have been if it were not for the brand she carried on her arm and in her heart. "Little brother," she said tenderly, "I must go. I must do this thing for our people. And for myself."

"Yes, sister," he scuffed the toe of his shoe against the tile floor, his chin quivering slightly. "But will you come back?"

"Yes." She lifted his chin higher and kissed his cheek lightly. "I will come back."

"When?"

"Soon."

"Tomorrow?"

"Soon. Just remind the professor to baste the lamb, eh? Promise?"

Yacov nodded. "I heard the captain, Luke Thomas, saying that it is very dangerous in the Old City. He says it is important that you come out soon."

"It is not good for you to listen in on private talks of Captain Thomas and Moshe and the professor," Rachel chided, turning back to her work.

"You told me to ask if they need more coffee. Can I help if they talk in front of me while I wait so I am not interrupting their conversation?" He sniffed and fiddled nervously with his eye patch again. "I heard what the English captain brought for you inside the meat and bread and cabbages. You must be very careful, Rachel. I would be very unhappy if you get blown up so soon after I have just found you again."

"So would I, little brother." She smiled and mussed his hair, then laughed aloud at the thought of all the things Captain Thomas had brought with him, smuggled inside tonight's feast. Inside the loaves of bread were two disassembled pistols. The chunk of lamb concealed a hand grenade and the cabbages carried detonators. Less than three hours from now, Rachel would board the Number Two bus, a courier carrying weapons to the nearly defenseless soldiers who clung to the besieged Jewish Quarter behind the ancient walls of the Old City of Jerusalem. There were other things that she hoped to accomplish there, among her people. But these were secret thoughts that she had not shared with

18

Moshe, nor could she share them with the bright young child who stood beside her now in the kitchen. "Tell me, Yacov," she questioned, "do they want more coffee?"

"Only the professor and Moshe. Captain Thomas would like tea if you have it."

With a sigh, Rachel filled the kettle, then hurried down the hallway to Howard's study where Luke, Howard and Moshe spoke in hushed tones about the defenses of the Old City.

"Fourteen rifles?"

"That is all. And they are all ancient, I'm afraid."

"And how are Israel's most ancient weapons?" Howard asked Luke.

Luke cleared his throat uncomfortably. "Safe. Hidden in plain sight." He hesitated a moment, then said, "Word is that both the Mufti and the British government are offering several hundred thousand pounds for the scrolls."

Moshe laughed bitterly, "The British would like to display them in London, and the Mufti would enjoy burning them at a Muslim rally, eh?"

Howard nodded. "I think we have nearly convinced everyone concerned that the scrolls were lost that night in Bethlehem."

"Good," Luke said softly. "A thought occurred to me." He frowned and twisted his moustache nervously. "I cannot even presume to know the worth of such things, but surely it would be enough to purchase weapons for an entire army."

A heavy silence filled the room until at last Howard spoke. "That is out of the question, Luke. I know you are offering a practical suggestion as a soldier but . . ."

Luke coughed and shrugged. "Just a thought," he said apologetically. "At any rate, Howard, I will be leaving for England in a couple of months. I can take them out to safety then if you like."

"I don't see any other way to smuggle them out of

Jerusalem," Moshe said. "I have the strongest feeling we are being watched."

"You need to know that if anything happens to me before I return home"—Luke lowered his voice—"I have left my shell collection to you, Howard."

Howard chuckled. "That would be nice in my display cases."

Rachel hesitated at the half-open door, gazing tenderly at the back of Moshe's head. His hair was mussed and he wore a bathrobe draped over the heavy plaster cast on his arm. A feeling of warmth filled her as she studied the dark hair and the tilt of his head. Her breath caught for an instant; then she looked away, suddenly ashamed of the emotion she felt for this kind and gentle man. *He deserves so much more than a woman like me*, she thought, closing her eyes tightly. *Someone better than I am.* She knocked softly on the door to announce her presence; then she moved quickly into the room, not daring to look at Moshe, although she felt his gaze on her.

"Just the girl!" cried Howard enthusiastically.

"Two coffees? And tea for you, Captain Thomas?"

"Yes, thank you." Luke cleared his throat, concealing his grin at the longing he read in Moshe's eyes.

Rachel gathered the empty cups onto a tray and hurried from the study back to the now empty kitchen. She was trembling and breathless, simply from being near Moshe. Setting the tray on the counter, she stared at the cup she knew was his. Slowly she wrapped her fingers around it, then raised it to her mouth, gently touching her lips to the rim where his lips had touched. "Oh, Moshe," she whispered, tears pushing against her eyelids. "I cannot come back here. I must not see you again. It can never be. I must not let myself love you. Not now. Not ever."

2 Zion Gate

Captain Luke Thomas pulled up the collar of his heavy gray overcoat and impatiently tapped the muzzle of his sten gun against his thigh. He and six British soldiers under his command huddled in cold misery beneath the arch of Zion Gate and peered out at the snowflakes that dusted Jerusalem. Snow clung to the rugged face of the massive stone wall surrounding the Old City, decorating the buildings of the New City like icing on a Middle Eastern gingerbread house. Two inches covered the cobblestone streets of the Old City as well as the muddy rain-rutted New City road that wound around Mount Zion and up the rocky Valley of Kidron to the gate where Luke and his small band of men now waited. *Beneath its white blanket,* Luke mused, *the Faithful City seems to be at peace. The bloodstains of Jews and Arabs are hidden.* Ragged mountains of twisted metal and shattered concrete, where only a week before the cries of the latest bombing victims had been heard, now blended in silent harmony with the soft contours of surrounding buildings. It was as if God had grown weary of watching the agony of hatred that divided Jew and Arab and Englishman; that contorted the face of the Holy City He had wept over.

"Oh, Jerusalem, Jerusalem," Luke said softly as he gazed through the white curtain toward the Mount of Olives. He sighed heavily; it would only be a short time before this beauty was once again stained red with the blood of innocents caught in the crossfire between the Jews and Arabs who sought to claim the land as their own.

"What's that you say, Captain?" asked gruff-voiced

Sergeant Hamilton, whose perpetually ruddy face and portly stature had earned him the nickname "Ham."

"Nothing." Luke glanced down at him and half-smiled. "Nothing," he finished lamely. "Just thinking."

"Beautiful, ain't it, sir?" The round little Sergeant shoved his hat down farther on his head and dug the toe of a spit-shined boot into the edge of the snow that ringed their shelter. "Must've looked like this when *He* was here, if you know what I mean, sir. Hard to believe the Jews and Arabs are out there now plotting ways to blow each other's brains out. And us in the middle, eh? One thing's for certain." He sniffed and wiped his nose with a fresh white handkerchief. "There's not a man among us won't be glad to be back in England and out of this mess, if you know what I mean, sir."

"Aye," agreed one of the men. "I'm for a bit of warm ale in an English pub."

"Only four months, lad, and we're bound for home and England," declared Ham.

A small cheer echoed from beneath the arch. "Home and England!" shouted the men.

"God save the King!" cheered another.

"And God save the Jews when we're gone, eh, Captain?" remarked Ham, stepping up beside Luke, who continued to gaze out at the falling snow.

"It will take God to save the Jews, Ham," answered Luke quietly. "The Arab irregulars are pouring into the country and the High Command has demanded the blood of every living Jew in Palestine. Indeed, God save the Jews. They dare not hope in anything else. I'm afraid that once we're gone, they'll have no other protection against five armed Arab nations."

"Not with the arms embargo against 'em, eh, Captain? Not that I'm questioning policy, you understand, sir, but don't you think it's somewhat of a shame that this won't even be a fair fight? I mean, the poor staggerin' beggars ain't got a rifle between 'em."

"Unfortunately, Ham, until England officially leaves, the Jews cannot be a sovereign nation. Which means

22

they cannot purchase arms for defense. And when we're gone . . ."

"It'll be too late for 'em then. Sam Baxter told me every Arab nation has tanks and men on the border waitin' to invade the moment the last British soldier heads for home. The Yids ain't going to have time to buy weapons then, if you know what I mean, Captain."

Luke nodded grimly, frowning at the memory of the Mufti's words, "*We will drive the Jews into the sea.*" Haj Amin Husseini, Grand Mufti of Jerusalem, had already begun to wage war against his most hated enemies, the Jewish population of Palestine. Supplied by the bordering Arab nations, his Jihad Moquades, the Holy Strugglers of Islam, had begun their assault against the infidel Jews through terrorism and sniping. Daily, as the bodies of Jews were carried to the Mount of Olives for burial, the Jewish terrorist gang, the Irgun, had begun to answer violence with violence against the innocent Arab population. *Crying out for an eye for an eye and a tooth for a tooth is about to leave Jerusalem blind and toothless,* thought Luke. The pious Hassidic Jews who lived and worshiped inside the walls of the Old City were ringed about by hostile Arabs and already virtually cut off from the rest of the Yishuv. Only one thin lifeline ran from Zion Gate into the New City.

Luke glanced at his watch, straining now to see its dial in the blue dusk of the first evening of the New Year, 1948. It was half-past five. The Number Two bus, the final bus to Zion Gate, was already thirty minutes late. It was the most dangerous bus ride in the city. The faded blue armor-clad vehicle left the safety of the Egged station in the heart of Jewish Jerusalem and wound through the Arab sectors of the city until it reached its final destination: Zion Gate, and the Old City.

Luke's men grumbled irritably beneath the arch of the locked gate. The armored British personnel carrier that escorted the bus also brought the guards who were to relieve them of their thankless duty guarding the only entrance into the Jewish Quarter of the Old City. A late

23

bus meant late suppers and half an hour longer of cold feet and noses.

" 'ow long we gotta wait, Cap'n? We ain't none of us slep' off last night's 'angover yet," moaned Smiley Hitchcock, whose unhappy expression belied his name.

"Aye," agreed the others. "Wha' gives those blighters the right to dally on our time?"

Luke sniffed and rubbed a gloved hand across his cold cheek. "Steady on now, lads. Perhaps the bus has gotten bogged in the snow."

The thought of the relief guards up to their knees in a snowdrift digging out a bus with army issue spades was a comforting one to the small band. They leaned back against the stone archway and silently contemplated the plight of their tardy companions with satisfaction. Here, at least, they were out of the bad weather.

"Better she bogs down comin' than goin'!" Smiley shuddered at the thought of battling a snowdrift while attempting to guard a Jewish bus through the hostile Arab territories that flanked the road to Zion Gate.

"Think the Arabs are up t' something, Cap'n?" asked a pink-cheeked young soldier named Harney.

"Ah, come off it." Smiley nudged him hard in the ribs. "Y'know the Mufti's called off the hounds since 'e blew up Ben Yehudah Street last week. 'e ain't goin' t' risk blowin' no paltry thing like a bus now, Harney. Not with the 'ole world out t' get 'im, 'e ain't."

"Well, then," chimed in a portly young man named Matthews. "I'm for taking that great long key in the captain's hand and nailing it to the gate here with a little note to the fellows: 'Gone to tea.' What do you say, Captain?" He stepped forward a step.

"There'll be time for that later, lads." Luke humored them to pass the time. He glanced at his watch again, worried at the bus's delay.

"They say the Mufti's gone t' tea," volunteered Ham.

"Gone t' Cairo, more like it, Sergeant," Smiley added. "And good riddance t' the likes of 'im, I say. I spent a day down on Ben Yehudah pullin' out pieces of kids from the rubble," he said bitterly, shaking his head.

"Jews. Arabs. It's all the same," snarled a grim-faced young man named Captain Stewart. He had come from England only two weeks before and was with the patrol as an observer. His eyes seemed to smolder in the deepening shadows.

"What's with 'im?" whispered Smiley to Ham.

Stewart spat into the snow and growled. "It isn't always this Mufti fellow blowing up things. Weren't any of ya here when the Jewish Irgun swine blew up the government wing of the King David Hotel?" The eyes of the men stared silently back at him.

"Y' got a point," nodded Smiley. " 'e's got a point. Killed Englishmen an' Arab Civil Servants aplenty, they did. Me an' Sergeant Ham 'ere was pullin' pieces of people off the wall of the YMCA building clean across the street. Wasn't we, Sergeant?"

He was answered by a stiff nudge in the ribs from Ham. "That'll be enough, Smiley," he said under his breath, noting the look of vacant horror that passed over Stewart's hard young face.

"A bloody mess it was," Smiley continued.

"That's enough," Luke interrupted.

"Well, sir, I was just agreein' with the cap'n. It was—"

"That is quite enough," Luke barked, stepping toward Smiley, who backed against the wall in confusion at the sudden displeasure of his superior officer. He snapped his heels together and saluted smartly.

"Yessir!" he said loudly, staring straight ahead.

Luke answered his salute, then turned to gaze across the rapidly darkening countryside, hoping to see the dim headlights of the bus.

All eyes remained on Smiley, who lowered his hand from the salute, then looked at Ham in confusion. Ham leaned toward the uncomprehending Smiley and whispered hoarsely, "Dolt! Stewart's brother died in the King David."

Her hands sweaty and shaking just a bit, Ellie Warne yanked hard to set the parking brake of the aging black Plymouth sedan.

"I just hate driving through the snow!" She smiled briefly at Rachel Lubetkin, who was gazing in wonder at the softly falling flakes.

"Where I am from, my friend," she said, her English thick with the accent of her native Poland, "this is only a little snow. Still, is it not a miracle that it should be here in Jerusalem? I do not remember a mention of such a thing in any of Grandfather's letters but one. And when she read it, my mother shook her head and told how only once when she was a young girl growing up here did it snow so much. They had let the Yeshiva schoolboys out to play and praise God in the streets."

"Next time, remember that I'm a California girl, and let's take a taxi, okay?" Ellie wiped her forehead and let out a long, slow breath.

"I think the taxi drivers are not so happy either." Rachel watched as the dilapidated Jewish taxis inched down Jaffa Road toward the drab, squat Egged bus station. At the curb, behind the faded blue hulk of the Number Two bus, cab doors opened and passengers tumbled out onto the sidewalk like circus clowns crammed into a miniature automobile. "And these days, who can fit in a taxi, anyway?"

Ellie squinted at the line of automobiles. "I guess their tire treads are as bare as ol' lizzy here." She blinked hard as she studied the tires of the Number Two bus. "Rachel, take a look at the bus tires, will you? You sure you want to ride in that thing? Bald as a billiard ball."

In the best of times the top speed for an Egged bus was ten miles per hour up the slopes of Zion. Heavy iron plating strained the engines to capacity even when the weather was good. This evening, Ellie guessed, the bus would be lucky to make it to Zion Gate.

"Perhaps the British escorts are thinking the same as you." Rachel turned her attention to two warmly dressed soldiers who alternately blew on their hands and stamped their feet as they argued with the adamant bus driver. Red-faced and angry, the driver gestured and wagged his gloved hand, pointing toward the Old City wall in the distance. He knew, as did Ellie and Rachel, that the cargo he carried to the threshold of the besieged Old City must pass through the gate tonight. The soldiers who normally searched Jewish passengers for weapons had already received considerable bribes from the Jewish Agency. Tonight and tonight only would they turn their heads as the thirteen young members of the Haganah boarded the bus with pistols and Sten guns strapped beneath their rough and bulky Orthodox dress. Rachel, the only female among the group was, as Uncle Howard had commented from his easy chair an hour before, "loaded for bear."

"Well, something's up." Ellie watched as two more British armored cars sped up Jaffa Road and lurched to a stop in front of the bus station. "You ready?"

Rachel nodded and stepped out of the car, pulling a small worn suitcase out after her. She hesitated for a moment as soldiers clambered out of their vehicles and precariously skated across the slippery sidewalk and through the revolving door into the tiled lobby. *Have all these members of the Mandatory British Government been bribed?* she wondered. *Or will they search and arrest me, as they have so many other Jews attempting to arm themselves against the coming Arab onslaught?*

Ellie took her by the elbow and walked with her toward the entrance to the building. "What is it, Ellie?" Rachel asked.

"Moshe warned us there would be soldiers swarming all over the place. Just act natural. I've got my trusty camera and my press pass. Nobody's going to get fresh with you and risk having his picture taken."

"Fresh?"

"They'll search the men, maybe, but these guys aren't going to be caught dead frisking a woman. *Life* magazine is published in London too, you know." She batted her eyes knowingly. "You think these fellas want their mothers to know they search innocent Orthodox girls for a living? I'll stick around until you get on the bus."

In the back of both their minds was the knowledge that the penalty for any Jew caught carrying a weapon was death. Regardless of the fact that Rachel had not the slightest idea of how to load a Sten gun or pull the pin on a grenade, simply the act of carrying such devices implicated her in the Jewish terrorist atrocities that had begun to rival the horror of the Mufti's attacks. For this reason, the Haganah, whose very name meant "defense," had resolved not to use their weapons except for protection. The holy sites of the Old City were by far the most defenseless. Housing two thousand Orthodox Jews whose sole goal in life was to fulfill the laws of Torah, the Old City concealed only a few outdated World War I rifles. Less than one hundred Haganah defenders had posed as Yeshiva scholars to slip past the British guards at the gates. Every day that passed, it became increasingly difficult for men and supplies to reach the Old City. Rachel knew that the ride she was about to take could very well be the last of the Number Two bus runs to Zion Gate.

The scream of an ambulance siren fractured the still air as Ellie and Rachel reached the door of the building. The driver and the two escorts looked up and peered down the road to see the brightly flashing light moving toward them.

"There's likely to be dead and wounded on the Tel Aviv convoy, you know," said a tall, lean soldier to the driver. "With the Arabs up in arms again, are you willing to risk it with your passengers?"

"So, maybe the Arabs are all busy down in Bab el Wad. Jerusalem is not Bab el Wad, you know," the driver said, referring to the narrow canyon gorge that climbed from the valley to Jerusalem. Jewish vehicles traveling from Tel Aviv had been the objects of constant attacks from the Mufti's Arab irregulars since the United

Nations' Partition of Palestine into two states one month before. Jerusalem, with a population of 100,000 Jews, lay deep in the heart of Arab territory. The narrow gorge of Bab el Wad was the city's only link with Tel Aviv, and every day that link grew more fragile.

Ellie glanced around the lobby at the men and women who awaited word on friends and loved ones who had traveled this day to Jerusalem. Small groups clustered near the door, their faces tight and drawn with worry. One young woman in a bright blue dress sat forlornly on a hard wooden bench and sobbed into her hands. An elderly man in a ragged wool sweater and fisherman's cap sat next to her, chain-smoking cigarettes and staring blankly at the chipped floor tiles at his feet. British soldiers, no less concerned about their comrades who had been sent to aid the Tel Aviv convoy stood along the wall by the drinking fountain. Words like "snipers" and "land mines" buzzed among them. Their rifles slung, they took no notice of the odd collection of Yeshiva students across the room who waited to board the Number Two bus. In their long black coats and broad-rimmed hats, they seemed a century apart from the heavily armed servants of the British Mandatory Government opposite them. Yet they too were soldiers and officers—of the Haganah. Ellie sized them up quickly, curious at the complete and effective concealment of the weapons she knew they carried. Under baggy trousers Sten guns were strapped to their legs. Under the tall hats, perhaps a grenade or two was hidden, and beneath the fringes of the talliths, bandoliers of bullets. She tried not to watch as one bearded, bespectacled Haganah man walked directly toward the soldiers.

He stepped between two officers and slurped noisily from the drinking fountain as they continued to talk over the top of him.

"That's what I call acting natural," Ellie whispered to Rachel as they found a seat on an empty bench near the ticket counter, a mere ten feet from the Haganah men.

The small man at the fountain wiped his lips on the back of his hand and adjusted his hat before he strolled leisurely back to the group. His face was expressionless as he spoke to a large heavyset young man who, to Ellie, looked for all the world like a wrestler. Ellie could not understand the language, but the wrestler's eyebrows arched slightly, then pulled down in a frown.

Rachel leaned closer to Ellie and whispered, "He speaks in Polish."

"What did he say?"

"The English are not certain what damage has been done to the convoy from Tel Aviv. There are wounded on board. Also there was some firing from the civilian transport at the attackers. They say they will arrest whoever had a weapon to fire at the Arabs."

"Did anybody arrest the Arabs who attacked?"

Rachel held a finger up to silence her as she listened to the two men speak. "The Arabs fled as the armored car approached. Possibly there are some Englishmen wounded. They are not certain."

A wave of anxiety washed over Ellie as she studied the aquiline profile of her young Jewish friend. The clothes of the Orthodox might hide weapons, but they could not conceal the striking beauty of Rachel Lubetkin. And now Rachel was about to become a target of Moslem Arab hostility.

"Are you sure you want to do this, Rachel?" Ellie asked.

Rachel sat back on the hard wooden bench and smiled brightly into the eyes of her worried auburn-haired friend.

"Ellie," she said softly, patting the hand that held a large black camera, "I will be very well. How do you say it in America? Okay, eh? I will be okay."

Ellie blinked back tears of concern. "Yeah, well, I wish they'd let me come."

Rachel raised her left eyebrow slightly and carefully

appraised her obviously American young friend. Ellie's teal sweater and black wool slacks gave her the appearance of someone about to head for the ski slopes. Rachel had seen pictures of such women in Ellie's American magazines. "You do not know the ways of the Orthodox Jews, my friend." She patted the plain navy scarf covering the satin sheen of her own black hair. "In Poland, when I was but a young girl, I belonged among the Hassidim. My own father was a rabbi. I will serve my people very well, and you, my sweet, dear friend, will serve in another way, will you not?" Her deep blue eyes fell on the camera that Ellie cradled in her lap.

"But the Old City, Rachel. It's so dangerous now. Just deliver your message and get out." Ellie ached at the thought of all the things that would surely befall those few chosen to defend the holy places within the Jewish Quarter of the Old City. Her eyes searched Rachel's finely chisled features; black-rimmed cobalt eyes gazed tenderly back at her. "Even this stuff you're wearing—" She flipped the lapel of Rachel's worn-out black overcoat. "You think some Arab guy isn't going to notice you if you're caught entering the Jewish Quarter? You think you're going to be safe if the Old City falls? Rachel, haven't you been through enough? Why don't they send homely women in there if they need someone to deliver a message?"

Rachel's hand unconsciously moved to touch her forearm where the ugly blue tatoo remained: *Nür für Offizere*. It had once proclaimed her the property of a Nazi brothel. "It is because I have seen so much and survived that I must go. Moshe and I have spoken long hours. He agrees with me on this. It is my mitzvah, my duty, to warn my people in the Old City. You cannot change this by your worry for me." She frowned and looked across the crowded lobby. "I ask only that you do one thing for me."

"Name it." Ellie eagerly leaned forward.

"As my grandfather is in the Hadassah Hospital here in the New City and I am going away to the walls of his

31

home in the Old City, it occurs to me that I shall perhaps not see him ever again." She paused and searched Ellie's face.

"The doctors say he'll be okay," Ellie said brightly.

"This I do not doubt." She waited until understanding filled Ellie's eyes. It was an understanding that punctuated the fact that Rachel was the one for whom each moment would be lived in danger. "If it should happen that I do not come out and one day there is no more Jewish Quarter for Grandfather and my little brother to come home to, and if you should find that my eyes will not look upon their faces in this life, I ask that you will somehow..." Her voice faltered and Ellie reached out to put a fingertip lightly on Rachel's lips.

"Don't say it, okay?" her voice quavered. "You are—" She took a deep breath and began again, nearly overcome at the thought that these might be the last moments she could look at the face of her friend. "You are really special to me, too, you know? So just plan on coming out of there in one piece, okay?"

"Yes, but..."

"No buts..."

"But if it is not to be, you must promise that you will help them, eh? Grandfather is so very old. And Yacov so very young. And we have only just found each other once again. I must know that if I am not here, you will be my sister, my little goy friend."

Ellie nodded, unable to speak for a long moment. "I just wish Moshe would let me go in there with you."

"Do you not have more important things to do?" Rachel tapped Ellie's camera again. "Is it not your mitzvah to be the eyes for the world and show our struggle here? Must they not see that this is our last foothold on a planet that murdered so many ... so many? Ellie, I tell you, if my people are denied this place, a homeland of their own, then there is nowhere in the world where we will ever be safe. You must show them all. With your photographs, eh? Then they will see that even now there are those who seek to destroy us." She touched

Ellie lightly on the arm. "Is this not an important thing for you to do?"

Ellie nodded reluctantly. "Then at least I wish that Moshe was well enough to go with you. Whom do you know in the Old City, Rachel?"

"I am the granddaughter of Rabbi Shlomo Lebowitz. It is enough. I will speak to the other rabbis of his condition and his desire that they assist those who will help save the Old City. They will listen." She slipped her hand into her pocket and touched the letter the old man had written for her from the hospital bed where he lay recovering from his heart attack. "And if they do not listen, well then at least I have done what I could do." She frowned at the thought of Moshe, still weak from the wound of an Arab bullet. "As for Moshe, when he is again well, he has much more to do than to look after me, I think."

"I have the feeling there's nothing he'd like better to do." Ellie raised her eyebrows.

Rachel looked quickly away, hoping that Ellie had not seen the hopelessness in her eyes. "He is a good man. A decent man. He deserves more than someone like me," she said, ashamed that Ellie had observed anything between her and Moshe. "I am not destined to love one man and be loved in return. You do not know, dear friend. You cannot know everything that has befallen me. But I thank you for seeing me through eyes that do not judge."

"How could anyone judge you for what happened at the hands of the Nazis, Rachel?"

"It is my own judgment that condemns me. Perhaps you will not understand this. But I will not love Moshe. I will not love any man as my own."

There was a finality in her words that filled Ellie with helplessness. Somehow she knew that Rachel had requested to serve as courier to the Old City not only to save this ancient Jewish Holy site but to lose herself as well. "Listen," Ellie said firmly, "I want you to remember something. It's a lot harder sometimes to live than it is to die, okay? And I'm not just talking about breathing and walking around. I mean really living. And that means knowing people need *you*, no matter what you think of yourself."

The ticket clerk behind the counter shouted loudly, "The Number Two bus is now boarding!"

Rachel stood quickly, nervously looking away from Ellie's imploring face. "I must . . ."

"Did you hear what I said, Rachel?" Ellie took her by the shoulder. "If you go in there, you're coming out from behind that wall again—alive. Because there are all kinds of people who need you now. And *living*, not dying, is your mitzvah."

Rachel shook her head slowly and smiled sadly back into the intense face of her friend. "Thank you, little shiksa. For everything."

"You're not getting on that bus until you say you understand what I'm telling you. We need you. We love you."

Rachel nodded again, then turned to file in behind the line of Yeshiva students who shuffled toward the door and the Number Two bus. Ellie remained standing by the wooden bench in the lobby. As Rachel turned and raised a hand in farewell, Ellie breathed a prayer that somehow her friend would find herself and find forgiveness so she could begin to live again.

3   The Celebration

Uncomfortable in the brace he wore, David leaned awkwardly forward in his chair and put his ear to the speaker of Howard Moniger's ancient Philco radio. As static popped and spit, he turned the tuning knob as delicately as a safecracker hoping to break into a bank vault.

"Come on," he coaxed, impatiently tapping a foot that stretched out far beyond the cuff of his too short pants.

Howard rubbed his bald dome with a pot holder as he surveyed the curious scene in his kitchen. Of the small group assembled there to share what was surely the last lamb roast in Jewish Jerusalem, he was the only one who was dressed normally—with the exception of his dish towel apron. He wore his own khaki trousers and a blue and white checkered shirt. His attire blended wonderfully, however, with Moshe and David, who both wore matching blue and white checkered bathrobes bought by Ellie. Their khaki trousers, borrowed from Howard, were several inches too large around the waist and several inches too short in the inseam. Furthermore, Howard was the only one in the group who wasn't sporting a bandage—with the exception of Shaul the dog, of course, whose adoring eyes were turned mournfully up to where David and Yacov crouched in front of the radio. Moshe's arm and upper chest were encased in a heavy plaster cast. David's neck and arm were held rigid in a brace designed to protect his broken collarbone from movement. Young Yacov still wore his black, pirate eye patch. Howard's cuts and bruises were healing, and the nasty gash on Shaul's front paw seemed to be responding nicely to the gentle licking Shaul had been faithfully administering.

Since the events of the week before, both David and Moshe had been released from the hospital and, at Ellie's insistence, brought back to the Monigers' Rehavia home for recuperation. Never had these men experienced such loving care. As Rachel made blintzes for breakfast, Ellie had administered warm shaves every morning. Howard winced as he noticed the tiny nicks on the faces of the young men in his kitchen. Finally, after a few days of enduring such tender ministrations, Moshe had insisted that he needed to grow his beard in the next few weeks—the better to identify with the Hassidic Jews he would undoubtedly be working with. David quickly followed suit; unable, however, to come up with a diplomatic excuse, he had simply explained that he was afraid she was going to slit his throat some morning.

Three days' growth of beard on the ruggedly handsome faces of his two young guests, then, gave them the appearance of a couple of adventurers—toughs who definitely needed the cuffs of their trousers let out.

"You know, you boys look like you deserve the Purple Heart," Howard said aloud.

Moshe rubbed a hand across his nicked chin. "I'll take several."

"Not for me, thanks." David frowned and continued to worry the knob. "I got my Purple Heart in the last war. All I need is aspirin and a little good ol' American news."

"But I do not understand why it must be American Armed Forces radio. The BBC of Palestine is easier to pick up." Moshe sat back in his chair and knitted his brow in frustration at David's attempt to tune in a station based on the other side of the Mediterranean.

Howard smiled and shrugged and banged the oven door open. He noisily pulled the steaming roast out and began to taste the pitiful chuck of lamb. "This was a little guy," he said under his breath. "Not a lot of meat here, boys, but enough's a feast, eh?"

"Quiet," David commanded, ignoring Moshe's question. "We gotta have quiet here."

Yacov sat watching David with wordless intensity. French words from Morocco and Arabic from Cairo drifted in and out of the static until at last a faint recognizable Yankee twang stammered in the distance. ". . . delay . . . broadcast . . . Times . . . are . . . and . . . Guy Lombar . . . his orchest . . ."

David slapped his one good hand on his knee and gave a whoop of delight. "We did it, Yacov, l'il buddy! Guy Lombardo and his orchestra! Now, that's what I call some kind of celebration. New York City! Times Square. So what if it's a few hours after the fact, huh?"

Yacov's face was alive with curiosity. "American New Year is for dancing? Celebrating?"

"Right. Parades. The Rose Parade. And football. Right, Howard? The Rose Bowl."

"Actually, David, you must remember I left the States when this Lombardo fellow was probably still in knickers. Probably not even old enough to hold a football."

"No! No! No!" David rolled his eyes in exasperation. "Lombardo is a band director."

The broken strains of an orchestra with a severe case of hiccups sputtered over the airwaves. "That must be your Mister Lombardo, I take it?" Howard questioned as he covered the roast and shoved it back into the warm oven.

"He should never have left football," Moshe remarked with an amused gleam in his eye.

"You gotta hear this guy!" David protested. "What we need is clothes hangers. Metal ones, and lots of 'em. Howard, the closet in my room is full. Do you mind?"

"Not at all."

"Come on, kid." David touseled Yacov's hair and marched from the kitchen, with Shaul following closely behind.

With David's enthusiasm moved to another part of the house, the kitchen seemed suddenly devoid of life.

For a long moment, neither Howard nor Moshe spoke above the radio. Moshe drummed his fingers nervously on the table as Howard puttered about the room, opening cupboard doors as if he were looking for something but wasn't quite sure what it was he wanted.

"Ellie should be back soon," Moshe said at last.

"It's a shame Rachel couldn't share supper with us." Howard took a glass from a shelf and filled it with water. "Especially since she cooked it. Ellie can't boil an egg, and since Miriam has been gone, I'm a regular Fibber McGee without Molly."

"There was nothing else to do." Moshe stared grimly at the worn slippers on his feet and tugged at the belt of his bathrobe.

"I know that, Moshe. Still, it's a shame she couldn't eat with us." Howard tried in vain to lighten the conversation.

"One more day . . . one more hour might be too late for anyone to enter the Old City."

"Well, she won't be in there long. Not to worry. Luke will see that she gets where she needs in one piece. And back out again."

"I only hope the rabbis will listen to her."

"The letter from her grandfather is pretty fair credentials, Moshe. So stop worrying. A couple of days and she'll be right back here."

"Yes," Moshe said quietly, his face tight with worry.

"Come on now," Howard chided. "Buck up. Remember whose hands Rachel is in."

Moshe raised his eyes gratefully to Howard's. "That is all I can think of; all I pray for since we decided to let her go. She is so vulnerable, Howard. Like all my people now," he added quickly.

"Well, I think she means a bit more to you than the others, eh? Or is that just the imagination of an old man?"

Moshe hesitated and gave an embarrassed half-smile. "You are not that old, my friend."

"She is a lovely girl, Moshe, but I won't say I'm not

38

a bit disappointed that you won't be a member of my family."

"Ellie and I have talked long these last few days, Howard. It is not me she loves. It has never been, I think. We are so different," Moshe finished lamely.

"Well I still say I'm disappointed. Even though I figured it out a few weeks ago."

Their arms full of hangers, Yacov and David banged happily through the swinging door, which swung shut just as Shaul squeaked through behind them.

". . . and I was right there in Pasadena for that one, pal. UCLA is my Alma Mater, see. Both Ellie and I went there," David explained enthusiastically to Yacov as they dumped the wire hangers on the table in front of Moshe. "UCLA Bruins. Unbeatable."

"And did UCLA win this Rose Bowl last year?" Yacov asked.

"Well." David bit his lower lip. "It was a put-up deal."

"That means they lost," Moshe grinned.

"Bad refs. The referees favored Illinois, that's all." David began to tinker with the back of the radio, attaching one hanger to the antenna terminals, then hanging the wire hangers on one another until the reception became louder. ". . . and this year's Rose Bowl promises to be a much more evenly matched game between Michigan and USC. Last year Illinois annihilated the UCLA Bruins in a lopsided game whose final score was an unbelieveable 45 points to UCLA's 14 . . ." the radio blared.

"Excellent reception." Moshe noted the chagrin on David's face as he continued to drape the hangers from the cupboard door handles.

"Bad refs?" Yacov asked, impishly.

"Ask Ellie. She was there, you little shrimp."

Yacov tapped his temple and glanced at Moshe. "Meshuggener, crazy man, eh?"

Moshe nodded in agreement.

David ignored them and pulled up a chair in front of the radio. "Speaking of Els," he said, suddenly serious, "shouldn't she be back by now?"

"The weather has no doubt delayed the bus departure. She'll wait with Rachel. There is no real danger between here and the station." Howard pulled a stack of dishes from the shelf.

"She ought to be back before dark." David glanced out the window at the still heavily falling snow. "I should've driven them."

"My friend," Moshe began patronizingly. "You are no more in condition to drive than I."

Both men sat in bathrobes, worn trousers and slippers. David was unable even to turn his head without turning his entire body. "I guess you're right. We are pretty likely candidates for the repple-depple."

"As I explained earlier, David"—Howard lowered his basting spoon and narrowed his eyes—"I left the States when people still spoke English . . ."

"Repple-depple. You know, the replacement depot. Sort of a clearing house for soldiers who have been wounded and separated from their outfits. A guy has to wait there until he gets reassigned. This is the Rehavia repple-depple."

"Well, it has a nice ring to it, anyway—wouldn't you say so, Moshe?" Howard repeated the word several times.

"Definitely." Moshe smiled in spite of his concern for Ellie and Rachel. "This is a word we must introduce to the Haganah handbook. As soon as we have such a thing."

The music of Guy Lombardo continued in the background as the men discussed the relative merits of wartime slang that had been lost over the centuries. David would say a word, and Moshe, Howard and Yacov would attempt to guess its meaning. Nearly a half hour passed before the Armed Services radio station in Rome interrupted its traditional New Year's broadcast.

As Howard held his hand up for silence, the grim news filled the room. ". . . After nearly a week of quiet in Palestine, hostilities have once again broken out. Partial news has reached us by wire from Jerusalem. A civilian convoy en route to Jerusalem from Tel Aviv has been ambushed near the pass of Bab el Wad. British forces routed the Arab attackers, but there are said to be a number of Jewish and British dead and wounded . . ."

4   The Number Two Bus

Protected from the weather by the stolen boots and heavy trenchcoat of a British officer, Gerhardt still cursed the cold and wet that seemed to tear through him and his disheveled, drunken companion.

"Another drink, Gerhardt," slurred the British deserter, "or I'm leavin' thish nasty business for you alone. Can't fancy you out 'ere all by yourself layin' these wires."

"I'll give you a drink when we are done, and not before," Gerhardt growled, unhappy that the Mufti had sent him on such an important errand with this lout.

The deserter grumbled loudly and dropped the shovel. "Then I'm done, mate. Can't expect a man t' dig a 'ole when the ground is froze. And without even a drop t' keep 'is blood warm." He started to turn and stagger back down the road.

"One more step and you're a dead man," Gerhardt coldly warned. All he needed was a drunken British Army deserter loose in the bars around Jerusalem. News of this mine set for the Number Two bus to Zion Gate would reach the front page of the *Palestine Post* before the bus ever left the station. Gerhardt pulled out his Luger and pointed it toward the retreating man.

"Ah, go on," said the deserter. "Fight your own war, y' bloomin' blanket 'ead!"

Without a moment's hesitation, Gerhardt pulled the trigger. His lip curled slightly in disgust as the bullet slammed into the back of the deserter's head, sending him to the ground in a heap.

Gerhardt sighed at the prospect of facing the cold evening without conversation as he waited to push the plunger on the mine resting just beneath the surface of the road. He reholstered the Luger, then walked deliberately to where the deserter lay lifeless in his own blood. With one fierce kick, he shoved the body off the side of the road and sent it plummeting into the Valley of Hinnom below.

———

Dim light flittered through the armored slit windows of the bus. The black garb of the Hassidic passengers blended into the interior twilight. Each man moved down the aisle, choosing an empty seat and stashing his battered satchel; Rachel carefully inched past them. Her eyes skimmed the tops of the broad-brimmed black hats as she moved instinctively toward the farthest back corner of the bus. The faces of the men on either side of her seemed almost ghostlike behind the frost-streaked masks of their beards. Breath rose in a cold vapor around pale skin, and dark brooding eyes were careful not to meet her gaze.

Eyes had a power to speak when words would fail; this Rachel knew. It had been the same on that first endless journey to the Nazi camps. Hearts searching for comfort through the tender glance of a loved one had often broken in anguish when eyes had betrayed the truth that this was a journey from which most would never return. Eyes had spoken wordless goodbyes; asked silently for forgiveness for failures; caressed without touching—all this as German soldiers had separated husbands from wives, children from mothers. And always, in seeing one another for the last time, it had been as though they were seeing one another fully and completely for the first time. Nazi gun butts and cries of *"Schnell! Schnell Juden! Hurry, Jew!"* had punctuated and finally ended those last eloquent goodbyes.

Rachel chose a seat on the aisle. She tossed her frayed satchel onto the empty window seat and resisted the temptation to peer out the narrow slit to where Ellie stood on the snowy sidewalk of the Egged station. She stared straight ahead, aware that Ellie's eyes were searching the steel armor that surrounded her. But she would not look out to meet the last loving gaze of her friend. This was a journey she had determined to make alone. She would not take with her even one more goodbye. There had already been too many in her life.

The red light atop the British armored escort blinked and flashed to life, washing the pale faces of the passengers in an eerie red glow. Grumbling beneath his breath, the bus driver bounded up the steps and pulled the heavy iron doors shut with a clang. He slammed the bolt hard with a gloved hand, then took his seat without once looking at the passengers behind him. The engine moaned, then roared to life as the bus seemed to shudder. Leaning far over the steering wheel, the driver squinted and peered out at the escort ahead of the bus.

"Oy Gevalt!" he exclaimed. "What are they waiting for? The angel Gabriel?" The sound of grinding gears reminded Rachel of an ancient horse that pulled the bookseller's wagon in Warsaw. Its grinding teeth had been louder almost than the sound of its hooves on the cobblestones. "So move it, already!" shouted the driver through the window slit before him. "Any longer and the Arabs can build a ski resort on Mount Zion! Gevalt!"

Passengers shifted nervously in their places as the bus finally lurched forward. The bald tires whined against the slick asphalt. Slowly the bus moved into the flow of cautious and complaining traffic, and only then did Rachel allow herself to look out at the darkening city. She recognized the three-story red stone structure of the *Palestine Post*, where only a week before she and Ellie had picked up detonators from a harmless-looking little man as the presses roared and the phonograph played the *1812 Overture*. Since then the building on Hasollel Street, just a few steps from Zion Square, had become very familiar to Ellie and Rachel. What photographs Ellie had not sent on to *Life* magazine, she had sold to the *Post*. Editors had exclaimed with delight over the work of the young American woman with the knack of being in the right place at the right time. Rachel smiled at the memory of Ellie's cries of protest when it was decided that she could not enter the Old City with her.

The driver carefully turned south toward Ben Yehudah Street where white-frosted barricades and coils of barbed wire began to thicken and grow like a briar patch. A motorcycle clattered by, its driver and sidecar passenger crouched in cold misery as they rode toward the headquarters of the Palestine police. Two police cars followed closely behind, and the wail of a siren approached and receded down a side street. The mute wreckage of Ben Yehudah Street stood behind yet another barricade. Snow-covered rubble spoke profoundly of the task before them. If this could happen in the New City, in the heart of Jewish Jerusalem, what would be the fate of the tiny Jewish toehold in the Old City?

"*Schnell Juden! Hurry, Jew!*" The wreckage seemed to mock their journey. *Once again,* Rachel thought, *we hasten toward what is surely our own destruction.* Moshe had carefully explained to her that most senior officers of the Haganah had declared the Jewish Quarter of the Old City indefensible. The evacuation of the area had been recommended by the British and demanded by the Arab High Committee. It was David Ben-Gurion who refused the idea.

As the bus rumbled past the pale stone compound of the Jewish Agency, Rachel imagined Ben-Gurion standing at his window watching them pass.

"Not one inch of Jewish soil shall be abandoned! Not one grain of sand!" the Old Man had said as Moshe pored over the Old City maps in his office.

And yet already, several hundred Old City residents had lost heart and left their homes and ancient houses of study. In her coat pocket Rachel cradled the letter written by the feeble hand of her grandfather.

"You must deliver this to the Council of Rabbis," he had instructed her. "Warn them that the advice of Akiva is not sound. Bid them stay. Speak for me."

Once again Rachel moved inexorably toward walls

45

and watchtowers of stone, through fields of barbed wire to a beloved prison on the holiest ground on earth. "*Schnell Juden!*" And this time she entered her prison willingly, hopefully. They would shut themselves in to keep out those who would destroy them forever. Surrounded by thousands of Jihad Moquades who called daily for the sacrifice of Jewish blood in their Holy War, she and these few who rode with her in silence would almost certainly be laying themselves on the altar.

"Deliver your grandfather's message and then get out," Moshe had instructed her. "Captain Thomas will help you. By no means are you to remain in the Old City, Rachel. Do you understand?"

She had nodded, fully understanding. How could she tell others to stay in danger and then escape to safety? Hadn't that been the very sin which had destroyed her soul? As her own people had died, she had lived for the use and pleasure of her enemies.

"Yes, Moshe," she had said, knowing all along that she would not come out willingly through Zion Gate. He had nodded and given his permission for her to travel with the small band of Haganah soldiers. It would be too late for him to stop her by the time he realized that she never intended to leave the Old City. She wondered if he would be angry with her.

Rachel gazed at the bobbing heads of the men in the bus. The small bespectacled Hassid leaned across the aisle and spoke in hushed tones to the wrestler who shrugged, then peered anxiously out the window slit as the last light of evening disappeared. As the bus passed through the familiar Jewish area of Rehavia and into Arab-mixed Talbieh, Rachel felt strangely unafraid. Soon they would reach the Valley of Hinnom and begin the slow, dangerous ascent up the slopes of Mount Zion toward their final destination. At Zion Gate, Rachel knew, the gentle British captain waited in the falling snow. This time there would be no guns and clubs to force them into their holy prison. Rachel only wondered if somewhere along the darkened roadside men with guns waited to keep them out.

5 Arrival and Departure

Ellie glanced at her watch as the blackened, bullet-pocked convoy vehicle from Tel Aviv limped into the Egged bus station. Three armored British convoy escorts followed, and Ellie raised her camera as a British soldier climbed wearily from the gun turret and called, "We'll need an ambulance for the wounded!"

Stretcher bearers, the folded stretcher between them, ran toward where the Tel Aviv transport rolled to a stop. Their faces tight with worry, men and women who had waited two long hours for their loved ones clambered toward the still-closed door.

Men ground out the last of their cigarettes. Women wept openly and wrung their hands or clutched their children to them as they strained to see who would be the first to walk down the steps.

The metal doors slid open too slowly and a cry arose as the passengers from Tel Aviv staggered out.

A woman screamed, "Eli! That's my husband, my husband, let me through!" The crowd parted as she ran to the steps and reached upward to help a middle-aged businessman whose doubledbreasted suit was smeared with blood. His head was bandaged with the remains of a red-soaked shirt, but he shouted loudly, "I'm all right! There are wounded here! Hurry! There are wounded!"

His face was grim beneath his makeshift bandage. He stepped down and quickly embraced his sobbing wife; then he shouted again, "Get a doctor! There are wounded." The man shrugged off the attention the ambulance attendant tried to give him. "I said I'm all right!"

The names of the expected passengers became desperate cries of hope and fear on the lips of those who waited.

"Let them through!" someone shouted as the medics shoved past the friends and relatives and into the vehicle itself. Beads of sweat formed on Ellie's brow as she snapped the shutter of her camera. One by one the injured passengers stumbled or were carried down the steps and laid on the floor of the lobby. From their wounds a red film seeped over the tiles, and their moans mingled with the cries of their loved ones, lending to the scene an eerie, unearthly quality. *I will never get used to this*, Ellie thought as her stomach revolted at the sights around her. *Never.*

There were nine passengers numbered among the wounded, and after they were taken from the transport, the others came. Weary and unwashed, the survivors stepped from the door. Their eyes searched the hysteria before them. Joyful shouts erupted as a quick glance scanned for injury and found none. "I am not hurt! It was terrible, but I am all right." Shoes tracked through the blood and left footprints on the floor as the uninjured walked to the side of the crowd to embrace their loved ones and thank God for safety. "Don't cry now, little one." A young bronzed Sabra took a weeping child in his arms. "Daddy is not hurt."

Ellie snapped a picture of their tearful reunion. *They are lucky*, she thought, turning her attention to the empty doorway. For a long moment no new faces appeared. Several families still waited. "They will bring the dead out last," someone whispered behind her. Then, as Ellie watched, a familiar, harried-looking face loomed from the dark interior.

"This is why I went to sea! At least in the ocean a man can jump overboard and swim or drown quickly!" cried the disgusted voice of Ehud Schiff. "No more will I ride in such a tin can!" He stepped from the armored transport and shouldered his way through the crowd, his voice rough and angry above the din. "No more will

48

Ehud Schiff be target practice for such as those Arab swine."

Ellie let her camera drop on the strap around her neck. Joyfully she called out to him and, carefully avoiding the sticky ooze on the floor, she inched her way toward the coarse yet gentle sea captain. "Ehud!" she called loudly. "Ehud Schiff!"

He turned and squinted, trying to see through the crush. At last his eyes found her, and in spite of his anger he smiled broadly and waved. A shrill cry erupted beside him as a young woman in a blue dress collapsed at the sight of her husband's body being carried down the steps. Ehud's smile disappeared as he reached out to catch her. "Doctor!" he cried, dropping to his knees with her in his arms. "Someone help this woman!" Instantly she was surrounded and as another young woman stroked her head, a thin worried-looking man snapped smelling salts under her nose.

Ehud rose slowly to his feet and looked around the room. His lips were tight and his eyes wide with the sorrow that surrounded him. He shook his head, then took Ellie by the elbow and led her out to the snowy sidewalk and away from the tragedy inside.

"Ehud . . ." Ellie began, wondering where he had come from and why he was in Jerusalem.

"Take me to Moshe's place, eh?" he answered quietly. "You have a car? Of course you have a car if Moshe has sent you here to fetch me."

"But, Ehud . . ."

"So." He breathed the cold air deeply. "It is good to see you all in one piece. I did not think any of us would be alive from that journey. The Arabs. They attacked just beyond Latrun. Where they always attack, nu? Just as Joshua did from the heights looking down over the Valley. Ah, we could have used Joshua today! Today it was the Arabs who made the sun stand still. Never have I felt the minutes crawl so long until the sun began to set. And the Britishers . . . they fought bravely for us or we should have no one alive at all, I think. It is only right

49

they should fight to save the life of Ehud, nu? Since it was they who destroyed my dear *Maria*."

Ellie nodded and smiled at the thought of the little ship *Ave Maria*, the leaky little vessel that Ehud still mourned for. "But we didn't know you were coming, Ehud." She finally got a word in.

"What?" he cried. "A message was sent to Moshe at his apartment."

"Moshe has been staying at our house in Rehavia."

"You did not come to pick me up, then? So how do you happen to be here?"

"I brought Rachel to the station. She is going to the Old City."

"Rachel? The selfsame little minnow that Moshe rescued from the sea? Rachel the beauty?"

"Yes," Ellie chided. "The one you told me about to distract me when I was about to win a chess game with you."

"Ah yes. Hmmm. I remember. And how does she happen to know you?"

"Moshe."

"And how came she to be in Jerusalem? Did she come from the refugee kibbutz by way of bus?" He took her arm again as they stepped between two ambulances and threaded their way across the street to the car.

"From Netanya kibbutz, yes. By bus, no. A friend of mine flew her in. In an airplane."

"A much safer way to travel than this, I think. A ship in the air, eh? Never more will I come to Jerusalem by way of Bab el Wad while the Mufti breathes his venom into the Arabs who live along the road."

"How many were there?"

"Perhaps a hundred. It is hard to say. They had a land mine. The lead car was blown up. Two Britishers dead, I think. The Arabs called 'Yehudah! Yehudah!' then fired their rifles through the slit windows. We were trapped for many hours until the Britishers came with more men and armored cars. Some Haganah aboard the transport used weapons. They are arrested now. One man who I do not know jumped from the transport while it was still moving through the outskirts of town and ran away. The English either did not see him or they did not care to chase him down, which is to their credit."

"Ehud"—Ellie felt a surge of emotion as she looked at the hairy, good-hearted seaman—"it is good to see you."

"Tonight I am glad to be alive, little one."

———————

The Number Two bus labored slowly up the narrow, rutted road toward Zion Gate. Mud from the tires of the lead British armored car splattered the front grill and coated the headlights. Softly falling snowflakes instantly melted as the wind slapped them against the hard metal plates. A howling sleet began to fall. It swirled in gusts and beat angrily on the roof above them, rattling like machine-gun bursts, while muddy water seeped through the rusty seams of the floorboard whenever the wheels hit a deep rut. Moshe had explained to Rachel that the buses of the Egged Bus Line were protected like the hide of a strange ancient beast with a hard and crusty shell. Only the underbelly was soft and unprotected. As the soles of her shoes became damp and the cold night air whistled around her ankles, she understood why the creature he had spoken about had become extinct. "We Jews are the same, are we not?" he had said. "To the world we have seemed so hard and unbending. Always they hooked us, turned us belly up, then gored. We can't let the world see our soft spot again, Rachel, or next time it may be the end."

She had nodded quietly, fully aware of both her own armor and the gaping vulnerability of her soul. *Never again,* she thought, *or it will be the end.* She thought about Ellie and Moshe. Both of them seemed to care so deeply. *Surely neither one of them would ever intentionally hurt me.* She had no fear of them or Yacov or Grandfather. *Why, then,* she wondered, *do I want to run away when I have only just found them once again?* She turned her eyes on the strangers she rode with and let the shell of her own armor close around her heart once again. In the past, trust had turned her over, and love had gored her. *Never again.*

The driver shouted and cursed as he worked the steering wheel like a wild little boy pretending to drive his daddy's parked car. Sweat poured down his face in spite of the frigid wind that whipped through his tiny slit-window. He shifted and cursed and ground the gears for what seemed like the thousandth time as the rear of the bus fishtailed again and again. Tires spun and wailed in the wheel well just in front of Rachel's seat until she could no longer hear the oaths of the driver. For an instant she dared to peer out at the soggy shoulder of the road. It was scarcely visible in the faint glow of the headlights, but she knew that where the road ended, the steep slopes of Mount Zion dropped into the ragged Valley of Hinnom. She closed her eyes as a rush of fear filled the pit of her stomach. Putting her face near the slit, she let the wet wind sting her cheeks until she could think clearly once again.

She remembered the stories her father had told her about the Valley of Hinnom. The ancients had called the place Gai Hinnom, which became another word for hell. As a child she had shivered under the coverlet at the very thought of the Valley where "the kings of Judah did evil in the sight of the Lord." Rachel remembered the faces of her small brothers as they sat in the lamplight and listened to stories about King Menashe, "who made his children to pass through fire in the Valley of Hinnom." Their bright eyes had grown wide and fearful as Papa had described the terrible god, Molech, whose outstretched arms awaited the sacrifice of small children to feed the roaring flames of his copper belly. And as the children were devoured by this god with the head of a bull, loud drums had been beaten to drown out their screams of agony. The sins of Gai Hinnom had given birth to the Hebrew word *gehenom*, a word that had become a real and terrifying hell for Rachel as she watched the smokestacks of Auschwitz belch out their blackened sacrifice into the air.

The appetite of the ancient god seemed small by comparison to the Nazi camps. Cannons and self-righteous denial by the world had for a time covered the screams of six million innocents, but Rachel could still hear their cries in the wind that howled up the Valley of Hinnom and surrounded the bus. She shuddered and closed her eyes, trying to shut out the memory of the insatiable Nazi Molech who had first devoured those she loved most, then consumed her own heart as she stood by and watched in helplessness.

The bus fishtailed and slid against the bank with a loud scrape and a jolt that sent three passengers sprawling to the floor.

"Careful, Yosi!" the wrestler shouted to a young sparsely bearded Hassid who fell again as he tried to regain his footing. "You want to blow us up, boy?"

Rachel watched with morbid fascination as Yosi's heavy overcoat gaped open, revealing three grenades precariously strung by their pins across a leather bandolier. Angrily the wrestler grabbed him by his shirt front and pulled his face close.

"Idiot!" the big man hissed. "What if one of those had jarred loose? What kind of fool carries grenades by the pins?"

"I—I wanted to be prepared. Snipers you know," stammered the young man.

"Bah! Snipers, in this weather? You want to be a hero. Throw a grenade, eh?" The wrestler shoved Yosi into his seat. "Blow us up, more likely. These are to conceal and carry into the Old City, you idiot!"

"I thought perhaps if there were snipers . . ." he tried helplessly to explain.

"Bah!" spat the wrestler.

Yosi clutched the precious cargo tightly beneath his coat. Rachel stared at his pale and distressed profile with a detached interest. Fragile and bookish, probably not yet eighteen, he did not look as though he should have been carrying anything heavier than a copy of the Torah. Perhaps that is why he had been chosen to smuggle weapons. He had the look of the underbelly. Surely there could be no armor on this Jew of Jews; Yeshiva student, Juden. *Did he come from the camps?* Rachel wondered. *If so, how had he survived?* How many boys, just like this one, had been shot on the loading platform before the death trains had even begun to fill? Sensitive, idealistic, young enough to still have hope, they had dared to defy their captors with a look, a mumbled word of disrespect. And so they had died; instantly or slowly, they were blotted out in the Final Solution. Rachel stared at his hands, clutched across his middle as if he were in pain from the discovery of his deepest desire. *You can't pay them back, you know, Yosi,* she thought. *You can never pay them back.*

The bus slowly rounded a sharp curve and the driver suddenly yelled above the din, "Everyone get to the back of the bus! Over the rear axle. We need more weight in the back. Hurry up!"

As the ascent slowed to a slippery crawl, eleven of twelve Hassidic passengers staggered toward where Rachel sat. Yosi remained where he was, staring silently at the empty seats in front of him. Clutching the backs of seats and one another, the men stumbled into the last rows over the rear axle. Rachel clutched her satchel to her and moved as far over as she could, leaning heavily against the cold metal wall as the wrestler crammed in next to her. He squinted and peered at her, momentarily curious about the only woman passenger on board. Then his eyes followed her gaze to Yosi.

"Yosi!" he shouted as other members of the group settled in. "Idiot! Get back here!"

The young man appeared not to hear him for a moment.

"Yosi!" the wrestler shouted once again. "Are you deaf?"

As Yosi rose to make his way carefully down the slippery aisle, another, much older man called out, "So, when we reach Zion Gate, we should drink a toast to the driver, nu? May he live to see his wife and child once again, Omaine!" he said with a laugh.

"Omaine!" repeated the little band.

"Omaine!" repeated the driver grimly.

Yosi clutched the grenades as the bus swerved and lurched up the mountain. His eyes were downcast and he did not call out when the others said "omaine."

Rachel felt a surge of resentment toward the big man who sat beside her. *He humiliated him,* she thought. *And enjoyed doing it.*

Suddenly a choked cry came from the driver and an eerie phosphorescent flash beamed through the windows ahead of him. He swung the wheel desperately to the side, and the whole bus rocked in a violent, drunken, slow-motion swing. The wrestler slammed against Rachel as Yosi screamed and fell forward, the force of his fall jarring a grenade free from its pin.

For one brief instant, Rachel saw his hand fumbling for the horned orb. His face was etched with desperation and anguish. Then as the light flashed and flashed again, the grenade flew from his grasp and landed with a loud thud just in front of the Hassidim "Grenade!" shouted Yosi, scrambling toward it.

"My God! Dear God!" Cries echoed through the reeling vehicle.

Yosi grasped the live grenade just as the bus swerved up on two wheels and began a tortuous roll, like the ancient wounded beast of Moshe's stories. Above the sickening crunch of twisting metal, Rachel heard the cry of Yosi as he tucked the grenade under his stomach. The roar of its explosion shattered the steel frame of the bus beneath him.

6   Gai Hinnom

As the snow turned to rain, Ellie fished Uncle Howard's rain slicker from under the seat and pulled it on.

"I'm going to be a little while, Ehud," she warned, peering out at the brightly lit building that housed the *Palestine Post*. "I've got two rolls to develop. You might as well come in."

The captain scowled and sniffed. "Can I have coffee?"

"Sure. And you can read the paper while you wait."

"Tonight I can write the news," he said sourly.

Ellie jumped from the car and sprinted up the steps into the familiar lobby of the *Post*. Ehud lumbered after her, stamping his feet noisily on the tiled floor of the lobby.

"Ellie!" cried the matronly receptionist. "We were just trying to reach you. The phones are out all over. Morrie couldn't get Dieter, either. There's been a terrible incident, you know. We need a photographer."

"I've got it." Ellie held up two rolls of film. "Just need the use of a darkroom. I'm about out of paper."

"You *got* it?" the woman asked incredulously.

"Right here. At least the stuff in the bus station. And if you want a fella who knows the whole story—" She turned to Ehud. "Come here, Ehud. Get Morrie out here. Ehud was actually in the convoy."

"Ah yes," Ehud stepped forward. "But may we not have coffee, and I will tell you every horrible detail. There is no place safe on land, you know. So these Arabs say they shall drive us into the sea and I say, well and good! Let them! For there is no place safe on land."

The receptionist looked puzzled and hurried to get

coffee and Morrie Rudnick, the editor. Morrie emerged from an office behind the lobby and extended his hand to Ellie. "You got the story already? Such a journalist you are, Ellie! Always in the wrong place at the right time. So don't get your head blown off someday, eh? Just for a picture, eh?"

"I want to pull a few for *Life*, but since this concerns the lifeline of Jerusalem I figure you ought to have first crack at it."

"And I was just calling you to stand in for Dieter. We only just heard about it a moment ago on the short wave." He held the door wide for Ehud and Ellie who took coffee from the still-puzzled receptionist.

"Only a moment ago?" boomed Ehud, feeling a sense of importance. "It was an entire day. The Arabs attacked just beyond Latrun. Like Joshua from the ridges. Only it was they who seemed to make the sun stand still . . ."

Morrie stopped in his tracks and turned, the excitement vanishing from his face. "Latrun? You say Latrun?"

"Yes. They attacked until the British—"

"I got shots of the convoy arriving at the station, Morrie," Ellie explained.

"You're speaking of the convoy from Tel Aviv to Jerusalem?" he asked.

"Sure, what else?" Ellie's smile disappeared.

"I wondered." Morrie pursed his lips. "Today has not been a good day for Jewish transportation. We heard about the attack on the Tel Aviv transport hours ago, Ellie."

"Then what—"

"The Number Two bus. The Zion Gate bus. There's been a terrible accident. On the short wave the British said they don't expect there will be any survivors."

————

Twenty minutes earlier, from their frigid outpost at Zion Gate, Luke Thomas and his men had spotted the tiny lights of the Number Two bus and the armored cars as they crept up the hill. Curses had rippled through the group as the searing flash of Gerhardt's land mine ripped up the road between the lead car and the lumbering bus. As Luke and four others ran to his armored vehicle, the faint pattering of submachine-gun fire began to sound above the falling sleet.

Now, as Luke stood beside the crippled bus, he rubbed his forehead in bewilderment at the sight before him. The front of the bus sat on the road tilted at a slight angle. The back half of the vehicle dangled precariously over the edge of the embankment. A gaping hole yawned in the floorboard, and as Luke shone a flashlight down the sheer hillside, he saw the twisted bodies of two men lying like broken dolls below him. With each gust of wind the rear of the bus groaned and swayed over the valley floor.

"There was nothing I could do," the bus driver wrung his hands and followed after Luke as he directed his men. "I was trying, you see, to avoid the mine."

Luke frowned as mud from the embankment crumbled and slid away in small clumps. The bus groaned and shifted slightly. "Tie her off, lads!" he cried as his men pulled cable from the winches of their jeeps and began to look for the most solid place on the bus to attach them.

"Cap'n, if she goes she'll take the cars with 'er!" cried Sergeant Ham as he scrambled around the deep hole left by the mine.

"So what are you waiting for?" came the angry cry of a male voice inside the back of the bus. Like an overloaded see-saw, the back of the bus groaned and swayed again. As Luke watched, the front wheel lifted slowly and the frame began a grinding slide toward oblivion.

"We're losin' 'er, Cap'n!" cried Ham.

The wind moaned like the sighs of a thousand dead, and a chill swept through Luke as he watched the cables stretch and tighten.

"She's takin' the cars, Cap'n!" cried a young relief

soldier as he scrambled from the path of the tortuous slide. Two other soldiers bailed out of the cars and scrambled to safety.

Dear God! thought Luke, *There are people in there!* Their fearful cries filled his ears; without thought he ran to his armored car. With a brief glance at the shifting beast that seemed bent on its own destruction, Luke slid into the darkness of the car and started the engine with a roar. He could feel the tortuous backward tug as he let out the clutch and revved the engine. Mud from the tires sprayed men who stood helplessly by. After a moment's hesitation Sergeant Ham called out, "I'm with ye, Cap'n!" and he stumbled to the second car to repeat Luke's maneuvers. With the pull of both vehicles, the bus steadied on its perch momentarily. "Come on, lads," Luke mumbled, unable to leave his post. "Get another cable on her. Tie her off to the boulder."

For a moment no one moved; then, as if they had heard the whispered orders of their brave captain, three men left the muddy sidelines and with frozen fingers secured first one cable between the bus and the boulder, then another. Only a few minutes had passed since Luke had run to the armored car, but it seemed like hours.

Luke looked up to see the happy face of Smiley Hitchcock shining down at him. "Y' can get out now, Cap'n," he said. "We got 'er secured t' the boulder all right. Don't know 'ow long she'll 'old though, sir. An' I wouldn't be surprised a bit if the back 'alf weren't gonna bust off all the same. She looks shaky at best, sir, an' the Yids is settin' up a squawk in there t' be let out!"

———————

A man lay in a pool of blood beside Rachel. He moaned long and loud, his cries rising and falling like the wind. Trapped partly by the heavy bulk of the wrestler and partly by another man, Rachel was desperately uncomfortable but, to her own amazement, unhurt. Only moments before, when the big man had attempted to shift his weight from her, their shattered prison had swayed and groaned until cries of fear had echoed off its metal walls. Except for the unfortunate Yosi, everyone who had boarded the bus seemed to be alive. The wrestler, who had a bloody gash on his forehead, had gasped out a roll call which had been answered feebly name by name with a word or sometimes the phrase, "he still breathes, thank God," or "I saw him move a bit."

Four men were unconscious. One wept quietly as he held his hands over his bleeding ears. Two others cried out at the slightest movement and another said he thought his leg was crushed but he felt no pain. Besides Rachel, only three others seemed uninjured and clearheaded. For them, perhaps, the awareness of the chasm below was the most frightening.

"Let me die!" cried the man who had been closest to Yosi when the grenade had exploded. He rocked his head in his hands.

"Shut up, Amos!" exploded the wrestler. "You tempt God when you pray like that!"

"Let me die!" repeated Amos.

"He cannot hear you," a voice called out. "His eardrums are shattered."

"Pay no attention to him, God," the wrestler called loudly. "This is Chaim, God. Pay no attention to Amos!"

Rachel felt an unreasonable urge to giggle at this giant of a man as he called out in the darkness. The heap next to her moaned once more and she tried to cover her own ears. *Pay no attention to Amos, God,* she thought. *He is only in pain, and death feels merciful to those who suffer.* How many times had she prayed to die, and the heavens had answered in stony silence? Yet tonight, she knew that perhaps her own prayer of pain might at last be answered. Soon perhaps it would all end.

The small man, whose spectacles had long since vanished into the hole beneath them, tried to reassure the big man. "You're worried about a prayer from

Amos?" he asked, his voice full of humor. "Amos prays for riches, yet he is poor. He prays for a wife; no one will have him. He prays to go to America; here he is in Jerusalem. Let your heart be at rest, Chaim. If Amos prays to die, stay near him. He shall be the first rescued."

"Your name is Chaim?" Rachel ventured.

The wrestler grunted a response.

"Chaim. Life. That is a good name to have tonight—"

"And when we are free," interjected the small man, "we shall drink Chaim! To life!"

"Shut up! You want to tempt the evil eye?" Chaim shouted.

"God did not bring me so far to die like this," said the small man.

"Then maybe you should be telling God to put wings on this bus," said the wrestler.

"Chaim," the small man chided, "you know better than that, nu? If God had wanted buses to fly. . ."

To Rachel's amazement, the big man answered with a deep chuckle. He drew his breath in slowly and released it with a sigh. "So what are they waiting for out there? Winston Churchill?" he said.

A light licked the darkness, and a strangely cheerful British voice called out to them, "Righto! We'll have you quite safe in half an instant. So sorry for the inconvenience, chaps. Just trying to keep the bus from tumbling on down the slopes, you know!"

"There, you see, Chaim. Winston Churchill nearly. So quit your kvetching already!" said the little man.

Rachel wondered what fears lay behind his own remarkable self-control. She felt like weeping and laughing, and once she wanted to push the crush of the injured away from her regardless of the peril to the bus. *Panic. I have known this before. In the cattle cars when they packed us in one against another.* The old and the feeble had died where they stood on the two-day journey to the camps. And when Rachel had thought she would go mad in the crush, her mother had calmed her.

"It will soon end, Rachel dear. They promised us a cup of water soon." But the water had not come until the end of the journey. Then promises of water and bread and jam after a shower had lured the thousands into the chambers. And their journey had ended in the crematoriums less than two hours after they had disembarked.

"I am thirsty," Rachel said suddenly.

"So open your mouth," growled the wrestler. "God has not lacked in the blessing of water."

Feeling foolish, Rachel cupped her hand and held it beneath a stream of water that poured through a jagged crack in the seam of the bus. She held her hand to her lips and sipped the icy liquid as if to quench the thirst of her memory.

"But, Mama," she had cried, *"I want to go with you."* She had turned to the guard and begged, *"Please, can I not go with my mother?"*

"Do you want a cup of water, girl?" he growled. *"Are you thirsty? Come here!"* he demanded. Then he stepped back and filled a dipper with water from a large metal drum on the platform. Her tongue had swollen in her mouth and she could no longer swallow.

"I want to go with Mama," she cried again, clutching her mother around her waist.

"And so you shall," he softened his tone. *"Woman,"* he demanded Rachel's mother, *"tell her to come."*

Rachel had looked searchingly into her mother's haunted eyes. *It is only a cup of water,* they seemed to say. But her mother had not spoken. Slowly Rachel had released her and turned to the guard where he stood smiling and holding the dripping cup.

"You see, girl," he had said as she drank amid the surging crowds who staggered from the trains. *"It is only water."* Twice more he had dipped the cup for her, and when she filled it once again to share with Mama, she had turned to find that her mother had vanished and she was alone among the fearful and the brutal who acted out their roles on the platform that afternoon. She

never saw her mother again.

Let me die, God, she had prayed. *Please let me die.* But she had lived.

Rachel recognized the calm voice of Captain Luke Thomas. "You're well secured now, but all the same it is important that there be as little movement as possible. We're sending down a sling on a rope." Rachel watched as the rope was fed down the broken aisle toward them. "Ladies and wounded first," he instructed.

"I can't," Rachel called back to him. "I am in the far back and there are several who must come out before me." There was an edge of panic in her voice that she had not known would be there.

"Well, then," he said, his voice calm and reassuring, "as soon as it is possible. You will be all right, Miss Lubetkin."

"He knows your name?" asked the small man.

"He is a friend. He has helped my grandfather, a rabbi in the Old City," Rachel answered defensively.

"And the rest of your name, please?" asked the small man without offense.

"Rachel," she replied, pulling her armor close about her.

"I am Dov." He answered simply a question that had not been asked. "So, when people are close enough to perhaps die together, it is good that they should know one another's names, nu?"

Dov seemed a strange name for one so small—in Hebrew it meant "bear." Suddenly Rachel remembered his courage in stepping up to drink the water near the British soldiers. *Perhaps Dov is a good name for one with such courage,* she thought. "I have always thought names mattered little when one was dead," she answered.

"Well, then, perhaps we should not die." He grasped the rope and carefully placed the sling over the head and beneath the arms of an unconscious man next to him. "So, there are eleven others in here," he called. "What are you waiting for, Winston Churchill?"

Wind whistled through the open belly of the bus as one by one the wounded and unconscious were disgorged. Rachel closed her eyes tightly when cries of agony echoed inside the iron chamber. As the weight was pulled away from them, the rear of the bus seemed to sway more violently and groan more loudly. Broken seams in the iron plate fractured the two halves of the bus. The sleet grew more fierce as it poured down on them. Rachel was not so sure that God had not brought her this far to die. There had, after all, been a pointlessness to her life; why should death not be pointless as well?

Amos clutched at the rope with one hand and his ear with the other as he was pulled to safety. "You see, Chaim," said Dov. "If you want to live, have Amos ask God to kill us all, nu?"

Only four of the uninjured remained. The wrestler shifted away from Rachel and Dov passed the sling back to her. "Women first, eh?" he said.

"You are ahead of me. It would be easier. . ."

Dov looped the sling awkwardly over her head. "Does God answer your prayers?" he asked with a half-smile.

"No," Rachel returned.

"Then pray we die, eh? And God will say, 'That's Rachel down there. Pay no attention.'"

She gasped as the steady tug of the rope lifted her over the broken seats and gaping bottom of the bus. Below her she could see the raw face of Gai Hinnom and feel the harsh wind that sought to pull her into the valley.

Lights and glare nearly blinded her as she crawled the last few feet out the exit of the vehicle. The grim face of Luke turned toward her and he nodded briefly, then returned to the task of freeing the three men still trapped inside the now dangerously swaying vehicle.

"We're about to lose a cable, Cap'n," a short sergeant said loudly.

"Then secure another!" Luke snapped with uncharacteristic irritation. "One of you men get Miss Lubetkin into some shelter. Fetch her a blanket out of my car."

Her knees nearly buckled as she leaned against a faceless soldier who escorted her to the shelter of an armored car. She sipped hot coffee from a thermos and watched as an ambulance and a transport drove down the slope and ultimately to Hadassah Hospital. When at last Chaim and Dov and an older, scholarly looking man stood huddled together on solid ground, Rachel rose and walked slowly toward the pool of light where they spoke in hushed tones to Luke.

"I will be fine," Chaim blotted his forehead. "It is not the will of God that we should come so far and not see an end . . ."

"As for the injured," Dov added seriously. "It was not meant to be so. But for me, I cannot go back."

"This is my home," said the older man. "I will not turn back because of such misfortune as a land mine. I also am needed."

Rachel stepped into the light. "I do not wish to turn back either, Captain Thomas. I do not know how, but I have come too far to end it thus. I have a message to deliver. For my grandfather"

High atop the broad wall of the Old City, Gerhardt stood serenely beneath the British-made umbrella held by a shivering Jihad Moquade. He held his field glasses to his eyes and focused on the four Englishmen below the wreck of the Number Two bus. He almost laughed at the expressions on their faces as they bagged the broken bodies of the deserter and the mangled Jew. Instead, he passed the glasses to Ram Kadar.

"He was nothing but English scum, anyway," he said, directing Kadar's gaze to the body. "So, the Jews shall say it was the English who placed the land mine and the English shall say it was the Jews who killed the English deserter."

"With Haj Amin in Cairo, it is just as well. No one

will say tomorrow that our forces had anything to do with this. You have done well, Gerhardt. Haj Amin, the Mufti, will reward you well." Kadar peered at the wreck below them.

"I need men. Courageous men that I might train."

"Men you can find here. Haj Amin will not deny you this."

"And money. For the souks of Damascus where a man might find anything he needs to exterminate vermin."

"You know well I have not agreed wholly with your methods. But if this"—Kadar gestured broadly—"will stop the flow of men into the Old City, then I will speak to Haj Amin on your behalf. You can train men to be competent in the use of explosives?"

"As capable as any man in the S.S."

Kadar smiled slightly and handed the field glasses back to Gerhardt. "The men of the Führer lost the war. Otherwise we would not have this problem. Perhaps you should train your men as a Muslim, not as a German."

Gerhardt glared at Kadar, then spit angrily on the rough stone floor where they stood. "Though my father was German, my mother raised me in the ways of the prophet. Thus you think less of me, but I will tell you, I killed my first Jew before Hitler was made Chancellor. In the Mufti's service and the service of Allah, here in the streets of the Old City, I killed first."

Kadar coolly appraised the angry young man beside him. Gerhard's ice-blue eyes burned in the darkness and his lip curled with hatred. Kadar did not like the Mufti's half-breed pet, but one could not argue with his success. Ben Yehudah Street was leveled, and Jews throughout the city lived in terror. "Yes, here in the Old City you killed first. But you also killed a man, a German officer, over a Jewish girl, did you not? And then you were sent to a concentration camp for five months as punishment. If it had not been for the Mufti's appeal to the Führer, you would have died in the gas chambers with the very people you now destroy. An interesting twist, Gerhardt. I have always thought so."

"The girl was a whore. Nothing but a whore!" Gerhardt shouted. "And the idiot I killed wanted to keep her for himself. They were provided for the pleasure of all of us. He was selfish. He deserved to die. I bore no feeling for the woman. I can kill a Jewish woman as easily as a man. And so I have."

"And so you have," Kadar sighed. "And so, no doubt, you will again. I will commend you to the Mufti tomorrow and tell him of your needs. Even now he is arranging the financing we will need for such *activities* as yours."

"And men. Tell him I need men. A Commando group of my own. Under my command. Tell him this when you see him."

Kadar bowed slightly. "Salaam. May the blessings of Allah be with you in our struggle."

"Salaam." Gerhardt bowed curtly, then turned back to the scene below him on the hillside as Kadar descended the steps into the darkness of the Arab Quarter.

Training the glasses on the frantically working English soldiers, Gerhardt knew that if he had a rifle he could easily pick a few off. But by order of the Mufti, his men were not to antagonize the British. *Let the Jewish terrorists do that.*

One by one the wounded Hassidim were loaded onto the waiting vans. In spite of the fact that he had detonated the mine a fraction of a second too early to destroy the bus completely, Gerhardt had a sense of accomplishment as he surveyed the scene. He focused on the three Hassidim who stood talking with the tall English captain whom he had seen many times in the streets of the Old City. The big Jew blotted his bleeding forehead as the little Jew talked. The older man had the look of a rabbi about him. *This night,* thought Gerhardt, *the vermin need a rabbi.* And on the edge of the group a woman stood with her back to him. He could just see her hands, delicate and white in the glare of the lights.

Her hair hung in long damp strands and she nodded as the others spoke. *Turn around,* Gerhardt whispered. He focused down on her and watched her for a long time. Then, as he was about to give up, she turned and he saw her profile. *Young. This Jewess is young and beautiful,* he thought. *Her skin looks soft as the breast of a dove.* Gerhardt lowered the glasses as the woman stepped from the pool of light. He turned away and touched the brand of Ravensbruk on his forearm as he remembered the face of the Jewish whore for whom he had killed.

7 Rachel's Choice

Ellie pulled to the far right-hand shoulder of the road as two ambulances and an army transport moved with cautious urgency down the slippery incline toward them. Red lights swirled and blinked, illuminating the rocks and barren soil on either side of the road. A sense of dread filled Ellie as the vehicles snaked past them with only inches to spare. She rolled down her window and called out to the driver of the first ambulance, "Is there an injured woman in your van?" The man did not stop or acknowledge her, and as the sleet poured into the car she slammed her fist on the steering wheel in frustration. "*Rachel*," she breathed, and the word named all her pain. *Dear God . . .* Her prayer remained unspoken and full of grief.

"We will not make it up the road in this, miss," Ehud sniffed and opened his car door. "Come on. We must walk, unless you are afraid."

Ellie retrieved her field boots from the backseat and pulled them on. Ignoring the downpour, she donned Uncle Howard's slicker and rain cap and plunged into the slush. Her camera was tucked safely beneath her coat; even as the sleet stung her cheeks, Ellie wished she had not accepted this assignment. "I should have driven straight to Hadassah!" she shouted to Ehud trudging a few feet ahead of her. Ehud stopped and stood staring at the twisted bus and the emergency vehicles surrounding it. The jagged hole in the bottom was visible even from fifty yards.

"What use is a hospital?" he said bitterly. "Who could survive such a blast?"

Far below the bus in the glare of the spotlights, soldiers loaded canvas-wrapped bodies onto stretchers and lugged them to the lower switchback where yet another van waited.

On the perimeter of the darkness, Ellie saw drenched soldiers standing alert with their Sten guns ready. Her mind reeled with the images of death she had seen since she came to Palestine. "Rachel," she whispered again as she stopped and stared at the bus. Her hands fell limply to her sides, and she bit her lip with the certainty of her friend's fate.

"Do you care to go on with this foolishness?" Ehud asked. "Or do we go now to your uncle's home and to Moshe?"

"I have to know." Ellie leaned into the wind and forced herself the last few yards of the road to where a wet and muddy young soldier stood staring out at the empty darkness.

"Halt!" he shouted as they approached.

"My name is Ellie Warne," she stammered. "I'm a photographer. *Life* magazine and *Palestine Post.*"

"Identification."

Ellie fumbled in her pocket for her press card. "*Life* magazine, eh?" The young man's demeanor changed instantly. "Want t' take me picture, miss?"

"How many were killed?" Ellie asked.

"Can't say for sure. They've picked up a couple bodies down below. Gruesome job, if ye ask me. I'd sooner stand out in the sleet all day an' night—"

"Was there a woman among them?"

"Can't say. They hauled a load down from 'ere, I can tell y'. Want t' take me picture now, miss? Standin' guard 'ere?" He noticed the angry-looking bulk of Ehud who grimaced and scowled at the Britisher. "An' who is this?"

"He's with me." Ellie grabbed Ehud's arm and pushed past the soldier.

"Takin' a bit of chance aren't ye, miss?" the soldier called out to them. "No tellin' 'ow many of 'em are out there. Sure ye don't want t' take me picture?"

A new surge of panic seemed to pull Ellie toward the wreck. Cable that seemed as fragile as sewing thread held the giant listing hulk on the brink of the embankment. She frantically searched for a familiar face among the men who moved purposefully about. "Have you seen Captain Luke Thomas?" Ellie asked a preoccupied-looking middle-aged man.

"Aye. 'e's round t'other side of the bus."

Tugging at Ehud's sleeve, she ran splashing through the mud to the front of the bus. She quickly ducked under the cables and called to the grim-faced captain. "Luke! Luke Thomas!"

He turned from the group of men he spoke with and shielded his eyes against the glare of the headlights.

He frowned, then smiled politely as Ellie ran toward him. "Ellie Warne!" he exclaimed. "Does your uncle know you're out and about on a night like this?"

"Rachel!" Ellie cried, spotting her friend and running straight past the captain into her embrace. "Oh, Rachel, are you okay? I was worried sick. We heard at the *Post* that there had been an accident. I stopped to drop off the photos of the Tel Aviv convoy and they said there had been an accident."

Rain mingled with tears of joy as the worry melted away. Rachel patted her on the back. "You shouldn't be here. This was not an accident. Many are injured. Moshe will be most unhappy that you have come here alone."

"I didn't come alone. I brought Ehud. Remember Ehud Schiff? Captain Schiff?"

A spark of recognition passed over Rachel's face. "In Jerusalem?"

"I didn't know he was coming. He just got off the Tel Aviv transport and there we were. He said he tried to reach Moshe."

"So this is not a day for Jewish convoys, eh?" said Ehud surveying the scene. "Three died on the way from Tel Aviv to Jerusalem. Nine wounded."

"Two dead here. Only four passengers of thirteen

71

are well enough to continue their journey," said Luke. "Some serious injuries, but when they left they were still breathing."

"You're going ahead, then?" Ellie took Rachel's hand. "You're going in there even with this?"

"What choice do we have, Ellie?" Rachel did not look at her face. "There is no one else left to go, eh?"

Luke lowered his voice. "Tell Moshe nearly everything has been confiscated or lost. We have only these four to carry for us. There probably will be no more buses to Zion Gate. All this"—he waved his hand—"was more likely done by one or two men at the most. It was a mine. We found the wires. They led to a plunger up behind those boulders. If only one man can do this much damage—"

"How much was lost?" Ellie asked.

"All but for what we four carry. We can bring no more with us," Rachel answered. "The young men who were to defend are all injured."

"I am not so very old, you know." Ehud stepped into the circle. "I am strong. As strong as any seaman on the coast. Have you weapons I might carry into the Old City? Might I join you this night?"

Dov, who had remained silent as he watched the newcomers, pursed his lips and frowned thoughtfully. "You are Ehud Schiff? Late of the *Ave Maria*?" he asked.

Ehud bowed curtly.

Chaim clapped his hands together. "I remember you now!" He cried, then embraced Ehud in a bear hug. "A brave fellow! A good captain, although I was sick from the journey."

"Old passengers?" Ehud grinned broadly. "I did not bring you to a haven of safety, I see."

Dov clapped him on the back. "We would be honored to have you numbered among us, Captain Schiff."

"What about me?" Ellie asked hopefully, still clinging to Rachel's hand.

The eyes of the Hassidim and Rachel and Luke focused on her in incredulous silence. "Ha!" exclaimed Ehud. "I think not."

"Just for tonight. I've—" She stopped herself and lowered her voice. "I've smuggled weapons before."

"Moshe would not allow it," Rachel said coolly, withdrawing her hand.

"What's with you?" Ellie felt a spark of anger. "Moshe's not here, and this isn't anything I haven't handled before."

"I am here," Luke said with a kindly sternness. "And I will not allow it. It is true you have been behind the walls before, but this is not the place for you now."

Rachel breathed a relieved sigh that the good captain had taken command of her impetuous friend.

"But I—" Ellie began.

"No, Miss Warne. I am a friend of your uncle's as well, and it is my duty to see you safely home."

Clearly beaten, Ellie stood in frustrated silence for a moment as the rain began a fresh deluge. Then she pulled her slicker off and handed it to Rachel. "You might as well take this," she pouted.

A half-smile on her lips, Rachel took the slicker from Ellie and slipped it on over her drenched coat. "Thank you."

"You want my field boots?" Ellie took her by the arm and led her to an armored car while Ehud was taken to a small cache of weapons that had been taken from the wrecked bus.

Inside the comparative warmth of the car, Ellie pulled her heavy boots from her feet and handed them to Rachel who sat quietly beside her.

"I just want you to know something, Rachel," Ellie began, her voice tinged with emotion.

"Yes."

"I figured out what you're up to. You aren't coming out again after you deliver your message and the weapons. You've decided to stay in the Old City, haven't you?"

Rachel's eyes remained downcast. "I must do what I can to help."

"But you decided not to come out again, didn't you?"

"Yes."

"And that's why you don't want me in there, isn't it?"

"Yes."

"Because I'll make you come out."

"No. You could not force me. I am doing this on my own, dear friend."

"Okay, so why don't you want me to go?"

Rachel groped for words, angry that she was forced to give an account of what she truly felt. "I don't know."

"What are you afraid of, Rachel?" Ellie demanded. "We are supposed to be friends, and still you don't let me or anyone else see what's going on inside you. Your walls are thicker than the walls of the Old City, I can tell you."

Rachel swallowed hard, feeling unhappiness push against her throat. "You are angry with me." Her voice sounded small and childlike. "That is why I could not tell you."

"I'm not mad. But why don't you want me in there with you? I could carry weapons as easily as anyone."

"I . . . I am afraid."

"Of what?"

"That I will see you . . . hurt. I cannot say goodbye even one time more, my dear friend. Better not to care. Better to live alone and die alone."

"It's a little late for all that now, Rachel. You have Yacov and your grandfather and Moshe—"

"No. Not Moshe. You must not say such a thing!" she said intensely.

"Yes, Moshe. What do you think it will do to him if something happens to you now?"

"Not Moshe." Rachel insisted.

"Suit yourself. But whether you believe it or not, the guy loves you, Rachel."

"There is nothing left of me to love. I must find myself here, Ellie, behind these walls. No one can do this for me, or even help me in this."

A sharp rapping on the metal door interrupted them.

"Miss Lubetkin." The voice of Captain Thomas echoed hollowly. "Miss Lubetkin."

Ellie looked deeply into Rachel's eyes. "I guess there's nothing I can say."

Rachel shrugged and tried to smile a reassuring smile. "No."

"Well, then," she sighed. Rachel opened the door and the howling of the storm filled the car with cold again. She glanced at Ellie one last time and started to climb from the car.

"Wait!" Ellie cried. She pulled Rachel to her. "Just don't let them kill you, Rachel. Please don't let them kill you."

Rachel laid her head on Ellie's shoulder, then patted her on the back and nodded.

"Miss Lubetkin," repeated Luke, "Rachel, we have to go."

8 Meetings in the Old City

One by one the nine rabbis filed respectfully into the dining room of Rabbi Akiva, mayor of the Old City. Only one small oil lamp hung from the ceiling above the long mahogany table. A thin ribbon of smoke circled around the ornate electric chandelier, severed from its source of power a month before, three days after Partition had passed. The household of Akiva was the only house that suffered loss of electricity, since no one else in the Old City had such a luxury. The distinguished mayor also possessed one of two telephones in the quarter, a privilege due his rank as mayor and head mediator among the Arab High Committee, the British Mandatory Government, and the citizens of the ancient Jewish Quarter. The telephone still worked, at any rate, with a direct line out to the headquarters of the British government in Palestine.

Rabbi Akiva sat in majestic silence at the head of the table as the men he had called together bowed slightly and took their places on either side of him in order of age. Snowy-white beards and sidelocks sat nearest, then gray-streaked, followed by black with gray, and last, jet-black. Each face was grim and eyes looked straight ahead instead of wandering enviously around the opulent mahogany-paneled room.

Thin and pinched-looking, Akiva's 17-year-old daughter Yehudit poured tea into delicate china cups set before the rabbis. A plate of Armenian baklavah pastry adorned the center of the white lace tablecloth, but none dared reach out to take a piece. The Jewish Quarter might have been under siege, but not the house of Rabbi Akiva. He still had friends and neighbors among the neighboring Christian and Muslim Quarters in spite of the fact that the militant Zionists had invaded his small empire.

Akiva tugged his beard, then took his gold pocket watch from his vest and laid it open on the table. "Well, gentlemen, there are ten of us here. We have a minyon and may begin, nu?"

A bronze clock ticked noisily on the sideboard as the men of Akiva's minyon shifted in their chairs and sipped tea. Each pair of dark and brooding eyes rested on the face of the man who now struggled desperately to maintain control of his city. "Yes, well," Akiva raised his broad head and lifted his chin with the air of one who is in control. "I have called you here, the most distinguished of Yeshiva scholars, to discuss a problem. It is the most urgent of problems we have suffered in many years—"

An ancient rabbi to his right cleared his throat and said as he pointed to the chandelier, "I see you have not gotten your lights to work again since the tragedy."

"No, Rebbe Raumgarten. Not since the Partition was voted."

"Such a shame, nu? To have such an expensive lamp that sheds no light."

The other rabbis cast their eyes toward the useless fixture and agreed with the old man. "Such a waste! Oy! What a pity!"

Akiva cleared his throat again and sighed. "It is a small thing compared to the troubles we all face here in the Old City since the Jewish Agency sent these Haganah Zionists into our midst."

"Are they not for our protection, Rebbe Akiva?" the black-bearded man at the far end of the table asked quickly. All heads turned toward him, and he stared at his hands in shame at his impudence.

Akiva's mouth twitched as he fought for control. Calmly he replied to the foolish young rabbi, "Our problem is not the need of protection from our neighbors. It is need of protection from those who would destroy our peace. Is this not so, Rebbe Gruen?"

The man with the gray beard in the center of the table nodded. "We have always managed on our own before. In the shadow of the wall of the Temple. In the shadow of danger, we are under the eye of the Eternal."

A chorus of "Well spoken! Omaine to that!" filled the dining room.

"For years we have lived at peace with our neighbors," Akiva began.

"Not so many years as all that," mumbled the white-bearded rabbi to his right.

"What is that?" Akiva demanded, his voice thick with irritation.

The old man answered with a toothless smile. "I was just remembering it is not so many years since the riots killed so many of us."

"But always the violence was brought in by outsiders, nu? Are we not men who seek peace and pursue it?"

Heads nodded all around. "Well spoken, Rabbi."

The old man raised his hand slightly and sniffed. "The very words of your dead father, may he rest in peace. Omaine. But still in 1929 and again in 1931 and '32 and '36 we buried the dead on Mount Zion and picked up the torn fragments of the Torah scrolls. Often it is not enough to seek peace. And there are other ways than dying to pursue it, nu?"

Another chorus of "Well spoken, Rabbi!" echoed around the table.

"That is true, true," Akiva smiled grimly. "But always violence has been brought in by outsiders. Now we again have outsiders in our midst. They come with money from the Jewish Agency and take control of our social programs. It is they who distribute the food brought into the quarter by the British convoys. They pervert the studies of our young men and give them broomsticks which they carry, pretending to have rifles. And they drive out those among our Christian and Muslim neighbors who have lived in peace with us these many years."

The white-bearded rabbi stuck his lower lip out thoughtfully and tugged his beard. "This is true. My Shabbes-Goy, the kindly Christian gentleman who always came to light my lamps for me during Shabbat, has departed his home only this week. Although he told me it is as much for fear of the men of Haj Amin as for fear of the Haganah."

"The Mufti fears for his people who might be caught in Zionist cross fire. As I fear for mine. It is not guns that will keep us safe, but reason and sanity."

"It has always seemed as though reason would prevail."

"We are men of peace, nu? And yet we number among us members of the Haganah. It is said that some rabbis have even allowed them to use our ritual baths." He glared hard at the young rabbi on the end.

"Well, well," the rabbi with the white beard chuckled, "is this so terrible? Better they should not stink as long as they are here, nu?"

Akiva's voice became more insistent. "But they jeopardize everything we have here. And do they look for the Messiah to deliver us?"

"I have not heard them say they do not look for Him," volunteered a voice from behind a black and gray beard.

"They look for deliverance at the muzzle of guns smuggled in in place of our food. They wear the coats of Yeshiva scholars, but they come here to fight and kill the innocents."

"Perhaps they might also kill a sniper or two, Rebbe Akiva," said a gray-bearded man to his left.

Akiva drew himself up and placed his palms on the table in front of him. His brooding eyes probed each face. "There are some among us who are pleased to believe that the Haganah offer us protection. Many shelter these strangers. Many students have forsaken the Torah studies to follow after their ways. But I say to you that unless they are turned over to the British authorities, they will bring destruction on our homes and synagogues. My friends, we do not need these usurpers to protect us. Protect from what? Do our neighbors not long for peace as much as we? We cannot let the Zionists stir us to passion in the Old City. We must not fail to remember that only one can lead Israel to freedom, and that one will be our Messiah."

Opinions were mixed as the rabbis gathered their coats from the arms of frail Yehudit. One by one they filed out the massive door and into the cold night air. And as Yehudit bolted the latch behind them, she turned to her scowling father.

"Will they help you, Father?"

"Some of them, perhaps. They do not all understand that it is more important to save the Old City than to shelter these Zionist fools who have come among us . . ." He drummed his thick fingers on the tabletop. "You can help me, Yehudit."

"Yes, Father." Her melancholy face brightened at his words. "Go among these Haganah. Perhaps at Tipat Chalav when they distribute food, nu? Make friends and find out what it is they are up to, eh?"

Dodging spouts of water that poured from the rain gutters overhead, Rachel moved closer to the fronts of the lifeless shops of the Old City Jewish Quarter. The snow had melted quickly under the deluge that streamed off the rooftops and down the cobblestones where she and her four companions walked. Faint light glimmered from an upper-story window of a large house of Chaim Street.

"There is the home of Rabbi Akiva," said the rabbi. "We will find no help from him."

"Then we will not ask," boomed Ehud.

Rachel involuntarily touched the pocket of her coat

where Grandfather's letter waited for delivery into the right hands. She glanced up at the heavy gate that led to the courtyard of Akiva. It was just as Yacov had described to her. *Tall stone walls surrounding a courtyard. The house of Akiva is the finest in the city. The door is carved with roses, and inside! Oy! Such a house you have never seen. But just the two of them live there. Rebbe Akiva and Yehudit. She will have many suitors because her father is wealthy, but I would not have her. She is not pretty like you, my sister.* She smiled at the memory of Yacov's words; then she reached out and touched the gate as the hands of Yacov and Grandfather must have touched it many times.

"How much farther?" stuttered Chaim, his hat soggy and dripping on his face. "I will need a cup of hot tea."

"Bah! This is but a small gale." Ehud spoke like one accustomed to shouting above the wind. "This is not enough to shake the mast of my sweet *Maria.* We have faced worse than this with our hold full of cargo and no fire to heat water for tea."

"Tipat Chalav is only around the corner," encouraged the rabbi. "They will gladly give a cup of tea for the cargo we carry, little though it may be."

Rachel did not regret the loss of the hand grenades and bullets she had tucked away in her satchel half as much as the loss of clean, dry socks and warm clothes. She realized that all she owned was what she wore on her back. She was grateful for Ellie's field boots, but wished she had thought to take her walking shoes with her. She raised her eyes as the rabbi shouted happily, "You see! There it is! Tipat Chalav, the Drop of Milk! I first came to this place as a babe in my mother's arms. And so it was with most of the others who have lived their lives here."

Lights poured warmly from the windows of the two-story building that served as the food distribution center for the hungry children of the quarter. "Listen!" the rabbi cried again. "Do you hear it?"

As Rachel strained to hear above the howl of the

storm, the faint sounds of an orchestra drifted clearly from the building.

"It is Tuesday night," he explained. "Leah Feldstein comes to play her phonograph on Tuesday night. Rachmaninoff, *Piano Concerto Number One in F Sharp*, I think." He smiled broadly as the music grew more distinct. "Ah yes, exactly."

Rachel smiled as she remembered what Yacov had told her about the woman Leah and her phonograph. *She is a teacher. She once played cello for a great orchestra in Vienna before the war. Sometimes she plays her cello for us. She calls it Vitorio, and once she let me hold the bow and play a note. And on Tuesday night . . .*

As Rachel passed the lighted window, she looked through the rain-streaked panes into the room that was as well known to her brother as his own home. Perched atop a wooden stand was Leah's battered hand-cranked phonograph. Small children clustered around it on the floor, and young and old women sat in hard wooden chairs around the room. Next to the phonograph a young woman sat with her chin lifted and her eyes closed in rapture as she listened to the music. Her back was very straight and her hands were clasped on her knees. Her light brown hair was cut to frame a round, pretty face that seemed to glow. The woman wore a frayed camel hair coat and a black shawl over that. *This is Leah*, Rachel thought, remembering Yacov's description of the woman who had been so kind to him. Suddenly the stories he had told her about the Old City and the people of the quarter became reality to her. This was the home of her family—her mother and father, Grandfather, Yacov; this is where they had lived and loved and scratched out a piece of the earth as their own. She was home!

She stood outside, her chin resting on the windowsill as her heart thirstily drank in the picture before her. Images that her mother had given her so long ago suddenly came to life. *Over there, by the kitchen door, Father first spoke to Mother. And at these tables Yacov and*

Grandfather have eaten many times while the dog Shaul waited outside the door just here . . .

The voice of Dov brought her back to the reality of the moment. "Rachel!" He called from the front steps of Tipat Chalav as the rabbi threw the door wide and stepped in. "Come on! Get out of the weather. We have arrived, nu?"

As the door burst open and they stumbled into the warmth of the large community room, heads turned in curiosity to stare at the five dripping vagabonds who stood at the back of the room. Leah opened her eyes and put her finger to her lips to silence the buzzing of the children sitting cross-legged on the floor in front of her. Then she stood and walked quietly around the fringe of the small audience to where they stood. Rachel noticed that Leah's coat gapped in the center and she walked with the rolling gate of a sailor. *Why, she is pregnant!* Rachel thought with surprise. This was the only detail about Leah Feldstein that Yacov had failed to mention. Rachel tried not to look at her bulging stomach. *The child will be here very soon,* she thought.

A pleasant smile lit up the moon-shaped face of Leah as she walked directly toward Rachel with her hands outstretched. Rachel had a sudden surge of panic when she realized that Leah's gaze was solely on her. She tried to hide her bewilderment from Leah and smile in return at this woman who acted as though she had known Rachel always. Leah grasped Rachel's cold hands. "You are the granddaughter of Rabbi Lebowitz," she said warmly.

"Why, yes, but how—"

"I was there. At the synagogue in the gallery when you came to find him. Is he well? We have had no news, you see, though we have prayed daily for him."

"He . . . he will live." Rachel felt almost overcome by the instant welcome of Leah.

"And Yacov? How is my Yacov?"

"He is recovering in the New City. He must remain

83

with Professor Howard Moniger and his niece—"

"The red-haired woman who was with you that night?"

"Yes. Ellie."

"I spoke with her briefly as your grandfather lay ill. A kind woman. She seemed quite concerned about the safety of my husband, Shimon, as he lay on the scaffolding in the cupola of the synagogue to keep watch for snipers." She still held Rachel's hands tightly in her own. "And now you must all be frozen." She at last looked up at the four dripping men who had stepped away from Rachel in amazement at the greeting. "A cup of tea?" Leah asked.

"Didn't I tell you?" beamed the rabbi. "It is good to see you, Leah. Some things do not change, nu?"

"Only some things, Rabbi Vultch." She shook each man's hand. "You must forgive my manners. It is just that to meet the granddaughter of Rabbi Lebowitz . . . God is gracious."

"You did not tell us who you were Rachel!" exclaimed Rabbi Vultch. "Rebbe Lebowitz was once my teacher in Yeshiva. Your dear mother—" He gazed tenderly into Rachel's face. "I knew her well. And your father. You favor her as I look at you now. Such a beauty. I hope you favor her spirit as well."

Rachel looked quickly down at the puddle of water that had formed around her boots. "It was always my wish that I would be like her someday," she said. Then she smiled at Leah, who still gazed happily at her. "Yacov has told me all about you. About Vitorio your cello and the Tuesday night concerts."

"I have an aunt in New York, America. She sends me these RCA Victor records of the symphony," she explained. "The children seem to enjoy them very much."

"As well as the adults." Rabbi Vultch surveyed the Old City residents listening raptly to the music.

Leah frowned as she noticed the gash on Chaim's broad forehead. "You are injured! Was there trouble?"

"An accident. Several injured," Dov answered quickly.

"Where are the others?" Leah asked.

"Hadassah Hospital by now." Chaim touched his forehead gingerly.

"Go down to the basement," Leah instructed. "The men are waiting for your arrival there. Have you lost your clothes as well? Have you nothing dry to put on?"

"What luggage we had is at the bottom of the Hinnom," said Rabbi Vultch. "Beside the young boy, Yosi." He glanced quickly at Chaim. "Molech has claimed yet another life, I fear," he mumbled.

"I am sorry." Leah took Rachel's hand again but her eyes moved from face to face. "It is by the grace of God that you stand among us, I see."

"Yes. By the grace of the Eternal," Dov said, a frown creasing his brow.

"Now we must get you all into some dry things or you may not be able to stand in the morning. Rachel, come with me while I brew some tea and we shall see what we might find for you to wear."

9   Coming Home

It was nearly one a.m. before Moshe switched off the BBC of Palestine. David's delayed broadcast of New Year celebrations in the States had lost out hours ago to repeated news broadcasts of the two attacks on Jewish transports. An hour before, Howard had wandered off to bed with the sleeping Yacov cradled in his arms; then David had yawned and said good night. Now only Ellie sat in the kitchen watching as Moshe paced the length of the small room, then turned and retraced his footsteps across the tiled floor. He tapped his fingers nervously on the hard shell of his plaster cast.

"Moshe." Ellie sipped the last of her coffee. "Don't you think you should give it up now and go to bed?"

"I couldn't sleep," he said. "I just couldn't."

"Too much coffee." She set her cup down and peered at the dregs of the cup. "This stuff will stand up without a cup, it's so strong." Moshe continued to pace. "Come on, pal. Call it a night."

"Not until I hear from Luke. He told you he would come by and report on their arrival. You go to bed, Ellie. I'll wait up."

"No." She took another sip and wrinkled her nose. "I couldn't sleep."

They passed a few moments in silence; then Moshe spoke, his face a mask of grim consternation. "Didn't she say anything else?"

"Like what, Moshe?"

"Perhaps about me?"

Ellie smiled slightly and drummed her fingers on the tabletop. "She said . . ." Ellie began then thought better of repeating the words Rachel had spoken about Moshe and the fact that she could never love a man as her own. Moshe was suffering, it was plain to see. Rachel's hopelessness was nothing he should have to bear tonight.

"Yes? What? What did she say?"

"Just what I told you. She's not coming out. She feels her place is in the Old City."

"Couldn't you have stopped her?"

"You think I should have sat on her or something? She's a big girl, Moshe—"

"Not really. In so many ways she is still a child."

"She did say something about you, Moshe—"

He pulled up a chair and sat across from Ellie, his face imploring her to help him understand. "Please . . ."

"She said you had better things to do right now than look after her."

"She said that? That is all I want to do." He gazed at the floor in front of him.

"I don't think that's what she wants right now."

He looked up quickly into Ellie's face. "But *why?*"

"She's going in there to prove something to herself. She is looking for something. Forgiveness, I think."

"But there is nothing to forgive—she was a child, just a child. The things that were done to her were not her fault."

"No, but they have become her memories. She told me the other day that so many died, and she couldn't figure out why she hadn't. She had wanted to die so badly."

"I have known this," Moshe nodded miserably.

"She said she felt like a traitor to still be living. She is looking for a way to make that up, I think."

"Even if it means her life? If it means dying?"

"In a way, it does mean dying—to those things that have happened to her. She is looking for a much bigger love than anything you and I can give her. I know. I've been there. Oh, Moshe, she needs the kind of love that will help her forgive herself. Nobody can make her accept that love, or really even make her believe it exists until she is ready. She still thinks she can make it all up somehow, that she can personally atone for the guilt she feels for being alive when her parents and brothers died. I had my own stuff, you know, my own failures I was trying to make up for, and for a long time I thought I could. Now I see for myself that only the love of God could have healed my wounds, Moshe. And only God's love can heal Rachel's heart. She has to walk through this on her own. You can't do it for her. And when she is ready to hear the answer, you love her and be there for her."

Moshe rubbed at the dull ache that throbbed in the back of his neck. "I suppose it is obvious what I have come to feel for her."

"To everyone but her." Ellie smiled, grateful that her affection for Moshe had translated so easily into friendship.

"What do you mean?"

"Did you ever tell her?"

"How could I?"

Ellie rolled her eyes in exasperation. "Watch me." She exaggerated each word. "You open that mouth of yours and say, 'I LOVE YOU, RACHEL.' "

Moshe smiled in spite of himself. "You are wonderful, do you know that? When first I met you I thought how marvelous it was that you didn't seem to think too deeply. You were happy all the time. But now I see you truly do have a deep understanding of the heart."

"I think you just complimented me."

"You are wonderful. Your David is a lucky man."

"Well, we'll see about that. We still have a lot to settle . . ."

"Your friendship for Rachel has touched her in a way that I have not been able to. And I love you very much for that."

"There! You see how easy it is to say?"

"To a sister one can say such things. But with Rachel . . ."

"It's hard to say because she really wouldn't believe

88

it right now. She doesn't love herself and can't imagine that anyone else could love her."

He nodded and rubbed his forehead. "I feel that I must go to her, Ellie. I cannot remain here when there is so much to say. I thought she was coming back and there would be time." His voice was filled with regret. "If I had told her how I felt, she would have had something to come back to, perhaps."

"Or something else to run away from. Don't forget, Moshe, your love might lead her to the love of God, but only the Lord himself can heal her heart. You can't make it all better for her. She and the Lord are going to have to work that out by themselves."

Moshe nodded again, then frowned, hating the feelings of frustration and helplessness that flooded him. Finally he raised his eyes. "You are right, of course. This is her journey alone and I cannot make it for her. Still, I want to be with her—walk with her as she walks, and when she reaches the end I want to be there. I will talk to Luke. Perhaps he can help me into the Old City."

"His orders were that no one else goes in. I heard it over the shortwave. He ignored it and took Rachel and the others through Zion Gate. But it's going to mean his head. You better find some other way."

"Perhaps in the food convoy."

Ellie thumped his cast. "Right. You can go disguised as a boiled egg. Moshe, the best thing you can do right now is pray for her. Then get yourself well, okay? There's not a thing you can do right now to help her. I figured that out, or I really might have sat on her."

Ellie's heart ached for her miserable friend. She gazed tenderly at him for a long time, watching the helpless worry for the woman he loved cloud his handsome face. "I only wish she had told me she was not coming out," he said slowly.

"If she had, would you have let her go?"

He shook his head from side to side. "No," he said simply. "No, never."

Rachel opened her eyes in the darkness, listening to the hiss and sputter of the Primus stove. For a long moment she could not remember where she was; then her uneasy sleep parted like a curtain. She reached for the tall glass of water on the night stand and drank deeply. Lying back on the pillow, she drew a breath and savored the faint odor of Grandfather's tobacco and the musty scent of the damp stone walls that surrounded her. The ancient springs of the old man's bed groaned and sagged as she turned onto her side and stared at the faint light that seeped through the shutters.

"Be sure to sleep in Grandfather's bed," Yacov had told her as he handed her the rusty iron key to the basement apartment. "And if you would like, under the bed there is a box where he has kept some things from Mama. On special days sometimes we look at them together. You are coming home, nu? That is a special time."

Hours before, juggling an armload of Leah's extra clothes, Rachel had turned the key to the empty apartment. Ehud had lit the kerosene stove for her, then left hurriedly. Rachel had sat for a long time beside the stove and stared at the corner of the box that poked out from under the bed. It was not how she had pictured her homecoming. Always she had pictured Grandfather sitting across from her and raising a glass of cognac with the blessing, "To Life! L'Chaim! My dear." Instead, she stared at the untouched box of memories, then undressed and climbed between the cool sheets.

Rachel reached out and touched Yacov's empty bed. She tried to feel what it must have been like for the boy to grow up with Grandfather. She closed her eyes again and imagined that she had been with them all along, that she could hear the even breathing of her little brother and the deeper sound of Grandfather's breath as he dreamed of prophets and Torah and mighty Jerusalem as it must have been in its days of glory.

She sighed as the long ache of loneliness filled her heart. After years of her own dreams, she had finally touched the face of Grandfather and held her brother in her arms once again; yet still she was alone.

They must never know what I have done, she thought, *or they would wish me dead with the others.*

She remembered the words and hostile glances of those who had traveled with her from the Displaced Persons Camp onto the deck of the *Ave Maria.* To them she had been the woman of the Nazis, the harlot who had chosen life over honor.

On the *Ave Maria* she had first spoken to Moshe. "I am different than the others," she had said. "I have a family." He had smiled and called her lucky. He had been kind to her from the beginning, and yet when she felt her heart begin to trust him, she had drawn back and run away from him—from all of them. She knew what they would say if they knew how far she had fallen. And in the blackness of Grandfather's little room, she knew there was no one who really understood the depth of her crimes. Even here, she was still searching for home.

Hot tears stung her eyes and rolled down her cheeks. "Mama," she whispered to the darkness. "Mama, can you hear me? I am still so very thirsty, Mama." She held her arms out and grasped the emptiness above her. "Hold me. Please hold me, Mama." Only the hissing of the Primus stove answered her until at last she turned her face into the pillow and grieved for the thirst that could not be quenched.

Mama. It was a name no child would ever call her. Rachel ran her hand across the flatness of her stomach and the roundness of her breasts and remembered: *I was so filled with milk after they took the baby from my womb. If only I could have held her. Even just a moment.* She had wept then, too.

"Do you not understand, girl?" the young major had asked her. "You cannot carry this child or you will surely be killed and the child will be cast into the fire.

91

It is regulations. You will both die a horrible death."

She had known this. A hundred times she had seen the women marked *Nür Für Offizere* die when they tried to conceal their pregnancies. And yet, for nearly five months she had carried her secret until the soft bulge of her stomach and the fluttering within had filled her with both joy and terrible anguish. Then she had told the major. He had been kind to her, brought her chocolate and extra rations. Perhaps he would help. In the purgatory of night he had taken her to a doctor in the town. "He is well paid. No one will ever know." Then the tiny flutterings had ceased, and after hours of pain the perfect form of a baby girl had been gathered up and carried quickly away into the arms of Molech.

Rachel had returned to her place at the house. The major had gone back to the front. There were a hundred others who came in his place, but never again had she felt the soft flutter inside her womb. She had sacrificed the only thing still innocent enough to live in her.

Wiping her cheeks, she lit the lamp on the table beside the bed. Flickering shadows filled the room, and Rachel lay alone with her memories. How often she had dreamed of the girl-child! Tikvah, she had named her: Little Jewel. How her arms ached to hold her dreams! She wrapped the quilt around her, then climbed from beneath the covers and knelt beside the bed. Carefully she pulled the ragged cardboard box from under the springs. Almost afraid to lift the lid, she stared at it a long time, then summoned her courage to face the things that were.

On top of the neatly bound stacks of letters lay a yellowed photograph cluttered with happy faces. Prim and straight-backed, Mama sat with baby Yacov in her arms. Papa sat beside her, pride in his young family radiating from his eyes. And there behind Papa stood her two brothers. Rachel held the photograph close to her eyes as she studied the young girl who stood among them. "Was this ever me?" she spoke aloud, astonished at the eyes that shone so full of happiness and free of heartache. "Oh, God!" she groaned, holding the photograph to her breast. She squeezed her eyes tightly shut, trying to stop the flow of tears that pushed past her throat and spilled onto the bundles in the box. Fighting for control, she put the photograph face down on the bed and chose a packet of envelopes with Mama's filigreed handwriting on the outside. She held the packet close to her cheek and breathed deeply, trying to catch the sweet scent of Mama, but it had faded and disappeared with the years. She untied the string and opened the first of the letters, dated April 15, 1936. She tried to remember what her life had been like on that day, but it was like a long-forgotten tune that played sweetly in the back of her mind. Unclear and elusive, she could not define the melody.

"My dearest Papa," the letter began. Rachel traced each curve and swirl of the letters with her fingertip. Then she read aloud Mama's words.

"Another Seder has come and gone and still we long for you and say, 'Next year in Jerusalem.' Perhaps the immigration papers will come soon and we may truly see you before the year is past.

"Our Seder was so beautiful. The boys did so well and you would be proud of Rachel. Such a cook she will be! She helped in the kitchen this year. Her father says when it comes time for her to marry, young Reuven will be happy to learn when he lifts the veil that his bride is not only lovely but she can cook as well. In serving she spilled a bit of gefilte and I thought she would weep, but Rabbi Voher said the fish jumped off the plate, and she laughed instead . . ."

Rachel leaned back against the frame of the bed and tried to remember. "She wore a white frock with lace at the cuffs . . ."

My hair was braided and done up with a pale blue ribbon.

"Our young daughter of Zion would have turned the head of Solomon himself. The rabbi said . . ."

And the rabbi said to me how pleased young Reuven

would be when he first laid eyes on me . . .

". . . just as Jacob was pleased to lay eyes on Rachel of old in the days of our fathers. Then Rachel blushed and nearly spilled the soup . . ."

Rachel laid the letter on her lap, unable to finish. The boy she had been betrothed to had never laid eyes on her. From the city of Lod, he too had perished in the ghetto.

If only we had known, Rachel thought, covering her face with her hands. *If only we had known.* Suddenly that which had seemed so ordinary became like a holy rite, a sacred act of the dying on the eve of their death.

PART 2

The Arrival
January, 1948

*"He who has children in the cradle
had best be at peace with the world."*

Old Yiddish Proverb

10 Connections from the Past

A single light bulb swung from a long cord in the center of Gerhardt's cheerless room. His disguises hung neatly on a metal rod in the corner. Haj Amin had offered him quarters more befitting his station, but sacrifice and simplicity made better soldiers of men who might be tempted by comfort and ease. Gerhardt prided himself in the selfless simplicity of his own life. Since his return to Palestine, disguised as a Jewish refugee, he had vowed to live only for one goal: the death of the enemies of Allah and his servant Haj Amin.

He stared up at the water-stained ceiling and thought about the woman he had seen at the bus. *Surely the face was a mirage, a demon sent to distract me from my purpose,* he thought. He sat up suddenly and pulled a wooden crate to the edge of his bed. There, among stacks of papers filled with designs for new weapons of terror, were sketches of faces he had known in the camps, victims he had killed with his own hands. Contorted with agony, mouths gaping and eyes wide with terror, these faces had become his companions in the long sleepless nights that he endured since his internment in the camp. Frantically he searched for the face of the Nazi colonel he had killed because of the woman, the demon who had pulled him from the focus of his life.

Near the bottom of the sheaf he found the yellowed re-creation of the scene that had marked the beginning of his torment. There among the dark scratchings of his pen was the face of the Nazi officer. His eyes were bulging and his mouth was opened wide in a soundless scream. Gerhardt's hands were clenched tightly around the officer's throat. Yes, Gerhardt could feel his rage as if it were yesterday. His eyes moved to the upper right-hand corner of the paper. There, distorted by his clumsy attempts to draw her image, was the very face he had seen at the bus, the Jewess for whom he had killed and suffered for so long. She was perhaps beautiful enough to turn a less dedicated man from his purpose, but— Gerhardt vowed for the thousandth time—she would not move him.

He thumbed through his drawings, revealing fifty scrawled caricatures of her likeness. Hers was the face that came to him in his dreams each night to implore and beg and accuse and testify and finally sentence him to the living death of Ravensbruk.

"You will not stop me!" he said aloud. "You are but a demon and a dream sent from the darkness of hell, and I will destroy you yet! I will destroy you all!"

He piled the sketches into a heap and threw them into a metal can near the head of his bed. Then he held aloft one final image of Rachel and struck a match. Deliberately he held the flame near enough to slowly singe; the pale white skin withered to brown until at last the eyes burst into flame. Then he threw the burning likeness on top of all the others until the flames danced high and licked the images with darkness.

"I will destroy you all," Gerhardt said quietly as he lay back against his cot and closed his eyes to see her face once again.

———

Rachel ran a brush through her hair as a sharp rapping sounded on the door.

"Rachel! It is Leah," she cried happily. "Open the door."

Rachel pulled her shawl closely around her and opened the door just enough to let Leah in and keep the cold of the morning out.

"It is good to see you." Rachel surveyed Leah, whose

stomach seemed even more pronounced than it had the night before.

"Did you sleep well? I thought perhaps you would not have anything to eat for breakfast since Yacov and your grandfather have been gone from here."

"I found a bit of cheese." Rachel pointed to the stale hunk of hard cheese lying unwrapped on the table. "It has kept well enough from the cold of the room, I suppose."

Leah grimaced and looked around the stark little apartment. "Ehud said it was cold as a tomb last night. But it seems warm enough now. Are you ready?" she asked.

"For what?"

"First breakfast, if we hurry. It is only hot mush, but the children eat it to the last drop. Tipat Chalav feeds most of the quarter's children. There is only powdered milk to drink now that the gates are under guard of the Mufti's men. We have to mix it quite a lot with water. That is one thing we have an abundance of. The cisterns are quite full; we shall not die of thirst."

"I shall not wish to deprive the children of their food." Rachel recoiled at the thought of taking what a child might need.

"Nonsense," Leah snorted. "They pretend to hate it, anyhow. But when one is hungry enough . . ."

Rachel finished dressing as Leah encouraged her; then, pulling her long coat on over the dress Leah had loaned her, she followed Leah up the steps and into the streets.

Children laughed and played, dodging among the crowds of Yeshiva scholars and stooped rabbis winding their way toward the Yeshiva schools and synagogues that cluttered the Old City. Harried women carrying straw baskets called after renegade boys who darted out of reach.

"It is hard to know that all is not as usual here, eh?" Leah remarked as Rachel followed after her.

"Very difficult indeed," Rachel agreed. Then her

gaze followed the hand of Leah as she pointed to the British soldier perched high atop a roof in a nest of sand bags. "He watches them." She pointed to a group of Haganah men who stood watch on a lower roof. "They watch the Arabs."

Rachel nodded, noting the Sten gun cradled in the arms of the British soldier. "And who watches him?"

"We do. And the children, eh?" Leah lowered her voice. "The children steal his bullets when he is not looking. One distracts him while another steals his bullets. Of course we have only two Sten guns of our own in the quarter, but bullets are important, nu?"

Rachel recognized the broad shoulders of the wrestler and the small form of Dov beside him. "And where are the guns of the Haganah?" She squinted and scanned the four men who played cards beneath the watchful gaze of the soldier.

"Shhh." Leah put a finger to her lips. "Beneath the tiles on the roof. Dov and Chaim have been there since 5:30 this morning. Your friend Ehud stood the watch all night last night." Leah grinned. "He said it reminded him of being at sea. When the wind stopped howling, he was ready to come down. He sleeps now in a room at the Warsaw Compound."

Rachel looked up at the sky as they descended the steps of the street that led to Tipat Chalav. Tall clouds, tinged with light and shadow drifted toward the azure mountains of Moab. Patches of blue shone through like small clean windows into heaven. "Ehud shall be disappointed if the storm passes before his next watch."

"A lovely day. I love to smell the air after such a storm." Leah inhaled deeply.

Leah was clearly out of breath by the time they reached the steps of Tipat Chalav. "Only three weeks and this little one will arrive."

Rachel smiled slightly and looked away, her own memories too raw to hear about the child Leah carried.

"They have a way of coming no matter what shape the world is in, eh? My husband says they are God's way of being an optimist." She touched her hand to her belly as they reached the top of the steps. "Oh, he can kick! He will make an officer in the Haganah!"

Warmth surrounded them as they entered the building. The room was filled with children and their mothers. Spoons clicked noisily against the tin bowls, and tiny ones held their cups with two hands as they sipped their watered-down milk. Eyes barely looked up from the scant breakfast, but here and there around the tables, happy greetings floated toward Leah. A long line formed from the door of the community kitchen, and Rachel and Leah took their places at the very end. Everyone who passed was introduced to Rachel with the explanation, "This is Rachel Lubetkin, granddaughter of Rabbi Lebowitz. Newly arrived from Europe."

Questions flitted briefly across the faces of those who met her, but good manners quickly concealed them and replaced them with other questions about the health of Yacov and Grandfather. Unlike the disdain she had felt among the other survivors, here there was a sense of respect among the women who greeted her. She could almost read their thoughts: *So this is the granddaughter of Rebbe Lebowitz. I thought all had been lost but Yacov. Perhaps this one escaped and fought in the resistance. She does not look like one of the Displaced Persons. Perhaps she fought in the ghetto of Warsaw against the Nazis.*

"It is good to have you among us," each woman would inevitably say. "God is good to bring you home to Jerusalem." The older women would touch her hand and tenderly remark, "I knew your mother, God grant her peace. How good that my eyes have lived to see her daughter standing here!"

Word filtered down to the front of the line that Rachel was at the back, and a small cluster of women nearest to where the food was being served spoke in hushed tones. A young woman with a baby in her arms left the group and walked timidly back toward Rachel.

"This is Rachel Lubetkin," Leah began.

"Yes, we know." The young woman nodded and blushed. "We thought perhaps she would like . . ." She faltered, and Rachel thought that she could not have been more than eighteen years old. The girl began again, directing her gaze to Rachel, "Would you like to come to the first of the line, please? We thought perhaps you might be hungry."

Astonished, Rachel glanced quickly at Leah. "Oh no, thank you so much, but I couldn't."

"Go ahead," Leah nudged her.

"Oh! You too, Leah!" the girl insisted.

"There are so many in front of me," Rachel protested, not knowing how to respond to such kindness.

The girl lowered her voice. "You are a defender, nu? You came in with the Haganah last night? Always we let the fighters eat first."

Nodding and smiling at the respectful faces that she passed, Rachel followed Leah and the young mother to the front of the line.

"After we eat," Leah explained in hushed tones as though she were divulging a great secret, "Rachel goes before the Council of Rabbis at the synagogue."

Eyes grew wide with wonder that a mere woman would stand before the Council, and the secret passed quickly through the room. Soon even small children stared with wonder at Rachel, the granddaughter of Rabbi Lebowitz, as spoons filled their mouths with mush.

"And what will she say to the Council?" the question returned.

"She has a message and a letter from Rebbe Lebowitz."

Rachel nodded affirmation as wondering eyes searched her face. "I am only a messenger. For my grandfather who cannot sit with the Council while he is ill." She tried to erase some of the awe that surrounded her mission.

"You survived the bus attack last night?" a small boy asked her. "And you survived Warsaw, too?"

"Shhh!" his mother cuffed him. "Don't be so nosy!"

"But you said—"

"I said don't be so nosy!" the woman hissed. "I said the granddaughter of Rabbi Lebowitz is a very brave woman who no doubt the Eternal has smiled upon for her bravery in helping her people."

Rachel did not reply, instead, she gratefully took her plate from the old woman behind the counter. She noticed there was an extra piece of toast with a pat of butter melting on it and one scrambled egg beside it. Not once had she seen an egg on anyone's plate. "An egg!" Rachel said, trying to hand the plate back. "No. Thank you so much, but someone else might need the nourishment."

"So take it, already!" the woman exclaimed, refusing to take back the plate. "You should eat something good for you, nu? So skinny you are! What's one egg?"

The kindness of those who surrounded her made Rachel want to bolt and run back to Grandfather's house. She felt as though every kind word and smile she accepted, she took under false pretenses. *If they really knew*, she thought. *If they really knew me, they would chase me from their presence.*

She sat beside Leah on a hard wooden bench and tried very hard not to show the shame she felt. She kept her eyes on her plate as Leah chattered away.

". . . Rabbi Vultch has told them you have come from a very terrible bus incident last night and how you would not be rescued until the wounded were taken out first. They are impressed that you are still alive from the wreck and still more impressed that you, a woman, are courageous enough to enter the Old City after such an experience as you had last night. The Eternal has been watching over you, nu?"

Rachel nodded and tried to change the subject. "Leah, where is your husband?"

"He is a teacher. He teaches the little boys in Yeshiva school. You will meet him soon enough. After the meeting with the rabbis." Leah glanced up as the door opened, and her face clouded as she eyed the girl who entered.

Rachel followed her gaze. "What is it?" she asked as she took in the frail mousy form of the young girl whose eyes darted around the room.

"Shhh. It is Yehudit Akiva. She is the daughter of the rabbi who most opposes the presence of Haganah in the quarter. She is here to spy for her father, most likely."

Rachel watched as Yehudit walked past women who turned their backs on her or expressed hurried, self-conscious greetings as they moved past her. There was something in the face of the girl that inspired pity in Rachel. Perhaps it was because she had often been the one who was shunned. Her eyes met Yehudit's for an instant, and the girl looked quickly down, then walked toward where she and Leah sat.

"Oh no! She's coming here!" Leah said under her breath. "Don't speak to her. I will do the talking."

Yehudit's thin lips turned up briefly at the corners, but her eyes did not smile. "Good morning, Leah," she said quietly.

"Hello, Yehudit." Leah's voice was flat.

Yehudit looked at Rachel then at Leah again. "I thought I might come and meet the granddaughter of Rebbe Lebowitz."

Leah did not respond and the silence became uncomfortable. "Hello," Rachel blurted out. "I am Rachel Lubetkin. You have known my grandfather?"

"Very well!" Yehudit answered eagerly. "Many times he has been a guest in the home of my father. I am Yehudit Akiva." She lifted her chin proudly and glanced at Leah, who continued to eat.

Leah put her spoon down and nudged Rachel again. "Are you finished yet? You musn't be late for the meeting, you know." She stood up between Yehudit and Rachel. "Good to see you, Yehudit," she said without emotion. "We have to go now."

Without waiting for Rachel's response, Leah gathered up the plates and started for the kitchen.

"It was good to meet you, Yehudit," Rachel said, feeling pity for the pale-stricken face whose eyes sadly followed Leah.

"Thank you," Yehudit mumbled, then she turned away and walked out the door.

11   The Council of Rabbis

The complex of four Sephardic synagogues where the Council had chosen to meet with Rachel looked much like the plain houses on the square Tiferet Yerushalayim.

"Tiferet means *glory*," explained Leah as she led Rachel down the wooden staircase below street level to the entrance of the synagogue. "From the outside there is not much glory in these places, for the builders could not have a building taller than a mosque. The Ottoman authorities forbade Jews and Christians from building new houses of prayer or to worship God in public according to our 'foolish tradition,' as they called it. So the outside is very plain. We do not want to arouse the wrath of the Muslims!" She winked and opened the heavy wooden door to the left of the staircase.

The long hall was covered by three vaults. Long seats stretched out on either side of the bimah, the pulpit where the Torah was read. On the east wall, the double arched doors of an ornate ark were seen, and to the right of the ark, Leah pointed to a high square window.

"There is our glory," Leah said. "You see the jug of olive oil and the *shofar*? Those remain from the days of the Temple. It is this shofar which will be blown to announce the coming of the Messiah. It would be good if He would come to us now, nu?"

Rachel nodded, feeling a lump of apprehension in the pit of her stomach at the thought of meeting the Council.

"Where are the rabbis?" Rachel asked, her voice resounding off the vaults of the empty room.

"This way." Leah walked to the door on the wall opposite the window niche where the ancient shofar rested. "They wait for you in the Central synagogue. It is called Kehal Zion because it is said there is a tunnel that connects it to the tomb of King David outside the walls of the city on the slopes of Zion."

Rachel raised her eyebrows. "Is this true?"

"Only a legend," Leah whispered. "These halls are full of legends, but do not tell the old men that they are legends."

A steady buzz of male voices filled the air as Rachel and Leah entered the long, narrow chamber of Kehal Zion. As the door slid shut behind them, all conversation stopped, and the eyes of the leading rabbis of the Sephardic, Ashkenazi, and Hassidic congregations turned with intense curiosity toward where Rachel stood. Nervously she fingered the note that Grandfather had given her. Her eyes darted from one face to another of the thirty who had gathered there.

"Don't be nervous," Leah whispered.

"Why not?" Rachel replied under her breath. For a long moment she stood motionless, and then a heavy-set Hassidic rabbi with a heavy gold chain across his vest and a glowering face stepped into the *bimah*.

"Well, girl," he said impatiently to Rachel. "Can you not see that we are busy men?"

"Don't be afraid," Leah whispered again as Rachel stepped forward. "Speak in Polish and I will translate."

The sound of Rachel's feet clicked loudly against the hard marble floor. She was grateful that Leah had found shoes for her to wear other than Ellie's field boots.

Her hands shaking, Rachel unfolded the letter from Grandfather. "I am Rachel Lubetkin, the granddaughter—"

"Yes, yes. We are aware of who you are. We have called you here, nu?" said Akiva. "I am Rabbi Akiva, mayor of the Old City."

Old and frail, a white-bearded Ashkenazi stood and spoke with a quavering voice. "Must you be so harsh

107

with the girl, Rebbe Akiva? She has been through much to come and stand before us."

A murmur of agreement rippled through the Sephardic and Ashkenazi rabbis. The Hassidim sat silent for the most part, not looking at Akiva.

"A little kindness, please. A little gentleness, eh? So it is not custom for a woman to speak? It will kill us to hear what she has to say?"

Leah whispered. "This is the chief Ashkenazi rabbi. They will listen to him."

"Most certainly it is important that we hear the words of the granddaughter of Rebbe Lebowitz," Akiva conceded, a near-smile playing on his thick lips. "Of course the rabbi himself, a respected member of our Council, cannot be among us personally for reasons the Eternal knows alone. We shall hope that his illness is not caused by some transgression, God forbid. And although we cannot know the mind of God, we can only hope that in His mercy He has understood the reasons for our brother to break the Shabbat." Again the Council buzzed with conversation as its members remembered how Grandfather had broken Shabbat to travel into the New City just the week before he was stricken.

A surge of indignation filled Rachel as she considered the accusation that Akiva had made against Grandfather. "Honored Rabbis," she blurted, astonished at the strength in her own voice. "As you well know, my grandfather traveled on Shabbat because the Mufti lifted the ban on travel from these walls only on Shabbat. It was an affront to God for the Mufti to do this. And so, knowing that the law of Leviticus demands that the laws of love be followed first, my grandfather traveled to give comfort to a very small and sick little boy. God did not punish Rabbi Lebowitz for this, but instead He has rewarded him."

The old Ashkenazi rabbi stood. "Well spoken, daughter of Zion. Well spoken! The Eternal has indeed rewarded our dear friend Rebbe Lebowitz to reunite him with you. For all these many years his heart ached for the loss of all those he loved—except for Yacov, who was left. Now you stand before us, a miracle! And we should hear the words of Rebbe Lebowitz that he has sent through you."

The members of the Council clapped their hands in a soft applause of agreement. "Well spoken, Rabbi." Only Akiva sat in mute disapproval, his eyes examining Rachel with cold disdain.

Rachel held the letter up and in a loud, clear voice she began to read:

"My Friends and Honored Council Members, How my heart yearns to be among you. And yet the Eternal has seen fit in His wisdom to let these old eyes behold one returned to my household from the grave to speak for me. Listen to her voice, for her eyes have seen much . . ." Rachel paused, her voice faltering. She had not expected Grandfather to say such things in his letter. *"Her mother prayed for peace. Her father prayed for peace and spoke with honest hope to those who in the end became the murderers of his family. They did not raise their hands in defense, but instead,"* Rachel felt the catch in her voice become a lump of emotion, *"instead, they believed the soft words of their tormentors. Their voices cry out to us that we should not leave these sacred stones again because of false promises. Those who seek to dishonor us and our worship of the Eternal are the same who spit on the name of the Almighty. Do not believe in false promises, but help those who will help you defend your houses of prayer and your wives and children from violation. I write this with all the truth that the Eternal has given me to see. Now listen to the words of Rachel Lubetkin, whose young voice can tell even more"*— she hesitated— *"than this aged Rabbi."*

Slowly Rachel lowered the paper. Feeling every eye on her she did not look up until she regained courage and the strength to speak.

"Well, Rachel?" asked the kindly Ashkenazi rabbi. "What have your eyes seen that might help us come to a decision here?"

She raised her chin and looked only at him, not the twenty-nine others who questioned her with their gaze. "I have seen the Third Destruction," she said quietly. "In Warsaw where all we desired was to be left in peace to study the words of our God, there is not even one Jew remaining among the million who prayed there. We lived in false hopes and broken promises. They kept us within walls without food or fuel to heat. They brought thousands there from all over the countryside and hoped that starvation would eliminate us."

Rachel blinked back tears. "We continued to live. There were schools and plays. Our musicians played concerts for us—only Jewish songs, because we were not allowed the music of German composers. In the winter the frozen bodies littered the streets. Always we thought if we would just live they would finally leave us alone."

She paused, exhaling slowly. "It was not to be. First came registration for work. Those with useful skills were given a yellow card. That card meant that the Jew who carried it was useful to the Reich. It meant life. People killed for the yellow card. A man could keep two of his dependents safe with him, safe from deportation, if he had a card. No one said what he was to do if he had five children instead of only two. People had to make choices about who would go and who would stay. The Nazis said, 'We want five thousand in the Square to deport by tomorrow. The old and the very young.' After that, they promised to leave us alone. No more would be deported.

"Our leaders wanted to believe, and so five thousand were chosen. A few days later they would come again and say, 'Ten thousand in the square, that is all. After that no more.'" She drew a deep breath and looked around at the men whose decision would settle the fate of the Jewish Quarter. "After a long time there was no one left to take. Then those who had hidden in basements and sewers came out and fought. They held the Panzers for weeks, I am told. Longer than the entire

Polish Army held the first attacks of the Blitzkrieg. The Germans brought their tanks and shelled and shelled until now there is nothing left of our homes in Warsaw but rubble and dead. They promised us. They promised, and we lost our lives inch by inch because we wanted to believe that reason would prevail. It did not. I stand here today and I tell you, there was no sanity or reason in any of it."

The room hung heavy in thoughtful silence. "Now I am told you bargain with a man who supped at the table of Hitler, Haj Amin Husseini, the Mufti of Jerusalem. And he promises that you will keep your homes if you have no defenders. He promises, and then he speaks of the end of all Jews. There is nothing left for us in Europe. Hitler and his promises destroyed everything. There are no houses of worship or little boys in Yeshiva anymore. This is the last place. The only place left on earth for us." Her voice was full of emotion. "Do not believe the false promises. Do not hold false hopes. Help the men who come here to preserve all that is left of what we once were. Do not bargain with the devil, for in the end you will lose your souls."

Completely drained by the force of her emotion, Rachel lowered her head and sighed as if a great weight had come to rest on her. Akiva sat gazing about in disinterest and disgust at her words. The rest of the Council stared at her in stunned silence, stricken by the truth. At last the old Ashkenazi spoke.

"Well spoken, daughter." He shuffled toward her, his gaze intent on her bowed head. Touching his gnarled hand to her shoulder, he motioned Leah to escort her from Kehal Zion. "May the blessings of the Eternal be with you," the old man called. "And with us all."

12   Call to Prayer

Field glasses dangling around his neck, Gerhardt bounded up the steps of the tall minaret that bordered the Jewish Quarter and towered high above the great Hurva Synagogue.

As he spiraled upward he could hear the clear call of the muezzin who had daily summoned the Muslims to prayer from this tower for over thirty years. Gerhardt knew the old man well, and when the prayers were finished he was willing to move aside and let the young Jihad Moquades take his place with their guns and grenades. There were few places in the Old City that provided such a clear view into the streets of the Jewish Quarter.

Perhaps in the light of day, Gerhardt thought, *I will see the face that haunts me. Perhaps I will see one who only resembles the one who follows me like a shadow.*

Breathless, he reached the platform beneath the onion-shaped dome of the minaret. The old muezzin smiled broadly, showing his toothless gums to Gerhardt. Then he bowed and touched his hand to his forehead in greeting.

"Salaam! A most honored visit!" he proclaimed. "While our people bow in prayer, you are ever watchful and vigilant."

"Salaam." Gerhardt returned the greeting. "I am searching the alleyways of the Jewish Quarter for one who would destroy the plans of our gracious leader, Haj Amin el Husseini."

"May Allah prevent such a thing!" The muezzin frowned and shook his head. "For years I watch these dogs below me and wished that the ways of the Prophet

112

could be practiced in purity and without defilement in this city. Some of our number mingle freely with them, but I hear their infidel prayers rising from their temples and pray that Allah and the Sons of the Prophet will strike them down. Look there." He pointed across the Jewish Quarter to the dome of Nissan Bek Synagogue. "They think perhaps these old eyes do not see, but in the night I come here and I can see the shadow of a Jew who lies upon wooden planks and stares out at us from behind the lattice work. He is nearly as high as this minaret and can, I suppose, see into our streets as well as I can see into the Jewish Quarter."

Gerhardt had already raised the field glasses to his eyes and began to focus down on the forms and faces of the Jewish women below his vantage point. Carefully he scanned the streets, systematically moving his search from block to block.

"Perhaps the face I seek is but a spirit, a demon," Gerhardt muttered.

"As with all the infidels, sir," the old man chattered. "As with any who would interfere with our exalted one, the Grand Mufti, eh?"

"Of course," Gerhardt said absently.

After several minutes Gerhardt slowly lowered the field glasses in disgust.

The old man's face twitched with curiosity. "Have you found the face of the man whom you seek so earnestly among the Jewish dogs?"

Gerhardt's jaw seemed to jut out even farther as he continued to scan the bustle of the quarter below him. "No," he said simply, reaching into his pocket and flipping a coin to the muezzin.

"May the blessings of Allah be upon you!" the old man cried in delight. He gazed at the coin for a moment as Gerhardt turned wordlessly for the stairway. The old man's eyes brightened with an idea that might net him even greater reward. "Most honorable sir," he called, "might I not be able to serve as your eyes? If you but instruct this old one in the features of your enemy, perhaps I could . . ."

Gerhardt paused midstep and turned to face the muezzin. His lips curved in a smile. "Of course! An excellent idea." He removed the field glasses from his neck and walked purposefully back up to the small platform. "The enemy I seek is in the body of a woman with the eyes of an angel . . ."

The last of the lunch dishes were dried and put away.

The face of Rabbi Vultch glowed with delight as he smiled across the battered wooden table at Rachel. "Only five rabbis of the Council sided with Akiva," he explained to the group that had gathered in the basement of Tipat Chalav to hear the news. "And I think it was the words of Rachel Lubetkin that swayed them in the favor of defense."

Ehud, Chaim and Shimon, Leah's burly young husband, clapped one another on the back.

"Well done, Rachel!" Leah cried, taking Rachel's hand. "Well done!"

"They argued for over two hours," Rabbi Vultch continued. "There is some compromise, of course. Of the Council members not siding with Akiva's point of view, twelve were solidly for the active arming of the quarter, and the other twelve walk the middle line of compromise."

"What are the compromises?" asked Dov.

"The convoys will continue to be searched by both the British and the Arab Irregulars together."

"That cannot be avoided," said Dov.

"We shall have to be as clever as cats," said Chaim.

"There is nothing to fear on that score," Ehud bellowed. "'Moshe Sachar is the King of Contraband among the Haganah. He is one who will conceal our supplies until even we will have to search the flour barrels to find them, eh?" He nudged Rachel, who nodded

114

slightly and looked away at the mention of Moshe's name. "Tell them, Rachel! Tell them how he tricked the British patrol the morning you were washed up on the beach!"

"Yes," Leah said quietly, a frown creasing her brow as she noticed Rachel's hands tremble slightly. "The fame of Moshe Sachar is legendary."

Rachel did not reply, but continued to look intently into her half-empty coffee cup.

"There was much anger in the Council over the theft of our food by the Arab Irregulars. If the food from the convoys is stolen, even cleverness will not help us save the Jewish Quarter. Akiva promises he will talk to the Arab High Committee and warn them that the theft must be stopped. He says it is a matter of good faith; that we must also give up something."

"But why should we give up anything," Chaim growled, "when it is our food they are stealing?"

"Well spoken," said Shimon. "Why, indeed?"

"In return for this," the rabbi explained, "we must not train our men at the synagogues any longer. The rabbis fear that we desecrate the holiness of the houses of prayer."

"That is one victory for the Mufti," Shimon said grimly.

Leah put her hand on his arm. "That is all right. There are other places, nu?"

"But it was as if the rabbis sanctioned the training when it was at the synagogues and Yeshiva schools," Shimon said. "And the British were not so eager to search the houses of prayer for weapons, or arrest a man whose head was covered in prayer."

"Even if he had a pistol under his tallith, eh?" laughed Ehud.

"It does not matter," Rabbi Vultch said firmly. "There are many places we can secretly train the young men of the quarter. They will come to learn all the same."

"Even if all they have to shoot is rifles made of broomsticks, eh?" Chaim said bitterly.

"My friend Moshe shall find a way for us to have rifles when they are needed, I think," Ehud said enthusiastically.

"The point right now is that Rachel has convinced the Council," Dov smiled at her. "And though most walk the middle road between appeasement and defense, they are willing to accept the presence of the Haganah among them."

"We are people of the Book." The rabbi sipped his coffee and then rubbed his forehead thoughtfully. "Somewhere in the middle of appeasement and violence there is the law of God, nu? For a man to seek peace and pursue it is a righteous goal. But if we seek peace at the cost of our lives and the lives of our families, then we seek the peace of a man who first kills his children and then takes his own life. Most of the rabbis recognize the need for self-defense, and yet all continue to pray for peace without defilement of those things the Eternal has given into our care. This is a difficult line for men of study to walk."

"So we must walk it as well," Leah said. She patted Rachel's shoulder. "You have not said a word to us. I know this has been a most difficult day for you, but you have done well in speaking about the things you have seen. So many among us want to believe that all will be well, and that there will be no need for us to defend ourselves against the Mufti. Those who live within these walls came to pray and study God's Word, not to fight. You have spoken to their hearts. This is truly the last place for us."

"How strange it is," said Dov quietly, "that it was from this very place our fathers were driven out to wander the world two thousand years ago; and now, there is no place left for us to go but back to where we came from."

"God spoke of this time," Shimon said. "The haftara reading for the day of Partition was from Psalm 137: *'How shall we sing the Lord's song in a strange land? If I forget thee, O Jerusalem, let my right hand forget her*

116

cunning. If I do not remember thee, let my tongue cleave to the roof of my mouth; if I prefer not Jerusalem above my highest joys.'

"And so, I read this to the little boys in Yeshiva and I thought how people who are not Jews have decided in the United Nations what the fate of Jerusalem should be. I said to myself, 'Shimon, most have never seen Zion, never walked upon this sacred Mount or prayed at the wall. And yet they decide by a vote of nations that Jerusalem will not be part of the Jewish state they created with a stroke of their pens.' Then I hear the Arabs shouting threats and deciding that there will be no more Jews at all. I would rather not fight, but I want my children to have a place they might call home." He took Leah's hand. "I want to be among those who decide the fate of the city of my fathers. I want to stand firm on this soil and make it safe for all the children who seek to know God. Unless I fight now, there will be no safety forever more."

"If we do not draw a line and say to the enemies of peace, *'This far and no farther,'* then someday this child I bear will be forced to fight an enemy a thousand times stronger than the one I face," Leah quietly agreed. "We could have gone to America," she smiled. "Perhaps I would not have had the trouble I have now in finding strings for my cello, eh? But if I had not come here, who would have? And if we do not stand now, then when will a stand be taken against evil? That is why we came."

"For the rest of us," Dov said, "there was no choice. We came because the rest of the world has no room in their immigration quotas for even one more Jew. But now that I am here, I am going to stay."

"I was apprenticed to a shoemaker," added Chaim. "Before the war I would look at the Polish farmers tending their fields and I always envied them. We could not farm or own land from the earliest days, you know. Anyway, I always wanted to plant and till the soil. At the camps I planted the dead of our people in the soil of the Reich. They chose me to do this because I was

117

strong and the job would break a small man's back. Only my heart was broken." There was a long silence in the group. "Someday I want to be a farmer. I want to help make the desert bloom again and nourish the children. But first I think that perhaps the war against the Reich goes on. A little Hitler walks the streets of God's Holy City, and we must put an end to his plans forever."

Rachel studied the lined face of the wrestler. His eyes were full of pain, yet still he spoke of hopes and dreams. Each heart gathered around that table had a purpose past mere survival; each heart but hers. *What hope exists in me?* she wondered. *What purpose can my existence have past simply continuing to breathe? The heart of Chaim has broken, but that will heal in time. My heart has died within me. Where is the hope that it will ever live again?*

"Tell us, Rachel," said the rabbi. "Why have you chosen to come among us to fight when there are so many safer places you might be?"

For a long time she said nothing, almost afraid of what her answer might be. "Everything was lost—everything I knew and thought I was. I was . . . I was looking for something. At first I thought it was maybe a part of my mother or my father. But I come here and all that I find of them are shadows of what once lived and breathed. Somehow I thought I was looking for my life the way it should have been. Instead I have only what is. I don't know what I am looking for anymore, or why I have come here. I will tell you though, Rabbi, if I find any answers." A sad smile played on her lips and she shrugged slightly and looked away, uncomfortable under his gaze.

Finally Leah spoke. "Well, I can tell you, Rachel, that it is a good thing that you are here. No one could have spoken better to the Council. Perhaps your words will make them understand."

Rabbi Vultch leaned forward on his elbows. "Your grandfather, Rebbe Lebowitz, would be very proud of you."

"Thank you," Rachel said politely, secretly doubting his words. "I said only what is true."

Leah stuck out her lower lip as she observed the sadness in Rachel's eyes. She cleared her throat and changed the subject, trying to pull the focus from Rachel. "And what was the response of Rabbi Akiva to the decisions of the Council?"

"The steam rose from him like incense in a Greek church!" laughed the rabbi. "He is not finished with the argument yet, you may be sure of that. Since the control of the quarter's charities has passed from his control into the hands of the Haganah, he is very angry. He is a man who is in love with power more than truth. The only power that remains for him is the privilege to pass through the Arab Quarter to pray at the Wailing Wall. This is a privilege granted by the Mufti and the Arab High Committee, of course. The undecided among our Council have hesitated in giving their wholehearted support to the Haganah because they fear losing that privilege. To pray at the western wall is the closest that one can come to standing before the altar of God. Akiva, it seems, holds great power in his hands if he holds the right to pray in such a holy place. It is no wonder some hesitate to disagree with his warnings."

"One can only wonder what he has given to the Mufti in return for safe passage to the wall," Shimon mused. "Surely the Mufti has not offered this right from the kindness and generosity of his heart for the Old City rabbis."

"On Friday a minyon of ten will walk through the Arab neighborhood to pray before the wall. Akiva says they pray only for peace."

13 Discovery

Akiva sucked on a peppermint and stared at the white sheet of paper on the green desk blotter before him. He moved his lamp closer, then dipped his pen in the inkwell and scratched out the message.

Yehudit knocked softly on the door of his study, then opened it a crack and peeked in timidly.

"Yes, Yehudit." Akiva did not look up from his work.

"The rabbis. They are here. They wait in the parlor, Father."

"Very well." He continued to write. "Tell them I shall join them in a moment."

Yehudit closed the door as Akiva finished writing with the flourish of his signature. He pursed his thick lips and adjusted his spectacles on his nose, then studied the cramped scrawl.

"Sehr gut!" he exclaimed, shaking a bit of sand onto the wet ink to blot it. Then he folded the paper several times until it seemed to be only a tiny fragment. He slipped it into his pocket along with his silver-bound prayer book and rose to meet the minyon of nine rabbis who had come to join him on his sojourn to the Wailing Wall.

Gerhardt's field glasses had become a symbol of importance for the old muezzin. Each day he walked to his minaret an hour early. Heads nodded in respect as he passed by. He lingered long in the cold tower with the glasses held to his eyes as he probed the streets below him. Faithfully he searched for the face of the woman in the drawing Gerhardt had brought to him. "I will find this infidel woman," he said each morning. "If Allah wills."

He called the faithful to prayer at four o'clock Friday afternoon, then quickly raised the field glasses to his eyes and began his search once again. Below him men and women bustled about in preparation for the Jewish Shabbat. He could see their faces clearly as they hurried about their business. Women gossiped together and he tried to read their lips.

Suddenly the old man drew his breath in sharply. Just beyond where a group of rabbis stood together on a corner, the slender form of a woman emerged from a basement stairwell. He dared not take his eyes from her as she waved a greeting to two young boys who called to her. *Hair as black as a raven's wing. Lips full. Teeth white. Eyes that shone bright and blue.*

Young and beautiful she was, as Allah had intended women to be in the first of creation. *The form of a woman and the eyes of an angel. But she is a demon.* The old man remembered the words of Gerhardt. He watched her walk down the street until she turned a corner and disappeared from view; then he swung the glasses back toward where he had first seen her walk up the steps. This would be worth great reward for him. He fumbled in his pocket and retrieved a note pad and stub of a pencil. With the eagerness of one who had just discovered a great treasure, he wrote down the landmarks that led to Rachel's basement apartment. There could be no mistaking that this was indeed the woman.

With one quick look down the street, the old man turned and ran down the stairs as fast as his old legs could carry him. He pushed and shoved his way through the crowded souks, unable even to acknowledge the stares of admiration from the merchants with whom he had shared the secret of his great mission.

When, at last, he came to the battered apartment house where long flags of laundry waved above his head and Arab mothers screamed out the windows, to their children, he was out of breath and unable to

121

speak. He ran into the dark and stinking hallway and stopped to lean against the broken stair railing. Another old man in stained trousers shuffled by him. "I am here to see Gerhardt, servant of the Mufti," said the muezzin.

The old Arab pointed upstairs. "First door," he mumbled.

The muezzin clutched at his rapidly beating heart; then he pulled himself up the stairs to the faded green door of Gerhardt's room. He banged loudly against the chipping paint. There was no answer. Once again he knocked insistently and waited. Still there was no answer. He looked around the crowded stinking hallway and lost much of his enthusiasm. *My own hovel is more gracious than this. What hope of reward should I then have?* He wondered.

Still, he remembered the bright coin Gerhardt had tossed to him, and he touched the field glasses that hung around his neck. He slid to the floor to sit and wait for the servant of the Mufti to return home to reap his good news.

14   The Shabbat Blessing

The tiny apartment of Leah and Shimon was above a grocery store that served as a meeting place for the women of the quarter to gossip and exchange bits of news. Their voices and laughter filtered up through the plank floors of the one-room flat.

Rachel stood at the window watching as the customers hurried into the store and out again, their shopping bags nearly as empty as when they entered.

"They are making last-minute purchases," she remarked as Leah spread the elegant lace tablecloth over the rough wooden planks that served as their table.

"God alone knows what there is left to purchase," Leah answered quietly. "Such a shame I ask you to make Shabbat with us, and there is not so much as one apple in the whole quarter for me to make a strudel with!" She placed both hands on her bulging stomach and sighed as she looked down at the tablecloth.

"Come sit down, Leah." Rachel moved from the window and picked up the silverware that lay on a small counter near the stove.

"What? Sit before a Shabbat meal? You are my *oyrech auf Shabbes*. I am not yours!"

"And you would deny your Shabbat guest a blessing?" asked Rachel, a twinkle in her eye.

"God forbid!" said Leah. "What blessing?"

"I want to help. You look tired. Sit down for a few minutes. I can set the table."

Rachel had already taken over the job and was carefully placing china and silver around the table. "I suppose . . ." Leah said, reluctantly sitting down.

"You're always doing *something* for everybody. You

and Shimon both. Next Shabbat you will be my guests, eh? Although I am not sure what Grandfather has in the way of Shabbat finery." She held up a delicate crystal wine glass to the light and looked through it. "Beautiful," she said. "Just beautiful!"

"Wedding gifts. All of this. All but four dinner plates were broken on the trip from Austria. My silver survived, of course. Some pieces we had to sell before Shimon got his job here at the Yeshiva. All in all, we have eaten very well on this silver, though now I cannot have more than four people to eat at my table."

Rachel glanced around at the plain little room. In the corner stood Leah's cello, and next to it her phonograph. On the opposite wall was a bed behind a blue floral curtain, and a small baby bed waited beside that.

"I think you are one of the most lucky women I know, Leah," she said quietly. "A beautiful home—" She gazed at the Shabbat table. "A fine husband and a baby soon to come. God has smiled on you, indeed."

"And someday I hope to play once again for the symphony. Then life would be perfect, nu?"

Rachel polished a knife with a linen napkin. "Would you play for me sometime maybe? Yacov told me you play like an angel."

Leah's face brightened. "Now?"

"You should rest."

"We have time before Shabbat!" Leah had already begun to unzip the cover from her instrument. "Now *you* sit!"

Rachel pulled out a chair and folded her hands in her lap as Leah began to tune the cello. She held it out from her stomach and sat a bit awkwardly. "The baby likes it," Leah smiled. "When I play he dances."

"What if it's a girl?"

"Then *she* dances. I'll have a little ballerina." She drew the bow slowly across the strings until the sweet mellow sounds filled the room with a tapestry of melody so intricate that Rachel forgot the plain walls and bare floors. Leah's music was as elegant and rich as the finest Shabbat table. Rachel watched the expression on Leah's face as she closed her eyes and felt the music come from her hands. The laughter in the store below fell silent as the customers listened to Leah welcome the Shabbat with her music.

Full of sweet sadness, the melody surrounded Rachel with memories. In the ghetto of Warsaw music had offered the only salve to her wounded heart. Now, as Leah played, Rachel closed her eyes and remembered the cold winter nights in Warsaw when the food was nearly gone and hope had almost vanished.

"Still we can hope, can't we?" Mama had asked Mrs. Rabinski. "Perhaps our papers will come and we will yet see Jerusalem."

Bitterly the woman had answered, "When there is nothing left to feed our children, we feed them hope until they sicken and die with the madness of it. Hope cannot nourish them."

Mama's lips were tight, Rachel remembered, *and she looked at baby Yacov and did not answer. That night we sipped what remained of the soup; then she and Papa bundled us up and took us through the snow to the community center. Mama held Yacov and her face glowed when she heard the music. Then I said, "Oh, Mama, is there anything more beautiful than this?" and she touched my hand and answered, "Yes, sweet Rachel. You are more beautiful. My children are more beautiful yet."*

Together they had listened as the finest concert musicians in Europe had played for them and nourished their hearts. Rachel had noticed the thin, frail arms of the woman who played the cello that night. In spite of her talent, she, too, was starving because she was Jewish. In the end, not even her music had saved her.

I was still hungry when we left the concert that night, Rachel remembered, *but my heart had heard beauty and was full. And Mama said, "When we are all with God, even the air will be filled with music."*

Leah drew her bow across the strings one last time. The note seemed to linger in the room for a long while.

Until the last sounds faded, Rachel did not speak.

"Yacov was right," she said. "You play like an angel. Such music may be the nearest I can ever be to heaven."

Leah looked down shyly. "You like it?"

"It is finer, Leah, than the richest Shabbat table. How satisfied the world would be if we could dine on music!"

Leah nodded and began to put away her instrument. "You know what I thought when we had to leave Austria and I heard later the fate of my friends who stayed? I wondered that the same music could fall upon the ears of Jew and Gentile and both could say 'how lovely,' and then one man could turn on the other and kill him— and also kill the one who played the music for him. It is a mystery, Rachel. God made us one and all, did He not? And was it not His pleasure to make us all different? And yet people try always to make everyone the same. Like them, eh? If I tried to be like someone else, then who would try to be like me?"

"Just because God made us all to be individual doesn't mean that people have to like the idea. My father used to say, '*If God lived on earth people would break His windows.*' If you live long enough pretty soon you stop being surprised about what people do to one another."

"Have you lived so long, Rachel?"

"Perhaps not." Rachel turned and gazed at the baby bed. "Kindness still surprises me, Leah. And music."

Leah sat down beside Rachel and looked searchingly into her eyes. "So deep are your wounds, then?"

Rachel nodded and looked away. "Yes. They are so deep. And yet, there is a third thing that surprises me, Leah." She tugged at the edge of her apron. "Sometimes I surprise myself because I want to hope. I still want to hope so badly."

"Then you will find hope, Rachel. As I have found it; and Shimon. There was a time in my life when I had nothing. I lied and stole to escape from Europe. I denied my faith and my people and left my friends behind to die. I thought there was nothing left for me to live for. Now I have Shimon. And the baby."

"You did these things?" Rachel asked in amazement. "And yet you can live with yourself now? I cannot, you see. I look in the mirror each day and I wonder why I am still alive. If, indeed I am." Rachel lowered her eyes.

"I understand." Leah touched her hand. "My very words. You see, I was hidden by a family of righteous Gentiles for a short time. They taught me much about forgiveness and love. God's love for me and my love for myself. There is no sin so great—"

"Yes, Leah. Oh yes, there is. If you gave the life of the child you now carry, you would feel differently."

Leah bit her lips and frowned. "Do you need to talk, Rachel? Can your heart trust in kindness long enough to speak?"

Rachel looked into the shining face of Leah. Her eyes seemed to radiate kindness and hope. "You remind me much of my friend Ellie. She is a righteous Gentile as well. She is filled with love, and yet I could not bring myself to tell her all that is in my heart."

"I understand."

"Yes. You were there. You know what it was like."

"And I, too, was once afraid to die, and then afraid to live."

For a moment Rachel wavered, then she held tightly to the hand of Leah—the hand that made such beautiful music, that worked so hard for the children of the quarter. For nearly an hour Rachel talked and wept with Leah as she told of her mother and the baby Tikvah. When at last she stopped, the sun hung low and Shabbat was upon them.

Leah dried her eyes and held Rachel like a small child. "Stay with us tonight. When we have finished our Shabbat meal, Shimon and I will tell you our stories. God has known us all, and still His love for us is great. Now, from my heart I want to tell you that your courage is to me a symphony. Perhaps it is not completely written yet, but the music from your heart will someday touch many lives, my friend."

"As you touch mine."

Like twin Gullivers among the Lilliputians, Ehud and Shimon walked toward home with two dozen of the quarter's children trailing after them. Small boys surrounded Ehud and tugged on his thick, calloused fingers, on the frayed hem of his sea coat, even on the fringes of his tallith.

"Tell us another story, Rebbe Ehud!" they cried. Then they turned to Shimon. "Make him tell us another story!"

"Go home now, children!" Shimon replied. "It is almost Shabbat and your mothers will be looking for you! Are you washed?" He mussed a young boy's hair, then straightened his yarmulke on his head. "Look at you! It's almost Shabbat and you aren't even washed yet. Your mothers will say we have made you into a collection of paskudnyaks!"

Two dozen dirt-smeared faces studied one another in horror. Could they be mistaken for paskudnyaks, the soldiers who didn't wash even on Shabbat and were late for the holiest and best meal of the week?

"God forbid!" bellowed Ehud. "God forbid that these small soldiers would forget to wash and would be late for Shabbat!"

"So go along home now, men," said Shimon, pulling a few of Ehud's more tenacious fans off his coattails. "Shabbat shalom!"

"Shabbat shalom! Shabbat shalom! Shabbat shalom!" echoed down the narrow alleyways as the children drifted reluctantly toward their homes and a basin of water.

"Well," said Ehud, "they'll be missing a few ears when their mothers get hold of them, I'll wager."

Shimon laughed loud and long. "That you can bank on. I know their mothers! Being late for Shabbat when you are a child is a quick way to avoid old age, eh? These boys stand more in fear of Mama than God himself! Oy vey! You tell stories too well, Ehud! I myself forgot the time, and Leah is as strict with me about Shabbat as my own mother, may she rest in peace!"

"So! Leah is about to become a Jewish mother herself, and it is all your doing, eh?"

Ehud's broad smile faded as he glanced up the street and noticed the grim faces of ten rabbis walking slowly toward them. Akiva was in the lead, and he raised his chin and peered down his long nose at Shimon and Ehud.

"They are going to the wall to pray," Shimon whispered. "As always on Friday afternoon."

"If God hears the brokenhearted and those cast down in countenance, He'll surely be listening to these, eh? They make one afraid to smile!"

"Shabbat shalom, Rabbis!" Shimon called cheerfully as they passed the black-coated entourage.

No words were spoken in response as they brushed shoulders and continued on their separate ways.

"Maybe they're late for Shabbat, too?" grinned Ehud.

"If they do not change their way of thinking, there may not ever be Shabbat for us again here," Shimon said quietly. "Old Akiva holds with the proverb that it is better to have a bad peace than a good war."

"Ha! Looking at him I would have guessed his favorite saying was *Better a live dog than a dead lion!*"

"He thinks he is right." Shimon tugged on his sidelocks and paused to look after the retreating forms of the rabbis. "From far off he fools everybody, but close up he fools only himself."

"Well, God," Ehud called, "then pay no attention to the old fool. Go right ahead and do what you want, God!"

"We are the chosen people, eh? I just keep wondering why God had to choose us for such a blessing as Shabbat with only Arabs having the key to the grocery!

129

Always by Shabbat there is barely enough left in the cupboards for a little snack."

"So? You can only ask me to dinner on Shabbat? I eat the rest of the week as well!"

They rounded the corner and Shimon led the way up the steep steps to his and Leah's apartment.

15 The Message

The wall lay one hundred yards outside of the Jewish Quarter, and access to it would have been impossible had Akiva not bargained with the Mufti and the Arab High Committee. The very fact that his voice alone had been heeded was enough to sway many in the Jewish Quarter; perhaps he was indeed right in his insistence that were it not for the Haganah, there would be no threat from the Arabs. But their good Arab neighbors themselves gave credence to the rising doubts about Haj Amin and his intentions. By the hundreds, Arab Christians had purchased tarboosh hats from the Arab hatmaker as identification lest they be assaulted by the violent strangers that now roamed the streets in search of Jews.

Right now, Akiva felt that he and the minyon had nothing to fear. He was under the protection of the Mufti himself as he walked through the alleyways beyond the barricades and finally stood before the stones of the western wall of the Temple. The wall loomed above them. Every crack and crevice was jammed with tiny slips of paper: the prayers of those who had come to pray at the holiest site in Judaism.

Akiva lifted his prayer shawl over his head and reached out to touch the stones. His voice rose and fell in prayer among the rabbis who had come with him. He opened his prayer book and read from the Hallel. Together they prayed for the peace of Zion and for the Messiah to come to Jerusalem and deliver them from the wicked.

When at last dusk began to envelop the city, Akiva took his tiny slip of paper from the pocket of his coat.

With great reverence he slipped it between the stones just at the end of the wall.

————————

From the deepening shadows on the steps of the alleyway Rehov Hakotel, Ram Kadar watched the Jews as they finished their prayers and lowered their prayer shawls almost in unison. They seemed dwarfed and fragile beside the massive stones that soared above them. "The help of Allah is more beyond their reach than stones at the top of this wall," remarked one of the three Arab Irregulars that accompanied him.

Kadar did not reply. Instead he lit a cigarette and watched the actions of Rabbi Akiva with interest. He noted the slow and certain placement of the tiny slip of paper, just below a large patch of moss that grew on the face of the sacred wall. He smiled as Akiva turned and searched the shadows for some sign of the presence of Kadar. Inhaling the cigarette deeply, Kadar felt certain that the rabbi caught sight of the brief orange glow before he turned away to return through the crooked alleyways to the Jewish Quarter.

"They are gone." One of his men began to descend the steps that led to the wall.

"A moment longer," Kadar snapped, throwing down the cigarette and grinding it out with his foot. "There is too much at stake to be hasty."

Dusk melted into black darkness before Kadar descended the steps. The hollow sound of their shoes against the stones echoed in the alleyway before the wall. He stretched out his left hand and ran his fingertips across the rough face of the holy Jewish shrine. His eyes searched the stones above him for the patch of moss that hung like a shadow. Then he reached up, his fingers touching the clutter of notes stuck in the crevices until at last he grasped the slip that had been left by Akiva. Checking for an expected mark but not bothering to open the note, Kadar placed it in the pocket of his flowing robes and strode from the place. Allah was indeed looking with favor on the plans of Mufti Haj Amin Husseini.

It was only a short walk to Bab el Silsileh, the Street of the Chain, that led to Bab Daud Gate, the entrance to the Temple Mount directly next to the residence of Haj Amin.

A vaulted roof covered the street, and the smells of the spice shops filled the air. Spice merchants huddled beside the fires built in metal drums. As Kadar passed their stalls they rose with respect and called out to the man who served the Mufti so well. Kadar nodded acknowledgment as his hand closed around the slip of paper in his deep pocket. On the faces of many lay the shadow of fear; many of the vendors' stalls were closed and locked tight behind iron grills. *All will be well again,* he thought, *when Jerusalem and Palestine are at last totally within the grasp of Haj Amin. And that will be very soon.*

"A gift! A gift to the captain of Haj Amin!" an old man shouted from his spice stall. Kadar stopped momentarily and savored the scents of peppercorns and cinnamon as the vendor hurried toward him carrying a glass jar filled with precious yellow saffron powder.

Kadar bowed slightly and touched his forehead. "You are gracious; Allah will reward you," he said serenely as the man handed him a note.

"Remember the shop of Ishmael Ibn Doud, Captain. Remember your humble servant to your Master Haj Amin el Husseini."

Three times the scene was repeated and with each gift, a slip of paper was handed to Ram Kadar to carry from the petitioner to the Mufti. Throughout the years, Haj Amin had granted gifts of land and civil positions with a wave of his hand. Death had been pronounced just as effortlessly upon his enemies. Only the Arab intelligentsia disdained the rule of Haj Amin—and they would pay for their soft notions of government in the hands of the people. Kadar looked up at the darkened windows of the house of Khalidi.

From the time of Saladin, when the first Moslem rulers had come to Jerusalem in the seventh century, the family of Khalidi had held positions of high honor and respect under the different rulers. And yet they had left their home for the safety of another city. For too many years they had objected to the methods of Haj Amin as strenuously as they objected to Zionist dogma. Now they were gone—gone with most of the intellectuals who had spoken out against a holy war. Haj Amin would have traded a thousand peasants for their support, but neither favor nor honor could win them to him. Now it was the vendors, the merchants, and the ignorant villagers that followed. On this foundation of saffron and petitions and small bribes, the kingdom of Haj Amin was being built.

They passed through one more vault, then emerged into a small square at the end of the street in front of the gate to the Temple Mount.

Kadar handed the armful of petty bribes to his men, then washed his hands in the fountain across from the gate. He smiled as he read the inscription that announced that the fountain had been built by Suleiman the Magnificent: *Our master, the Exalted Ruler, King of the Nations, the Strength of Islam, the Defender of the Shrines . . .* How many times had he watched Haj Amin wash at this very basin before entering the Temple Mount to stir his people to the passion of Jihad, Holy War! And always, the eyes of his leader had scanned the inscription of Suleiman, *the Strength of Islam*. The Koran demanded the eradication of the Jews, yet was not Allah a God of peace? This very gate was called "Gate of Peace," but when Haj Amin passed through the doors of the gate, there was no peace. Kadar pushed away the doubts that crowded his thoughts. He dried his hands on his robe, then took the note of Akiva from his pocket before he entered the mansion of the Mufti Haj Amin. The men who had accompanied him remained outside and sat on the long stone benches on either side of the great doorway. Kadar left his bribes in their arms and, bowing graciously, entered the huge mosaic foyer of the house.

The house itself was filled with the history of the city. To Haj Amin it seemed fitting and proper that he lived in a house built on the foundation of the Chamber of Hewn Stone, where the Sanhedhrin, the Supreme Council of the Jews, once sat in judgment. The eastern wall of the house was built against the stones of the western wall where the Jews prayed to their God for mercy and deliverance. Often, Kadar had heard Haj Amin say that they had more need of praying to him, for he held their fate in his hands. "If Allah wills," Kadar said softly as he looked around the room.

Gerhardt lounged moodily in an overstuffed chair across from the double doors of a room where two tall black Sudanese bodyguards spoke in hushed tones. They looked up as Kadar entered, then resumed their conversation as they waited for their master to finish whatever business he conducted behind the closed doors.

Kadar sighed and rubbed his neck as he gazed up into the shadows of the vaulted ceiling.

"Will you tell him that I am back?" he asked a guard. "I came the long way, as he instructed."

"The Mufti cannot be disturbed," the guard said with a thick accent.

"Tell him."

The guard ignored him and Gerhardt laughed a bitter laugh.

"He will not see you now," Gerhardt said menacingly. "He is weary from his trip from Cairo, they say, and has much yet to do. He will not see you."

Kadar sniffed and looked disdainfully at Gerhardt. "You mean he will not see *you*, eh?" Kadar knocked softly on the door. After a moment a short turbaned servant opened the door slightly and examined Kadar. Then he closed the door and Gerhardt guffawed from his chair until the door opened again and the servant

135

stepped aside to allow Kadar to enter the majestically furnished room.

Haj Amin sat behind a broad-topped desk studying a sheaf of papers in front of him. He did not rise when Kadar stood before him, but waved his hand to indicate that Kadar was to sit in one of the two leather chairs in front of him. Haj Amin continued to scan the papers for five minutes, then sighed deeply, shoved them aside and looked up at Ram Kadar. His ice-blue eyes were the legacy of some ancient Crusader ancestor, and tonight the lines around them spoke of his weariness.

"You have done well in our absence, Ram," Haj Amin said quietly. "Both you and Gerhardt. Although it has not escaped our notice that the two of you share a common passion."

"What is that, Haj?" Kadar asked.

"Your hatred of one another. And of the Jews, of course."

Kadar looked down at the note from Akiva. "Yes."

"Gerhardt waits in the foyer, does he not?"

Kadar nodded. "He seems quite unhappy having to wait."

"Impatient man, Gerhardt. But you—patience is your greatest quality. Although you and Hassan failed us once, still, we are reasonable, and we appreciate men with the quality of reason. And patience. We also possess the quality of patience. Allah smiles on those who wait, does he not? We have waited long for what is soon to be delivered into our hands. We discuss and reason with our Arab brothers in Egypt, Jordan, Syria, and this is not an easy task. However, they also have come to listen to reason." Haj Amin leaned back in his chair and clapped his hands twice. The servant beside the door jumped to attention. "Admit our friend Gerhardt," he instructed. "Then fetch coffee."

The servant bowed and backed from the presence of Haj Amin. Kadar did not look up as Gerhardt stalked into the room.

"Dear friend," Haj Amin smiled an oily smile and

held his hand palm up toward the chair beside Kadar. "Please be seated."

"Why do you seat him and admit him before me?" Gerhardt's voice was full of indignation. "Have I not succeeded where he has failed? Yet you keep me waiting while you entertain him."

Haj Amin continued to smile. "Salaam. Peace, please. You are an impatient man, Gerhardt. This has nearly cost you your life many times—"

"It has cost the lives of Jews," Gerhardt interrupted.

The eyes of Haj Amin flashed like fire. "You interrupt!" He sat in silence while Gerhardt shrank back beneath his gaze. "As we were saying, you are a man who must learn to wait, Gerhardt. You will come when you are summoned, not before. You will leave when you are told to do so, not before. You will act only on our word, on none other. Is this clear?"

Gerhardt nodded, his mouth angrily turned down at the corners.

Haj Amin's patronizing smile returned. "Good. Then we understand one another?" He paused. "Both of you are our faithful servants. We are pleased with your actions—except for some minor failures."

He paused long enough for Kadar to squirm at the memory of Moshe Sachar's escape with the ancient scrolls only two weeks before. "Thank you, Haj."

His elegant hands touching at the fingertips, Haj Amin continued. "We have the money now, acquired from our Arab brothers, to fully arm you, Gerhardt, for the kind of war you know best how to fight."

Gerhardt smiled smugly and looked at Kadar. "And men. I need men of my own, under my command."

"A reasonable request. But first we have a small list of priority targets for you." Haj Amin handed a sheet of note paper to Gerhardt. "These should not be too difficult, eh?"

"The water mains?"

"We are aware that killing Jews is more to your liking, but you must think of the long-term effect, Gerhardt. To cut off the water supply to the Jewish sections of the city is victory."

"Brilliant!" Kadar said enthusiastically, relieved that there was to be a reprieve in the terrorist activities.

"We must make certain that our own water supplies are untouched. That is your job, Kadar."

"As Allah wills, Haj."

Haj Amin directed his gaze once again to Gerhardt. "The other things on the list shall be more what you have been trained for. As for the Jewish Quarter of the Old City, Rabbi Akiva assures us that soon the Haganah will be ousted."

Kadar cleared his throat and passed the note across the desk. "Another message from Akiva. He left it in the usual way just this evening."

Haj Amin stared at the folded paper in front of him. "Please read it for us, Kadar. Let us see what peaceful assurances the fool offers us tonight."

Kadar opened the note layer after layer until the cramped scrawl of the rabbi was revealed.

"Honorable Mufti, Haj Amin Husseini:

"Together we share a great responsibility—that of keeping the sacred stones behind these walls free from further bloodshed. Of late there have been some tragic occurrences that only make our situation more diffi-cult. I have granted your men permission to search the food convoys for Haganah and weapons as you re-quested; however, your men are stealing food. This causes much unrest among my people, and many are coming to believe that our quarter is indeed in danger. Only this week a young woman has come into this quar-ter from surviving the bus attack on Mount Zion. She is much admired and very beautiful." Kadar paused as Gerhardt leaned intently forward in his chair. He glanced sideways at Gerhardt, then at the face of the Mufti, who was watching Gerhardt with curious amuse-ment.

"Go on," Haj Amin instructed.

Kadar cleared his throat and continued. "She is

named Rachel, the granddaughter of a rabbi here, and a survivor of the camps. The people have listened to her. She has spoken for the need for defense, and I say to you that unless the pilfering ends, perhaps the entire quarter will hearken to her. Respectfully—"

Haj Amin interrupted. "What is it, Gerhardt? You have gone pale. You have killed a thousand, and yet this note about the petty pilfering by our men of food convoys, written by a fool who deludes himself that he will save his people—"

Gerhardt gripped the arm of his chair. "I saw her," he said grimly. "The woman he spoke about. I saw her the night I blew the bus."

"Can she be so beautiful?" Haj Amin was amused.

"She can be. She is. She is the whore. The Jewish whore from the Commando school."

Haj Amin hid the surprise he felt. "The woman for whom you suffered in the camps?"

Gerhardt's eyes narrowed. He nodded curtly. "It is the whore he writes about. I saw her. I was unsure at first. Then I remembered her face."

Kadar laid the letter on the desk of Haj Amin. The Haj picked it up and smiled as he scanned the words. "You are invaluable to us, Gerhardt. Allah smiles on us. We shall give this foolish rabbi what he needs to survive a while longer. And in return, he shall deliver to us what we want—the Haganah."

"How can we do that?" Kadar asked, genuinely puzzled by the exchange.

"It is a simple matter to discredit this girl whom he seems so threatened by, is it not? Gerhardt, is there a way to prove she is the woman you believe her to be?"

Gerhardt motioned to his forearm. "On her arm. On the inside she will bear the S.S. mark and the words, *Nür Für Offizere*."

Haj Amin clapped his hands together. "Marvelous! So simple. You shall be rewarded for this, Gerhardt. If, indeed, Akiva assists us because of this, you shall be rewarded."

Gerhardt rubbed his fingertips together with anticipation, his surly mood dissolving with the good fortune
that had fallen into his lap. "I want the girl," he said simply. "Give the girl to me."

16 Grandfather's Shabbat

Rabbi Shlomo Lebowitz sat very straight and tall in his bed at Hadassah Hospital. His Shabbat coat was buttoned neatly over his nightshirt, and a large black hat shaded his eyes from the glare of the table lamp as he recited his Shabbat prayers.

Yacov sat on his bed as the others stood in a solemn circle around it. David, Howard, Ellie, and Captain Thomas represented the Gentiles. Moshe, wearing a yarmulke that perched precariously on his head, shifted from one foot to the other.

Grandfather's voice was much stronger this Shabbat than it had been at the last, Yacov noted with satisfaction. The old man prayed:

"With ever-enduring love hast thou loved thy people of the house of Israel: Law and commandments, statutes and judgments has thou taught us. Therefore, O Eternal, our God! when we lie down, and when we rise we will discourse of thy statutes and rejoice in the words of thy law and in thy commandments forever. For they are our life, and the length of our days . . ."

Grandfather's eyes were full of life once again, and there was a smile beneath his white beard. He was going to be well again. The boy sighed with relief.

"HEAR, O ISRAEL, THE ETERNAL IS OUR GOD: THE ETERNAL IS ONE!" the old man said forcefully.

Moshe and Yacov repeated his words, while the rest of the tiny congregation wondered what they should say.

"And thou shalt love the Eternal, thy God, with all thy heart, and with all thy soul, and with all thy might . . ."

Thank you, God, Yacov prayed silently, *for returning the health of my grandfather to him. Help us to be able to go home soon. And bless my sister Rachel on this Shabbat. Also, God, a special blessing on these goyim who are my friends, eh? They are nice people, good people, even if they aren't Jews.*

"OMAINE!" said Grandfather loudly. He tugged on his sidelocks and peered earnestly at Ellie. "Did you remember to bring the candles, young woman?"

Eagerly Ellie pulled a brown paper bag out of her purse and laid the candles on the bed. "You bet! Just like you said."

"So are you going to light them on my bed? Such a Shabbat we will make, eh? You will burn the hospital to ashes and this old rabbi with it? Oy!" he teased her.

Quickly Howard pulled the night table to the foot of the bed, and Ellie set out the silver candle holders and the long white candles. "How's this?"

"Okay!" said Grandfather. "Is that how you say it, Yacov? Okay!" The old man looked around the group until his eyes rested on Captain Thomas. "So, you promised to have Shabbat with us sometime, eh? I remember this. Did you bring the challah?"

Luke held out a bag with two long braided loaves of white bread poking out the end. "I did not forget my promise, Rabbi Lebowitz, but I was afraid for a day or two that you might go off and forget yours!"

"Who, me? What would God want with such an old man, eh? I have too much yet to do." He sniffed and tapped his chest. "My creditors would chase me to the gates of heaven. I owe God for my soul and the butcher for the meat, eh? They would come and repossess that dog of Yacov's!"

Luke laid the challah next to the candles, and Moshe pulled one last package out from beneath his coat. "We musn't forget this!" He handed the small bag to Grandfather, who peeked in, then cried with delight.

"Oy Gevalt! Such a wine you bring for Shabbat, Moshe! Mogen David! I have not tasted wine since I

142

woke up in this sanitary prison! And who brought the glasses?"

Howard shrugged and raised an eyebrow, then reached down to retrieve yet another bag at his feet. "I thought we might need something to drink from."

"*You*, Uncle Howard?" Ellie asked, astounded.

"Before you get too excited . . ." Howard pulled out a small bottle of Coca-Cola. "Yacov and I can share!"

"This is not the most elegant of Shabbats," laughed Grandfather, "but it will do. It will do." He directed his gaze at Ellie. "So, you are the woman of the house, so to speak. You are supposed to light the Shabbat candles, nu?"

"Just a minute!" Ellie dug through her purse. "I forgot the matches!"

Confidently David reached into his flight jacket pocket and pulled out a small box of matches. "I figured," he said with a grin.

Ellie rolled her eyes and took them from him as he winked back at her.

"Do not strike your match yet!" instructed Grandfather. "First I will tell you a little something, yes?" He glanced at the group. "Some of us grew up with Shabbat and so we know what a day it is! Now when we share our Shabbat with the rest of you, it is a good idea if you know, too." The old man pursed his lips thoughtfully and tugged on his sidelocks again. "Shabbat is a day when even a poor man is a king and his wife is a queen. This is the day when we are favored by God's special attention. To remember the Shabbat is God's fourth commandment, a commandment He gave not for himself but for man. Six days we labor but on the seventh we rest, like God did, and we remember who made us, nu? Are there questions?" He paused and waited as all shook their heads in a definite no. "Such a bright group, eh, Yacov? Now, Yacov, open the window shades."

Yacov scrambled off the bed and pulled up the shades, revealing a soft dusky glow and the gleaming dome of the Temple Mount. The Old City below seemed serene and silent.

"Beautiful," Howard whispered as reds and golds reflected off the stones of the city.

"Each Friday evening when the sun sets, the Shechinah, the Divine Presence, descends into our homes and upon this Holy City, as it did of old," Grandfather continued. "And the angels come to earth and walk among us." His voice fell low as the sun sank beyond the brim of the horizon. "Now, young lady?"

"Yes?" Ellie nodded.

"Don't be impatient. It is nearly your turn, eh? Cover your head with the scarf."

"It is Rachel's scarf," Ellie said. "I thought it would be nice."

"Very nice indeed." The old man smiled at her as she draped the shiny satin scarf loosely over her head. "The Talmud says that the soul is the Lord's candle. And so as you light the candles you pass your palms over the candles, always toward yourself. Then you say these words: *Blessed art thou, O Lord our God, King of the Universe, who has sanctified us by thy commandments and has commanded us to kindle the Shabbat light.* Easy, eh? And then you ask God's blessing on your loved ones."

He gazed at Ellie over the tops of his spectacles. "You can do this? Then begin, please."

Ellie glanced out the window at the gathering dusk and imagined Rachel sharing Shabbat somewhere behind the wall. She sighed and struck the match. Holding the little flame high, it seemed to be the brightest thing in the world for an instant, and she thought about her own soul, the Lord's candle; she touched the flame first to one wick and then the other.

"Blessed art thou, O Lord our God, King of the Universe"—she passed her hands over the flames—"who has sanctified us by thy commandments, and commanded us to kindle the Shabbat light." She bowed her head and took a deep breath, wondering what blessings to ask for those gathered around the old rabbi's bed.

144

She cleared her throat and began, "Lord, you see our little flames flickering down here in the darkness. I'm glad for that; glad you see my heart. You have promised in your Word that you will not put out a light that is smoldering or break off a branch that is bruised. Thank you for your tender love. And I ask for those I have come to care for so deeply." She opened her eyes and looked out toward the Old City and thought of Rachel. "For those you have brought into my life, that you will walk with them and stand guard over them in a way I cannot. Tend to the little candles that wish so much to burn brightly for you and your kingdom. Fill us with your love for one another. I pray these things in the name of your son Jesus who died for my sins and the sins of the world. Amen."

Ellie raised her eyes to the surprised faces of the old rabbi and Yacov. Luke and Moshe covered their grins with their hands, and David chuckled openly. "Not exactly an ecumenical prayer, Els," David remarked.

"A good Shabbat prayer, young lady!" Grandfather exclaimed, silencing David. "So you think the mother of Jesus didn't light the Shabbat candles, David? For a Gentile Christian this is the very best kind of Shabbat prayer. So! I say to that, OMAINE!"

Smiles vanished, and the word *omaine* rippled through the group.

"And now it is for Moshe to say Kaddish before we drink the wine and break the bread. This old voice grows weak in favor of a younger man, eh?" He handed his silver-bound prayer book to Moshe, who held it up to the light of the candles. He too could think only of Rachel, and his voice was thick with emotion.

"Blessed art thou, the Eternal our God . . ." He swallowed hard and lifted his eyes to the outlines of the synagogues of the tiny Jewish Quarter far below Mount Scopus. *Keep her safe for me, Lord,* he silently prayed. *Hold her heart with gentle hands.* ". . . and found pleasure in us, and caused us to inherit His holy Shabbat in love and favor, as a memorial of the work of creation;

145

for that day ranks first . . ." *Heal her, Lord. You made everything, you can do anything. I ask you for a miracle for Rachel, my Rachel.* ". . . For us thou hast selected, and sanctified us from amongst all nations . . ." *In the name of Jesus the Messiah, I pray.* ". . . Blessed art thou, O Eternal! who hallowest the Shabbat!"

"OMAINE!" the tiny group said loudly.

"A rabbi you should have been!" exclaimed Grandfather to Moshe after the wine was sipped and the challas eaten. Moshe nodded and hung back as the others filed out into the hallways of Hadassah Hospital and Yacov hugged the old man one more time.

"I would like to speak with you, Reb Lebowitz," said Moshe.

Grandfather waited until Yacov shut the door behind him and they were alone in the room. "About my granddaughter, Moshe? About Rachel?"

"Yes."

Grandfather sighed and took off his spectacles. "Then you should maybe sit down, eh?"

Moshe sat awkwardly on the edge of his chair and tried to find a place to begin.

"You want to make small talk first?" asked Grandfather, finally breaking the silence. "How's your arm?"

"Getting better. How's your heart?"

"It would be much healthier if I knew my granddaughter had a fine Jewish man who would take care of her."

"You have a way with small talk, Reb Lebowitz."

"After so many years there is not a lot of time for skirting issues, nu? So. Do you have something to say?"

"I would like very much . . . I mean I have come to feel very deeply for your granddaughter. I would be so honored if I might ask for her hand in marriage." Moshe mopped his brow.

"What?" the old man cried. "Without a matchmaker you are asking to marry my granddaughter?" He smiled. "First there are some things you should maybe know, eh?"

146

"Sure."

"She is a poor girl. She has no dowry."

"I make a good living."

"Hmmm. Yes. I remember. You're in the business of old scrolls, eh?"

Moshe shrugged. "So are you."

"Well spoken." The old man tugged his beard. "Now I will tell you something serious. My son"—he frowned and looked out toward the skyline—"she has been wounded. Deeply. I cannot say how I know these things, as we did not speak of them in the short time she was with me. But my heart knows she has seen too much. Perhaps there is great risk in what you ask. Both for you and for her. I have letters that tell me of Rachel as a young girl. The young woman who has come home is not the same person. The Germans killed my only daughter, Rachel's mother. They killed also her two brothers and her father. I thought only Yacov had survived, and now Rachel has returned—from a path that led her to hell and back again. Her heart still is singed from the smoke of that place. I do not know what they did to her."

Moshe stared at the toes of his shoes. "God alone knows, Rebbe Lebowitz. I know enough. That doesn't affect the way I feel about her. I love her. Like God loves His bride Israel."

"Well, then," the old man sighed. "Israel too has seen much and strayed afar. Yet God still loves her, nu?" He rubbed his gnarled fingers over the cover of his prayer book. "If it is the wish of your heart, . . . and *hers*, you have my permission to marry."

17 Rachel's Home

Gerhardt nearly stumbled on the sleeping body of the muezzin. He squinted in the darkness and grasped the old man by the shirt collar.

"Wake up, old man!" He pulled him to his feet. "What news do you have? Have you seen her?"

The old muezzin blinked and stammered in fear at the force with which Gerhardt grasped him. "My m-m-most excellent—"

"Just give me news!" Gerhardt shook him hard. "Have you found her? Have you seen her?"

"Yes, most exalted—"

"Where? Where is she?" he demanded.

The old muezzin fumbled in his coat pocket for the slip of paper and held it out to Gerhardt, who snatched it from him; then let him go. Gerhardt rushed into the room and pulled the chain to the electric light bulb. Obsessed with the thought that the woman was alive and near, he studied the scrawl of cramped writing as the old man trembled outside the open door.

"What is this?" screamed Gerhardt. "Chicken scratching?"

"I-I can show you where you might find this woman. This enemy of Allah and the Mufti. This infidel dog."

"As well you should!" Gerhardt grabbed him by the back of his coat and half-dragged him down the stairway and into the streets. Merchants still hawked their wares, and the nighttime bustle of the souks was only slightly less than it had been during the daylight hours.

She is not a spirit, then, thought Gerhardt. *But flesh and blood. And Allah will himself deliver her into my hands for justice. No more will she haunt me and torment me and accuse me.*

The old muezzin was exhausted by the time they reached the tall minaret. "I cannot walk up the steps," he wheezed to Gerhardt. "Or I shall surely die."

"If you do not, then you shall die more surely." Gerhardt shoved him toward the long spiral stairway and threw him roughly against the steps.

The old man cried out and when he looked up at his benefactor, he was filled with fear. *The eyes of Gerhardt are the eyes of a demon*, he thought as he scrambled ahead of the servant of the Mufti.

He held the field glasses up and located the dark house where he had seen the woman only a few hours before. "It is there, most gracious your honor," said the old man. The woman came from the steps that lead from the basement."

Gerhardt smiled and seemed instantly to relax. "You have done well, old man. You have done well for me and for our master the Mufti. Your reward shall be great." He pressed a gold coin into the withered palm.

"Most honorable! Most gracious!" the old man exclaimed as he struck a match to view his treasure. "May Allah grant you every desire for your generosity."

"I have only one desire old man, and it is soon to be fulfilled."

A white silk shawl trimmed in blue covered Leah's head as she stood before the candles. The soft light illuminated her face as her arms briefly encircled the candles in a gesture that seemed to pull the warmth of their glow into her heart.

Rachel's eyes remained steadily on Leah as Leah spoke softly:

"O God of your people Israel,
You are holy
And you have made the Shabbat
    and the people of Israel holy.
You have called upon us to honor
    the Shabbat with light,

With joy,
And with peace,
As a king and queen give love to
    one another,
As a bride and her bridegroom—"

Leah's eyes fell lovingly on Shimon, who winked in acknowledgement.

"So we have kindled these two
    lights for love of your daughter
The Shabbat day.
Almighty God,
Grant me and all my loved ones
    a chance to truly rest on this
Shabbat day.
May the light of the candles drive
    out from among us
    the spirit of anger
    the spirit of harm.
Send your blessings to my children—"

Leah touched her stomach and smiled. "Oh, he kicked!" she said with surprise. Then she continued. "Excuse me, Lord . . . where was I? Oh yes . . ." Rachel noticed that her cheeks were flushed with embarrassment.

"Send your blessings to my children
That they may walk in the ways of
Your Torah, your light.
May you ever be their God
And mine, O Lord,
My Creator and my Redeemer.
Omaine."

"Omaine!" boomed Ehud, and each person repeated the word as Leah took her place at the table.

"A beautiful Tehinna, Leah," Rachel said.

"A good omen, eh?" beamed Shimon. "My son kicked when you prayed for God's blessings."

"Or your daughter . . ." Leah chided.

"Whatever!" Ehud raised his wine glass. "A toast to the little one, whatever he may be. May he be born to peace and happiness and the love of a happy mother and father! L'Chaim! To life!"

The glasses clinked together and Shimon slurped his wine happily. "A good toast. The toast of a righteous man!" He raised her glass again. "And now I wish to toast my friend an oyrech Shabbat. May the blessings of the Eternal rest upon Ehud. May he dwell in safety and may be once again find himself on a steady ship in a calm sea! Omaine!"

Rachel sipped her wine and quickly searched her mind for a blessing for Shimon and Leah. "A toast to my Shabbat hosts!" She thrust her wine glass toward the center of the table. "May this house be filled always with joy and happiness and the noise of many children! L'Chaim! To life!"

"My turn!" cried Leah, raising her glass. "This is easy, eh? I raise my glass and ask a blessing for Rachel Lubetkin. May her heart find peace and happiness here among her people. And may God grant her a fine strong husband and many small blessings to tug at her skirts and call her blessed!"

"Omaine!" shouted Ehud. "And I know just the man!"

Rachel's hand trembled slightly as she sipped her wine.

"Just the man?" cried Leah. "You did not tell me about this, Rachel."

"Perhaps Ehud knows more than I know myself." Rachel tried to smile as she dipped the ladle into the dumplings and began to spoon them into the dishes.

"Why, I speak of Moshe, girl!" Ehud said loudly as he took his plate.

"Not the Moshe I know," Rachel replied.

"He is a moonstruck calf. Sick with love. Like Solomon in his song. If ever I saw a man in love . . ."

Rachel felt an overwhelming sense of panic at Ehud's words. She toyed with her fork and did not reply, instead wishing she could run out the front door and hide somewhere.

Leah frowned slightly, then deliberately interrupted Ehud's train of thought. "Well, Ehud, tomorrow the convoy will come and we can feed you a little better."

"Yes! The convoy! This is the *very same Moshe* I was speaking of when I said he will find a way to smuggle arms into us! This is the *same Moshe* who loves Rachel."

Shimon noticed Rachel as she bit her lip and squirmed uneasily in her chair. "Always the Arabs allow the convoy on Shabbat, nu? And we must carry burdens on the day when it is forbidden." He attempted to direct Ehud's attention to another issue.

"This *very same Moshe* is he who will conceal weapons until we have to hunt to find them ourselves." Ehud continued, oblivious to Rachel's discomfort. "Why, it was he who rescued Rachel from the sea on what was nearly to be the last voyage of the *Ave Maria*. Tell them, Rachel! It is such a story!"

"How many immigrants did you smuggle into Palestine on the *Ave Maria*?" asked Leah.

"Together, Moshe and I smuggled in a few, I can tell you! But I never knew him to go overboard for a girl!" He guffawed at his own joke. "Loved her from the moment he saw her, eh, Rachel? Don't tell me he didn't tell you! Oy! Always he was a bit backward when it came to women. You'll have to take him in hand, girl. You'll have to teach him a thing or two, Rachel!"

"Leah has trained me well." Shimon attempted to distract Ehud again, certain that Rachel was near to tears.

"Well, Moshe is overboard. First I thought it was the American girl he was in love with; then along came *this* little one!" Ehud attacked his supper. "I wouldn't be at all surprised if we didn't open a flour barrel tomorrow and find him inside in search of a bride!"

"Ehud." Rachel stammered. "Please . . ." She laid down her fork.

"What . . ." He paused mid-bite. "You might as well

152

face it, girl. As soon as he makes up his mind—"

Shimon kicked him beneath the table.

"What?" Ehud asked. "All I'm saying is—"

"Shut up, Ehud," Shimon said.

"What?" Ehud was ever more bewildered.

Rachel stared steadily at her plate, unable to reply.

"Well, maybe Rachel hasn't made up *her* mind," Leah said pointedly.

"Not made up your mind?" Ehud exclaimed. "No woman can find a finer man than *Moshe*. And you know the old saying, 'The best of horses need a whip; the wisest of men, advice; the chastest of women—a man!' Well spoken, nu?"

Rachel stood up quickly, unable to stay in the small room any longer. "Excuse me. I need to go. I am not well. No! Don't stand up. I have not felt well all day."

Shimon rose, bumping the table and spilling a bit of Ehud's dumpling on his lap.

"Oh, Rachel!" exclaimed Leah. "Can I get you anything? Shimon! You must see her home."

"No! Please!" Rachel cried, groping for the door. "I just need to be at home now. Thank you. I'm sorry."

She hurried out the door and down the steps, leaving Shimon and Leah to stare at Ehud in disgust as he continued eating his dumpling.

"Good food," he said when he looked up and noticed their eyes on his face. "Well, what is it?" he bellowed after a long silence. "You couldn't tell she didn't want to talk about this Moshe fellow?" Leah chided.

"Not want to talk?"

"Not even a little bit!" exclaimed Shimon.

"As God is my witness!" Ehud defended. "As He guides my lips—"

"God never told anyone to be stupid!" Shimon shook his head as Leah rose from the table and hurried to the window to watch Rachel retreat into the shadows toward her own home.

Quietly moving from rooftop to rooftop, Gerhardt inched his way toward the perimeter of the Jewish Quarter. To his right he could make out the vague outlines of British guards who stood watch for the Jews who quietly supped at their Shabbat tables, peacefully unaware of the menace that surrounded them. *The fools*, he thought as he ducked behind the dome of a rooftop. *Do they think the world will stop for their Shabbat?* The empty stations of the Jewish checkpoints only accented their stupidity. Even if the British soldiers spotted his lurking form, he was reasonably certain they would do nothing as long as he did not threaten them. But they would not see him. They played bridge within the safety of their tiny sandbag nests and only glanced in his direction every few minutes.

He snipped through the barbed wire that covered the rooftop border between the quarters. Only once did he snag his black sweater as he employed the techniques he had learned in the commando schools of Adolf Hitler only a few years before.

He quickly gained the Jewish side of the wire and crawled on his belly to the edge of the roof.

He glanced toward the British guards, noticing from the corner of his eye a movement. A guard stood and stretched, then climbed down toward where Gerhardt lay against the black asphalt roof.

"Right!" yelled one of his companions as the guard moved nearer and nearer to Gerhardt. "Hurry it up Smiley, will you? We ain't got all night."

The guard waved back, laughed and stopped at the edge of the rooftop just a few feet from Gerhardt. He muttered clear enough for Gerhardt to understand every word. "Time's all we do have . . . all night long freezin' up here." The guard spit over the edge of the roof, looked down, and then, still muttering, turned and climbed back into the nest of sandbags.

Gerhardt did not wait long before he continued his slow crawl to where a wooden ladder clung to the side of the house. His eyes on the guards, he swung himself over the rain gutter and clambered quickly and noise-lessly down the ladder. Then a few feet above the street, he heard a sound that made the hair on the back of his neck bristle. The low, menacing growl of a dog threat-ened his next step and he quickly scrambled back up the ladder a few steps. Yellow eyes glared up at him in the dark. "Go on!" he hissed, but the dog's lips curled back, revealing rows of gleaming white teeth.

The dog barked loudly and jumped upward, hook-ing a fang in Gerhardt's trouser leg as he kicked at the dog.

"What's 'appening over there?" he heard a guard yell.

Gerhardt pulled his pistol out of his jacket and cocked it, cursing silently at the dog as he scrambled back up the ladder and rolled onto the roof under the safety of the barbed-wire field.

The dog continued to bark and snarl as the guards ran with their flashlights scanning the rooftops. Ger-hardt ducked behind a dome on the Arab side of the wire and waited in breathless anticipation as the guards searched the entire area.

"Smiley!" a voice called as lights played on the sev-ered wire. "Sergeant Ham! There's somethin' amiss 'ere! The wire's been cut!"

Disappointment and rage filled Gerhardt. He could have easily tossed one grenade and wiped out all the idiots who stood between him and his goal. But he would wait. *Patience* was the one characteristic Haj Amin had denied he possessed. Now he would show the Mufti what a patient man he could be when the oc-casion called for it. There was time. Lots of time. And Gerhardt would wait to fulfill his highest desire. He would prove himself to be a man of patience.

18   Shaul

Tiny Shabbat candles beckoned through every window of the Jewish Quarter, and above Rachel's head the crystal stars of the Milky Way glistened. Fragments of song and Shabbat chants mingled in the streets, swirling around her like a wind, then rising in wisps toward heaven.

"Welcome to you, O ministering angels. May your coming be in peace, may you bless us . . . Ah, Father—Father—Father in heaven, look upon us . . ."

It is Shabbat, Rachel thought, *as it has always been. As it was in the shetl when I was a child. Can it be so unchanged when the world is so changing? When I am changed forever?*

"His love endures forever . . . Give thanks unto the Lord, for his love never changes . . . Though I descend into the deepest sea, lo thou art there."

As she passed the low buildings of the Sephardic Synagogue, the muffled chant of the cantor and the murmured prayers of the congregations seemed to follow her.

"His love endureth forever . . ."

She stumbled on a step and fell, crying out as her palms struck against the cold stone. A rush of pain pushed against her chest and tears spilled over from her soul.

"His love endureth forever . . ."

"I don't believe you!" she cried aloud, half choking on the force of her anger. "If you loved me so much, then why am I still alive? Why did you leave me in hell?"

"Lo, though I descend into Sheol, thou art there."

Rachel lay her head down in her arms and wept as

the sweet sounds of Shabbat surrounded her, mocking the bitter ache inside her own soul. Shabbat would never be a day of rest for her. The intimate smiles of Shimon and Leah and the tender gaze of Moshe lingered in her mind, sharpening the edge of her loneliness. Mama and Papa had also looked at one another in such a way, but it was never to be for her. "Oh, Moshe," she sobbed. "Oh, God!" The love of both God and man seemed as distant as the stars above her. So beautiful, so unattainable.

"His love endureth forever."

Rachel raised her head and wiped her eyes. The stones around her still echoed with songs of peace, yet for her there was no peace. She braced herself against the wall and slowly stood. Pulling her thin coat tightly around her, she turned the corner and hugged the faces of the buildings as she made her way toward the apartment. She grasped the iron key and descended the steps, hesitating only a moment as the darkness surrounded her.

Suddenly she heard a movement in the shadows to the right of the door. Her fingers searched for the key hole, panic welling up inside her. She fumbled and dropped the key with a clatter.

"Who's there?" she cried, her heart pounding wildly.

For a moment only the sound of the cantor answered her. ". . . for his love . . ." Then she heard a slight scratching sound and a low whine.

"Who is it?" she asked again.

From the shadows the dark form of Yacov's dog Shaul emerged. He yawned and stretched slowly, then sidled up to Rachel and bumped against her legs.

"You!" She knelt and buried her face in the shaggy neck. "What are you doing here?" She groped for the key, then found the keyhole and opened the door with a crash.

Shaul scrambled past her and joyfully jumped up on the sagging iron bed that belonged to Grandfather. He circled twice, then thought better of it and jumped to the floor again.

"Thank you for coming." Rachel wiped tears of relief from her eyes. "I was feeling alone, you know? Thank you for coming."

Kneeling on the floor, she embraced the dog once again and wept into his fur while he sat very still, looking self-consciously around the room.

Shabbat morning the streets of the Jewish Quarter seemed almost desolate in the silence that enveloped them. But beyond the sandbag and barbed-wire barriers that marked the beginning of the Muslim Quarter, the clatter of wooden-wheeled produce carts wakened Muslims and Christians to market day.

Rachel stood on the top step of the apartment entrance and watched as Shaul raced full speed down the empty street and cleared a sandbag barricade with one leap. A feeling of utter loneliness once again settled on her. She stayed out in the cold morning air for a long time, listening to the muted calls of the Muslim produce sellers one hundred yards and another world away.

She remembered the stories Grandfather had told about the old Arab man who had come each Shabbat to kindle Grandfather's fire and bring him vegetables from the souks. Today there would be no Arab friends or neighbors to pay calls. No Shabbes Goy to perform the work forbidden on this day to faithful Jews. This Shabbat the Orthodox, young and old alike, would spend their time in cold and hungry contemplation of the day of rest and He who made it.

Rachel scanned the rooftops to the lonely outposts where Dov, Chaim and Shimon stood their Shabbat watch on flat rooftops. As the first light gleamed against the Dome of the Rock, Rachel imagined that she could see their lips move in silent prayer welcoming the morning.

"To Him who made the greater lights shall praise be

given, for His mercy endureth forever. A new light upon Zion may thou cause to shine, and may all of us long enjoy its radiance . . ."

The silhouettes of four young British guards were plainly visible. They watched from a higher vantage point, Sten guns propped against their hips. It seemed hard to believe that these were the same men who had rescued them from the bus only days before.

"Do not wonder about it," Dov had said to her over lunch at Tipat Chalav. "Not many believe as the Captain Thomas does. He is a righteous Gentile, nu? But he cannot be among us and with his own men each moment. Oh yes, Rachel. These men who stand guard over us would kill us indeed if we had need to use a weapon."

"Then why do you stand guard?" she had asked. "You hide your guns and cannot use them in any case. Why stand guard at all?"

"The Jihad snipers do not know we cannot fire our weapons. And it would not be wise for them to think we depend only on the English for protection. Someday soon the English will be gone. If the Jihads knew what little we had to defend ourselves with, they would come with boards and broomsticks to take the quarter. We will fool them, eh? Like Gideon."

"The English protect us from snipers, and yet they would protect the snipers by shooting you if you pulled out a gun for defense?" she asked, uncertain of the sense of the entire situation.

Dov laughed at the expression on her face. "A confusing plot, indeed! Of course, the English do not know that I would shoot at them just as easily as I would shoot a Jihad Moquade if my right to self-defense is denied. I have seen enough that I do not take kindly to *anyone's* bullets flying in my direction. English. Arab. It makes no difference to me. I have grown weary of standing duty for target practice!"

For a full fifteen minutes Rachel stood motionless on the step and watched the sky turn from soft pastels to vivid blue. Shaul did not return. Finally she sighed and descended into the cold apartment. She scraped the chair closer to the unlit stove, hoping for a remnant of warmth.

What difference would it make to me if I lit a fire? Why should I not work on Shabbat? I have violated every other law. I could kindle a thousand fires on Shabbat, and none of them would make my niche in hell any hotter. It all seems like such a small thing. God must laugh when He watches men work so hard at not working. And yet perhaps He weeps when He looks at me. With or without Shabbat lights, I am still dark with guilt.

Aware of those around her who would pass the day without warmth, Rachel sat still and stared at the stove. "It makes no difference to my soul, but for them I will remain cold also today. And God," she added softly, "if you can hear me, I ask a Shabbat of warmth and peace for Grandfather and Yacov and for Moshe. For Moshe . . ." her prayer remained unfinished as her breath ascended in a cold vapor.

———

The morning slipped in crisp and cold, with bright sunlight streaming over the rain-washed city. Yacov hugged his bathrobe around him as he jogged in place on the front steps. His bare toes ached with the cold, but still he stayed, his eyes scouring the farthest horizons of the street.

"Shaul!" he called loudly, his shrill voice certainly to awaken the neighbors. "Shaul!" he called again and again, his words alternatingly demanding and pleading with the dog to come home. "Stupid dog!" he muttered. "Grandfather was right. He is nothing but a jackal. To be gone all the night through!" He was about to turn and go back into the house when a shaggy black speck turned the corner of the street and paused to lift a leg against a lamp post. "Shaul!" Yacov shouted, skipping down the steps and onto the sidewalk. "Come on, boy!" He whistled loudly, and the shades of the house across the street lifted as an angry face squinted down at Yacov.

Shaul seemed not to notice. He sniffed his way along the railing that lined the walk and weaved his way home from lamp post to lamp post.

"Shaaa-aul!" Yacov stamped his foot angrily. "COME!"

With total unconcern, Shaul glanced up and wagged his rump, then scampered full tilt toward Yacov. The boy knelt down and spread his arms wide as Shaul bounced and licked and wriggled his greeting.

"You! You are a bad boy, Shaul! I have worried half the night after you! Where have you been? Have you found another girlfriend? Grandfather says you have found a girlfriend when you go away overnight. Well, I do not like it! You must not run away like this anymore. Things are very bad and dangerous, you know. Some hungry Arab soldier might see you and—Yacov ran a finger over his throat in a cutting motion. "Then you would be somebody's breakfast, nu?"

Shaul sat patiently panting with his tongue hanging out as Yacov reprimanded him. Then he sneezed three times, rose and padded quickly to the front door to be let in. Yacov scrambled after him, oblivious now to the numbness in his feet.

"I found him!" he shouted joyfully as he threw open the door. "Hey, everyone—I found Shaul!"

David's door cracked open and squeaked softly as he peered out at the boy and dog in the hallway. "Pipe down a little bit, huh?" he moaned.

"But Rebbe David, I found Shaul."

"Great. Great, kid," he yawned. "You want some coffee? I could use some coffee." He glanced at his watchless wrist. "What time is it, anyway? You know what time it is?"

"After six."

David's lower lip stuck out and his eyes narrowed. "We were up until three last night. Three this morning, I mean, talking about this convoy thing, y'know? Now you've wakened the whole house up. You wanna make me some coffee?"

Yacov sighed and shrugged. "Sorry, Rebbe David. A Jew you are not. Today you can make your own coffee. This is Shabbat, eh? I am forbidden to work."

"You call making coffee work?" David asked incredulously.

"Of course I may drink it if a goy makes it."

"You remind me of the story of the Little Red Hen, kid. You'll drink it but you won't make it, eh?"

"This is something I have learned very well from you, Rebbe David." Yacov thumped Shaul and trotted off toward the kitchen.

He pushed the kitchen door open a crack and peered in. Moshe sat in the same chair that he had been in the night before, his head resting on a table littered with lists and piles of papers. Yacov frowned and sniffed as he stared at Moshe's sleeping form.

"Are you awake, Rebbe Moshe?" he asked softly. When there was no answer he tiptoed in, followed by Shaul. "Rebbe Moshe?" He tapped Moshe on the shoulder. "Are you awake, Rebbe Moshe?"

Moshe opened his eyes and rubbed a hand sleepily across his face as he sat up. "Must have dozed off. What time is it?"

"Morning. Shabbat morning. I found Shaul."

Moshe cleared his throat and rubbed the back of his neck. "That is very nice. Good. Yes. You found him."

"Are you hungry?" the boy asked.

"A bit."

"I woke up Rebbe David. He can fix us breakfast before Ellie wakes up, eh?"

"Don't think I have time, Yacov. I have work to do."

"Work, Rebbe Moshe? On Shabbat?"

"The convoy, Yacov. Unless it is ready today, all those in the Old City will go hungry and cold the rest of the week as well."

"Ah yes." Yacov noticed the cold cup of coffee that

sat beside a stack of papers. "Rebbe Moshe? You are up so early or so late?"

"I fell asleep where I sat, I'm afraid." His eyes wandered to Shaul. "The wanderer is home early and late, I see." He offered Shaul his hand palm up, then scratched the dog behind the ears. "Have you found a girlfriend, old chap? These are dangerous times to wander the streets, you know." Then he winked at Yacov. "He must be truly in love, eh? One does not risk everything unless he is in love, eh? Or a meshuggener, crazy dog."

"I think you are maybe a meshuggener, Rebbe Moshe. It is after six and you have not slept in a bed. And this is Shabbat. You are supposed to rest."

"Are you resting?"

"No."

"Why not?"

"I was worried about Shaul," Yacov said defensively. "I got up to find him."

"I also have a worry, eh? About your sister. About those she is with now. God would count it a greater sin if we were not to do what we can for those we love, even on Shabbat."

Yacov nodded, his face clouding. "I have missed my sister these last few days."

"And so have I."

"A funny thing. All these years I didn't miss her because I didn't know her. I thought she was dead, and all I knew of her was the picture. Now that I have seen her and touched her and she is in my life, I am missing her. And also Mama and Papa and my brothers. Before I didn't know. You know?"

Moshe toyed with his pen. "A funny thing, Yacov." He shoved a chair out with his foot and gestured for the boy to sit. "I had never seen her face before I met her on the *Ave Maria*, but I always missed her. Somehow God told me she was in the world. Each day I looked for her and prayed for her. Now that I have found her, it is very hard to know that she is only a few kilometers away and I cannot be with her. It is . . ." He closed his eyes for a moment. "It is very hard, indeed."

"I thought perhaps you would marry her."

"Perhaps. Someday."

"Since Grandfather has already given you permission—"

Moshe's eyes widened. "You would make a fine spy. You listened to my conversation with Rebbe Lebowitz!"

"Such a fuss you make! You think I didn't notice this? That you look at my sister and she turns red—"

"Does she?"

"Oy! You didn't notice?" He slapped his hand against his forehead.

"No. No, I thought she—"

"Oy! When you talk, you can talk about nothing. But when you just open your mouth, her eyes do this." Yacov batted the eyelashes of his good eye. "And does she ever turn red! Like a tomato. And her ears turn red like little flowers." Yacov turned to Shaul in amazement. "Can you believe this grown-up meshuggener, Shaul? He doesn't even know when a girl has gone twitters over him. No wonder he is so old and still has no children, eh?"

"For one so young—" Moshe sputtered.

"Everyone noticed. Not just me and Shaul." He sniffed and crossed his arms. "So how come you let her go in there?"

"You sound angry, Yacov."

"For a whole lifetime I have no sister and now here she is, and then she is gone again because you said she could go."

"It was her own decision."

"She would have stayed here if you had asked."

Moshe frowned and bit his lip, wondering at the truth of Yacov's words. "I thought it was for the good of . . . of the Old City."

"And if the city lives and my sister dies, what good does that do me, Rebbe Moshe? And you? You will be alone like before."

"You are right. Of course you are right. But I . . . I didn't expect her to stay."

"But you let her go. So how will you get her back?"

Moshe shrugged and tapped the papers before him. "I am searching for a way, Yacov. I will tell you and Shaul something because I think you will understand, eh? When one is in love it is easy to risk everything for the person you love, eh? To do less feels like death itself. But I must be very careful in my decisions now. So that my head rules and not just my heart. If I do less, my actions could hurt a lot of people. Perhaps even your sister, eh?"

"Such a shame you cannot be a flea and ride on the back of Shaul into the Old City, Rebbe Moshe." Yacov sighed and gazed sadly at Shaul. "He would know just where to take you, nu?"

Moshe rose and poured his cold cup of coffee into the sink. "This would be a clever plan, Yacov. I have sat up through the night trying to find a way that I might become a little flea among the Old City souks." Moshe pursed his lips and stared for a long time at the dog sleeping at his feet.

19 Changing of the Guard

Luke clasped his hands behind his back and paced the length of Colonel Black's crowded anteroom. Officers and non-coms read the morning paper or smoked and stared absently out the window as they waited their turn to be ushered to the other side of the solid walnut doors. The sound of a Mozart symphony drifted out from the colonel's office. Five times the symphony played through until the men in the office looked at one another and rolled their eyes as if to ask whether the infamous Colonel Black couldn't afford any other records.

An officious-looking lieutenant sat shuffling papers at a small desk just to the right of the double doors. Occasionally an officer would glance at his watch, then walk to the little man at the desk and whisper. The Lieutenant would then look at his own watch and study the appointment book in front of him. Then he would answer, "As soon as possible, sir, I assure you."

At last the sixth playing of the symphony finished; every head raised in silent hope that Colonel Black might possibly have a Glenn Miller record in his stack. When the music began again, the Lieutenant smiled and said smugly, "Ah, Mozart! *Symphony Number 39 in E-Flat Major.*"

A portly sergeant sniffed and shifted in his seat, "The colonel never heard of Guy Lombardo I suppose?"

"The American fellow who plays jazz? Saints preserve us!" exclaimed the lieutenant.

"Well, we was allies in the late war, wasn't we?" blustered the sergeant. "Now we got t' listen t' German music, begging yer pardon?"

The lieutenant narrowed his eyes and was about to comment when the black intercom on his desk crackled to life and the music of Mozart blared out, accompanied by the precise voice of Colonel Black. "Captain Luke Thomas, please," said the colonel.

"Yes, sir," the lieutenant flicked the intercom switch, then rose to open the door for Luke.

"See if the colonel's got 'alf a mind for takin' requests," the sergeant called after him, and a twitter of laughter filled the waiting room.

Tall and angular, Colonel Black leaned back in his chair and returned Luke's crisp salute with seeming nonchalance.

Luke then stretched out his hand toward Captain Michael Stewart, the newest replacement in the command.

"You two know one another, I assume," commented the colonel briskly.

"Of course," Luke smiled. "Captain Stewart was assigned as an observer the night the bus to Zion Gate was blown and wrecked." He nodded at Stewart, who returned his nod with a tolerant smile.

"Quite a few Zionist sympathizers among your men, I dare say," said Captain Stewart drily.

"Quite right," said Luke. "They have been here quite a long time you see, and—"

"Which brings us directly to the point," interrupted the colonel. "Just this morning we received this." He tapped a stack of papers marked *priority* across the top. "You and the men under your command have done some good things, even heroic things, during your tour of duty here in Palestine. Your actions during the bus incident saved a number of civilian lives, to be sure."

"It is no more than what had to be done," Luke said, feeling the intense gaze of Stewart on him as he spoke.

"Yes, well, I suppose so." The colonel packed his pipe with care and lit the tobacco until a halo of blue-gray smoke drifted around his head. "Now, I want to tell you there has been a change of policy in regard to how

167

we are to handle the Jewish question. Our main concern, of course, is to get our own lads safely back to England."

"Of course."

"What that means, Captain Thomas, is that you are not to interfere anymore."

Luke looked first at the colonel's grim face and then to the smirk on Stewart's face. "I am not quite sure I understand, sir," said Luke quietly.

"British lives come first. You are not to risk your life or the lives of your men for any purpose whatsoever. The British Mandate is effectively coming to an end. We want no more English blood spilt on this godforsaken soil."

"But, sir, if I may be so bold, when the lives of the innocent—"

"Exactly." The colonel pointed his pipestem at Luke. "The men waiting to return to England are the innocents now."

"But, sir, the Old City residents are like ducks on a pond. The Mufti's men will—"

"They have been offered safe escort from the Old City. If they choose to stay, that is no concern of ours. They stay at their own risk. Our order of the day is to protect British lives."

"A shortsighted order, sir."

The colonel's face grew red with anger at Luke's comment, and he snatched the pipe from his mouth. "That is no concern of yours. Not any longer, Captain Thomas. As of this moment you and your men are relieved from your duties in the Old City. Captain Stewart will be taking your place, and his main purpose is to fulfill the last orders of the British Mandate—"

"Is that all?" Luke asked, feeling the ground fall from beneath him. *Dear God, how can I help your people now?* he prayed silently.

"You will be assigned elsewhere, Captain Thomas. A post that will assure that you and your men will indeed make it back to England in one piece."

"We have gotten on quite well with the Old City rabbis. This may make things more difficult in that location."

"It has been duly noted how your men have fraternized with the Jewish population. This cannot help but be detrimental to our purposes here."

"And what are those purposes, Colonel Black?" he asked, ignoring the look of triumph on Stewart's face.

"To bring our men home in one piece. That is my goal and the goal of His Majesty. The rest is up to Almighty God." The colonel swiveled in his chair and stared up at the map behind him. Palestine was represented by a tiny patch of red amid a Middle-Eastern quilt of violence and upheaval. "In my opinion this place is much ado about nothing," he said after an uncomfortable silence. "Do you know how many Englishmen died defending this territory against Rommel?" He looked from one man to the other. "Of course, Captain Stewart here was not involved in 1942 during the battle of El Alamein. Too young."

Stewart looked down at his hands. "My brother was there."

"Yes, of course. A shame about your brother's death. To die at the hand of Jewish terrorists after fighting the Nazis so bravely." The colonel shook his head. "And you were right in the thick of it, weren't you, Captain Thomas?"

Luke nodded and smoothed the corners of his mustache. "With Field Marshal Montgomery. We lost 13,500 men. Rommel lost 55,000. Churchill called it *the beginning of the end*. We turned the Nazis back. In the end, the oil fields were saved and Palestine was never invaded. Possibly it saved yet another death camp from being built by the Mufti to eliminate the Jews of Palestine." He cleared his throat. "That was the plan, you know. And it still is."

The colonel bristled as the music finally ended. He did not get up to turn the record, and his voice could be heard clearly in the outer room. "Only a bit more than three years ago, we pulled this place from the fire. England has lost enough good men for the sake of these ungrateful Jews. Enough is enough. Now here we are back at it again. Fighting everyone! The Jews! The Arabs!"

"We have built our own camps for the Jews," Luke allowed his own voice to rise.

"For the good of Palestine! For their own good as well. How long do you think we could keep the peace if half a million survivors staggered into Palestine!"

"There would have been many millions more who would have survived if we as a government had allowed them to emigrate to Palestine before the war. We have not done such an excellent job of keeping the peace, have we? The war has been over for three years and these people *still* have no home. They have to have a place to go."

"To hell!" the colonel snapped. "Let them go back to where they came from!"

"Then that would indeed be hell." Luke was certain that every word he spoke punctuated the end of his career, but somehow it didn't seem to matter anymore.

"I feel as sorry for them as anyone. The war crimes trials going on right now in Nuremburg prove that the world has a conscience. But we are marking time here, and the Jews are marking time for their own survival. There is nothing left to do but get our own men home!" The colonel's argument was finished. So, Luke felt, was his career. In the colonel's mind there was nothing left to argue. Home and England and the survival of his own were all that mattered now.

"Yes, sir," Luke finished.

"Well, I'm glad we agree." The colonel sniffed. "You will assist Captain Stewart in taking command of the Old City."

"Yes, sir. But—"

"One more question," the colonel interrupted, tapping his pipe against his teeth. "This fellow, Moshe Sachar, the fellow in charge of supplies to the Jewish

Quarter. What sort of fellow is he?"

"A good man. An archaeologist."

"An archaeologist?" exclaimed Stewart in disdain.

"Yes," replied Luke with difficulty. "He was educated at Oxford. A good chap."

"At Oxford?" The colonel seemed impressed. "Well, then."

"You can never trust a Jew no matter where he is educated," Stewart said, shifting uneasily in his chair.

Luke exhaled loudly and continued to look at the colonel. "During the war, it was Moshe Sachar who played a key role in the battle of El Alamein, Colonel Black." His voice was thick with anger. "Professor Sachar traveled extensively behind the German lines, mapping water supplies and a possible route of escape for the British army in the event we were defeated by Rommel. All this he did for England at great risk of his own life."

"Well, we weren't defeated, were we?" quipped Stewart with disdain.

"Educated at Oxford, eh?" the colonel said again. "Sounds like a decent enough fellow."

"He is, sir. Will that be all?"

"All for now, Captain. Your transfer orders will be coming through shortly, I imagine. Dismissed."

Luke saluted and strode toward the door. As his hand grasped the knob, he turned back toward Colonel Black. Stewart smirked at him triumphantly.

"Colonel, sir?" Luke said.

"What is it, Thomas?"

"I just want to clarify one point, sir. We do *not* agree." Luke saluted again and closed the door behind him.

Yehudit Akiva smiled briefly at the new British officer who had come to visit her father.

"Quite pleasant to meet you too, Rabbi Akiva." Captain Stewart shook the rabbi's outstretched hand. "It is always good to meet with a reasonable man—no matter what his personal religious beliefs."

Akiva's smile faltered for a moment; then he regained his composure. "I had thought for a time that the British government had gone mad in their support of these troublemakers. I am only a rabbi, not a Zionist. I would recommend that at the first sign of trouble, these Haganah be expelled from my quarter."

"Certainly. With your support we will be happy to teach these men a lesson. And what about the woman?"

Akiva stuck his lower lip out and shook his head from side to side. "That would not be wise. She is a relative of an old rabbi, and quite popular. She has roots here in the Old City, unlike these upstart immigrants. We want no martyrs. There is another way. My daughter Yehudit can help restore order. She knows what to look for and will be most happy to supply information. If you need any help . . ."

"Thank you both. I will certainly keep in touch." He bowed slightly to Yehudit and slipped out the door.

Akiva's smile immediately faded. "Yehudit!" he snapped. "Come into my study!"

Obediently Yehudit followed her father into the dark room. "What is it, Father? You told the Englishman I could help, but what can I do?"

Akiva lit the lamp and sat down heavily behind his desk. He toyed with the edge of a tiny slip of paper, then opened it and studied it for a moment. The light reflected on his spectacles, hiding his eyes from Yehudit as she fidgeted nervously in front of him. At last he spoke. "The woman Rachel," he began slowly, "may not be all that she seems to be. Or perhaps she is much more than she appears to be." His mouth turned up in a half-smile.

"What do you mean, Father?"

"We must be sure of these things." He glanced at the paper again. "On her forearm, her left forearm, there is a mark. It looks like this." He handed the paper to Yehudit.

"What does it mean?" She studied the strange black

mark and the words, *Nür Für Offizere.*

"It means the end of opposition to me." Akiva took the paper back and grinned into Yehudit's bewildered face. "For Officers Only."

20 Convoy

"There isn't a thing I can do to help you, Moshe," Luke said grimly as he stirred his tea. "I have been given notice by the Colonel himself. Everyone is going to be watching how you behave at the cargo transfers this afternoon; there isn't a man in the army who hasn't heard about this. Down to the lowliest private, they all know the new policy. Moshe, if there is even a suspicion that I have helped, it will all be over."

"Certainly. I understand, Luke," Moshe replied in quiet disappointment. "You have done more than enough for any one man. I can't expect you to—"

"If you lay low for a week or two, perhaps . . . just perhaps you can smuggle a few items in here and there. But you must understand that the new directive says that every loaf of bread is to be torn open, every bean counted for bullets. Your kerosene deliveries will be personally checked. And not by me. Not by me. The man inspecting is as much for the policies of the Mandate as you are for Zionism. His brother was killed when the Irgun blew up the King David. Nothing is going to get by him." He rubbed his chin as Moshe let out a low whistle. "Especially not a man in a flour barrel. Especially not a man with a cast on his arm *hiding* in a flour barrel. It is much too risky, Moshe. Do you understand?"

Moshe nodded his head. "You are right, of course. I was not thinking with this." He touched his finger to his temple. "A foolish idea."

"I am not sure why it is you are so desperate to get into the Old City, but I am certain you have good taste in women."

Moshe grinned. "Yes, I do."

"She is quite lovely. Even wringing wet."

"Yes, she is."

"There is more than one way to skin a cat, as the Americans say. Would you like me to have her arrested? That is a certain way to get her out."

Moshe smiled and slowly shook his head. "Not the best way. But thank you. She has some reason, I am sure, for wanting to stay. Just as I have my reasons for wanting to be with her."

"You are quite intoxicated with this girl."

"Roaring drunk is more like it. I feel like I will go crazy if I don't see her. If I can't tell her—" Moshe ran his fingers through his hair in frustration.

"You'll never make it through Jaffa Gate dressed like an Arab. You'd be searched in a minute."

"That's just it. I don't hope to smuggle anything but myself. I won't carry in weapons. I speak Arabic with the best of them—"

"And your arm and chest are in a cast, Moshe. Questions will be asked."

"I can think of something."

"Half the British command would spot you as the fellow who has been hanging around the convoy loading."

"I'll shave." He rubbed the newly grown beard on his chin.

"A good start." Luke leaned forward. "You went to Oxford. How good is your British accent?"

Moshe took a deep breath and spoke in clear, crisp tones, "Quite good, actually. Difficult to tell I'm not a native Brit."

"Not bad. But I doubt we could find a coat big enough to fit over that monstrosity you're wearing." Luke's brow creased with thought. "Can you speak Armenian? Syriac?"

"Fluently."

"Excellent!" Luke slapped his hand against his knee with delight as a plan began to take shape. "Yes"—his

175

eyes narrowed as he appraised Moshe—"you do have the look of a righteous man. The proper gown, a little incense, and you'll slip in Jaffa Gate while the guards are all over at Zion Gate inspecting the cargo from the convoy."

Moshe tried not to let his excitement show. "How difficult will it be to get me the necessary clothes?"

"Difficult enough, but I'll be back after lunch. Don't shave; that beard and your ability with language is a sure passport, old chap."

———

Dressed in his British-made tweed suit, Gerhardt looked every bit the part of a minor English official out for a stroll among the covered bazaars of the Old City Arab Quarter. Sunlight streamed into the vegetable market through small square windows cut into the top of the vaults, and the noise of the bargaining crowds was almost deafening. Gerhardt smiled with satisfaction at the abundance of fruits and vegetables available in the Arab-owned stalls. An old Arab woman held a plump ripe orange high above her head and called to him as he passed. A thin carrier, lugging a basket twice his size filled to the brim with fresh vegetables, followed a fat, affluent-looking restaurant buyer from one stall to the next. Everywhere rose the din of arguing about the quality and price of the produce, and everywhere the price was eventually settled to the satisfaction of both the merchant and the customer.

The only thing missing from the usual market-day bustle was the presence of the Jews. Jewish dinner tables were sadly lacking the abundance of the Arabs. Gerhardt was pleased with the thought that it was his competent, one-man warfare that had finally frightened the last of the Jews from the streets. He was grateful to Allah that the vermin were hiding away in their shanties, as he planned yet another surprise for them.

———

As Howard's black Plymouth pulled away from the curb of the Jewish Agency building, Moshe waved at Yacov, who smiled out the back window.

I will tell Rachel you are well, Yacov, he thought as the battered car passed three British cargo trucks, then turned on its way to Hadassah Hospital.

David had already disappeared inside the Jewish Agency for a scheduled meeting with members of the air services, and Ellie wandered throughout the stacks of barrels and crates that littered the parking lot. Her camera was focused on the story that there was no day of rest at the Jewish Agency. Moshe turned and watched her turn her camera on the sweating face of a young man who lifted a fifty-gallon drum marked *kerosene* onto a dolly. Sacks of beans rested safely under the eaves of the building, and wooden crates of anchovies were nearly hidden under a mountain of freshly baked bread. For the first time in several weeks, the cargo now being inspected was just what it seemed to be. As Luke had warned, a squad of British inspectors wandered from one stack of boxes to the next, prying open lids and sifting through the contents in search of bullets and grenades.

"Smile, fellas!" Moshe heard Ellie say as she snapped the shutter of her camera at the dour faces of two inspectors who sifted through a sack of powdered milk. She then moved on to an officer who was busy tearing open each individual loaf of bread before it was stuffed into a large burlap bag and tossed onto the waiting truck.

Feeling useless, Moshe wandered around the parking area with his clipboard in one hand and the butcher-paper wrapped package that Luke had brought him tucked tightly beneath his cast.

As the inspectors checked off each item, Moshe ordered it loaded onto the truck. His feeling of frustration was nearly overwhelming when he thought about the desperate need for munitions in the Jewish Quarter. Still, as he watched the bread being torn apart, he was grateful for Luke's tip-off as to the extent of today's inspection. If only one weapon had been found, the convoy privileges would have been stopped. And today, Moshe knew, the Arab High Committee would have inspectors of their own at Zion Gate to repeat this procedure as the food was unloaded. Most of the guards from Jaffa Gate would be on hand at Zion Gate to observe and attempt to pilfer food from the convoy. He was grateful the agency had alternate plans. Moshe smiled slightly and touched the package beneath his arm. He was counting on the distraction to help him slip into the Old City through Jaffa.

"Moshe!" Ellie called, irritation welling up in her voice. "Look at this!"

Hands on her hips, she stood beside the bread inspector. "You don't have to rip it into such tiny pieces, do you?" she shouted at the man. "Nobody in there is going to be taking communion with it, you know! Most likely, they'll want to use it for more practical stuff, like sandwiches—if they can find two pieces big enough after you're done."

"You are here in what capacity, miss?" the inspector asked coolly as he continued his work.

"I'm a photographer, pal, and unless you want your face plastered all over the—"

Moshe interrupted. "What seems to be the difficulty, Ellie?" he asked calmly.

"Well, look at it!" she protested. "Who's going to want to eat that? He's made mincemeat out of a perfectly good stack of bread."

"Checking for detonators." The inspector continued ripping.

"Never mind, Ellie," Moshe grinned. "If the fellow finds a detonator while tearing into the bread like that, we'll have a bit of difficulty sorting him out among the pieces as well, eh?"

The inspector blanched and stared wide-eyed at the stacks of bread yet to be searched. Moshe heard him swallow hard; then taking Ellie by the arm, he led her to a stack of anchovy crates and sat her down.

"Wait here, my little shiksa. There is nothing to be done. What these men do not tear apart, the Arab guards will attempt to steal at Zion Gate. For a short time we must endure this. Only for a short time, eh?"

"But it just makes me so mad, Moshe." Ellie fumed. "I think about Rachel in there and it just burns me up, you know?"

"Yes," Moshe answered softly. "But perhaps that can also be remedied. Don't worry, Ellie."

"What's that supposed to mean?" she asked. "What are you up to, Moshe?" Her voice was too loud.

"Nothing." He put a finger to his lips. "Nothing for you to be concerned about."

"I know you well enough—" An inspector walked by.

"Please—" He frowned and touched her check lightly. "Just wait here for David, eh?"

Ellie sniffed indignantly and stared after Moshe as he strolled back through the shouting, jostling crowd that heaved crates like a bucket brigade into the trucks.

Suddenly a shout came from across the street. A short burst of gunfire erupted as a blue police van sped away from the curb and inspectors dropped what they were doing to race out into the street.

"They've stolen the van!" A young, pink-cheeked officer shouted and waved his arms. "Get them! Two Jews! Get them! They've stolen the van!"

A motorcycle roared to life and another inspector hopped into the sidecar as it sped away after the stolen van. Two more official cars joined in the pursuit, and Ellie snapped the shutter of her camera again and again as angry English soldiers shouted and sputtered and stormed back to their work.

Moshe rocked back on his heels as he eyed the newly placed sack of uninspected beans in the back of the lead truck. He tipped his hat to the muscled young porter who had just hefted in the cargo, unseen by the inspectors. Many small items had been slipped into previously inspected food. And this afternoon, Moshe knew, a similar diversion would be used to draw the attention of the Arab guards from their duty at Zion Gate.

Moshe glanced at his watch. An hour and forty minutes had passed since the blue van had been stolen. David strolled out of the double glass doors of the Agency and onto the cleared parking lot where the loaded convoy trucks waited.

"Hey, David!" Ellie called. "You missed all the excitement! These inspectors are animals. Absolutely tore everything apart. And two guys stole an inspection van. Quite an afternoon. I got it all right here." She tapped her camera.

"Ready to go?" David asked Moshe.

"In a bit. Why don't you catch a taxi and take Ellie home. I'll be a while yet."

"I want to stay," Ellie protested.

"I think not." Moshe stared hard at his clipboard and sniffed, pretending not to notice the look of indignation that crossed her face. "I have quite a lot to do, David. I think it would be best if you took Ellie home now."

"Sure. Sure, Moshe. Come on, Els." David took her by the arm.

"Wait a minute!" Ellie yanked free. "You guys know something you're not saying. And you're saying something I can't figure out."

"You think we're going to let the press in on everything, Els?" David teased as he took her arm again.

"Oh, knock it off, David. Come on. What's going on around here, anyway?" She asked lowering her voice. "Are you going in there with the stuff, Moshe?"

"No," he answered truthfully. "I really have a lot to do. I'll see you both at home, yes? Take care." He patted Ellie on the back, his eyes meeting David's, who returned his look with understanding. Without another word, Moshe spun on his heel and hopped up into the back of the nearest truck.

Ellie was still sputtering protests as David shoved her into the back of a cab and kissed her into silence.

Moshe smiled to himself as they drove off toward Rehavia, David's arms embracing the now-quiet Ellie.

By tonight, God willing, he thought, *I will embrace my Rachel. Dear God, please be willing.*

He stepped back into the shadows of the cargo area and pulled the heavy canvas flap down after him. Moments later the engines roared to life and the convoy of five trucks lurched into motion.

Moshe quickly unwrapped the package that Luke had given him and, balancing like a sailor in a rough sea, pulled the long robes of a Copt Monk over his head. His heavy plaster cast was completely concealed except for the plaster around his hand. He slipped his hand inside one of the voluminous pockets of the cassock, pulled a cap onto his head and then covered it with a hood.

His was the last truck in the column, and he peeked out at the last afternoon sky, noting that they were only moments away from Mamilla Cemetery.

He listened to the whine of the gears as the trucks ahead downshifted in preparation for the long turn that would lead them toward Mount Zion, and ultimately to Zion Gate. The monuments of Mamilla, the Muslim Cemetery that marked the border between the Jewish and Muslim districts of the New City, were plainly visible. Moshe slipped a large, ornate cross around his neck, then parted the canvas flap a fraction as he looked out the back of the truck once again. To his disgust a small green taxi followed closely behind. Moshe could see the angry face of the driver, who honked his horn impatiently and cursed the slow-moving trucks. As the gears of the truck whined down, the taxi driver honked and sped out to the side of the convoy. The cargo truck lurched from side to side as the taxi narrowly missed an oncoming car. As the wheel of the truck bumped noisily over the curb, Moshe spotted a large mausoleum that would serve as cover for him. The

181

driver braked; Moshe crouched and jumped just as cases of anchovies tumbled down around him.

He hit the ground like a cat, only slightly out of balance from the heavy weight across his chest and arm. Quickly he darted the few yards into the cemetery, then scrunched down behind the large monument nearest the road. The convoy rumbled on, completely unaware that Moshe had ridden with them deep into Arab territory.

He adjusted his robes and pulled his hood close around his face. Then he walked slowly through the monuments as if on a holy pilgrimage. Above him he could see the Tower of David and the Citadel that marked Jaffa Gate. Just outside the wall lay the blackened remains of the Jewish Commercial District, burned by an Arab mob the day after Partition had been signed. Moshe raised his eyes toward Jaffa Gate and prayed silently. *Close their eyes to me, O Lord. Lead me inside the gate. Guide me safely to Rachel.*

An old woman placed flowers beside a weathered gravestone. Her eyes glanced briefly at Moshe, then turned back to her task. On the road that bordered the wall, Moshe could see a large group of Arab Irregulars moving from Jaffa toward Zion Gate, where the convoy would soon arrive. *Protect those of your servants who carry defense to your holy places. Guard their lives and protect their cargo. Make it work, Lord. Oh, God, make it work!*

He reached the edge of the cemetery and passed another smaller group of Jihad Moquades also drawn away from Jaffa Gate. Close enough to touch him, they did not even look at the monk who walked so quickly toward the open square outside the Gate. Moshe glanced at his watch. In five minutes the Number One bus would arrive, and the diversion would be enough for him to slip unnoticed inside the Old City.

21 At Jaffa Gate

Gerhardt glanced at his watch. It was nearly four-thirty. He had only a few minutes to catch the Number One bus from Jaffa Gate. He stepped up his pace and wove quickly through the throngs that pressed and jostled around him. A black-robed monk walked slowly ahead of him, browsing the stalls. Impatiently, Gerhardt pushed past him and half-jogged down the narrow twists and turns until at last he entered Omar square just to the left of the massive stones of the Citadel of David. Jaffa Gate lay before him.

A couple holding hands stepped out of the Petra Hotel and moved in front of him just as he passed. They were British, he noted, wondering why anyone would come to Jerusalem by choice during these bitter days. *Missionaries,* he thought, *or petty government officials.* As the throng moving toward the gate surrounded the couple, he was unable to pass them. He quietly cursed in Arabic as he looked above the young woman's head toward the crowd just beyond the gate. Chances were slim that he would get on the bus, and it was a full half hour before another would come to Jaffa Gate again.

"We'd better hurry!" the young man said to the woman, tugging her hand and attempting to weave through the crush.

Yes, Gerhardt thought. *An Englishman.*

"If we miss this one we'll be late for supper at Trudy's, won't we?" the young woman asked.

"Pardon me," Gerhardt said, trying once again to squeeze by. His errand was far more important than a dinner party. The woman ignored him, intent on making the bus.

Irritation welled up within him. For a moment as they passed beneath the pedestrian archway, past three disgruntled-looking Arab guards, he actually contemplated knocking her down.

"Has the bus come yet, Tom?" she asked her companion as she stood tiptoe and tried to see over the sea of bobbing heads.

"No. Not yet, darling."

Gerhardt spotted the bus moving slowly up the road; far behind, a blue Palestine police van tore recklessly around it, heading for the bus stop. Instinctively Gerhardt paused. The van was in too much of a hurry to be on a routine patrol. They were after something . . . or someone. Gerhardt reached for the pistol inside his coat pocket and hung back as the young couple pressed on.

———

Moshe had just begun the climb up the incline to Jaffa Gate when he heard the sputter of the bus engine on the main road to his left. The crowd waiting for the bus seemed especially heavy this afternoon, and Moshe was reasonably certain he could pass through without any problems.

Only three Muslim guards remained on duty. Their faces reflected disappointment as they smoked cigarettes and stared off in the direction of their comrades at Zion Gate. None of the three even glanced up as the bus groaned slowly toward the waiting queue of jostling passengers.

Moshe looked back over his shoulder at the retreating forms of the Jihad Moquades. There were no other pedestrians walking the road between the two gates. He paused for a moment and searched for the stolen blue police van scheduled to approach from the south along the wall. He frowned briefly, looked back toward the bus, then suddenly stopped and drew his breath in sharply. From Jaffa Road in the northwest, he could clearly make out the van speeding recklessly up behind the laboring bus. *What are they doing? Why are they coming from that direction?* The van swung around the bus and passed it on the uphill incline. The bus swerved slightly as the van nearly clipped its front bumper. Moshe stepped up his pace. Still a full fifty yards from the square in front of Jaffa Gate, he knew he would not make it through before the van roared past him to its target along the nearly deserted section of the wall. Still moving, the van would dump a bomb along the road just behind the Jihad Moquades. This would hopefully draw the attention of guards at both gates, allowing the contraband cargo to pass Zion Gate unnoticed and Moshe to slip through Jaffa Gate. It seemed like a foolproof plan, except for the fact that the van was a full five minutes too early. The convoy had most certainly not yet reached Zion Gate.

"What are you doing?" Moshe muttered involuntarily as the van screeched to a halt in the square in front of the waiting queue of bus passengers. To his horror, the deadly answer came immediately. The back doors of the van flew open with a clang. Inside Moshe could see the large metal drum and a very frightened young man trying desperately to strike a match. For an instant the crowd stared blankly at the Jew in the back of the van. Then a wail started at the front nearest the van as someone screamed, "It's a bomb!"

"What are you doing!" Moshe shouted at the top of his lungs. Instinctively he ran toward the van as if to stop the tragedy unfolding before him. The fuse sputtered to life and the van roared away as the barrel was shoved out among the people, who clawed and scrambled to get away.

Too late! Too late! Too late! The words ripped through Moshe as he dived for the hard asphalt of the road.

Gerhardt recognized the threat instantly and pressed himself flat against the ground just as a roar and a flash consumed the square. The young couple in front of him disintegrated into a thousand pieces. The concussion slammed Gerhardt back against the stones of the pedestrian archway. He lay still and fought to regain his breath as an eerie silence enveloped the bodies that littered the smoldering square.

Gerhardt slowly raised his head, his eyes meeting the sightless gaze of a dead Arab woman. "The Jews!" he gasped to the dead and dying. "It was the Jews!"

At that same instant Moshe rolled awkwardly onto his back. For a moment he lay with his eyes closed to the carnage just beyond him. Then he opened his eyes and watched as a vapor of smoke drifted across the blue sky. Moans and weeping filled his ears. "Dear God!" he cried as he looked toward the square. A dozen yards from where he lay, a woman cradled the body of her son in her arms.

"Help me," the woman sobbed. "Help me, please."

Moshe rose with difficulty and stumbled toward her. His cast had shattered around his chest and dropped from beneath the cassock in white chunks as he moved. *Run, Moshe,* he said to himself. *You can make it into the Old City easily. Run, you fool!* Instead, he knelt beside the woman. Her left arm hung limply at her side as she rocked the child back and forth and wept. The boy's eyes were wide with horror, and his mouth gaped open as a small trickle of blood flowed from the corner.

"Help me, Father," moaned the woman. "Don't let him die! Dear God!"

Moshe bowed his head, stung by the grief of a woman he had never seen before. He reached out and closed the eyes of the dead child.

"Someone will be here shortly," he said softly in Arabic. He put his arm around her shoulder and listened as the wail of approaching sirens filled the air. "Someone will come in a moment, sister," he said. Then he moved on to a wounded man whose leg was nearly severed. Blood pumped in spurts from his gaping wound, and quickly Moshe pulled a shoelace from his shoe and tied a makeshift tourniquet above the artery of the unconscious man. Like a shadow, Moshe moved from form to form, doing what little he could to help the wounded until finally the ambulances and medics arrived on the scene. The entrance to the gate was by that time completely cordoned off by two dozen hostile Irregulars.

Moshe stood at the edge of the square and looked toward the Old City. "Rachel," he said softly. "My Rachel." Then he turned and walked slowly back toward Mamilla Cemetery.

22 Life After Death

What had begun as a quiet Shabbat ended at sunset Saturday with a thick spray of sniper fire raining down on the Jewish Quarter from the tops of Muslim roofs and tall minarets. Occasionally a British Sten gun was fired into the air as a warning, but there was no other answer to the fury that burned in the Arab sectors of the city.

Under cover of darkness, the cargo from two of the convoy trucks was unloaded. The remaining three trucks had been turned back at Zion Gate by an angry mob before the smoke had even cleared from the square in front of Jaffa Gate.

Rachel moved quickly toward Tipat Chalav, holding her hands over her ears as if to shut out the high-pitched, undulating wails of the Arab women. White with rage, Arab men gathered just beyond the sandbags and barbed wire that marked the border between Arab and Jewish quarters. Curses against Yehudah echoed from the walls. Rachel glanced up toward the guard posts; she could see the British guards glaring angrily at their Jewish counterparts, who sat at rigid attention, expecting the worst to happen at any moment.

There was still no word on the number of dead at Jaffa Gate. Someone muttered that several British citizens had been killed as well, and it would not be surprising if the Englishmen turned their Sten guns on the Jews.

A shudder went through Rachel as she entered the dining hall of Tipat Chalav. Although the room was packed, a heavy silence rested on everyone, even the very small children. In the corner of the room she noticed the dark, brooding face of Yehudit Akiva as the girl stared intently back at her.

Rachel hurried down the narrow stairs to the basement where the food supplies were being carefully checked and logged in a little notebook by Leah. Leah's face was lined with concern as she checked off the supplies one by one.

"Only two trucks, Rachel," she said. "The fools! Why did they choose this day to blow up an Arab bus stop?" Her voice was ripe with frustration. "One of the English guards went berserk. It took three of his companions to hold him back from beating an old rabbi."

"This is a black day," Rachel said. "For everyone— Jews, Arabs, English. Everyone."

An old woman shuffled up with a wooden bowl filled with rifle cartridges. "In the beans, Leah dear. A miracle, nu?"

Leah tried to smile. "Yes, Shoshanna. Perhaps we have need of a miracle tonight. Take them to Shimon, please. He is in the back room."

"Indeed," said the old woman. "Then I will search for more little miracles."

Silently Leah counted a stack of anchovy crates. "Sixteen. Not nearly enough. No powdered milk. Nothing fresh. No vegetables or bread. They say the Arabs looted the other three trucks. Luckily there were British drivers or they would have been killed."

"Do they know yet who bombed Jaffa Gate?" Rachel asked.

"I asked Yehudit Akiva. She knows everything, which makes her good for something. Her father spoke with a British officer shortly after it happened. Two men, Jews, were caught and shot down. The English say they are Haganah. Imagine! It all makes me so angry. It was so unnecessary."

Shimon stepped into the basement and frowned when he saw Leah's weary face. Two men crowded around him with news or questions, but he walked through them and took Leah by the arm.

"You need to go home, Leah. To rest. You have worked far too hard tonight. Surely this cannot be a good thing with the little one coming so soon."

"Nonsense," she protested. "If I don't do this—"

"Rachel will."

"Of course," Rachel volunteered. "I can take inventory here. Shimon is right. Go home and rest."

"I rested all day today," Leah protested, as Rachel took the notebook from her. "But my feet do hurt."

"There's a good girl." Shimon hugged her quickly. "Sit down for a minute until I get my coat. I'll walk you home."

"Don't worry, Leah," Rachel said. "There is nothing more important right now than you and the baby, eh? I would enjoy helping." She searched the room, taking in the activity of Ehud and Chaim and Dov along with a half-dozen others she did not recognize.

"Just be sure you tally every cartridge, Rachel," Leah instructed as she rested her arms on her stomach. "Thank you. I really am tired, you know, and so very sad for those Arab families whose loved ones are missing from their places at the dinner table tonight. There has been so much senseless killing. I just wonder when it will . . ." Her voice trailed off and her face blanched as the clatter of boots sounded on the stairs. Shouts filled the basement as six British soldiers stormed into the busy room. Their faces were rigid, their jaws set in anger, their Sten guns poised and ready to shoot if even a hint of trouble arose. A young, surly-faced captain led the group, and each man looked to him for instruction as the bustle in the basement grew still.

"By order of His Majesty. . ." the captain began.

"By what right do you come here?" Dov shouted angrily.

Rachel deftly concealed the little notebook and sat down slowly next to Leah.

"By right of the British Mandate in Palestine, friend," Captain Stewart returned. "Your cargo slipped by us at the gate this afternoon, and we're here to finish the job."

"The cargo was inspected once already at the Jewish Agency. You won't find anything," Shimon said loudly as he stepped out of the back room with his jacket in hand.

"Enough has been found already," the captain said with an air of cool indifference. "The three trucks that didn't make it to your quarter were thoroughly searched by the men of the Mufti. Listen." He raised his chin and cocked his head slightly. "Tonight the Arabs shoot at you with your own bullets. Too bad they couldn't have done it before your murdering Haganah blew up Jaffa Gate and five British citizens with it." His eyes were red with anger, an anger that Rachel had seen before in the faces of her captors. Somehow the hatred they held in their hearts was an all-encompassing indictment against everything and everyone Jewish.

"It was not us who murdered them, friend," said Shimon.

A scrawny private stepped forward and said loudly, "Where shall we begin, Captain Stewart?"

A half-smile curled the lips of Stewart into a cruel grin. "With him," he pointed at Shimon. "Our big *friend* over there."

Instantly alive with the order, three soldiers rushed toward Shimon. One hit him in the stomach with the butt of his Sten gun while another grabbed his beard and slammed his head against a wall. Leah screamed and tried to stand as Rachel held her back.

"Just a minute!" roared Ehud, stepping forward, his voice a menacing growl.

Sten guns instantly cocked and aimed in the direction of the sea captain.

"You were saying something?" Captain Stewart jerked his head toward Ehud, and the three soldiers dropped Shimon, letting him slide to the floor next to a barrel of kerosene. Then they turned their fury on Ehud. Gun butts and fist and curses slammed against him until he fell unconscious to the floor.

"Shimon!" Leah moaned, sobbing as she broke free

191

from Rachel's grasp and ran to his side.

"Everyone against the wall!" shouted the captain. "Get up!" he kicked Shimon hard in the ribs.

Leah screamed again. "Leave him alone!" she cried as Shimon doubled up with the force of the kick. She lunged for the captain, who grabbed her by the throat and threw her back against the wall.

"For God's sake!" Rachel shouted. "Leave her alone!" She stood and lunged between Leah and the captain. The rage in her eyes matched his own and she stared hard at him, her fists clenching and unclenching. He looked as if he might easily kill her, and her expression dared him to pull the trigger. "She is pregnant, Englishman," she said at last. "Are you an animal, too?"

"Shut up, or I will kill something in this room!"

"Then you might as well begin with me, because you will not lay a hand on her or her husband again."

He turned his Sten gun point blank into Rachel's stomach, and his hands trembled with unreasonable hatred. "Get up against the wall, woman," he said sullenly.

Rachel stepped back among the others as the soldiers tore through the crates and kicked sacks of beans and flour onto the floor. Somehow Shimon had managed to hide the weapons that had been pulled from the crates and bags, and for a full twenty minutes, though they looked, the soldiers found only one detonator tucked into a small bag of coffee beans.

"This is all we found," a young soldier brought the detonator to the captain apologetically.

"It's enough," Captain Stewart said triumphantly. Then he raised his voice and glared around the room. "Think you can live outside the laws of the government, do you?"

Rachel searched the faces of the Jews who stood beside her. Eyes were downcast, not daring to meet the brutality that raged at them. *Smart,* she thought. *He would kill you if you defied him. Do not meet his eyes,* she silently warned the men.

Each person in the basement seemed to understand. Only Shimon dared to stare back, defying the man who had hurled Leah against the wall. Rachel saw his pursed lips and the white knuckles of his clenched fists as he stared at the major. *Don't speak,* she thought. *Please Shimon, remain silent. The animal waits for an excuse.*

Leah remained where she had fallen, her hand clutching her belly. "You are no better than a Nazi," Shimon said quietly.

The captain pivoted and stared at the big Jew. He smiled a smile that showed his teeth but no emotion. "I could arrest you and have you all carted away to prison. But I won't. I will show you that I am a man of reason. You think you can murder innocent Englishmen and women, eh? Is that what you think?" His voice grew louder. "Well, it isn't so. We have laws. You have to keep them. Like I have to keep them." He turned toward Chaim, who stood quietly controlling the anger burning within him. "You!" shouted the captain. Chaim did not raise his eyes. "You there! The big fellow."

Chaim sighed and glanced up.

The captain strode toward him. "You look big enough to take care of yourself. And you," he turned to Shimon. "Sergeant Miller, these two men are under arrest—"

"No!" sobbed Leah.

"For concealing a weapon." He held up the detonator. "In violation of His Majesty's laws of the Mandatory Government of Palestine."

Soldiers roughly grasped Shimon and Chaim, locking their wrists in handcuffs.

"Please don't take my husband. Please. Not Shimon," Leah begged as they led them up the stairs with their Sten guns still cocked. The captain paused at the top of the steps and turned to the men and women who waited in silence below him. He swept the barrel of his gun around the room. "As for the rest of you," he said malignantly, "I would not dare to follow if I were you."

Then he turned and slammed the door after himself.

For a long moment only the soft sobs of Leah were heard in the room. Rachel ran to her and embraced her. "Come, Leah," she said softly. "Come sit down."

The old woman Shoshanna came alongside. "She should be home in bed. I will see to it."

"Oh, Rachel," cried Leah. "They have taken my Shimon. What will they do to him?"

"Take him to a police station," offered Ehud. "He will be safe. He has done nothing to convict him." His troubled gaze met Rachel's. She shook her head from side to side and her chin trembled as she fought to hold back the tears.

"I have to know," begged Leah. "Please, I have to know what they will do with him." She doubled over with the pain of a contraction. "Oh, the baby! The baby is coming!"

"I will see where they take them," said Ehud.

"And I," offered Dov.

"Please, Leah. You need to go to bed now. Shoshanna will take you home." Rachel embraced Leah.

"Rachel, please don't leave me." Leah's voice came in soft gasps.

"Only for a little while," Rachel soothed. "I will be back soon."

Rachel turned to Ehud. "'We have to hurry. My brother told me of a way to travel in the Old City without walking on the streets." She clambered up the stairs, with Dov and Ehud following closely behind her. She ran out into the darkness and was startled by the glow that filled the sky in the Arab Quarter.

Like breakers against the rocky shore, the loud chant of "JIHAD! JIHAD! JIHAD!" echoed throughout the alleyways of the Old City. *Holy War!*

Two blocks away, the vague forms of the soldiers and Shimon and Chaim disappeared around the corner.

"Dear God!" shouted Dov above the din. "They aren't taking them out through that!"

194

Leah emerged from Tipat Chalav and stood for a moment, her face stricken with grief and fear. Gently the old woman led her away.

"Come on!" Rachel cried. "We don't have much time." Quickly she sprinted across the street and ducked down an alley to where a rickety wooden ladder stood propped against the wall. Rachel tucked her skirts around her and climbed up while Ehud held the ladder; then Dov held it for him as Rachel crouched and moved rapidly along the edge of the flat rooftop.

Beyond the edge of the quarter, Rachel could see what looked like a thousand torches burning brightly, illuminating the bitter faces of those who held them high. "JIHAD! JIHAD! JIHAD!" One block ahead of where she sat, she saw the guards shove Shimon to the ground, then kick him hard. Chaim struggled against his handcuffs until a Sten gun in his stomach calmed him. "DEATH TO THE JEWS! JIHAD! JIHAD! JIHAD!"

Ehud and Dov ran up behind her. "They'll never get them through that!" shouted Ehud. "The mob will think they are the ones who bombed the square. They'll never get through alive!"

"They know exactly what they are doing," Dov replied, desperation etched deep on his face. "This is a sacrifice."

As they watched from the rooftop, the soldiers passed into the streets of the Muslim Quarter. Rachel could see the fear on Shimon's face as the crowd fell silent and parted for them to pass through the torchlit mass.

"What can we do?" cried Rachel. "Isn't there something we can do to stop this?"

A thousand hostile eyes stared at Shimon and Chaim as the soldiers continued through the crowd. The silence seemed to speak louder to Rachel than the chants of a few moments before. Then an old Arab man leaned close to Shimon and spit into his face. "DEATH TO JEWS!" he wailed, and the cry echoed from every corner of the quarter. "DEATH TO JEWS!"

For an instant, as Chaim and Shimon stood back-to-back within a ring of British guards, Rachel thought that perhaps the guards would protect them. Then, one by one the guards stepped away and melted into the crowds. Shimon and Chaim stared face-to-face with their executioners, and silence fell.

Tears flowed down Rachel's cheeks as Shimon squared his shoulders and lifted his chin high. His voice rang out like a bell, "HEAR, O ISRAEL!" he cried. "THE LORD OUR GOD IS ONE LORD!" His voice was answered by the high-pitched undulating wail of a woman and then the frenzied cry of "DEATH TO THE JEWS!"

Arabs swarmed over the struggling forms of Shimon and Chaim, who stood like mountains, then fell beneath the surge of hatred that overtook them in an instant.

"Hear, O Israel," gasped Dov, sobbing at the sight of Chaim being lifted above the heads of the crowd and torn bit by bit by the curved daggers that struck and slashed at him. "Hear, O Israel," Rachel wept as Shimon cried out and went down a final time beneath the crazed mob.

". . . the Lord our God is One Lord." Ehud covered his face with his hands and sobbed like a small boy.

"Shimon," Leah said softly as she turned her face into the pillow.

Rachel quickly shut the apartment door behind her and drew a deep breath to compose herself before she had to face Leah. Old Shoshanna sat behind Leah's bed and patted her hand. The blue flowered curtain was pulled back, and Rachel could see Leah's face clearly even in the candlelight. Sallow and grief-stricken, she seemed as small as a child beneath the quilts.

Two broad-hipped women, their dour faces as lined as road maps, worked silently in the kitchen area. *Midwives,* Rachel remembered. Leah had told her about them. Between the two they had given birth to over a dozen children and had delivered nearly every child born in the quarter for the last forty-five years. Her own mother had been brought into the world with the help of these experienced hands. Leah would be well taken care of; Rachel was thankful for that. But even with the presence of these women, by far the strongest feeling in the room was that of loss. *Shimon should be here, God. Shimon should be with her now.*

Leah opened her eyes and smiled weakly at Rachel. She stretched her hand out toward her. "Did you follow them?" she whispered.

Rachel nodded and went to her side. "Yes."

"And what of Shimon? Did you see him?"

"Yes, I saw him." Rachel searched frantically for words to say.

Leah's forehead creased and she closed her eyes again. "Here is another one. Stronger."

Shoshanna leaned close to her ear. "Breathe deeply, my dear. As I have told you. Think of pleasant things. Of spring flowers and—"

"Shimon!" Leah cried. "Oh, why can he not be here?"

"Breathe deeply." The old woman breathed in slowly and exhaled to show her how to best manage the pain.

Leah squeezed Rachel's fingers tightly and then released her grip as the contraction eased away.

"There now," Rachel said gently, remembering her own pain. "That's better, isn't it?"

Leah nodded and sighed, then opened her eyes and gazed wearily up at Rachel. "Why are you crying, Rachel?" she asked.

Rachel wiped her cheek, unaware that tears had flowed freely down her face. "I just do not like to see you suffer, my friend," she answered, forcing a smile.

"The midwives tell me this is the only path to the joy of little ones. Imagine! I will speak to Shimon about this—" Her expression changed as a wave of fear seemed to wash over her. "You saw him. He is all right, isn't he?"

Rachel patted Leah's hand and glanced at the faces of the midwives as if expecting them to help her with the grim news that Shimon was gone. "He is . . ." she began haltingly. ". . . fine," she lied, certain she had done the right thing when relief flooded Leah's face.

Leah closed her eyes and smiled. "Thank God," she said softly.

Rachel looked away, her gaze resting on the shelf that held the china and silver candlesticks from last night's Shabbat meal. She remembered the words of Leah that had been spoken in sympathy for the families of the Arabs killed at Jaffa Gate: *I feel so very sad for those Arab families whose loved ones are missing from the dinner table tonight.* How empty the little room felt without the broad, smiling face of Shimon! His strong, eager arms would never hold the firstborn child he had loved without seeing. Rachel's heart ached when she thought about the moment when she would have to tell Leah the truth. *Not now,* she thought. *Not yet. Wait until she holds the child in her arms and touches a tiny hand that will make her want to live even though he is gone.*

Throughout the night contractions came closer and closer and filled with an intense fierceness that made Leah cry softly and cling to Rachel's hand. Time and again she called out for Shimon.

"The baby is turned," the midwife explained when Leah's water finally broke. "He faces up instead of down toward the spine. He is a big baby. This will be difficult," she explained in hushed tones to Rachel.

"But how long will this go on?" Rachel pleaded.

"Until it is finished," the midwife shrugged. "There is little to do but wait. The baby's head is still high. His shoulders block the way. There is little to do. In a hospital with a doctor, this would not be serious. But here . . ." her voice trailed away. "But will she be all right?" Rachel's worried gaze fell on Leah, whose damp hair clung to her face in wisps.

"This is for God to say," said the old woman, shaking her head.

"Please," Leah cried. "Rachel, come push against my back again. The pains are so close . . ." She gritted her teeth and pulled her knees up tightly as she rolled onto her side.

Rachel rushed to her side and pushed steadily on the small of her back as the pain became intense and then subsided. "Breathe deeply, Leah," Rachel said gently.

"Oh, why does it not come?" Leah cried as her breath exploded from her. "Shimon!" she moaned as the pain peaked, then relaxed.

Hot towels on Leah's back and bulging stomach eased her discomfort only slightly through the long hours. Her face was a mask of exhaustion. Black circles hung beneath her eyes, and she became too tired to speak even the name of Shimon. Twice Rachel stood to make tea and Leah cried out for her and reached to grasp her hand. Finally she muttered, "I want to push."

Quickly the midwives rolled her onto her back and propped her up. Strips of cloth were tied off to the headboard and then to Leah's hands.

"You must help her. When the pain becomes strong, help her to sit up and bear down with the contractions."

"We are almost finished, Leah," whispered Shoshanna. "Soon you will have a baby, and this will be forgotten."

"Now!" Leah shouted. "Another one!"

"Help her!" The midwife instructed Rachel as the other old woman cleaned the red fluid from Leah.

Rachel placed her arms beneath Leah's back and helped her sit as she struggled up and strained against the straps that held her hands. She expelled her breath with a cry, and the contraction subsided; then she fell back into Rachel's arms.

"Soon, soon," the old midwife crooned. "This is very hard." Her eyes met Rachel's and she shook her head from side to side. "But God will give you great joy in place of pain. Soon, soon."

"Again!" cried Leah, sweat pouring from her, soaking her nightgown and the sheets. Rachel helped her raise up.

"Push," Rachel encouraged. "Push, Leah!"

"I'm breaking!" Leah exclaimed. Then straining hard, she threw her head back and pushed until the veins in her slender neck bulged and her face turned dark red with the effort.

For nearly an hour the scene was repeated until Leah lay nearly unconscious, and the midwives shook their heads in frustration as they attempted to turn the baby with each contraction.

"He is moving!" shouted one of the old women at last. "Praise be to the Eternal! Push, Leah! Push, Leah dear!"

"I cannot," Leah said softly. "Oh, let me die."

"Soon you will have a baby to live for," Rachel said, propping her up once again. "You must push when the pain comes. Bear down, Leah, only a few more times."

"Now!" Leah's face contorted and she clamped her teeth together as she pushed with all her strength.

"I see the head!" an old woman exclaimed. "Push hard, Leah!"

A groan of effort sounded in Leah's throat. Her eyes were shut tight and her head again was thrown back.

Slowly the head of the baby emerged, wet and rosy gray in the dim candlelight. Rachel gasped with joy and sobbed as she saw first the tiny wrinkled face and then little hands attached to spindly arms. "The baby, Leah! Push now!"

With one final effort Leah bore down, though the contraction was waning. Rounded belly and umbilical cord emerged and then—

"You have a girl child!" an old woman cried with delight as the baby slipped into her hands. "Praise be to the Eternal!"

Quickly the midwives went to work; one cleared the baby's mouth of mucus while the other cleaned Leah with warm towels. Rachel laid her down and held tightly to her hands. Leah's teeth chattered, and she seemed not to hear the first cry of the tiny baby girl.

"She is shaking all over," Rachel said with alarm.

"It is the loss of blood." Shoshanna watched as the second midwife tugged gently on the cord until the placenta finally emerged.

The flow of blood from Leah was heavy and bright red. Rachel looked at the rapidly expanding pool and then the ashen face of Leah.

"We must elevate her legs!" the midwife ordered, lifting Leah's legs and propping them on a pillow. Then she gently pressed on the soft, empty abdomen of Leah as the baby wailed in the background.

"My baby!" Leah said weakly, holding out her arms. The second midwife brought the angry little one to her side.

"You have a beautiful, healthy baby girl." The old woman smiled a toothless grin.

Leah touched her soft cheek with her fingertip. "Shimon will be so proud—"

"I cannot stop the hemorrhaging," the first midwife said, her voice edged in panic.

"Look, Rachel," Leah trembled all over and seemed as pale as death. "A baby girl." Her voice was almost too soft to hear. "Her name is Tikvah."

"Little Jewel." Rachel tried to smile back at Leah, but a well of fear had sprung up in her as she saw the life of Leah ebb away in the deep red stain that now spilled over from the wooden bowl and onto sheets and towels and the hands of the frantic midwives.

Leah's voice became a whisper. "You must care for her for me, Rachel," she sighed. "I have prayed for you that you will find our Messiah. As Shimon and I have. And you will tell Tikvah about Him someday."

"Quick, more towels!" cried a midwife to Shoshanna. "We must try to stop the flow."

"You will tell her yourself, sweet Leah." Rachel's eyes filled with agony and helplessness. "You *must* care for her yourself!"

"She is . . . beautiful." Leah's gaze lingered on the

baby. Then she looked just beyond Rachel and her face became alive with tender recognition. "Oh, Shimon!" she cried. "You have come! Look! We have a little girl!" Her smile faded slightly and the light left her half-open eyes. Still they gazed at the empty spot where she had seen Shimon.

"Leah!" sobbed Rachel. "Oh, Leah, don't leave now! Please!" she begged, laying her head down on the lifeless hand of Leah.

Weary and drawn, Shoshanna put her hand on Rachel's shoulder. "She has gone to God, dear. Now you must care for the child. Sit up. Dry your eyes. She has gone to a better place."

Slowly Rachel sat up as one of the midwives closed Leah's eyes. Then the old woman picked up the baby from beside her dead mother and laid her in Rachel's arms.

"Leah and Shimon had no family," said the old woman. "There are orphanages that can care for the little one if you cannot. No one will condemn you."

Rachel sniffed and wiped her eyes as she carefully studied the tiny form she now held. "Tikvah," she said, emotion crowding her voice. "I once knew a little girl named Tikvah." She touched the thick black hair and then half-smiled as the toothless mouth opened to bleat a protest.

"She is a beautiful child, to be sure," said Shoshanna.

"But how will I care for her, feed her?" Rachel asked.

Quickly Shoshanna padded to a cupboard in the kitchen. "Leah had nine months to prepare for this." She swung the cupboard door wide, revealing row upon row of canned milk.

Rachel gazed tenderly at Leah, whose face had grown peaceful and full of joy even as she watched. "I will care for little Tikvah; do not worry, Shimon and Leah. I will care for her with all the love I would bear for my own."

PART 3

The Passage
Late January, 1948

"The more a man loves, the more he suffers. The sum of possible grief for each soul is in proportion to its perfection."

Frederic Amiel

23 Decisions

His shaggy head on his paws, Shaul's amber eyes followed the course of Yacov's top as it spun toward the dark wooden door of Howard's study. The big dog blinked, then yawned lethargically as Yacov scooted nearer to the door and leaned his ear against the heavy wood. The top spun, then died inches from Shaul's nose, but he did not move.

"Tragic!" exclaimed the voice that Yacov had come to recognize as David Ben-Gurion. "Tragic! They were both survivors of the camps, and in their bitterness denied God. In denying God they lost their humanity and have done a world of harm to our cause by their actions. Suddenly we are at the level of animals, who kill for the sake of killing."

"Don't worry, Shaul." Yacov reached out to pat the dog's head. "He does not really mean *animals*; he is talking about men, nu?" he whispered.

"So now the Arab High Committee has closed access even to the food convoys." The angry voice of Moshe drifted out. "All because of the rash revenge of a few psychotics."

"The whole cause of Zionism is endangered by this," said Howard. "It is not just the few in the Old City anymore. The United Nations is reconsidering Partition. Not even the United States believes this can work. Why, Harry Truman said—"

"Truman says something different every day," David chimed in. "Nobody can count on what he says any longer."

"Come on, David," Ellie said loudly. "Will you lay off Truman? Who's talking about Truman, anyway!"

"Everybody's talking about Truman!" David retorted.

"In a way you are correct," said Ben-Gurion. "Much depends on his support. Chaim Weisman has spoken with him and is assured—"

"That was before this incident!" exclaimed Moshe. "How many Arabs killed at Jaffa Gate—Christians and Muslims? I spoke to a man who grew up not far from me. It was his anniversary. He and his wife almost missed the bus. She was killed in the explosion! To what purpose, I ask you? For whose benefit was this done?"

"Revenge."

"They called it retaliation! The driver's brother was murdered in the Ben Yehudah bombing."

"Then life is worth very little in Jerusalem if our own men—"

"They were not our men. They were Stern Gang. And they're dead now."

"It hardly matters now. But it has created an immediate problem—the problem of how we will supply the residents of the Old City," Moshe said.

The voice of Ben-Gurion replied, "The British Captain Thomas feels that perhaps in time we can renegotiate for the food convoys. That will take time, of course. The men of the Mufti are flexing their muscles, showing us that they can completely shut down the route at will. They are giving us a taste of what it will be like when the British evacuate."

"What can be done?" asked Howard.

"We must find another way into the Jewish Quarter," Moshe answered, concern making his voice sharp.

"We could try dropping supplies by air," volunteered David.

"Is not the space too confined? It could drift wrong by ten feet and end up in the Arab sectors."

"If we brought her in low—"

"You'd get your rear shot off," Ellie interjected.

"She is right, of course. The Arabs grow bullets on

trees, it is said, and spit them at Jews like watermelon seeds."

Yacov laughed at the words of Moshe, then covered his mouth with his hand and laid his ear back against the door.

"Does anyone have any other suggestions?" asked Ben-Gurion. "Moshe, I came here in hopes that you have had time to think during your recovery."

"I have some ideas," Moshe answered thoughtfully. "I have looked at some old maps. Possibly there is a way . . . I need a little more time."

"Time is something we have little of, my friend."

"Right now we need some way for getting messages into the Old City. There is no communication as of yesterday, and I am afraid that there may be panic unless the people are informed of the events and efforts on their behalf."

"That we can help you with," Howard said cheerfully. "Yacov's dog—"

"You mean the beast that tried to eat my leg?" asked Ben-Gurion. "Does he not belong to an Arab?"

Yacov leaned over and rubbed Shaul's ear protectively. "You are no Arab!" he said soothingly. Shaul wriggled his tailless rump in acknowledgment, then drifted back to sleep.

"Yacov has trained him to go from the New City to the Old. There are a thousand dogs in the souks. He could pass unnoticed."

"Rachel, Yacov's sister, is staying at the apartment where the dog lived with Yacov," Ellie volunteered. "We talked about this before. Maybe now is the time to use him. I can tell you one thing, the mutt knows the Old City. He led me out after dark!"

"What will the boy say?" asked Ben-Gurion.

"Shall we ask him?" Moshe's footstep clicked on the wooden floor, and when he opened the door, Yacov smiled up at him.

"I say Shaul and I shall be most happy to help." Yacov grinned back at the shocked expression on Moshe's face.

———

Days of frustration and worry slipped into first one week and then two. The day after Arab riots rocked the Old City, the water mains in the Jewish sectors of Jerusalem were blown, leaving taps and toilets dry. Each person in the affected areas now lived on a water ration of two gallons a day drawn from the storage cisterns.

Howard rubbed a hand across the stubble on his chin and watched a young woman fill his water cans with the precious liquid. No man in the Jewish sections of the city could afford to waste water on the luxury of a shave. Now that Rabbi Lebowitz had been discharged from Hadassah Hospital to the Moniger household, their ration was twelve gallons a day. The amount was manageable; the recommended portion had been suggested to the Jewish Agency by Moshe, based on the barest ration required by each worker on an archaeological dig. Howard and Yacov carried their water containers to the donkey-drawn wagons each afternoon to stand among the irate women of the city who cursed the rationing, cursed the two-gallon limit, and cursed whatever foolish, thoughtless man had decided that a mere two gallons of water per person was sufficient. When women laden with teapots, buckets and roasting pans had begun casting envious glances at Howard's insulated five-gallon water cans, he had sworn Yacov to secrecy that he had sat in on the decision about the water ration. He was convinced that angry housewives could possibly turn into an ugly mob and lynch him at a moment's notice. Howard peered up at the cloudless blue sky and prayed for rain to fill the buckets perched hopefully atop every roof and doorstep in the Jewish Sector. Then he gazed sadly at the mute walls of the Old City and prayed that perhaps today Shaul would return with some word of Rachel.

Each morning Moshe and Yacov had sent the

shaggy messenger to run past the keffiyeh-clad guards that ringed the Old City; each evening Shaul had wearily returned with the untouched message still tucked in his ear. Even as Moshe worked on the plans for food rationing and the defense of Jewish Jerusalem, Howard and others had expressed concern as Moshe grew more and more haggard with the anxiety he felt for Rachel. Often as he spoke he would stop mid-sentence and walk to the window to stare out at the grim wall that separated him from her.

Occasionally bits and pieces of news from beyond the walls would drift out by way of one of the new British soldiers. Reports of low morale and severe rationing told a desperate tale. Two men and a woman had died the night of the riots; the stories had circulated quickly and filled Moshe with despair. The names of the dead had not passed outside the gates of the quarter, and Moshe was haunted by the fear that the nameless woman, now buried in an unmarked grave at the end of the muddy alleyway known as Gal'ed Road, was indeed the woman whose name he held as dear as his own life.

Only two days before, Moshe had questioned Luke about the possibility of bribing an English soldier to get word to Rachel.

"It would be too risky for her," Luke had answered. "These replacements are not sympathetic to man or woman. It would not be wise to draw attention to her at this point, I think."

"Of course," Moshe had nodded, sinking down into a chair with his head in his hands. "Rachel," he had whispered, and Howard had turned away from the suffering of his friend and left the house in search of the water wagon.

Yacov gazed thoughtfully up at Howard as if he had heard his silent memories. "Professor," he sniffed, "perhaps today will be the day that Shaul comes back with news of my sister. I am worried. Grandfather and Ellie and David are worried. But Rebbe Moshe looks as though his heart is breaking, nu?"

Howard nodded and took his full water can from a curious young Sabra woman. "We will pray that Shaul returns today with word that Rachel is well."

The woman cleared her throat and said, "You are Professor Howard Moniger, yes?"

Howard nodded and smiled hesitantly.

"So I thought! Two years ago I worked on a crew at the dig you were head of! Yes? You remember?"

"Why, yes, of course." Dim recollection sparked in his mind.

"Yes? You remember? I am Cassandra!" She filled the second container. "You are carrying your own water now? Often I think of you, Professor, as I fill the jugs with water! Such a miserable, dirty, hot job just to find old pots and such! Oy gevalt, how we suffered!"

Howard nodded now, definitely remembering the young student who had worked only two weeks and then dropped the course. "You didn't do well in the heat, as I recall."

"It was the rationing! The water ration! Oy gevalt!" she said loudly to the long queue of women. "You think this rationing is bad!" The women stared at Howard as the young woman's voice grew louder. "Two gallons a day! In the sun! In the heat! In the dirt!"

"It is enough when water is rare," Howard defended.

The woman smiled brightly. "Don't tell me, Professor, you're the man who recommended two gallons a day, eh? Admit it, Professor. You must be the man!"

Howard grinned sheepishly as all eyes glared at him after her playful accusation. "Enough joking, young woman. I'll take my ration now."

A small whisper filtered back through the line, "There's the man in charge of rationing . . ."

"She is joking, of course. I'm an archaeologist."

She pointed at him and said loudly, "Two gallons a day!" Then she smiled sweetly at the uneasy professor. "You should have given me a better grade," she whispered. He snatched his container from her and hurried away.

"Ah, women!" said Yacov indignantly as they rounded the corner. "A man could die from them, nu?"

"Well, one with a sense of humor like that could certainly get you killed!" Howard set down the water jugs and mopped his brow. He glanced up the street and a new concern filled his face. In front of his house was parked a large black limousine with tiny American flags waving above the headlights. Two motorcycles were parked in front and two behind, and a detachment of Marines from the American delegation stood outside his doorway.

"What the—" Howard picked up the heavy water cans and hurried toward home.

"What is it, Professor?" Yacov's small legs churned to keep step with Howard.

"Trouble, I think, Yacov. Or taxes. I've been here over a quarter of a century and never had anyone from the American Embassy just drop in for a cup of coffee. We'll see."

As he approached the Marines, they eyed him suspiciously, fingering their weapons. "Halt!" exclaimed one very large man as Howard started up the steps.

"Halt yourself!" Professor Moniger exclaimed indignantly. "We happen to live here. What seems to be the problem?"

"Your name please, sir?"

"Howard Moniger. Professor Howard Moniger, and I demand—"

"Of course, Professor." The men stepped aside, one taking the water canisters from him as he passed.

Yacov followed him into the house where two neatly groomed men in dark pin-striped suits sat in the parlor opposite David, Ellie, and Moshe.

Howard could see by the angry expression on David's face that the Embassy officials had not come to pay a social call. The handsome young flyer's jaw was tight, and he zipped and unzipped his leather flight jacket as

211

the Embassy official spoke to him in insistent tones. Every face looked up as Howard slammed the door behind him loudly.

"Ah! Professor Moniger!" one official said.

"I do not believe I have had the pleasure?" Howard walked into the room as the officials stood and extended their hands—too eagerly, it seemed to Howard.

"Edmond Tharp," said a balding middle-aged diplomat.

"Paul Green," said the other, a younger man. "U.S. Embassy."

"I guessed as much." Howard shook their hands. "And to what do I owe the honor of your unannounced visit?"

"The phones are impossible, you see. We tried to reach you but—"

"Understandable. I take it this is not a social visit."

"Oh, Uncle Howard!" Ellie blurted. "They say if we stay here we could lose our passports. Our citizenship. They say we must return the scrolls to the British government, that they have the legal right to—"

Howard smiled confidently. "And did you explain that we don't *have* the scrolls?" He chuckled and sat down.

"Of course," Moshe said quietly. "They do not seem to—"

"Professor Moniger," Tharp began, taking his seat but sitting rigidly on its edge, "we are simply trying to avoid a possible political incident. As a citizen of the United States and a well-respected scholar, it reflects badly on our government if you—"

"How can we give up that which we do not have?"

"Not simply the scrolls. Those are, obviously, artifacts which should belong to the British National Museum since they have been discovered while the English still have possession of Palestine. The Arabs are claiming them as well, and it might be better to let them haggle it out among themselves."

"Perhaps you are right," Howard said, wrapping an

arm around Yacov, who stood very close and wide-eyed. "But as Professor Sachar undoubtedly explained, we simply do not have them in our possession. Perhaps you should speak to Haj Amin if you would like to mediate between Arabs and British."

"The Arab High Committee claims that two men, one American"—he gazed sternly at Howard—"and one Palestinian Jew"—he looked at Moshe—"stole them several weeks ago."

"Propaganda," Howard sniffed. "When you've been in this country as long as I have, you learn not to believe every word you hear from the mouths of the Arabs."

The diplomats both glanced at one another; then each offered the other the chance to speak. "After you, Tharp."

Tharp straightened his tie and said nervously. "Well, then, if that's the way you wish to play your hand. There is another matter, of course. That of the curious presence of an American flyer in Palestine. In Jerusalem. In your home. Not just any flyer, but David Meyer, who as we all know was a top American ace in the late war. Can you explain that?" He looked from one face to another.

"Well, it's nice to finally get a little recognition!" David crossed his arms and raised his eyebrows in satisfaction. "Does this mean you guys are going to raise my G.I. benefits?"

Tharp directed his gaze steadily at David. "No. As a matter-of-fact, Mr. Meyer, it means that if any American hires out as a mercenary to the Zionists, he will lose his citizenship. If there is any involvement whatsoever from any of you, you will have no country to come home to. I am certain you are aware of the law passed by Congress only last week—"

Howard cleared his throat angrily. "Mr. Meyer happens to be a guest in this house. He is engaged to my niece, Ellie Warne, who is a photographer for me with The American Schools of Oriental Research."

David nudged Ellie and whispered. "Listen to your uncle, sweetheart."

"Furthermore," Howard rose. "I am ashamed to think that my government would enter a private home and make unreasonable accusations, threats, and demands on her citizens at the request of a foreign power."

"That was not our intention! We simply felt that we must warn you of the consequences if you choose to stay here or assist the Jews in any way. . ."

Howard eyed them both with silent disgust, causing them to squirm uncomfortably. Finally he picked up their coats from the back of the chair and said softly, "I am so sorry we cannot offer you tea. There is water rationing in our city now, you know. Two gallons a day. Barely enough for us to make a pot for this household, let alone uninvited guests."

The men stood and took their coats. "If you find yourself in difficulty," said Tharp, "you know we cannot help you."

"I doubt that any one of us would ask," Howard returned, leading them to the front door. "Good day, gentlemen."

David called from the parlor, "And give my regards to President Truman, will you, fellas? I'll invite him to the wedding."

24 The Vigil

From high atop his minaret, the ancient muezzin stared down into the streets of the Old City Jewish Quarter. Occasionally when a young and slender woman passed near the place where he had first seen the enemy of Gerhardt and the Mufti, he would raise the field glasses to his eyes. But since that first afternoon when she had ascended the steps, she had not returned while he had stood his duty. *Perhaps she was but a demon, after all,* he thought, watching the streets in boredom. *Perhaps she was sent by Shatan himself to distract the man who served the Mufti with such dedication.* But now Gerhardt had offered great reward to any Jihad Moquade who dared steal into the Jewish Quarter by night and bring her back. And so in hopes of capturing at least a part of that reward, the old muezzin watched for her day after day, though she never came. Only a dog came to the door each morning; a shaggy vicious-looking dog who descended the steps and remained by the door until the evening prayers were said. It had occurred to the old muezzin that if the demon could take the form of a beautiful woman, it could perhaps also live in the form of a dog. *If one were to kill the dog, would not perhaps the demon vanish?* He spit and made a sign to ward off the evil eye. Gerhardt would not reward a man who brought him the dead body of a dog, even if it was attained at great risk. It was the body of the woman Gerhardt required, and he demanded that the body be alive for his own purposes. The old muezzin sighed. Life had become so full of complications since the late troubles. His old bones had grown weary of his cold vigil. He longed for the peaceful days when he could raise his voice to call the faithful to prayer, and then return to the coffeehouse for thick Turkish coffee and a long afternoon of smoking and conversation with his friends.

Gerhardt, it was rumored, had gone to Damascus to purchase weapons for the Holy War. And every young sniper and Jihad Moquade carried in his robes the scrawled likeness of the woman with instructions from Gerhardt himself as well as great promises. The old muezzin had seen her first. If Allah willed he would see her again and the acclaim would be his. Then would he sit in the coffeehouse and tell of his own exploits: how he watched daily for the woman in spite of great hardship to himself.

He cleared his throat and spit out the opening of the minaret; then he raised his field glasses curiously to his eyes as a rough, burly-looking Jew approached the stairwell. The man wore a sea coat and a fisherman's cap. He walked with a swagger, and his bearded face seemed grim and thoughtful. He stepped onto the first step leading to the basement apartment, then leaped back as the snarling dog lunged up the steps toward him. The dog's ruff was spread like a rooster in a cock fight. His fangs were bared and his head lowered for the attack. The Jew backed quickly away, then snatched a broken board from a garbage pile. The old muezzin laughed at the sight of the gruff-looking Jew held at bay by the mongrel dog. The dog continued to bark, then sat on his haunches near the top step as if to dare the Jew to come near.

The muezzin focused the lenses on the face of the Jew, whose mouth was working hard with the curses of a seaman. "Run, you fool," chuckled the muezzin. "Run, Jewish dog, or the Jewish dog will have you for supper."

Still holding the broken board, the Jew inched his way along the wall of the house. His eyes never left the face of the dog. Then, as the man retreated from the animal's territory, the dog stood and once again padded down the steps. At that, the Jewish seaman lobbed the broken board into the stairwell and shouted curses loud enough that the muezzin thought perhaps he could almost hear them. With that the Jew disappeared down a side street.

"This must be the dog of a Jihad Moquade," the muezzin muttered. "A bright animal, to be sure."

Rachel cranked the phonograph briskly and carefully balanced the needle on the edge of the record. The crackle of static was immediately replaced by the clear strong strains of the Mozart *Hafner Symphony*. French horns, violins, cellos— all blended together, filling the tiny apartment with joyful sound. Rachel glanced tenderly at Leah's silent cello, then at the tiny cradle where Tikvah lay happily sucking her thumb.

"Is there anything more beautiful than your music, Leah?" Rachel whispered quietly. "Only this." She bent over the cradle and lifted Tikvah gently into her arms. She touched the velvet-soft hair and rosy cheek of the baby. "You are more beautiful, my little Tikvah. You are more beautiful yet." Tikvah opened her rosebud mouth and turned her face instinctively toward Rachel's breast. Rocking her softly to the music, Rachel danced across the floor and retrieved a bottle from the kitchen counter. "Here you are, sweet love," Rachel soothed as Tikvah squawked and shook her tiny arms impatiently. Instantly she relaxed and sighed as the warm liquid filled her mouth. "There, you see?" Rachel sat down in the rocking chair and held the bottle carefully so Tikvah would not end up with a stomach full of air. "You don't need to worry. Mama will take care of you, little love. Sweet love."

A tender joy filled Rachel as she held the baby. The deep-blue eyes were still unfocused, but Tikvah turned her head expectantly to the sound of Rachel's voice. Contentment radiated from the little one, and as the music played on, her eyelids began to droop. The sweetest music of all to Rachel was the sound of the baby's happy sighs as the milk slowly disappeared from the bottle. Rachel took the bottle from Tikvah's lips when the baby closed her eyes in sleep. The tiny mouth trembled a bit as though she were still sucking, and a trickle of milk escaped the corner of her lips. Rachel stroked her cheek, unable to take her eyes away from the sweet face. "Maybe someday you will play your mother's cello. I will keep it for you. Or maybe you will be a teacher as your father was. I will see that you have a fine education. And perhaps one day I will learn about the Messiah, as Leah said. And I will teach you about Him."

In the two weeks that had passed since Tikvah had come into Rachel's loving care, Rachel could hardly believe the happiness she had found simply in touching the little bundle. She had not returned to Grandfather's apartment in all that time; instead, she had stayed in the apartment of Shimon and Leah, feeling somehow that it would be best for Tikvah to begin her life where happy dreams had been dreamed of her. Each day she let down a basket from her window and Shoshanna placed a few meager groceries in it. Small children came with milk still in their cups and offered them to the baby of their beloved Leah. Ehud had become a courier and a water carrier for her. Even Yehudit Akiva had come with food several times and had offered her help in acquiring extra diapers and a beautiful sky-blue blanket.

Often Rachel stood over the sleeping child and gazed with wonder at the precious gift Leah had bequeathed to her. In the night she would listen to the sweet breathing of Tikvah, and her heart was filled with a love she had not known existed. Spindly red legs and round tummy filled her with delight as Tikvah lay in the same position she must have had in the womb of her mother. "You are a miracle, little one!" Rachel would whisper. "Perhaps there is a God, and perhaps you are His way of being an optimist as Leah said, eh?"

But with all the joy of Tikvah there was also a fear in Rachel. It ran as deep as her soul and as strong as her heartbeat. Often the fear clutched her in the night when Tikvah's breathing was so peaceful that Rachel could not hear it. Then Rachel would throw back the covers and light the lamp and touch the soft cheek. "Are you still breathing, little one?" she would whisper, panic thick in her voice. "You have not left me, little Tikvah? Mama's heart would break, sweet love." Then Rachel would hold her and rock her gently—not to comfort the peaceful child, but to soothe her own fears. And although the women of the quarter had stopped by to ask her when she would bring Tikvah to the synagogue, she had shaken her head and said, "It is too cold," or, "There might be snipers," or "She has a touch of colic."

And so Rachel stayed in the apartment, surrounded by a tide of joy that at times ebbed into a fear so profound she did not know how she would survive it.

She held Tikvah just a moment longer before she reluctantly placed her in her bed. Carefully she tucked the blue blanket around her before she went to the stove to check the steady flame that warmed the apartment.

Suddenly the sound of soft but insistent knocking came from the door.

"Rachel!" came the loudly whispered voice of Ehud. "Does the little one sleep? Rachel?" The knocking continued until Rachel cracked the door and let the burly captain slip in.

"Shhh." She put a finger to her lips.

Ehud nodded and tiptoed over to the cradle where he peered in. A tender radiance lit up his rugged features. "Beautiful little one." He wagged a thick finger under his chin. Tikvah wrinkled her face as if to cry; then as Ehud drew back in remorse for having disturbed her, peace again filled her features. "Well, she does not look like her uncle Ehud, God be praised!" he whispered in what would have been a loud-speaking voice to any other mortal.

"Shhh," Rachel insisted again. Then she noticed that Ehud had returned empty-handed. "And where is the sewing basket? And the extra blankets?"

"Oy Gevalt!" Ehud slapped his palm against his forehead in dismay. "An impossible mission you send me on, Rachel," he cried, his voice becoming even louder.

"Shhh, Ehud!" she exclaimed as Tikvah opened her eyes with a start and began to cry. "Now see what you've done?"

Ehud shrugged. "She wanted to see Uncle Ehud anyway." He bent over the squalling child. "Such a gale! Such a wind! Oy! My little darling," he crooned as Rachel bumped him out of the way and picked her up.

Bouncing and patting Tikvah on the back, she eyed Ehud with disgust. "Well, *Uncle* Ehud! Where is my sewing basket and the blankets?"

"A demon met me on your doorstep! I swear it!" He raised his hand solemnly as she narrowed her eyes threateningly. "I intended to retrieve the booty—"

"You talk like an old pirate!" she exclaimed; then she leaned closer and sniffed. "You smell like one too. What have you been drinking? No wonder Tikvah woke up, with the breath of a sea dragon filling her nose!"

"Only a little cognac!" Ehud hung his head. "The last cognac in the quarter. I was offered just one sociable drink. It would not have been right to waste it, eh?"

"From the scent of it, you might have brought it here and we could have burned it in the lamps for a week!" She glowered at him as Tikvah continued to wail. "There now, my little one. Mama will not let Uncle Ehud suffocate you with his nasty breath!"

"Only one drink, I swear it!"

"At a time, you mean." She raised her chin in disapproval. "Now, where are my blanket and sewing basket, please?"

"I promise! Before the Eternal! I was met on your doorstep by a mad dog! A vicious beast! The most vicious of dogs I have ever met! Why, I was lucky to have escaped with my very life."

"A dog?" Rachel said, suddenly serious. "On my doorstep?"

"A demon!" Ehud boomed. "Teeth like a lion! A growl like a great bear! As I stepped upon the stairs, he charged me like a bull and cornered me against the wall! I was lucky to escape with my very life!

"Was he black and tan with gray? Without a tail?"

"The very dog! A vicious mongrel, to be sure!"

"And his eyes?"

"Cruel and full of violence!"

"Their color, Ehud?" She stepped forward, holding Tikvah to her.

"An unearthly yellow! As cruel as—"

"Shaul!" Rachel cried. "Oh, Ehud! You saw Shaul!"

"Shaul?"

"My brother's dog. The very one sent to me from Moshe. Oh, Ehud!" She looked frantically around the room. "I must go to him! Oh, Tikvah!" She looked at the tiny baby whose steady bleating continued. "Ehud, you must stay here with her."

"Alone?" he exclaimed as she laid Tikvah in his arms.

"Ten minutes, Ehud! Sit here!" she demanded, shoving the rocking chair behind him. "Rock her!"

Obediently Ehud began to rock Tikvah as Rachel ran out the door without her coat or shawl.

She glanced over her shoulder to the west. The sun had begun its final dip behind the horizon. *Perhaps he will still be there*, she thought; passers-by stopped to stare after her. Quickly she darted up the Street of the Stairs and turned the corner past the Great Hurva Synagogue.

———

The muezzin watched the daylight slip away. Twice he nearly turned from his vigil to descend the stairs, but still he remained, his eyes on the streets of the Jewish

Quarter below him. Occasionally he glanced down to where the dog had chased the Jew from the steps where he had seen the woman. When at last the movement of a small coatless figure had caught his eye, his bones ached with the cold. He raised the field glasses to see why the woman ran past the synagogues and shops of the quarter. A gasp escaped from his lips!

"Praise be to Allah!" he exclaimed as her features became clear to him. "It is she!"

He was certain where her steps would lead, and he followed her progress toward where the big dog waited. As she neared the house he watched her mouth move in a soundless cry. He smiled at his good fortune and said once again, "Praise be to Allah!"

"Shaul!" Rachel cried, still a half block from the apartment. "Shaul!"

She laughed out loud as the head and shoulders of the dog appeared above the top step of the apartment stairs. He looked keenly toward her, then bounded down the street, meeting her hugs with a flurry of wet and happy kisses.

"You! You wonderful old thing!" she cried, burying her face in his ruff. "You frightened Ehud nearly to death!" she scolded as Shaul broke free from her grasp and ran in tight circles around her. He started to head back to Grandfather's apartment when Rachel called to him.

"I don't have the key, my friend! Come! Come, Shaul! I have a great surprise for you!" she called to him and quickly retraced her steps back to Tikvah and Ehud.

The room was silent except for the cooing of Ehud and the gentle gurgle of Tikvah as he balanced her carefully across his lap.

"Ehud's precious little darling! My sweet baby girl!" he said in a voice as quiet as any Rachel had ever heard come out of his mouth. He glanced up with a broad smile across his face. "Back so soon? Ah! As you can see, the child and I got on wonderfully!"

Rachel turned and called over her shoulder, "Shaul! Come here, boy!"

Ehud gathered Tikvah up in his arms protectively. "You are bringing such a beast into this house?" he bellowed.

Shaul bounded up the stairs and into the room where he sat down quietly while Rachel closed the door behind him. "He is all right, Ehud," she said, nearly out of breath. "And I see you have done a splendid job with Tikvah while I have been away these . . ." She looked at the clock. "Seven minutes? Was I gone so long?"

"She no longer bellows like a Nor'wester!" Ehud said. "Uncle Ehud is a good substitute Papa for her, eh little one?" He chucked Tikvah's chin.

"Thank you. And now, Ehud, I would like you to meet Shaul!" She took Tikvah from him.

"No thank you, I have met this shark in dog's fur once before today."

"Shaul," Rachel called, "this is Ehud."

Shaul rose and Ehud drew back in his chair. "Nice dog," his voice trembled. "Good and friendly beast."

Rachel tucked Tikvah into her cradle. "He won't hurt you, silly man," she chided, putting her hand out to Shaul, who moved immediately to her side. He sat down and began to scratch his ear feverishly.

"There, you see!" said Ehud triumphantly. "He must go out! The beast is not only vicious, he has fleas as well."

Rachel reached out to scratch behind Shaul's ear, and the dog continued to thump her hand with his paw. "He has something here," Rachel said with concern as she lifted the dog's ear to see what was bothering him so badly. As her fingers probed the soft inner skin, she drew her breath in sharply. "There is something here!" she exclaimed, her fingers touching a small metal lipstick tube taped deep inside the ear.

Ehud leaned forward as the light gleamed on the

cylinder. "There's a good dog!" he said with new respect for the furry messenger. "What does it say?" His voice was harsh with anticipation as Rachel pulled the tightly rolled note from inside the tube. Shaul moved toward Ehud and leaned against his outstretched hand.

Rachel held the note up to the light and read Moshe's cramped handwriting.

Send word whereabouts Rachel and Ehud. Needs of quarter. Condition of supplies and morale of men. All are well. Doing what we can to provide lifeline. M.

"Well, not exactly a love letter, eh?" barked Ehud.

"It is exactly that," Rachel said, clutching the note to her heart.

"It is enough. It is a link."

"You must take this to Dov and Rabbi Vultch. I will keep Shaul here until you return with a reply that we can send back."

"Good!" Ehud sprang to his feet and snatched the note from her. "And you might add a note of your own to this, eh?"

Rachel nodded and looked toward Tikvah, wriggling happily in her bed. "And if I told him, Ehud? Would he believe all the things that have befallen me since I came to this place?"

His hand on the doorknob, he smiled down at her. "Perhaps not. Perhaps you must tell him face-to-face, eh?"

"A more sensible idea."

Ehud shut the door behind him and hurried back toward Tipat Chalav where Dov was busy training the Yeshiva students to lay aside the ways of peace to take up the ways of war.

25   Escape

"YEHUDIT!" The voice of Rabbi Akiva boomed throughout the large, empty house.

Yehudit wiped her hands nervously on her apron and hurried down the hallway from the kitchen to her father's study.

"YEHUDIT!" he demanded once again.

"Coming, Father!" She opened the massive door and stood trembling before him in the dim lamplight of the room. She knew he was angry, his voice having told her even before she saw his brooding face. Now the flame of the lamp reflected on the thick lenses of his spectacles, shielding his eyes from her. The corners of his mouth were turned down in disgust as he impatiently tapped his sausage fingers on the desk blotter. He did not speak to her but sat with his face turned stonily toward where she stood fidgeting.

"Would you like some tea, Father?" she asked finally.

"Would you like some tea, Father?" he mimicked her cruelly. Then he slammed his fist on the desktop. "NO!"

Tears of confusion filled her eyes, and she searched her memory for the sin she might have committed that had brought such rage her direction. *Beds were made properly. Water for washing was just the right temperature. Prayer book laid out just so.* "What is it, Father? Have I done something?"

"The trouble is that you have done NOTHING!" he screamed. "Two weeks have passed! Two weeks and you have taken food to the woman Rachel and that orphan child. You have given them our best challah to eat and still you have no news for me! Still you have not seen the mark on her forearm as I instructed you to do!"

"What is this mark?" Yehudit asked, quietly shamed.

"It is proof! Proof that she is not what she seems!"

"But, Father, if you could only see her with the child," Yehudit pleaded. "She seems so loving, so—"

His face contorted in rage, Akiva leaped from his desk and lunged toward Yehudit. As he raised his arm to strike her, she covered her face with her hands. "You dare contradict me!" he screamed. "The fate of everything we hold dear hangs in the balance, and you dare to presume that you are wiser than your father?"

Yehudit had seen his rage many times before and felt his anger over her small failures around the house. But never had she known him to be so desperate in his fury. "No, Father!" she dropped to her knees. "Please, Father!" she sobbed in fear.

Akiva towered above her, his fist trembling with the anger that pulsed through him with every heartbeat. Slowly he gained control of himself. "You are worthless!" he said in disgust. "God has seen fit to curse me to a life without sons. And you are worse than having no children at all." He nudged her with the toe of his shoe. "Now crawl from my sight." She did not move; only her sobs penetrated the infuriated silence.

"I'm sorry, Father!" she pleaded. "Please—"

"Get out of here!" he shouted, returning to his desk.

"I will do better!"

"Then do not return before me until you have done so!"

Yehudit pulled her shawl closer around her shoulders as she hurried through the darkening streets toward the apartment of Rachel and the child. Over her arm she carried a small basket with an unopened tin of English tea and half a loaf of fresh white challah that had been brought by the British Captain Stewart when he had met with her father that afternoon.

She hoped the gifts would open the door of Rachel's home while closing her eyes to any suspicion. As she reached the top of the road, she saw a small light gleaming from the apartment window. Yehudit stopped for a moment as the shadows of three figures moved on the shades. *Two men. One large. One small. And Rachel alone in the apartment with them. Perhaps Father is right about her,* she thought as she pressed instinctively against the stones of a building just opposite the apartment. *I will wait and watch.*

Only a few moments passed before the door at the top of the steps flung open and a big dog scrambled down to the street. Yehudit gasped with surprise as she recognized Shaul. *Why, it is the dog of little Yacov,* she thought. *What is he doing here without the boy?*

A surge of excitement rushed through Yehudit as she imagined all the news she would have to offer her father before the night was over.

She watched as Rachel stood in the light of the open doorway for a long moment, her hand raised in farewell to the big, scruffy animal. *Indeed,* thought Yehudit, *this night I will have news for my father.*

Yehudit could hear the distinct pop of gunfire coming from the Arab Quarter of the city. It had become such a common sound lately that she paid little attention. Only a quarter of an hour passed until Dov and the big man known as Ehud descended the apartment steps. They talked quietly as they looked off in the direction in which Shaul had run. Ehud laughed and shook his head as Dov tugged his sidelocks and murmured something Yehudit could not quite make out. "We'll ... by morning. Perhaps he can ... in ... by morning."

They turned and began walking directly toward where Yehudit stood shivering in the cold. Quickly she stepped farther back in the shadows of a doorway and waited, hardly daring to breathe as they passed within feet of where she stood. When at last the click of their footsteps receded and faded, she stepped from her hiding place and ran quickly up the steps of the apartment.

Darkness had engulfed the city by the time Shaul

was sent away with a hastily scrawled message tucked in his ear. He paused only a moment to look back at Rachel with what seemed to be almost human understanding in his eyes. Then he trotted quickly up the street toward the sandbag checkpoint that marked the end of the Jewish Quarter.

He moved silently through the garbage-littered alleyways, now deserted but for the Jihad snipers who lurked behind darkened windows and waited on flat rooftops. Shaul could sense the ominous presence of humans he had not known before. A pack of four hungry dogs scavenged through the refuse of a closed Armenian restaurant. Their leader turned on Shaul, snarling with fierce possessiveness over his meal. Any other time Shaul might have met his challenge, but this evening he scrambled out of reach of the snapping jaws. He darted from the alley, the other dogs not bothering to pursue him.

As he emerged onto the crooked road that led to Jaffa Gate, another more terrifying sound greeted him. Shouts of excited and angry voices rang in his ears. Suddenly the staccato crack of rifle fire sounded above his head. Bullets struck the walls above him and the stones just behind him; then more curses filled the air as he lowered his head and ran with a speed he had never known. Quickly he turned into a narrow space between two buildings, close enough that a man could not easily pass through it. He and Yacov had used the passageway a dozen times to escape the British officers and soldiers who had turned to find their wallets gone while a young boy and his dog darted away through the Old City throngs. On those occasions, too, the heavy sound of boots had slapped against the cobblestones and Yacov had put a finger to his lips and said, "Hush, Shaul, or they might find us and hang us at Acre Prison, eh?" Shaul, of course, would have died before any man would have laid a finger on his youthful master.

Now, Yacov was not with him, but Shaul knew full well what he must do. He lay down calmly among the stench of the garbage and watched as first one, then two, then three cloaked figures ran past. Last came a wheezing old man, his face pale in the gathering darkness. His hand was raised as if to stop the strong young men who had gone ahead without bothering to look between the two buildings.

"Wait!" he gasped. "He is here! It is the same dog I saw with the woman!" His voice was weak and did not carry to the men, who turned the corner and dashed away in pursuit of Shaul. "Wait!" the old man cried in desperation. "He ran in here!"

Shaul laid his head on his paws and watched from the darkness as the old man crouched and peered into the lair.

"You are in there, dog," he crooned. "Aram has seen you, though the young fools have run off with their guns. I know where you hide, and I shall wait." He put his hand up as if to shade his eyes even though the shadows grew darker by the minute. "Come to Aram," he said. "And then you shall not be killed." He took a step forward; a low, menacing growl escaped from Shaul's throat, causing the old man to gasp and stumble backward. Inspired by fear, the old man raised his chin and called loudly in the sing-song chant of one accustomed to calling thousands to pray from all parts of the city: "The dog is here! I have found the beast who belongs to the enemy of Allah and the Mufti!" His voice ricocheted off the stones and carried over the rooftops.

Shaul sprang to his feet and growled once more; then he charged the old man, knocking him to the ground. The man screeched and wailed as two of the Jihad Moquades rounded the corner and ran toward him and Shaul. Without a moment's hesitation Shaul charged toward the men, whose panic-stricken faces blanched at the sight of his bared fangs and wild yellow eyes. The Jihad Moquade in the lead attempted to raise his rifle to his shoulder as Shaul brushed past his legs, but the shot went wild and struck the ground a few feet from where the old man lay weeping with fear.

"Get him!" Voices pierced the darkness as Shaul followed an old and well-practiced route to safety. "Shoot him!" He dodged around a collection of metal garbage cans, toppling them onto the narrow street and into the path of his pursuers. "Shoot! Shoot! Kill him, you fool!" More shots exploded from behind him, popping the ground around him as he leaped over a high stone wall and into a courtyard littered with decaying vines and an assortment of empty and broken packing crates. Often he and Yacov had found refuge here behind a broken trellis that rested precariously against a wall leading to the rooftop. Twice they had escaped when Yacov had lifted Shaul partway up and the big dog had scrambled clumsily up the slanted trellis. Yacov was not with him now and there was nothing to do but hide and wait for the approaching footsteps and the chorus of curses as the men helped one another over the wall into the courtyard.

"I know the beast is here!" one of the men muttered. "It jumped the fence as if it knew where it was going. As if Shatan himself were guiding it."

"Perhaps it is as the muezzin said, and the dog is but a spirit."

"It is no spirit who attacked the muezzin. Did you not see the claw marks on the old man's face?"

"Do not the demons of hell have claws?" The voice of the man quavered, and Shaul smelled the fear that seeped from his pores. The other, too, was afraid, but his voice was more confident and angry.

Dead leaves crunched beneath their feet as they walked slowly from crate to crate, lifting each box with their gun barrels. Shaul suppressed his instinct to growl as they moved between him and the trellis. The more frightened of the two men brushed the dead vines with the toe of his boot.

"We must go!" he cried. "I tell you this is not a thing of flesh. Perhaps even this woman of Gerhardt's is not of flesh!"

"Shut up!" shouted his companion, moving cautiously toward the crate where Shaul lay. "The dog may be flesh or demon, but we will have his pelt!"

The first man lowered his rifle and backed against the trellis. "I tell you there is something unearthly in all this!"

"Coward!" shouted the other man. Then he kicked the crate where Shaul hid, sending the dog scrambling out with a snarl and a howl.

"It is he!" screamed the first Jihad in terror as Shaul leaped high toward his face and shoulders. "Aiiiiii!"

Shaul flailed against the broken trellis with his claws as the man fell from beneath him. For an instant Shaul saw the face of Yacov and heard his voice urge him upward as he had done before; then the angry cries of the men below him crowded his consciousness as he scrambled precariously upward to the roof.

"He flies!" wailed a voice. "You see, we pursue a devil from the mouth of hell!"

With one final effort, Shaul pulled himself onto the roof and darted across the flat asphalt where he jumped to yet another roof and then still another.

26   The Watchers

Rachel gently tapped Tikvah on the back until the tiny baby burped with a gusto that seemed too mighty for her size.

"My goodness!" Rachel laughed, lowering Tikvah from her shoulder and laying her down across her lap. "No wonder your tummy hurt." She stroked the velvet head and smiled.

A soft rapping sounded at the door, and Rachel pursed her lips, not wanting to get up and unlatch the bolt. The afternoon and evening had become far too busy and full of interruptions.

"Your uncle Ehud has forgotten something," she said to Tikvah. "Perhaps we should make him wait until morning, eh?"

The knock grew more insistent and Rachel wrapped a small blanket around the baby before she went to open the door.

"Is it you again, Ehud?" she cried with mock disgust. "What do you want this time? No, you can't hold the baby again—"

"It is Yehudit!" came the muffled reply. "Yehudit Akiva."

Rachel hesitated a moment before throwing the latch bolt back and opening the door. As Yehudit's pale face appeared in the crack of the door, Rachel frowned with concern. Never before had the young girl come after dark.

"Come in, Yehudit!" Rachel said with alarm. "Does your father know you are out after dark? Why, look at you! You are in nothing warmer than a thin shawl and shaking like a little bird! Is something the matter? Have

232

you gotten some word of my grandfather? Is he—"

"No. No word. There has been no word." Yehudit scanned the apartment for Yacov, certain that if the dog was near, the boy could not be far away. "I brought you this," said Yehudit, her words coming in a nervous rush as she held the basket out.

Rachel smiled briefly, then frowned. "Thank you. How very kind. But perhaps you should have waited. You know how unsafe the streets are after dark."

Yehudit shrugged. "There is challah for you. And tea!"

"Well, then"— Rachel laid Tikvah in her cradle and hugged Yehudit warmly—"you should have waited until daylight. And worn something warmer out in this cold. Come, sit down. I will brew us both a cup of tea."

Yehudit sat nervously on the edge of her chair and stared at the long sleeves of Rachel's brown dress and tan sweater.

"The sweater you are wearing looks quite warm." Yehudit pulled her shawl closer around her.

"And so it is." Rachel measured out exactly two cups of water into the kettle; then she took her sweater off and handed it to Yehudit. "I am warm enough. Wear it a bit until the chill is off, eh?"

Yehudit smiled for the first time since she entered the room. "Thank you. You have warmed it for me." She quickly pulled the sweater on. "Are you sure you do not need it?"

Rachel shook her head as she opened the tin of tea. She breathed the aroma of the fresh tea leaves and sighed with pleasure. "Wonderful! How very kind of you, Yehudit!" she exclaimed, offering the tin to Yehudit for a sniff.

Self-consciously Yehudit breathed in the sweet, rich smell. "Yes. It is good," she said, wondering what her father would say if he knew she had taken one of his tins of tea to Rachel. *Perhaps*, she hoped, *she would have news for him to savor instead.*

As Rachel sliced thin slices of challah, Yehudit silently watched her delicate hands. "I have a tiny bit of jam in the cupboard. Perhaps we might share some," Rachel offered as the kettle whistled.

"I'll get the tea," Yehudit said as Rachel rummaged to find a small jar of strawberry jam.

"And here is the teapot." Rachel set the small blue pot on the counter as Yehudit moved toward her with the kettle of boiling water. Before Rachel could pull her hand away, Yehudit seemed to stumble and fall forward. The young girl's eyes never left Rachel's outstretched arm; as Rachel reached out to steady her, the glowing kettle slammed into her arm.

"Be careful!" Rachel shouted; then she gasped in pain as the steaming liquid spilled out of the kettle, soaking through the sleeve of her dress to the skin.

The kettle clattered to the floor and Yehudit regained her balance. "Oh, Rachel!" she cried, grasping Rachel's burned arm. "Quickly. We need to soak it in cold water before it blisters."

"I'm all right!" Rachel pulled her arm away. "I'm all right." But her eyes were bright with tears and she had to lean against the counter to steady herself.

Yehudit quickly dipped cold water from the pitcher and again grasped Rachel's arm. She poured cold water over the sleeve, and then, before Rachel could protest, pulled the sleeve of her dress up to the elbow. There, just below the nasty red burn on the tender inside of her forearm was an ugly black mark bearing the words, *Nür Für Offizere*.

"No, please!" Rachel cried, covering the mark with her hand. "I said I am all right!"

Yehudit smiled a slight smile of satisfaction. Her eyes narrowed as she appraised Rachel, whose head was lowered in pain and resignation. Empty teacups and untouched challah lay on the counter next to her. Slowly Rachel raised her eyes to meet Yehudit's gaze, almost pleading. Then she looked toward the cradle where Tikvah lay. Anguish and shame filled her face.

Yehudit frowned, suddenly sorry that she had

stripped so completely bare the soul of one so kind. "I am sorry I burned you," she said, turning away. "I am . . ."

Slowly Rachel tugged on her sleeve, pulling it over the cruel mark. She pulled herself up with dignity and said quietly, "I suppose it could not be helped. I am all right," she repeated. "Will you tell your father? Will you tell him about the mark on my arm?"

Yehudit took Rachel's sweater off and laid it across the back of the rocking chair. "He says you are not what you seem to be."

Rachel drew her breath in and let it out slowly, aware that Yehudit's gifts and friendship had not been offered in kindness. "Is that what he says?"

Yehudit nodded, uncertainty filling her eyes once again. "Yes. He says you are a bad woman."

Rachel smiled sadly. "I suppose he is right." She held Yehudit's empty basket and shawl out to her; then she opened the door and stepped aside as Yehudit walked quickly past her into the night.

Together they stood at the window and gazed into the nearly deserted Rehavia streets. Moshe put his arm around Yacov as the boy anxiously searched the dark shadows for some sign of Shaul.

"He is so very late tonight, Rebbe Moshe." Yacov leaned his head against Moshe's arm.

"What is it your grandfather says? Shaul has a girl-friend, perhaps?" Moshe patted his shoulder. "He is a clever thief. Trained by the best, eh?"

David's laughter floated down the hall from where he and Ellie played a game of chess. Ellie's loud protests made Moshe smile; it was obvious who was winning. Their playful happiness made Moshe's deep ache for Rachel seem even that much more intense.

Suddenly Yacov stiffened. "What is that?" he asked.

"What?" Moshe scanned the darkened street below.

"There." The boy pointed to a large black sedan

parked across from the house. "You will see. A small orange light."

A tiny gleam from a cigarette glowed for an instant, then disappeared.

"I don't know, but I can guess." He studied the car, then called for David, who came quickly, a broad grin still on his face.

"What're you guys doin' in the dark? Come on in the parlor and watch me wipe Ellie off the board."

"Don't turn on the light," Moshe quietly instructed. "We're being watched."

David's smile faded. "I figured as much. This afternoon some goons followed me from the airfield after I landed. Trailed me all the way to the Jewish Agency. A guy can't even deliver the mail around here without somebody breathing down his neck." David pulled the curtain back and stared briefly down at the car. Thumbing his nose at them he said loudly, "Nuts to you!"

"Americans? English?" Moshe asked.

"Who knows? But I'm about to give them a crew cut with my propeller. Look," he pointed. "There's another guy on the corner over there." Moshe and Yacov strained to see the shadowy figure leaning against a lamp post. "I wouldn't want to be him. It's cold enough out there to freeze the asbestos coat off a fireman." David rocked on his heels and narrowed his eyes slyly. "Well, as Sherlock Holmes said to Watson, 'The game is afoot.' " He twirled an imaginary mustache and winked at Yacov. "Speaking of games, you wanna come watch me beat the socks off ol' Ellie, kid?"

"It's nearly time for bed," Moshe answered for him.

"No, please, Rebbe Moshe," Yacov pleaded, "let me stay at the window just a while longer. Shaul is so late. I worry about him."

"You're worried about the mutt?" David asked. "Ah, he's just got himself a new girlfriend. He may not be home until morning now. Besides, if he does come, I'll wake you. Either me or Moshe."

"Just ten minutes more? Only ten? He turned his imploring gaze upward and Moshe shook his head in resignation. He pulled Yacov's yarmulke down over his forehead and winked.

"Okay. As the American flyboys say, Okay."

David returned to the chess game and Moshe left Yacov to his lonely vigil in the dark room.

He returned to the kitchen where Howard and Grandfather washed and dried the dinner dishes while they discussed points of scripture.

"Ah, you Christians," chided Grandfather. "You all have forgotten your Jewish heritage! True? Of course true! And so you miss much of what the great rabbi Jesus was speaking of, eh?"

"You're right Shlomo," Howard nodded vigorously. "But you're missing a thing or two as well, you know."

"So maybe the only ones who know it all are the *geshmat*, eh?"

"Geshmat?" Howard rubbed his head and peered curiously at Grandfather.

"Oy Gevalt! So long you have lived in Jerusalem and you don't know the word!" he exclaimed. "Don't you know that the first Anglican bishop of Jerusalem was *geshmat?*"

"Hmmm," Howard mused thoughtfully. "Is it possibly a Jew who converts to Christianity? A Yiddish word, isn't it?"

"Of course Yiddish! What else?" exclaimed the old man. From the corner of his eyes he spotted Moshe leaning against the doorjamb, quietly watching as the two men bantered back and forth.

"An interesting word, *geshmat*," said Howard.

"And here is Professor Sachar who can maybe help this poor goy with a little Yiddish, eh?" Grandfather teased.

Moshe cleared his throat. For him especially, the word geshmat was a tragic word, born in fear and bitterness from its Hebrew mother tongue. "It comes from the root *shemad* in Hebrew, Howard," he explained. "Meaning destruction or annihilation."

"Oy!" Grandfather tapped his fingers over his mouth. "Is this so? Such a smart man you are, Moshe. You should have been a rabbi. Who knows such things about words anymore?"

"Well, it's not a common word, is it?"

"Common!" exclaimed Grandfather. "As common as dust! Half the jokes in the life of a Jew are *geshmat* jokes, eh, Moshe?"

"That is true, Howard."

The old rabbi waved his dish towel in delight. "You mean you haven't heard the geshmat jokes, Howard? He hasn't heard the geshmat jokes!" Grandfather raised his eyes toward heaven. "For weeks I lay in the hospital bed across from a Jewish cab driver and next to a Jewish shoemaker! Not one new joke in all that time! A man could die from such boredom! We talked about the weather. We talked about the nurses. We talked about the Torah. We talked about the food. Oy! A man could die! True? Of course true! So God has placed me in the home of a man with the ears of a virgin! So. Howard, listen to this one, eh?"

Howard nodded and continued to carefully rinse the dishes, preserving every drop of water. "Go on."

"It was a cold night! Oy! Such a night it was with the wind howling and the snow blowing as it blows in a Polish winter, eh? Old Salkowitz, feeling that his time had come, called to his wife: 'Golda!' he says, 'please, send someone to fetch the priest and tell him to come right away—I am dying!' 'The priest! You must have a fever!' says Golda. 'You mean the *rabbi*!'

" 'I mean the priest!' snapped Salkowitz.

" 'May God protect us! Are you secretly a *geshmat*?' "

Grandfather paused and rubbed his hands together in anticipation of the punchline. Then he looked at Moshe. "You have heard this joke, young man?"

Moshe grinned and nodded. "Many times."

"Don't tell!" Grandfather continued. ". . . are you secretly a *geshmat*?"

Just then Yacov's shouts were heard throughout the

house. Grandfather tossed the dish towel on the stack of dishes. Howard laid down the last plate and wiped his hands on his trousers.

"He's home!" Yacov shouted, shoving the door open and jumping into the center of the kitchen in one leap. Shaul followed happily behind him, obviously spent, and plopped down on the floor in front of the stove.

"Good! Good boy!" Moshe knelt beside him. "Did you check his ear yet?" he asked Yacov.

"No. You look, Rebbe Moshe. He has been gone such a long time. Maybe this time . . ."

Moshe felt inside Shaul's ear for the small lipstick cylinder. Carefully he untaped it and as all eyes watched, he opened it. He drew his breath in sharply and bit his lip as he held the small silver container in the palm of his hand. "He made it through this time," he said quietly. "This time he got through."

"How do you know?" asked Howard, kneeling beside him.

"The paper is different."

"So open it!" demanded Grandfather. "What are you waiting for?"

Moshe pulled the paper from the lipstick holder and quickly unfolded it. His eyes hurriedly scanned the page, and his face flooded first with relief and then with concern.

"What is it?" Howard asked.

"She is well," said Moshe quietly. "She is alive and well. Rachel is well." He rubbed his hand across his cheek and began to read aloud. "Rachel Lubetkin inspires many to courage, but morale wanes daily. Akiva regaining powerful influence as lack of supplies and isolation demoralize residents. Send shortwave radio. Food supplies and weapons. Since the deaths of Shimon and Leah Feldstein—"

"Oh no!" cried Grandfather as Yacov gasped and clung to him. "May they rest in peace. She was carrying a child, poor thing."

"Oh, Grandfather," Yacov cried. "And all this time I

239

thought of Leah as alive. I thought of her with Rachel!"
Tears streamed down his cheeks as Grandfather patted
him on the back and Moshe read steadily on.

". . . we are in desperate need of leadership and supplies. Soon it may be too late." Moshe swallowed hard.
"Food supplies low. Send assistance soon." Moshe
passed the note to Howard, who scanned it quickly.

"You'll need to show this to Ben-Gurion immediately," Howard stated when he finished reading.

"And then what?" Moshe asked, his voice racked
with frustration. "What can we do? The English allow
only the barest trickle of food and medical supplies in
since the Jaffa Gate bombing. All of it is supervised by
their own men. Luke Thomas has been shuffled away
to duty in ordnance. There's no help there. What are we
to do?"

"I will tell you this. If something isn't done," Grandfather embraced Yacov and stroked his head, "the Old
City will be mechuleh! Pfft! Finished, eh?"

"Then maybe we should start by consulting the one
who has all the answers. God knows the way into the
Old City, gentlemen, and if we but ask Him, perhaps . . ."

"An excellent idea," agreed Grandfather. "We are
not a minyon, yet God did not always require a minyon
to pray, eh? We four shall pray like ten."

Moshe bowed his head and the others followed.
There was a long silence, which was at last broken by
Howard. "Almighty God, it was you who chose this city
as your own and her people as your people. You have
known every problem before it was a problem and you
can see the answers before we even look up from our
despair to seek your help. Lord, we do not know the
path that you would have us take into the Old City, but
you do. You know the need, you hold the answer. We
ask that you will show us the way. Amen."

"Omaine," whispered the old rabbi, raising his eyes.

Moshe sat back on his haunches and pursed his lips.
"For days I have been poring over the old maps of the

city. The records of archaeological digs from the nineteenth century."

Howard nodded. "You mean Warren?"

"Yes. And Bliss and Dickie after him." He looked at the old rabbi to explain. "You see, there were several teams of archaeologists who actually carried on quite a bit of exploration of underground Jerusalem late in the last century."

"Yes," said Grandfather, nodding his head vigorously. "I know. My father knew Captain Warren quite well. And I knew Mr. Bliss and Mr. Dickie as well. The underground of the Old City is like a rabbit warren, full of tunnels and cisterns and passageways of ruins built on ruins. I know about such things."

Howard leaned forward intensely. "You *know* of these things? You knew Bliss and Dickie personally?"

"So! You think I was born yesterday?" the old man exclaimed. "What year is this?"

"1948," answered Moshe quietly as a light of understanding filled his eyes.

"Yes. And when were Bliss and Dickie digging up Jerusalem?"

"1895." Howard answered.

"How old am I, Yacov?"

Yacov stuck out his lower lip and peered at the ceiling for a moment. "Very old, Grandfather."

"Indeed I am. I have reached the fullness of a man's years. I am seventy-two, Yacov. I was but a young lad of nineteen when I helped the gentlemen from England explore the tunnels beneath my city. But I remember them well, and I remember the passages well. They are a fearsome, contorted web in some parts. A young boy of ten was lost when he played a game and hid from his friends. No one of us could find him and his bones rest beneath the Old City with the bones that Titus himself crushed when he destroyed Jerusalem two thousand years ago. There is a city still beneath this city, but it is safe only for the rats, eh?"

"I was studying the charts and drawings," Moshe began eagerly. "Warren's tunnel shaft and the notes left by Bliss after he and Dickie traversed the length of the city underground . . ."

"Ah yes," the old man nodded. "Beneath the arches of the ancient causeway that once led to the Temple Mount when it was ours. This journey I remember well. Too well. It is mostly sewer now, you know. It runs directly beneath the Street of the Chain. Beneath the very house of the Mufti and then onto the Temple Mount itself."

"You have seen it?"

"Not all, but I saw them when they came out. They were gasping for breath. Pale as death itself from the breath of those fumes. They traveled by using three boards, you see, which they laid on top of the sewage. They would hop from board to board, then pull up the last board and lay it in front. Mr. Bliss said that if either of them had fallen, it would have been instant death. But this cannot be of help in this case, can it?"

"Possibly," Howard said.

"That path will not take you into the Jewish Quarter. Only beneath the house of the Mufti and the Dome of the Rock." The old man sighed. "It is a path that leads near the edge of death."

"Fascinating." Howard shook his head in wonder. "You knew them."

"Knew them! Of course! And were times easier I could show you the way into that foul stinking hole! I have walked over it a thousand times or more. There is a manhole cover just outside Jaffa Gate . . . but that is not what you need." Grandfather sighed and slowly shook his head. "If you were inside my quarter seeking a way out, I could help you without any difficulty. At least I could show you the way to the shaft. I do not know, alas, where it opens to on this side of the wall."

Moshe blanched, his face a mask of wonder. "But, Rebbe Lebowitz," he exclaimed, "I know the way in from this side! I was just uncertain where it would lead me once I entered."

"There are a dozen tunnels in that maze which lead nowhere. I could not tell you where you might wander if you tried to enter the Old City underground. But if you wandered far enough and if the Eternal were with you, you might find yourself trapped behind a locked grate in the women's mikveh—the ritual bath. Many years ago I was given the key to that grate for safekeeping. I could give you the key if only I were in the Old City to do so, nu?" The old man sighed. "But you see, I am here. You are here. The key is there. Even if you could by some small chance find your way to the iron grate, it is hopeless."

Moshe stared long and hard at the dog sleeping at his feet. "Not hopeless, Rebbe Lebowitz. Complicated, perhaps, but never hopeless."

———

Throughout the long night, Tikvah slept peacefully as Rachel sat, cross-legged, on the floor beside her cradle. The wind had come up, strong, from the north. It howled around the corner of the house and shook the windows fiercely. Any moment Rachel expected a group of indignant rabbis to slam their righteous fists against the door and demand that Tikvah be taken away and placed in the care of an honest, godly woman. Hours inched past and still no one came to accuse her; no one but the wind.

Her sleeve was pulled up over the elbow and she held her injured arm gently in her lap. The blistered burn on her soft white skin ached; worse, the ugly black letters just below it were a searing, white-hot flame that burned her very soul. Sometimes she would stare at the words etched on her flesh; then she would turn again to gaze tenderly at the innocent child sleeping beside her. "Maybe it is better if you grow up with someone else to rock you, little one." She reached out to touch the tiny hand of Tikvah. "Oh, Leah"—she lowered her head, feeling as though her heart would break—"why did you leave her with me to love and cherish? And now surely they will take her." She brushed persistent tears away with the back of her hand. "Was I ever so tiny, Mama?" she asked quietly. "And did you ever love me as much as I love this little one? Yes. I remember. Then it is good they took you away. Good you did not see. Once I was your Tikvah, wasn't I, Mama? It is better you did not live to see what I have become. Maybe better that Tikvah not ever know . . ."

She rose stiffly from the floor and held her arm at the wrist, studying the mark and the burn. *Only an inch lower, and the kettle would have healed my wound.* She touched the brand and winced. Still holding the arm as though it did not belong to her, she walked slowly to the kitchen and placed the kettle over the small flame of the stove. She stood for a moment with her hand still on the handle until the metal became hot to the touch, then she stepped back and watched until the water suddenly boiled. Steam hissed from the spout and pushed angrily against the lid; drops of water escaped and flung themselves against the stove top, then vanished in little puffs of hot vapor.

Empty teacups, challah and jam still waited on the countertop. Rachel filled the tea strainer with the fresh tea from the pantry of Rabbi Akiva. *Only one inch.* She took the pot holder from its little hook above the sink and reached for the kettle as the water screamed and boiled away. Tikvah woke and cried loudly, protesting the wind and the screeching kettle. For a moment Rachel turned toward the child; then she drew her breath and raised a teacup as if to pour the water. She moved her arm nearer to the spout, feeling the steam reawaken the pain just above the brand. *Nür Für Offizere.* The kettle radiated warmth as she poured the remaining drops of water into the cup. Slowly, as though in a dream, she put the kettle down next to the cup as Tikvah wailed unhappily in the background.

Only one inch lower. "Just a minute, little love," Rachel called. "Only a minute more and Mama will be finished." She hesitated an instant, then snatched the long sharp knife from beside the challah. Its blade gleamed in the lamplight as she placed its tip into the blue flame. *And then the major told me how he had stopped the bleeding of his leg when he was wounded in the field.* The tip of the knife glowed red around the edges. *My soul is an open wound. Nür Für Offizere. Bleeding.* "Only just a moment, Tikvah, and it will be gone," she said as she grasped the knife and held the glowing steel close to the jagged black mark of the S.S. *Courage.* She drew her breath sharply, intent on her purpose; afraid only for an instant. "Mama!" she cried out loud as she held the smoking blade flat against her skin. And then the world spun in darkness around her.

27 Messenger

It was still a cold half hour before sunrise.

"There now." Moshe tucked the message into Shaul's ear. "I may even come to have affection for you"—he patted the dog's ruff—"if you promise not to take my leg off."

"He likes you," said Yacov cheerfully.

Moshe stared down at the cold yellow eyes. "How can you tell?"

"He doesn't take your leg off." Yacov frowned thoughtfully. "You see. I told you he would not have trouble. There are a thousand dogs like him, nu? No one has even noticed."

"I am just happy that he has been going where he was told. I thought perhaps he had been creating a thousand more puppies like himself instead of attending to duty."

"He will see Rachel." Yacov scratched him under his chin. "Many times before I will see my sister again. I wish that I could go too. With him. With you, Rebbe Moshe."

"Then who would be here to receive the messages when we send Shaul out?"

"You will have the radio to talk. You will not need Shaul any longer. I know this."

"Wrong. Send him in as often as you can. He will carry your words to Rachel."

"And tonight when you enter the tunnels, will you . . . carry words to my sister for me? And the love of my heart?"

"And that of your grandfather. And my own love as well."

"Good. Then she will not be alone. I have had much worry for her since we have heard about Leah." His young face flooded with thoughts that seemed to Moshe far too heavy for a child to bear.

"I will tell you this, my young friend." He draped his arm over Yacov's shoulder and lifted his chin. "God has seen Rachel. He has heard our prayers and she is not alone, eh? She is not alone," he repeated. "And now, with the help of God I shall see her and tell her so." He turned to the big dog. "Be true to us now, Shaul. Go straight like an arrow and tell Rachel our secret, eh?" Moshe stood and stepped back as Yacov whispered softly in Shaul's ear, then tapped him lightly on the head and sent him on his way.

Shaul scurried from the steps, this time not stopping in the rain-soaked streets to look back. He ran through the charred remains of the Commerical District and up the road toward Jaffa Gate. Barbed wire and sandbags housed unhappy soldiers who stood their pre-dawn watch beneath dripping umbrellas. Shaul stood for an instant and sniffed the air. Only a few yards from the barricade, a pile of dead dogs blocked the pathway. Dozens of Old City mongrels had been shot through the night, and Shaul's keen nose told him this was not the safe path for a dog to travel. Before the guards even had a chance to glimpse him, he wheeled to the right and trotted easily beneath the massive wall to Zion Gate. Bolts and locks and half a dozen soldiers blocked the way through Zion Gate. Shaul clambered down the slope of the road and furtively moved beyond their view.

Through ancient cemeteries and past long-forgotten Crusader monuments, he ran. When he heard the familiar bleating of sheep, Shaul quickened his pace and raced the sunrise to the Dung Gate, where animals were brought into the Old City marketplace by shepherds each morning.

The constant yapping of sheep dogs and shouts of Bedouin merchants bargaining for top prices greeted

247

Shaul's ears. He moved quickly into the confusion, parting sheep as he ran through the filth of the gate and into the teeming market beyond. Only a few Jihad Moquades stood nearby. They seemed to pay no attention to Shaul as he scrambled past irate camels and bleating sheep.

Carcasses of newly slaughtered sheep hung from hooks inside the butcher shops. A young, strong porter who would have seemed more at home with a rifle slung over his shoulder, pushed a huge wheelbarrow filled with sheep's heads through the crowds of restaurant buyers and early morning meat merchants. A steady stream of blood and muck trickled down the gutter that traced the center of the street. Life inside the Dung Gate was strangely normal.

Shaul slowed his hurried pace and hungrily eyed the scraps of suet being tossed into a large metal container. An ancient Arab butcher whistled happily as he carved the carcass of a lamb, while his assistant wrapped stacks of chops for a portly restaurant buyer. Shaul had learned long before that dignity was the key to begging. He did not skulk or sneak when begging, but rather sat down slowly and watched each move of the butcher's hands as though he were learning the trade. Only a few moments passed before the butcher noticed the big dog sitting patiently on the sticky cobblestones. A quick slice and a flick of the wrist directed a thin slice of fat directly into Shaul's mouth. He caught it effortlessly, then licked his chops contentedly as he waited for more.

"A handsome beast for a jackal!" said the butcher as he directed every other piece of suet into Shaul's mouth. The man seemed to enjoy the one-sided game of catch, at times tossing one piece after another in quick succession to see if the dog would miss. Shaul did not miss, instead swallowing the pieces whole. Occasionally the butcher tossed a piece purposefully too far to the right or to the left of where the dog sat, hoping to make him move from his spot. Shaul did not bother to even look at the fallen booty, but sat steadfastly until the butcher was thoroughly impressed.

"Throw it high. See if he can catch it," said the assistant.

The butcher sliced a thin piece of meat off with the chunk of fat and pitched it a good ten feet above Shaul's head. Shaul watched calmly as the delicacy whirled down and slightly to the left; then he opened his mouth and caught it effortlessly.

His eye having caught sight of the thin red ribbon of flesh attached to the last missile, the portly restaurant buyer stepped forward cursing loudly at the butcher and his assistant, and finally at Shaul. He drew his foot back in a well-aimed kick, and only then did Shaul scurry out of the way and continue contentedly down the noisy stinking marketplace. He belched once, then turned up a street lined with the shops of pot sellers on his way toward the Jewish Quarter. Abandoned crates and overflowing garbage carts littered the once-busy street. Shops and houses where he and Yacov were both known by name were now boarded and deserted. Absent were the small Arab boys who had played stick ball with him and Yacov in this very street. And ahead, rolls of vicious barbed wire blocked his way into the quarter.

Just beyond, Shaul could see the outlines of the Warsaw Compound in the gray light of morning. But there was no way past the barbed barricade that wound layer upon layer across the street. Shaul sniffed the width of the obstruction, lifted his leg briefly, then trotted back the way he had come.

For nearly an hour the dog trotted through the souks of the Arab Quarter, turning up first one alleyway and then another, finding that all the eastern approaches into the Jewish Quarter were blocked and abandoned. On the rooftops of the Great Hurva Synagogue, he saw the faces of men he knew from home. Their eyes gazed steadily down toward the Arab streets. He barked long and loud, but they did not seem to notice him. As he headed north past the deserted Wailing Wall and to-ward the Street of the Chain, instinct warned him to turn and run from the souks where he had been chased the night before. The smell of dead dogs rose once again, strong in his nostrils. Twice he stopped and whined anxiously, looking back over his shoulder. *Yacov had told him to go home. In spite of the danger, the boy had told him.*

Through the stalls of the spice merchants, the scents of those humans who had pursued him drifted. Past the fruit markets, patches of blood stuck to the stones. He followed close on the heels of a man in long black robes, stopping when he stopped to bicker with an old Arab woman over the price of her lemons. Calmly he followed when the man started through the souks again. The scent of his pursuers grew strong again as church domes and minarets loomed above him. He bumped through a thousand bustling legs, keeping his head low and nearly against the robes.

"Hey you!" A voice cried out from the crowd behind him. It was a voice from the darkness of the courtyard the night before. "Monk!" The black robes halted and turned. "Yes, you! Is that your dog?"

Shaul whirled and ran through the crowds, pursued by the sound of running footsteps. Angry curses fol-lowed him as he dashed against legs and beneath the wheels of loaded carts. Only a block away was Haye-hudim Street; a low barricade and a short dash away waited the world he and the boy and the old man had known. And beyond that was his goal. His nails scratched against the stones as he tore past the long building with many doors. Human feet still slapped be-hind him; shouts still chased him. Any moment he ex-pected the angry pop of bullets and the sting of gravel against his skin.

Jumping a wall of upturned garbage carts topped with a thin strand of barbed wire, he left tufts of his heavy coat to mark his trail. And there ahead of him were the sandbags and the face of the large, rough man he had chased from Grandfather's door the day before.

―――――――

Ehud cupped his hands around the hot tin cup of steaming coffee for warmth. It had been a long, dull morning on duty with two Yeshiva students who had heard all of his sea-faring tales at least twice during their weeks together. Moods were gloomy and irritable. Ehud inhaled the steam and sipped slowly as he calculated the hours before he could visit Rachel and the baby Tikvah again. *The tiny baby never tires of hearing my stories,* he thought with satisfaction. That was the beauty of children. They forever begged a story. And though the infant now begged only milk and warmth and dryness, he knew she would one day sit on her uncle Ehud's knee and plead with him for a story. For now, his great gravelly voice seemed to calm her, and the tiny cherub face blinking up calmed him. He remembered his own children squealing with delight as he returned home from a fishing trip and swung them high over his head. *It is good,* he thought, *that there is still room in this world for Jewish children.* He looked up at the garbage cart barricade fifty yards beyond. *At least, with God's help we will make room.*

Suddenly, the large shaggy frame of the dog cleared the barricade at the far end of the street and galloped toward them. Angry Arab voices followed, and the faces of three Jihad Moquades appeared on the opposite side.

"It's the dog you told us about!" shouted Reuven.

Ehud dropped his coffee cup as a Jihad Moquade raised a rifle to his shoulder, aiming it at Shaul. "Run, beast!" he shouted. "Run, jackal!" With only a glance at the now-empty British checkpoint above them, Ehud scrambled for the revolver that lay hidden under the sandbags.

The first round of rifle fire exploded and hit the stones only inches to the right of the dog's shoulder. Shaul stumbled and dodged to the left, as the curses filled the air around the Jihad Moquades. A second Arab pulled the rifle from his friend and took steady aim on the back of Shaul's broad head.

Ehud clambered up the sandbags and cocked the pistol; then holding it steady in both hands he aimed at the cursing Jihad who followed the dog with the barrel of his gun. "Run, dog!" shouted the Yeshiva students. *Too far to shoot with a pistol.* Ehud gently squeezed the trigger as Shaul leaped over a garbage can, only yards from his destination.

The barrel of the rifle exploded at the same instant as Ehud's pistol kicked, hurling a bullet into the wood of the garbage cart.

Tufts of white hair standing up on his head, Ben-Gurion seemed for all the world like the very image of the Wizard of Oz. David smiled and watched the heated exchange between Moshe and the Old Man, who did not take kindly to being contradicted.

"There are a dozen men in better position to carry a radio receiver into the Old City!" The Old Man's face was red, a bright contrast to his white, open-necked shirt.

"None are as qualified as I am," Moshe said quietly. "I know at least part of the way in. Rabbi Lebowitz has drawn maps and diagrams of the rest of the way."

"And when did he last stroll through the sewers? Fifty years ago!"

"And who has been down there to change their course?"

"You are needed here."

"You have Joseph. A dozen others. You have my notes. My suggestions."

"You can save the Old City?"

"You said yourself that not one inch of ground would be taken without a fight. But those inside the walls are losing the will to fight. A small faction of the Orthodox rabbis grows more militant each day. If they

252

sue for peace with the Arab High Committee, we will lose the Jewish Quarter and the western wall. For two thousand years those stones were the only link we had with the land of our fathers. The Old City was our foothold! I grew up there, boss. They know me; they knew my family. I can make a difference."

The Old Man pursed his lips and rested his chin in his hands. He appraised Moshe coolly and was silent for nearly a minute until David coughed loudly and squirmed in his chair. "When I was a kid we used to call this a stare down," he said glibly. "Whoever blinks first loses."

The Old Man smiled slightly, then blinked hard at Moshe. "So. You win, eh?"

"Thank you," Moshe said simply. "At least, I was hoping. We already sent word by way of the dog." He shrugged and smiled.

"You will enter the tunnel through the ancient aqueduct, you say?" he asked. "And how will you reach it without being stopped or apprehended by those men—" He jerked his head toward the window that looked out on the street. "They shadow you everywhere, do they not?"

David sighed and fiddled with the zipper on his flight jacket. "That's where I come in. I've been ditching these guys for days now, you know. I have a plan."

"That is always good. Good plans make miracles, eh?" The Old Man directed his attention to the list on his desk. "And you think one man can carry all this through that maze?"

"I didn't say this will be easy. Only *possible*. The shortwave radio will need to be completely waterproofed. There will undoubtedly be enough dampness that it could be ruined."

"Water is not all you will find, I am sure." Ben Gurion leaned back in his chair. "God go with you. For the sake of His Holy City, may you find success."

Holding the requisition tightly in his hand, Moshe

walked quickly down the drab hallway, with David close at his heels.

"Man, you've got some kind of brass, buddy." David thumped him stoutly on the back. "How'd you know he'd let you be the one to go in there?"

Moshe raised his eyebrows and grinned knowingly. "I spoke to Ben-Gurion's boss about it this morning before we sent Shaul."

"Huh? Ben-Gurion's *what*?"

"Never mind." Moshe threw his head back in a laugh. "Thank you, Lord." He touched his hand to his forehead in salute.

The warehouse of the Jewish Agency had always held a wealth of miscellaneous supplies for the Jews of Jerusalem and Palestine. U.S. Army Surplus tents were mingled with British cots and spades. Flashlights and snow boots were heaped in boxes next to one another. Canned C-rations were covered by blue stocking caps and piles of woolen socks that disappeared from the storeroom at an alarming rate. Medical supplies occupied a special closet all their own; in the very back, beneath boxes of gauze, two bulky shortwave radios were stashed.

"These are German," explained the heavy-jowled warehouse supervisor. "Left behind after El Alamein. One of our fellows stole them from the English and now here they are. Pure gold, these days. Pure gold."

Moshe nodded. "We'll keep the other here?" he asked.

The man shook his head and gazed at the gray-green metal boxes. "Doubtful. The British could locate it, you know. Best in a private residence. Needs an antenna, though. The fellows in Tel Aviv run theirs through a clothesline and hang their laundry on it to dry. Very effective." He rooted around for a coil of wire, then thumped it down on top of one of the radios. "I just don't know what you're going to do about the batteries. They won't last forever, you know." He studied the list as David knelt to examine the radio. It was oversized, broader than Moshe's back; it would be difficult to carry on the aluminum framing of the Army Surplus packs. Difficult—but with luck, not impossible.

"So, how are we going to waterproof this baby?" David frowned.

The man thought for a minute. "Body bags. Quite resistant to moisture and muck, you know. Now this way, if you please." He walked briskly across the warehouse to a mountain of rubber boots. "You're about size 11, I would guess."

Moshe pulled a boot from the stack and peered into the interior looking for a size. "Or 10??/??."

"They're mismatched, anyway," shrugged the man. "You might as well start trying them on. There are only so many sizes available, and none of them has a mate." He shrugged at Moshe's wondering stare. "We got them cheap."

As Moshe rummaged for matching rubber boots, David disappeared for a moment around a pile of mattresses, then returned looking for all the world like a fly. "Gas mask," he said, tapping the black rubber mask that covered his face. "Where you're going you may need it."

"The Old Man is right," Moshe said gloomily, tossing a too-small left boot back onto the mountain. "One man cannot carry all this in."

"So don't try." David slipped the mask off. "Get yourself and the radio in. Request what you need and I'll sail over and drop it to you."

Moshe shook his head in amusement. "I thought we already decided you would get yourself killed that way."

David shrugged and playfully slipped the mask on. "Is this a worried face? I ask you, do I look worried?"

Moshe eyed the giant fly-like creature cavorting before him. "David, have you ever heard the word *mutche*?"

Sure. Granddad used it when he talked about my grandmother."

"Yes. Yiddish. It means to nag, nu? To torture. Make yourself useful, will you?"

"What do you think I'm doing? You won't find another gas mask in the place."

"Logical." Moshe held up two boots to match for size. "There hasn't been poisoned gas around since World War I."

"Are you going into the sewer or what?" David protested. "Take the gas mask!"

"That's not on the list!" said the warehouse supervisor.

Stealthily David wrapped the mask into a long coil of rope and packed it onto the backpack beneath C-rations, Spam, small flashlight, and a canteen of water.

All the supplies were then neatly arranged in the black rubber body bag and loaded onto an Italian Army surplus stretcher.

In full view of the men who had tailed Moshe and David so faithfully, the stretcher was loaded onto a commandeered Red Cross ambulance backed neatly up to the warehouse entrance. David and Moshe, in the meantime, hurried out the front door of the Jewish Agency offices and drove slowly home, grateful to see the grim faces of their escorts in the rearview mirror as the ambulance slipped quickly away to its destination.

Like an aged buzzard, the old muezzin watched the drama calmly as it unfolded before him. The crack and flare of gunshots had pulled his weary eyes to the bleeding dog. And as the very men who had fought to save the animal now cowered at his snapping jaws, the muezzin laughed loudly. Only the wind could hear his laughter, but surely Allah himself shared his amusement.

The dog stumbled and fell, then pulled himself painfully toward the steps of the apartment as the three Jews cooed to him and tried to get near him. The big, burly Jew drew the revolver and raised it now toward the head of the animal. Then he lowered the barrel of the gun and tugged his beard as he studied the drops of blood on the cobblestones.

I will wait, sighed the muezzin. *Allah rewards the patient of spirit. I will watch and wait. The woman of Gerhardt will come now.*

The big Jew handed the gun to his young comrade, then after one more look at the dog, he turned and trotted awkwardly down the alleyway.

He will come back with the woman of Gerhardt. And I will be rewarded for my faithfulness. The muezzin blew his nose loudly, then stepped back to escape the cold wind that had sprung up. *Allah rewards the patient.*

The creak of the rocking chair matched the slow deep breaths of Rachel as she fought against the pain in her forearm. Gently she cradled Tikvah in her good arm and held the bottle carefully with fingers that almost refused to move. The muscles in her arm and shoulder rebelled against the agony of the deep, open wound. Rachel's head throbbed and dark semicircles hung beneath her eyes, her white skin now ashen and ghostlike. She spoke to the baby in a voice etched with strain. Twice through the morning hours she had played the soothing music of Brahms on the phonograph, but now the needle scratched and thumped at the end of the record. Rachel did not have the strength to rise and start the music again.

The window over the kitchen sink revealed a flat, gray sky. Once again the heavens were cheerless and cold, like the smoke above Auschwitz. *I never said goodbye.* She listened to the contented sighs of Tikvah and studied the bright blue eyes that blinked happily and gazed up at her. *They will come soon and take you from me, little one. Surely a righteous woman will take you, and someday perhaps we will pass in the street. Perhaps they will tell you that I am a bad woman, and that you must not speak to me. And so I will say this to you now, little Tikvah, and pray that somehow your heart remem-*

bers. Rachel propped the bottle against her and put her thumb inside the tiny hand, smiling gently as the fist squeezed around it. "Perhaps your heart will remember," she said aloud. "And though you may not speak to me, I will pray for you each day. God will hear my prayers if I pray for you and not for myself. If ever the sky above you is gray and cheerless, if ever you feel alone, may your heart remember what joy you have given to me. And how I love you." She wiped a trickle of milk from the corner of Tikvah's mouth. "Remember you are loved."

For a long time she sat, unable to take her eyes from the sweet face. Suddenly a loud, insistent knocking interrupted her thoughts. She frowned and touched the baby's face again. Fists slammed against the door. "I will not say goodbye."

She raised her eyes to the gray sky and put Tikvah over her shoulder. "God, if you are there behind the clouds, hear me. Hear me, God." Her voice shook. "I cannot say goodbye."

"Rachel!" came the booming voice. "Rachel! Open the door! It is me! It is Ehud!"

Rachel clutched Tikvah to her and covered her face with her hand for a moment. "Ehud?" she gasped.

"Yes! Yes! Open the door!" returned the muffled demand.

Covering Tikvah's head with a blanket, Rachel half-stumbled to unlatch the bolts of the door, opening it just a crack and stepping back as Ehud burst into the room. Beads of perspiration hung on his forehead and he panted heavily.

"They are coming for Tikvah," she said dully, taking in the agitation on his grizzly features.

"Tikvah?" He gasped. "Who will take Tikvah?"

"Have you come to warn me?" she asked softly.

Ehud blinked at her in bewilderment. "By the Eternal, Rachel!" he cried. "You are not well, girl. Your face is so pale. Are you ill?" His eyes fell on the burn on her forearm. His face a mask of concern, he took Tikvah from Rachel and ushered her to a chair. "What have you done? How did this happen?"

"An accident. The tea kettle," Rachel replied lamely.

"This must have attention. A doctor. Such a deep burn." He patted the baby gently and put her in her cradle where she wailed a protest. "Quiet, little one. Your mama is hurt."

Rachel leaned her head against her hand in misery. "Have you come to warn me?"

"Warn you?" boomed Ehud, genuinely puzzled. He rummaged through the cupboards and drawers, looking for an ointment for the burn. "Warn you? You are delirious, poor girl. Small wonder." He triumphantly pulled a small bottle of olive oil from the cupboard. "I came to tell you. The dog." He poured a small amount onto the burn. "The beast who tried to eat me yesterday. The one by whom we sent the message to Moshe. He was faithful! He was a faithful brute!"

Rachel winced and drew a sharp breath. "You mean Shaul?"

Ehud's face lit up and he sat back on his haunches. "Yes. The very same. He returned this morning among flying bullets and the curse of the Arabs."

"Did he bring word? A message?" Rachel felt some strength return in her excitement.

"I cannot say. He lies bleeding. Shot."

"Dead?"

"Not yet. A snarling angry beast he is. He lies at the door of your grandfather's house and will let no one near him. I thought perhaps you—but you are ill. We shall have to shoot him to get the message, I fear."

"No!" Rachel shouted, getting up quickly and stumbling to her shawl.

"You cannot—" Ehud began.

"Stay with Tikvah. Stay with her, Ehud. Keep her safe for me. Don't let anyone take her, do you understand?" Her face white with pain, she pulled her sleeve down over the wound and wrapped her shawl tightly around her. Without a word she slipped out the door, clicking it quietly behind her.

The cold of the morning stung her cheeks and filled her lungs, reviving her. The two guards from the Yeshiva stood at the stair railing looking down to where Shaul lay still.

"Is he dead yet?" one asked as Rachel hurried toward them.

"He is quiet."

Out of breath Rachel grasped the rail and looked down at the big dog. He lay across the threshold of the door, his fur matted at the neck from the flow of blood.

"Shaul!" Rachel cried.

Almost imperceptively, the dog blinked, then opened his eyes at the sound of her voice.

"Shaul!" she cried again. She hurried down the steps as Shaul whined once, then tried to struggle to his feet and fell back against the door. Blood dripped freely from his wound.

"Beware of the beast. He is vicious," one of the men called after her.

"Shaul?" Rachel asked softly as she knelt beside him. Pain and grateful recognition filled his eyes and he bumped her outstretched hand with his nose; then he whined and licked her fingers.

Rachel stroked his head, careful to avoid his wound. "Poor Shaul. Poor dear fellow." She pulled Grandfather's iron key from the ribbon around her neck, fumbling as she unlocked the door.

"Is there a message?" shouted one of the men.

"Quick," Rachel called to them as they hovered on the top step. "Help me move him inside."

The two frightened guards looked doubtfully at one another and remained on the step.

"He won't hurt you! Help me!" Rachel shouted.

Slowly they descended the steps and cautiously lifted Shaul into the cold apartment as Rachel lit the lamp and shoved matches into the hand of the smaller of the two.

"He'll die," the man stated flatly.

"Light the Primus. He needs warmth."

"Get the message from him so we can go."

"Shut up and light the stove," Rachel snapped, surprised at the force of her words. The man obeyed as she held the light and studied the wound that passed from the back of Shaul's neck and out through a larger wound in the front just above his right shoulder. "The bullet has passed through. He is dying from loss of blood." Rachel grabbed a heavy wool blanket from Grandfather's iron bed and wrapped it around Shaul. Then she pulled a flannel sheet down and, wrapping it around her hand, shoved her fingers into the wound. Red stained the fabric, then gradually lessened its flow as she hovered over Shaul and pressed against the hole.

"You must not die," she said softly. "Remember Yacov, Shaul. Remember you are loved and needed, and live, eh?"

The Primus sputtered to life and the two men stood awkwardly by as Rachel continued to work on the dog. "There is a sewing kit beneath the bed," she instructed, afraid to move from the side of the big dog.

The large Yeshiva student adjusted his spectacles and knelt down, pulling the brown cardboard box from beneath the frame. "Here it is." He stepped forward and stumbled, dropping the box. It tumbled to the floor, spilling precious letters and the photograph onto the stone floor. "I am sorry!" The young man scrambled to pick up the mess.

"Never mind that," Rachel said. "The sewing kit." The yellowed photograph fell near her knee. Faces smiled up at her. Young brothers. Mother. Father. The beautiful girl who was Rachel when she was young and fresh. And the tiny baby on Mama's lap. Rachel gazed at the hands of her mother, holding the little one so gently. "Remember you are loved," she said softly, thinking of Tikvah. "Remember the baby and live." She stroked Shaul. "And *you*," she said. "Remember Yacov and live."

She took scissors from the ragged basket and began to clip away the hair around Shaul's wounds as the two men shrugged and slipped quietly out the door. For several hours she worked over the dog, bathing the wounds and dousing them first in Grandfather's cognac, then stitching them, careful to leave a small hole for the wounds to drain.

When at last he whimpered and licked her hand, she smiled and sat back, weary from her long vigil. "If you truly are as mean as you would have us believe, Shaul, you will not die." She had forgotten for a time the pain in her arm—and in her soul. Slowly she climbed onto the bed and thought of Tikvah in the gentle care of Ehud. *She will be safe. He will let no harm come to her.* Then she closed her eyes and slept.

28 The Plan

Light rain dripped down the windowpanes of Howard's study. Ellie tiptoed as she carried the tray of cheese sandwiches and steaming coffee to the broad desk where Grandfather had sat between Howard and Moshe for most of the afternoon. Before them, spread out like a place mat, was a cotton square of white cloth that contained the final sketching of the map of underground Jerusalem.

None of the men looked up from their work as Ellie wordlessly left the room. Moshe flipped through the pages of a dog-eared copy of the works of Flavius Josephus. "I have read this passage about the final assault against the Temple and the caverns below it that were ancient even then, but it had not occurred to me . . ."

"Josephus," Grandfather mused. "A Jew who knew the passages, eh? Back to the first century."

"His work gives us valuable information," Moshe agreed, pointing to the woodcutting of the battering rams slamming against the Temple gates. "A Jew. A rebel against the Romans in the first century. He loved life and in the end joined the Romans in their conquest." Moshe tapped the page with his index finger and began to read the ancient words:

This Simon, during the siege of Jerusalem, was in the Upper City; but when the Roman Army had gotten within the walls, and were laying the city waste, he then took the most faithful of his friends with him, and let himself and them all down into a certain subterraneous cavern that was not visible above ground. He looked up, his eyes studying Grandfather's sketches. "The cavern must be here, then."

"Indeed," said the rabbi. "Its height is well over thirty feet from the floor to roof. It is all hewn stone, and when you come to it you will know you are near. Just beyond is a long, broken pillar that spans a deep chasm. It must have been a well. I dropped a torch once and watched as it fell and finally the light went out. When you cross the pillar, there is a dangerous climb that you must make, and you will find yourself at the top of an archway marked by a cross. Do not climb to the right of the archway. The earth will slide away under you. Just beneath the cross you will see a small opening." Grandfather eyed Moshe's broad shoulders. "It will be difficult for you to pass through. But from there you will crawl until you come to the ladder. This will take you finally to the grate." Grandfather took the pen from the small bottle of indelible ink. "It is here"—he marked the cloth with an X—"that you are most likely to lose your way. The tunnel was blown just beyond the cavern."

"But why?" Howard asked, incredulous that the find had not been reported in any archaeological journals. "There must be a wealth of archaeological information there."

"Unhappily," sighed Grandfather, "it was I who first found the cavern. It was, indeed, full of artifacts. I gathered them and sold many, not revealing my source. Later, when the little boy became lost, I regretted what I had found. The Englishmen had gone away by then. After a week of searching for the lost child, we knew that he had died somewhere in the tunnels. Jew, Christian, Arab—we all live together in the Old City as neighbors, nu? We all love our children. We knew that there was a great danger to them in these caverns. What boy will not explore a forbidden tunnel if dared by his friends? And so we took a collection—Jews and Arabs. And we hired a young Turk, a madman, to descend and block the tunnel forever. He, too, was killed. Then the grate was installed, only to be opened in the event of life or death. How could we know then what those words would mean to the Jewish Quarter fifty years later? Since the time of the destruction of the Temple, there has always been some remnant of our people in the shadow of the wall. Who could guess that without this tunnel, that might all end for us?"

His face clouded. "There are some among the Arabs, the old ones, who also know of these tunnels. But that is not where the danger lies, Moshe." He gazed steadily at the face of the young man beside him. "Beware of the tunnels themselves. They will whisper to you, they will deceive you and lead you where they will. In the end, if you listen to their murmurings, you will lose your life. Mark your path that you may retrace your steps if you become lost in the maze. Beware of the ancient cisterns and wells, for they are deep, nu? And often hidden by only a thin layer of debris."

Howard rubbed his bald dome and pursed his lips. "Moshe, I want you to rethink this."

"No." Moshe shook his head firmly. "I appreciate your concern, Howard, but . . ."

"You need another man with you, Moshe. Someone to help. To go into that place alone . . ."

Moshe smiled and narrowed his eyes knowingly. "You're still the archaeologist, aren't you, my friend? No doubt there is a lifetime of material to study down there. But I am only passing through."

"You must admit, it sounds intriguing. I'd like to go along, Moshe. After all, I managed quite well on our little jaunt to Bethlehem."

"This is different."

"Two heads are better than one. What if you get into trouble? Your wounds have not completely healed, and—"

"Howard, you're over fifty. You have heard the descriptions of Rabbi Lebowitz. This is a difficult journey even for a young man."

"I have to help in some way!"

"Then pray. I will not be alone, Howard. I believe that."

Dark evening blew in with the wind from the north. Alone in his room, Moshe pored over the charts and written records of the first intrepid explorers of underground Jerusalem. Silently he recalculated the length of rope he needed and the equipment required for the first treacherous descent into the earth outside the Old City walls. Ancient stone vaults, cisterns, and sewers formed a complicated stairway nearly 1,400 feet long into the heart of the Old City—hopefully to Rachel.

He closed his eyes as he remembered the skepticism of Ben-Gurion and Howard. The way was difficult enough for two able-bodied men working together. He had only one good arm, and he would be alone. Doubt surfaced and spun around him. Had he fallen victim to his own foolish desires to stand beside Rachel once again? If so, his heart had been victorious over his mind, it seemed, and there was no turning back. *If I am a fool, dear God, still you know my path. You have written down my every footstep, eh? Go before me as a light. And until I am near enough to touch her myself, put your arms around my Rachel.*

A soft knocking on his door brought him back to the small room and the charts in front of him. "Yes?" he answered the knock.

Grandfather opened the door and stepped in. "I am disturbing your study?" he asked quietly.

"Just a few last-minute thoughts." Moshe gathered up the stack of papers on the bed.

"Well, yes." The old man tugged at his beard and reached into his pocket. "It occurred to me that possibly one of two things could happen tonight, nu? Maybe you will not make it into the Old City, or maybe, then again, you will."

"Logical possibilities, Rebbe Lebowitz," Moshe grinned. "And?"

"So. If you die tonight I wanted to tell you what a fine young man I think you are, eh?" The old man winked. "*But* if you should happen to live, then perhaps you will be my grandson. In which case I should tell you 'Mazel Tov' now. I certainly will not be at the wedding unless I follow you through the hole. So, here." He stretched out his hand and pressed a white envelope into Moshe's palm. "You might need this."

Moshe studied the scrawled handwriting on the outside of the fresh white envelope. Hebrew letters spelled Rachel's name beneath the Polish words, *Beloved daughter of Zion*. "What is it?" Moshe asked, puzzled by the smile on the rabbi's face.

"If she should say *no* to your proposal, young man, give her the envelope. And have a happy life together, nu?" He started out the door, then paused and turned, frowning thoughtfully. "My prayers go with you, Moshe. Surely God on His throne has seen the depth of your love."

"Thank you . . . Grandfather." Moshe tucked the letter into the oilcloth along with the charts and maps.

"So. The others are leaving. David and Ellie. They are going to dinner at one of those fancy places where men and women dance together! Imagine! Such a world!" Grandfather shook his head.

"Tell them I'll be right out, will you?" Moshe laced up his field boots and tucked his package of charts into his shirt front.

———

Dressed for an evening on the town, David and Ellie waited by the darkened window of the front room. Howard peeked out through a slit in the draperies. "They're still there."

"What if they don't follow David and Ellie?" Yacov asked, crowding in front of Howard to stare at the men in the black sedan across the street. "Will they follow Moshe?"

"Come on, kid." David slipped his arm around Ellie's shoulders. "If you had a choice between following a gorgeous girl or Moshe, what would it be?"

Yacov blushed and looked up at Grandfather for direction. Grandfather shrugged and chuckled as Yacov answered. "Who is the better cook?"

"Don't worry about it." David laughed at the look on Ellie's face. "These guys don't know she can't cook. They'll follow us, Yacov. At least the two in the car will. It's that other guy I'm worried about."

"He came back?" Moshe stepped to the window to search for the shadowy figure on the street corner.

"Like clockwork. As soon as the sun went down. I don't know if he's with these other two or not. Just watch your rear, buddy."

"Be careful, Moshe." Ellie looked as though she might cry for a moment. Then she embraced him and kissed him lightly. "Give her my love," she said quietly. "And your love, too."

Moshe gazed at her with warm brown eyes. "Little sister," he said, feeling the reality of their farewell. Then he shook David's hand. "God go with you both."

"Tomorrow," David said quietly. "During the Muslims' morning prayers, go to the Square Tiferet Yerushalayim. Got it? Good luck, buddy."

Moshe put his arm around Yacov as they watched David open the door of Howard's Plymouth for Ellie. Ellie bent to enter the car, then, as though she felt the eyes of Yacov and Moshe, she turned for a moment and smiled, raising her hand in tender goodbye. David closed the door after her, then loaded his flight bag and Ellie's camera cases in the trunk of the car.

"Will they be all right?" Yacov asked in a small voice as the Plymouth roared away.

"Of course." Moshe patted him on the back and stared after the red taillights. "I have flown with that crazy American. He is a very brave and clever fellow, Yacov. He gathers bird eggs from the treetops without any effort at—" He paused mid-sentence as the black sedan started and followed after them. The man in the shadows did not move; instead, he crossed his arms and leaned against the lamp post. *So this is the one I have to get past. English? American? Or Arab?*

"Well, I'll just have to make the best of it." Moshe buttoned his rain slicker over the warm, fleece-lined jacket he wore. "It will take me the better part of an hour to make it to the entrance of the tunnel. I can't wait any longer."

"What will you do if he spots you? If he follows?" Howard asked, glancing out at the man who waited in the street below.

Moshe frowned and tucked a long bayonet into his boot top. "I'll do whatever I have to do."

Howard nodded and shook Moshe's outstretched hand. "I'll go out the front and walk a ways up the street. Maybe that will pull his attention enough ... Good luck." He shook Moshe's outstretched hand and nodded curtly, harnessing the emotion he felt.

"Oh, Rebbe Moshe!" Yacov cried, clasping his small arms around Moshe's waist. "Please, please don't let them kill you!"

Gently Moshe pulled himself free from Yacov's embrace. The old rabbi took the sobbing boy by the shoulders. He motioned for Moshe to slip away as he spoke in quiet tones to Yacov, "Remember the story of King David, Yacov—as written in the second book of Samuel, nu? He sent one of his men to climb up the water shaft and enter the walls of Jerusalem to smite the Jebusites. And what is the rest of the story? Tell me, boy." He lifted Yacov's trembling chin.

Yacov sniffed and wiped his nose on his sleeve. "The city was so strong that the Jebusites said even the blind and the lame could defend it." He sniffed again, enjoying the memory of one of his favorite stories. "But Joab climbed up the shaft and entered the city through the well. And then he became captain and chief of the king's armies and David took Zion for his capital," he finished, the tears diminishing.

The sound of the back door clicking shut caused him to look down the hall to where Moshe had slipped quietly away. Grandfather embraced Yacov, holding him close and stroking his head. "Perhaps this is the same shaft Joab scaled, Yacov. And he won the city for the king, eh? David did not weep for him as he went. He only prayed and believed. Our Rebbe Moshe is a mighty man of valor too, is he not? And so we will pray for him." He brushed the tears from his own eyes. "And so we will pray."

29   Betrayal

Lightning flashed above the mountains of Moab and thunder rolled down to Jerusalem like a distant artillery. Along King George Avenue a strong, cold wind tore at the hedges and bent the saplings almost double. Moshe looked back over his shoulder at the rapidly approaching storm. The lights of the King David Hotel and the YMCA building sparkled and winked. Ahead and to the left, atop a small knoll, the giant Montefiore Windmill marked the beginning of the Valley of Hinnom. Huge blades spun in the darkness and gears moaned like a tormented monster as Moshe passed beneath it. Beyond lay Mount Zion and David's Tomb, a rocky, creviced landscape that Moshe knew like the creases on his own hand. The wall of the Old City loomed above that, lined, Moshe knew, by Arab warriors whose billowing robes only half-concealed their ancient Turkish and German rifles. Their eyes searched for any movement in the valley below.

The flash of lightning moved closer now and the thunder boomed just beyond Jerusalem. Moshe scrambled into a gully, grateful that the searing flash of lightning caused the watchmen on the walls to look away from where he moved.

The smell of imminent rain countered the rank odor of sewage coming from the murky water flowing in the open ditch. Reeds and swamp grass bowed against the force of the approaching storm, while tall palm trees rocked violently like chained lions trying to escape their prison.

Moshe climbed over a succession of boulders, descending deeper into the ragged valley as he avoided

271

the road. Above him, the lights of a British patrol car crept along beside the wall.

Suddenly the hair on his head and arms bristled. He threw himself flat as lightning cracked to the ground, splitting a palm tree just outside the wall. Moshe shielded his eyes against the flash, but in the instant of light, etched on his eye was the furtive movement of a man scrambling down the face of the hill after him. Lightning split the blackened sky three times in rapid succession as Moshe strained to see his pursuer against the white glare of the colorless landscape. The man moved in the strobe light like a character in some old-time silent movie. Moshe crouched behind his boulder and pulled the bayonet from his foot as thunder shook the ground around him.

Fifty yards behind him the silhouette of a tall, lean man bobbed and jerked over the rough terrain. Twice he stumbled and slid down the embankment, his eyes alternating between studying his precarious path and searching the gloom ahead for Moshe. Again and again lightning tore the curtain of darkness. *If I move he will see me,* thought Moshe, *just as I have seen him.* He fingered the cold blade of the bayonet. *And yet he is a man, as I am a man. Still, he will kill me unless I strike first. Then who will take my place? And what will become of Rachel?* He steeled himself against his doubts. Never had he killed a man with his own hands before, never close enough to see his enemy's eyes or feel the blade scrape against hard muscle and bone. He watched as the sky lit up once again behind his pursuer. *How awkward he seems, uncertain of his footsteps. And yet how determined to chase me down. Turn back, fellow, or these will be your last heartbeats. Turn back.*

Still the man came on with dogged determination. He paused once by the edge of the rank stream, his head was raised as though he were sniffing the air. The rain came suddenly, hitting him full in the face, causing him to tuck his head against the deluge. Moshe clung to the face of the boulder, grateful for the rain slicker he wore, but unwilling to move even enough to pull the hood over his head. His hair clung to his face and water dripped down his neck as he waited for the man to come alongside.

Not a full minute passed before the sound of sliding feet approached from just above him. He could hear the heavy breathing of his pursuer only a few yards away. *Go back, or you are a dead man.* Head and shoulder appeared in the shadows beneath Moshe's ambush. The man paused again and listened, his eyes scanning the horizon as he hoped for another burst of lightning to illuminate the bleak hillside. Then he lowered his head again and started forward. Bayonet in his right hand, Moshe sprang onto the man's back, grasping him around the neck and pulling him backward onto the ground. The man shrieked and fought back, elbowing Moshe hard in the stomach as they fell together. Moshe slammed his struggling adversary hard against a rock and raised his arm to plunge the sharp knife into his heart.

"Moshe!" the man cried in a half-strangled voice. Lightning flashed beyond them, and in that instant Moshe recognized the frightened face of Captain Luke Thomas, his eyes riveted to the raised blade of the bayonet. Realizing how near he had come to killing Luke, Moshe threw the knife, sending it clattering off the embankment and onto the rocks below.

Angrily he grasped Luke by his collar and shouted at him over the din of the pouring rain. "You idiot! Do you know how close I came to—"

"I was waiting," Luke tried breathlessly to explain. "Your house was being watched. Telephone tapped. The fellows followed David; then Howard came out and told me where you were going, what you are up to. Moshe"—he struggled to free himself from Moshe's grip—"I came to help."

"You were almost a dead man!" Moshe shook him again.

"And so I may still be, old chap, if you don't let me up out of the muck."

Slowly, Moshe released his grip and sat back, sighing heavily. "I thought you were . . ." He helped Luke stand. "Well, I didn't know who you were, but I was bent on killing you."

"You mustn't fire until you see the whites of your enemy's eyes. Or so says Rudyard Kipling, anyway. Come on, then. Hurry up, or they'll spot us." He jerked his head at the wall. "They're thick up there, the Mufti's men. We'd make an easy target." He scrambled off deeper into the gully and this time Moshe followed *him*.

Rivulets of water streamed down creases in the face of the valley. The trail became more slippery with every step. "How did you find me?" Moshe shouted to Luke.

"Followed my instincts." He patted his pocket. "And a little map Howard sketched for me. I figured if I didn't find you along the way, I could catch up with you at the shaft." The officer's heavy coat flapped in the wind, and Moshe thought of all Luke had risked to follow him. "You'll never make it alone, my friend," Luke said. "David is off leading British agents astray and Howard is too old. You need my help. You're still recuperating, even though that arm feels pretty strong." He rubbed his neck ruefully. "And you're only one man. I won't take no for an answer."

"Did it get too boring for you in ordnance?" asked Moshe as they picked their way cautiously down the side of a steep ravine.

"I happen to believe in what you're doing. Remember, I have spent a bit of time in the Old City. And I've heard how bad it's getting for the Haganah in there. If I can't help you get through the wall, and *they*"—he looked to the top of the craggy wall beyond—"won't let you *over* the wall, then there is only one thing left to do. I will help you *under* the wall."

Somehow Moshe felt a tremendous sense of relief as Luke took the lead and scrambled up the other side of an embankment past the Tomb of David. "You're a fool, Luke. I might have killed you. If your people catch you, you'll be branded a traitor and hanged. But I'm glad you're along. For the fellowship of it." He grinned. "If we do not hang together, we will no doubt be hanged together, eh?"

Just beyond the tomb of David and Mount Zion, the road wound upward in a series of switchbacks. Above them the remains of Rachel's bus lay like the bones of a long-dead dinosaur on the side of the hill. Armored transport lights gleamed as a British vehicle made its way slowly toward them. "Get down!" Luke shouted. "It's the relief guards for Zion Gate!"

Both men huddled in a shallow rain-filled ditch beside the road as the engine whined slowly toward them. Lightning illuminated the eerie scene again and again as the vehicle droned closer to them. "The ditch is not deep enough," Moshe said quietly. He pressed himself tight against the bank and prayed that his body would melt into the stones.

"Your tunnel will feel like a stroll along the Strand compared to this." Luke wiped the water and sweat from his face. "I am nearly ready," he whispered, "to ask the mountains to cover me."

The transport lumbered nearer, shifting gears only a few feet from where they huddled. Then it moaned on, taking no notice of the conspirators.

"Cross now!" Luke dashed across the muddy road and rolled into the ditch opposite. Moshe followed an instant later, tumbling in after him. "It's a good thing I lost my cast in the Jaffa bombing," he muttered, "or I'd surely lose it now!"

The hillside was dotted with tombstones. Crusaders, Jews, Christians, and Muslims slept side by side beneath the double gate that had been walled up so many centuries before.

"The entrance to the tunnel is almost directly in line with the Golden Gate," Moshe explained as they moved quickly from tombstone to tombstone. "The equipment should be stashed at the bottom of the culvert."

"Where the sewage from Silvan empties? Good choice. I don't know many men who would want to search there."

Cautiously, they crossed a low ridge that dropped steeply into a culvert where the road crossed three huge pipes that formed a bridge. The stench rose and fell with the wind. Moshe slid down the embankment, tucking his slicker beneath him and using his feet to brake a slide into the muck. He pulled a small flashlight from his pocket and beamed it near the edge of the bridge. There, half-hidden by broken reeds, lay a neatly packed bundle. Tied securely to it was an enormous coil of rope and a grappling hook.

"Well done, lads," Luke smiled and followed after Moshe, helping him shoulder the pack. Then he untied the heavy coil of rope and draped it over his own shoulder. "Lead on!" He smiled and clapped Moshe on the shoulder.

A crash of thunder jolted Rachel into wakefulness. "Tikvah!" she cried, sitting up with a start. For a moment she looked around the room in confusion; then the pain in her arm reminded her of Yehudit and the night before. *Tikvah is safe with Ehud.* She listened to the ragged breathing of Shaul. *The wound. I stitched the wound.* She glanced down at him, certain that he had not moved. Only then did she remember the reason Shaul had run the gauntlet of Arab rifle fire. *The message. Moshe has sent him with a message.*

She climbed from the bed and knelt beside Shaul. He opened his eyes and gazed soulfully at her as she gently probed his ear for the lipstick cylinder. "This small thing is what you risked your life for. And I had nearly forgotten about it," she said, removing the tape and twisting the lid off to reveal yellow notepaper rolled tightly and crammed inside. Rachel pulled it free with trembling hands, suddenly aware that only a few short hours before, Moshe had touched the paper she now held. On the outside of the paper she recognized his familiar scrawl.

Rachel Lubetkin. The note was only for her eyes. Excitement filled her as she unfolded each layer of the note.

Tears clouded her vision and she laughed aloud as she read the cramped words before her.

My Darling Rachel:
    What joy God has given to my heart today! You are alive! All of us are well. Grandfather is here with Yacov at the home of Howard Moniger. All send their fondest love. In the apartment of your grandfather, behind the mirror above the washstand, there is a loose stone. Take the key and go to the women's mikveh beneath Nissan Bek. Wait there. Help is coming tonight. Greetings to all my brothers. With all my heart I pray that I may soon see your face once again, my dearest. Remember you are loved. Moshe.

"Remember you are loved," she repeated softly as she pressed the letter against her heart. She closed her eyes and saw his face, felt his hand gently touch her cheek. "Oh, Moshe, how can it be? How can it be that you could love me?" she cried. Her eager eyes scanned the letter again and again; then she looked up to the rickety washstand and the blotched mirror that hung crookedly above it. She bent down and touched the shaggy coat of Shaul. "Thank you, my friend," she said quietly. "Thank you."

She stood before the mirror for a long moment, gazing in wonder at the weary face that looked back at her. Like missing pieces in a puzzle, the flaking silver left dark spots on the face in the mirror. She turned and looked at the young girl in the picture who smiled serenely back at her. She smiled at the woman in the mirror, and the image smiled back at her, but the pieces were still missing, the doubt still in her eyes.

"How can it be, Moshe," she asked again, "that you could love me?"

She took the small mirror from the nail and laid it face down on the bed next to the picture of her family. Her fingers probed the stones, searching for loose mortar, until at last a small round stone jarred free in her hand. She gripped it tightly and pulled, sending it clattering to the floor. She peered inside the dark hole, unable to see what, if anything, was hidden within it. Moving quickly to the lamp and holding it close, she probed inside. Her hand closed around a small velvet bag of coins with the Hebrew letters scrawled on a note with the name, *Yacov*. A few slips of paper tumbled out next, and a round gold band, her grandmother's wedding ring. In the very back, a long iron key rested against the stones. She drew it out and read the writing of a note wrapped around its handle. *Pikuach Nefesh*, said the words. *Life or death*. She clutched the key to her. "Life or death," she repeated.

Rachel tucked the blanket tightly around Shaul, then checked the Primus stove. "I will be back for you, old friend," she whispered to the dog. "In the meantime, stay alive for me, eh?" She shut and locked the door, then ran quickly up the stairs and into the darkened street. It was only a few twisting blocks to the Nissan Bek Synagogue, but the wind whistled and howled around her, blowing her skirts and pushing her back with strong and stubborn hands.

She lowered her head and pushed back against the unfriendly bursts. *Life or death*. She gripped the key to her and broke into a slow jog. *Help is coming tonight*. Rachel glanced up at the heavy black sky. *When tonight? Am I too late? Did I linger too long?* Fighting against her own weakness and the fresh pain that throbbed in her arm, she climbed the steps of the Street of the Stairs. She braced herself against the rough stones of the buildings that lined the way. Once she stumbled, catching herself before she fell. Ahead of her the lights of the synagogue shone brightly, glistening and winking in the wind-scrubbed air. The colors of the stained-glass windows beckoned to her. *Coming to-*

night. Women's mikveh. Key. Pikuach Nefesh. Struggling for breath she pressed on, never stopping to wonder at the cadre of black-cloaked rabbis who walked ahead of her up the steps and into the building.

As she ran up the steps they stepped back from her and stared blankly at her anxious face. She smiled, attempting to straighten her windblown hair. A look of contempt crossed the face of a young rabbi who blocked her way into the lobby of the synagogue.

"You have come as a witness on your own behalf?" he asked grimly.

"Witness?" She frowned, her smile fading as the realization of the purpose of their gathering flooded over her.

"Of course. We have searched for you today. No one seemed to know where you had gone. Including that lout of a seaman with whom you left the child—"

"Tikvah!" Rachel cried. "Where is she?"

"Is the seaman not one of your stooges? He sent two of our learned rabbis to the bottom of the stairs, causing them great—"

A heavy hand on his shoulder interrupted him. Rabbi Akiva pulled him to the side and smiled coolly down at Rachel. "Well, I see that you have decided to come out of hiding, after all. Perhaps you are even more clever than I have imagined, Miss Lubetkin. Of course, we can settle this issue without difficulty, eh?" He glanced back over his shoulder toward two strong young men. They stepped forward, and behind them Rachel saw the tortured face of Yehudit as she gazed tearfully at Rachel. Rachel answered her eyes with a sad smile. Yehudit looked quietly away.

"As I was saying," Akiva tugged at his vest. "This is a matter easily decided. Easily proven." The crowd of rabbis clustered around her. "You may choose to answer our questions voluntarily. It will be easier. We prefer that you not enter the synagogue until we have some answers." He sniffed and drew himself to his full height. "As you know, the laws of God and the Torah are quite liberal. In the case of Pikuach Nefesh, life or death, nearly all the laws may be set aside for a time. Except those which regard denying the Eternal, and the loss of chastity, eh? It is said that perhaps you are not what you seem to be, Miss Lubetkin—"

"Please, let me go . . . I must . . ." She stepped back, but strong hands grabbed her roughly by the arms. She cried out in agony as they touched the ragged wound beneath her sleeve. They let her go and she crumpled to the floor in a heap.

From the rear of the crowd came the anguished voice of Yehudit. "Father, stop! Please stop!" She pushed her way through the wall of black coats and hard faces. "Leave her alone!"

"Yehudit!" Akiva shouted, his eyes wide with rage. "Go home!"

She rushed to Rachel's side and wrapped her arm protectively around her. "I came. I tried to warn you," she whispered.

"Yehudit! Obey me. Instantly."

"I told you, Father!" Yehudit rose to meet his rage. "She is a good woman. I saw nothing that changes that fact. I cannot speak against her!"

"Then she shall speak against herself! I have proof that this woman, Rachel Lubetkin, is nothing less than a traitor to her people! To all who died in the war! And a traitor to her God. To the Torah! Get up! Did you hear me, whore? Get up!"

Rachel remained seated unable to stand. As though she had fallen into a nightmare, she stared up into the faces of her accusers. The same two men pulled her roughly to her feet. "Did you not hear the Rabbi Akiva?"

"Father!" cried Yehudit. "Stop!"

Akiva slapped her hard against the cheek, hurtling her back against the crowd of angry men. "Silence!" He stepped toward Rachel. "The question is simple." He smiled. "Did you indeed serve as a whore in a brothel that serviced the S.S. of Nazi Germany?"

Rachel cried out against the brutal grip on her arm. "Please!" she cried.

"Pull her sleeve up, please," instructed Akiva. "She wears the verdict on her arm."

Again Rachel gasped as the men who held her pulled the sleeve roughly past the wound, revealing the burned flesh beneath it. A murmur rippled through the crowd and Akiva frowned, then cleared his throat loudly. "There, you see. The woman has mutilated herself in order to hide the brand of the S.S."

"That's not true!" shouted Yehudit, pulling free from the hands that held her. "It was my fault! I stumbled with the kettle last night. I fell against her arm. I told you how it happened, Father! I told you there was no mark! I told you!"

"Shut up!" Akiva shouted, enraged.

"Learned rabbis," begged Yehudit. "I speak the truth! This woman is falsely accused. Falsely. I myself burned her arm. I was sent into her home to befriend her, to spy on her." She turned to Rachel as the crowd fell silent. "Forgive me, Rachel. I didn't know."

Blood oozed from Rachel's reopened wound and dripped on the mosaic floor. The world spun crazily around her as the murals of Moses on Mount Sinai throwing the tablets in rage to the ground loomed before her.

"Obviously, to my shame"—the voice of Akiva echoed hollowly—"my own daughter has fallen under the spell of this evil woman. I do not doubt that were he here, even her own grandfather would convict her and deny her."

The sobs of Yehudit accompanied the chorus of voices that rose up in agreement against her. *Guilty. Guilty. Guilty. Guilty. Guilty.* "The righteous judges among our elders convict you. No longer are you of the living of Israel. Your name shall no longer be spoken. You are dead to us. As though you were never born." The words fell like hammer blows against her. "Practice your trade far from us, for we tolerate no evil and no deceit within these walls."

The rabbis tore the edges of their coats and turned their faces from her as she pulled free from the cruel grip of the men who held her. She bent slowly to pick up the shawl that had fallen from her shoulders; then she reached into her pocket and touched the key. *Help is coming tonight. Too late, Moshe. Nothing can help me now.* Tears of humiliation streaming down her face, she steadied herself and turned away from the black wall that blocked her way into the synagogue and the mikveh. She put her hand against the doorpost of the great Nissan Bek and stared out at the windswept streets and the black sky beyond. *Even your grandfather would condemn you.* Slowly she descended the steps and the voice of Yehudit followed her into the street below. "Forgive me, Rachel! Forgive me!"

————

Haj Amin pressed his fingertips together and smiled serenely at Gerhardt. "You have done well in Damascus?"

Gerhardt nodded gloomily. "The souks are full of weapons. I told you if I had the money—"

"And you think you can penetrate the heart of Jewish Jerusalem a second time? As you did Ben Yehudah?"

Gerhardt shrugged irritably and sighed. "Of course. The *Palestine Post* is an easy target. Their boasts and propaganda can be silenced. A caravan of explosive trucks is on the way from Damascus even now."

"Good. Good. Your work for us will help the world to understand very soon that the lunacy of Partition cannot be enforced. We are pleased, Gerhardt. Very pleased." Haj Amin shifted in his chair. He leaned back and appraised Gerhardt's surly, unwashed features. Concealing his own disgust, he smiled and continued to gaze silently at his lacky.

"What are you looking at?" Gerhardt snarled at last.

"You are tired, my friend? The journey to Damascus has been most difficult for you. That is obvious."

"What if it has?"

"Or is it the woman who tears at your mind?" Haj Amin leaned forward, putting his elbows on the desk. His eyes narrowed as he studied Gerhardt's tormented face. "And does her face and the thought of her body keep you from hours of sleep?"

The scowl on Gerhardt's face became deeper, but he did not answer.

"Hmmm. As I thought." Haj Amin paused thoughtfully for a moment, then relaxed. He raised his chin slightly and called, "Kadar! Bring the old man!"

The door opened and Kadar swept in, holding the old muezzin by his arm. The old man was dripping wet and disheveled; he bowed time and again to the Mufti and to Gerhardt.

"He is somewhat like a stray cat, Gerhardt, no? And you have sent him to prowl the alleyways and sit upon the rooftops in search of little mice, eh? For the sake of Allah? For the sake of the Mufti? And perhaps for the sake of Gerhardt?" Haj Amin laughed at Gerhardt's discomfort. "Perhaps your alleycat has at last got news for you." The Mufti motioned to the old muezzin to step forward. "Howl for us, alleycat. Tell us what you have seen. A mouse? Or perhaps a she-cat?"

Kadar released his grip on the old man, staring at Gerhardt with disgust. The old man stepped forward and bowed low once again. "Salaam!" he said enthusiastically. "This time there is no mistake! I have seen her! The streets are nearly deserted because of the storm, you see. But I waited and watched. I stayed until after dark and she did not leave."

Gerhardt jumped up and grabbed the old man by his collar. "Where is she, you old fool? Where has she gone?"

"Do not strike me, Captain, and I will tell you!" The old man held his hands protectively in front of his face.

Kadar shook his head at the madness of Gerhardt

and stepped back against the doorjamb as Haj Amin clapped his hands loudly. "In our presence, please, Gerhardt—dignity. Let go of the muezzin. You may damage his throat—then how would he call the faithful to prayer?"

Gerhardt shoved the old man back and took his seat again. "This is a joke to you, eh?" he snapped. "I am the mouse and you are the cat. But if I were not here to light the fuses, what would you do?"

The eyes of Haj Amin grew cold with anger. "Find another."

"She is at the apartment," the muezzin continued, rubbing his neck. "She did not leave. The light still burns there. I saw her." The old man stuck a wrinkled palm out. "May I not receive my reward now, kind and honorable . . ."

The Mufti nodded slowly, regaining his composure. "You have been most faithful to us. This fellow would speak to no one but you, Gerhardt. Except for me. He insisted, waiting until the guards had to let him in. Perhaps you should pay him for his information."

Grudgingly Gerhardt drew out his money pouch. The old man's face lit up with a toothless smile. Gerhardt took a few shillings out and tossed them at the old man. The smile faded.

"Thank you, kind sir," said the old man without enthusiasm.

"Surely this is not enough reward for one so faithful!" Haj Amin smiled pityingly. "And such important news he brought, eh? At least a gold sovereign, Gerhardt. Pay him at least that much."

"Oh, most honorable Mufti!" cried the old man.

Gerhardt stared into the eyes of the Mufti; anger reflected on the faces of both men. "I said pay him," warned Haj Amin.

His eyes never leaving the face of his leader, Gerhardt pulled the coin from his purse and flipped it at the old muezzin. "If your information is false, old man," Gerhardt said quietly, "it is you who will owe me."

"Most honorable, most gracious sir. What I tell you is—"

"Get out!" Gerhardt turned on him with unrepressed fury, causing the old man to shrink back, then fumble for the door latch and hurry out. Kadar shut the door behind him.

"You pay your spies well, Gerhardt," Kadar laughed. "We will hope that they are worthy."

30 Descent into Hell

It took the strength of both Moshe and Luke to move the heavy concrete cover from the deep shaft in the cemetery outside the Golden Gate. As they hefted the slab to the side, Moshe breathed a silent prayer of thanks for Luke's presence. Quickly Luke fixed the grappling hook securely onto a large marble monument, then turned to watch Moshe loop the end of the rope through the straps of the pack and lower it carefully into the darkness. Yards of rope were quickly devoured until at last Luke rubbed the rain from his face and asked in disbelief, "How far to the bottom?"

Moshe wordlessly handed Luke his flashlight. "Look for yourself."

Leaning carefully over the edge, the light stretched into darkness that swallowed the pack beyond the reach of the beam. Luke gave a low whistle and sat back suddenly from the edge. His face was as white as a tombstone.

"Still want to come along? For the fellowship?" Moshe asked without amusement in his voice.

"Have we enough rope?" Luke asked after a moment's hesitation.

"Only just. The shaft here is eighty-three feet straight down. This rope is seventy-five. We can drop the rest of the way. We'll need to leave this rope here in case we can't . . ." He paused. "The smaller rope is fifty feet long. I don't know that we will need it, or how much we might need. Luke, I will think no less of you if you opt to bow out. I may even gain a bit more respect for your common sense. At least I knew what I was getting into. You are coming into this cold."

286

Luke tugged on the line, checking its anchor one more time as the pack hit the end. "My mother used to reprimand me for not having much common sense." He saluted, then grasped the rope and began his descent into the darkness.

A huge branch of lightning lit the sky behind the Dome of the Rock, silhouetting the guards along the wall. The rumble of thunder shook the ground; rain stung Moshe's cheeks as he looked upward into the angry heavens, then slipped over the muddy edge after Luke.

Hand over hand they lowered themselves into the blackness. The pressure on Moshe's bad arm caused him to gasp with pain, but he looped the rope around his good arm and continued down. Above his head Luke saw a small square of sky that blinked like an eerie neon light. The air around him pressed in, suddenly still and cold like an ancient tomb. The crash of thunder grew more distant and the labored sound of Luke's breathing seemed as loud as steam from a locomotive.

Bits of gravel crumbled away, plummeting noise-lessly into the depths. The postage stamp of light still flashed above them, but no beam penetrated the shaft where they now hung.

"You're sure?" Luke panted. "Eighty-three feet?"

"According to the records."

"Hold it a minute!" He shouted. "Here's the pack! We're at the end of the rope!"

Moshe wrapped his legs tightly around the rope. "Jump! I'll untie the pack and hand it down to you."

Luke remained silent and unmoving. "It's so dark, old chap. Are you sure I'm only eight feet from bottom?"

The darkness was oppressive, and the feeling that they had shinnied down into a bottomless pit filled Moshe. Holding on with his good arm, he carefully reached into his pocket for the flashlight. He switched it on and shone it down onto the top of Luke's head and beyond. The waterproof pack dangled a mere three feet from the ground, and Luke's feet were just above it. Moshe laughed out loud at the sight of the big British officer hanging on for dear life a mere three feet from the bottom of the shaft.

"Ah!" said Luke with relief as he stepped onto the rocky floor. "Might just as well been a hundred feet, the way it felt." He grinned up at Moshe, who slid down the final eight feet of the rope.

While Luke untied the pack, Moshe studied the workmanship of the shaft. Strong horizontal beams the size of railroad ties lined the interior of the shaft and the six-by-six area where they now stood. A five-foot high opening led to a tunnel that seemed to climb gently in the direction of the Old City.

Moshe shouldered the pack and ducked beneath the framed archway into the tunnel. Both men had to stoop to walk through the narrow passageway. Heavy timbers supported the sides and roof, but still the air itself seemed to press against them with a weight that made Moshe's ears throb against the pressure. Iron hooks hung on the beams where lanterns had once lit the passage for the men who had first entered the Old City through this passage. Moshe could easily touch both sides of the tunnel with his fingertips. He had often been in tight places before in his work, and he was accustomed to the closeness. But he was concerned now with Luke, who had followed silently for some time. "Are you still all right, my friend?"

. . . *my friend?* his echo returned.

"It's not nearly so bad as a coal mine."

. . . *coal mine, coal mine* . . .

"Now, that is the edge of sanity itself," Luke continued as his words overlapped and chased one another down the passageway. "And if you don't mind me asking, why did the archaeologists go to all the trouble of digging these shafts, anyway?"

Grateful for any conversation that would divert his thoughts from Rachel, Moshe explained the story of the first intrepid treasure-seekers to Luke as they moved up-

288

ward toward the base of the wall itself. ". . . and so, you see, the Sheik would not allow excavation beneath the Dome of the Rock itself; therefore they had to find another way in. No doubt the Archbishop of Canterbury would not hold kindly to archaeologists digging up the grounds of his cathedral, eh? The Muslim leaders did not like the idea of us poking around, either. We have become a sneaky lot. Some have accused us of being part mole. But the fellows who did this," Moshe said with awe, "were men who had heard of the glory of Jerusalem, and they wanted to see for themselves."

Suddenly the tunnel opened into a passageway that towered fifteen feet above their heads. Moshe shone the light on the huge stone blocks that made up the long-buried wall of Herod. "And here are the stones at the base of the city wall. Eighty feet below the surface. What a city she must have been! How she must have shone! The wall stood over the valley at a height of one hundred and seventy feet, Luke. No wonder Jesus wept when He saw what was coming upon Jerusalem, His beloved, eh?"

Luke reached out and touched the stones, then hurried after Moshe, whose light was already disappearing down the gallery to the east along the base of the wall.

Far below the surface it seemed impossible that the storm raged above their heads. The cold perpetual night of the tunnel filled Luke with a sense of unreality. Time and again he brushed the rough stone blocks with his fingertips and wondered what the city must have been like.

Moshe fell silent and intense now, searching the stones at the base. "Just as the notes describe it," he said at last as he knelt in front of a block two-feet square that was set loosely between two massive stones. There, on one corner, were the initials B&D chiseled into the stone. "Bliss and Dickie," said Moshe quietly as he set down his pack and shoved against the stone with his foot. It budged inward ever so slightly. "Help me," he instructed Luke, who had already laid his shoulder against the stone and begun to push. Slowly it moved, revealing a space behind it half filled with dirt and rubble. Here the way becomes very dangerous and difficult, Luke. I am not sure what is ahead. You have come this far with me. Perhaps it would be wise for you to—"

"In for a penny, in for a pound, eh? I'm afraid you're stuck with me, Moshe."

Moshe nodded curtly, then rubbed his chin. He raised his eyebrows slightly and smiled. "I'm glad," he said at last.

Shoving the pack through first, he wriggled into the small opening between the blocks of stone. They crawled for a full ten feet until they reached the remains of what looked like a stone-and-mortar flume. "The aqueduct," explained Moshe as Luke puffed after him. "This will lead us to a sewer, and then . . ." He pushed ahead, holding the light in one hand as he shoved the pack before him onto the narrow aqueduct. The side of the water conduit closed tightly around Moshe's broad shoulders and he turned sideways to force his body through its path. Echoes of tiny drips of water were magnified a thousand times until the air around them was filled with an unearthly sound, like ancient spirits wandering the broken streets of the old Jerusalem, searching for her lost glory. Rats shrieked and scurried away from the beam of Moshe's light. Rocks and broken rubble tore at their clothes and scraped their skin.

Neither man spoke as he crawled through the contorted pipe. Above them, Moshe could hear a ghostly wind howl past the opening. The old rabbi had warned him, *beware of the tunnels themselves, Moshe. They will speak to you and lead you where they will.*

He came to a sharp Y bend in the pipe. To the right, rubble blocked the way. To the left, the path seemed open, though narrow. "Just a minute!" he said to Luke, who grasped Moshe's boot and halted, grateful for the rest.

Awkwardly, Moshe pulled his bundle of maps out

and opened it amid the crushed rock in front of him. He pored over the notes of Bliss, searching for words he knew he had seen.

"What is it?" asked Luke.

"I thought we were supposed to take the path to the right. But it seems to be blocked. The left branch is open."

"Well, then, go ahead. The rats are nibbling my boots back here."

Moshe folded his notes, a frown of consternation on his face. He crawled forward, pushing the heavy pack through the rubble. Suddenly his light gleamed against a small cylinder that lay in the way of the pack. Moshe stopped again, shining the beam of the flashlight directly onto the golden object.

Impatiently Luke called to him, "What now?"

"I found something," Moshe answered, rubbing the mud from the surface of the inch-and-a-half long piece of ancient jewelry.

"What is it?" Luke asked.

Moshe turned the object over again and again in his hand. "A mezuzah."

"A what?"

"A kind of charm. Worn by Jews, like a star of David; like Christians wear crosses."

"Well, whoever lost it down here must have taken a wrong turn somewhere."

Studying the tiny Hebrew letters for a moment, Moshe sighed. "Whoever she was, I hope she found her way out."

"What?" Luke called, exasperation thick in his voice.

"It is very old. Very old, indeed. Proof that someone traveled this way long ago."

"Well, if you don't mind, Moshe, I don't want to become an archaeological relic myself. May we move along now?" He sneezed. "Before my boots are eaten, and me with them?"

Moshe shoved the tiny gold mezuzah into his pocket

and started forward. He smiled at the words written in the delicate filigreed charm.

The stench became stronger, and the screech of rats more violent as they crept along. Moshe flashed the light ahead just in time to see the hairless tail of a rat the size of a cat disappear out an opening a mere two yards ahead of them. He crawled faster now, hefting the pack out the opening. He breathed through his mouth and tried to ignore the patter of scrambling feet. His light reflected off the top of an ancient stone water cistern. Shadows of moving animals dashed to and fro in the soft glow.

"Dear God! The rats!" Moshe pulled himself out of the pipe. Huge, yellow-toothed creatures had already claimed his pack. Moshe kicked at a huge rodent and snatched his pack from four who sat up defiantly on their haunches. "Luke!" Moshe yelled as the pack swarmed around his legs. "Hurry!" In the corner a large rat roosted on the small skull of a child, and all around a thousand thousand eyes blinked hungrily at them.

Luke scrambled out, kicking at the creatures as Moshe scanned the walls of the cistern for the way out. "We've come the wrong way!" he shouted against the din when the light showed solid stone walls. "Quick!" He did not need to say even one more word to Luke, who was already disappearing back down the pipe as he shouted at the creatures who pursued them. Moshe swung the pack violently, beating back the rats as he slid after Luke. He slammed the pack down hard on the head of a large animal, who was then finished off by a frenzy of his hungry fellows. Blocking the upper end by pulling the pack after him, Moshe slid rapidly downward after Luke. Coming once again to the Y in the pipe, Luke had begun tearing at the stones with his hands, pulling away the rubble that blocked the path. Stone by stone, Moshe and Luke dammed up the cavern of rats behind a wall, crushing the more aggressive creatures who screamed and flashed their yellow teeth.

Wriggling ahead into a broader section of the ancient aqueduct, Luke sighed at last as he took the lead. "I thought you had a general idea of where we were going," he accused, only half joking.

"This is a maze," Moshe said as the sound of rats diminished and a hollow echo reached his ears. "I know only where I am going. Not entirely how to get there."

Luke pushed through another heap of rubble, and the smell of sewage filled their nostrils. He squirmed forward through a small opening and stuck his head and shoulders out of the pipe. "Well, we're somewhere, old chap." He shone the light against damp stone walls that sloped upward to a domed roof. Sewage flowed from three high tunnels into a larger shaft that led downward in a rank river of muck. He pulled himself onto a narrow, slippery shelf and carefully inched to the side as Moshe followed.

"Not even the rats come here," Moshe said, his eyes burning from the fumes.

"Where to now?" Luke's face was filled with disgust.

"Along this ledge. Another seventy-five feet. There are handholds. A sort of ladder to climb. Don't fall, Luke. This is one dive you wouldn't survive."

Slime on the ledge coated the soles of their boots and threatened to send them headfirst into the deadly sludge below them. Moshe pressed himself tightly against the walls as they inched along far beneath the Old City streets, guided only by God and the memories of an old rabbi.

Hiding in the cold shadows of a doorway, Rachel watched as one by one her judges left the synagogue. She counted ten grim men and finally the weeping Yehudit, held firmly by the arm of her father. He was the last to leave, extinguishing the lamps and locking the door behind him.

And did their words speak more harshly than your own heart, Rachel? Are they more cruel to you than you

*have been to yourself? Hadn't your heart died long before
they pronounced you dead?*

Yehudit's sobs echoed in the wind and swirled
around her like dry leaves. "You are forgiven, Yehudit,"
she whispered. "Do we not all sell pieces of ourselves
for a price?"

"No, Father! Please!" the trembling voice drifted
back.

Your price was approval. Mine was life. Rachel could
find no room inside her to hate. No anger argued with
her grief. Her judges had shown her the law, revealed
how far short she had fallen. Their verdict was just.
Death of her name, her place among them. She had
meant the wound on her arm to hide her guilt. But the
guilt remained.

She gripped the key tightly. *Life or death.* For Moshe
she would stay. For the sake of Moshe's love, she would
find a way into the mikveh.

For a full hour she waited, shivering cold. The streets
were desolate, deserted. In the distance the sound of
rifle fire popped. Lightning flashed and forked to the
ground, illuminating the tall, now forbidden synagogue. Thunderclaps drowned out the gunfire, and a
steady rain began to fall, soaking Rachel to the skin as
she scanned the building for a way in. Windows high
and bright with stained glass were covered by bars. A
sense of panic welled up inside her as she imagined
Moshe locked behind some dark impenetrable door in
the mikveh. *Life or death.* She looked up the steep stone
steps that led to the roof of the building. Lattice work
concealed the scaffolding in the dome where Haganah
men had watched over the city before the unhappy rabbis had shut them out. Rachel remembered the long
ropes that hung from the high dome to the floor below.

Her soaked shawl fell from her shoulders as she
straightened herself and stepped into the full force of
the gale. Lightning exploded the sky; she ran to the
steps and gripped the railing with both hands. Pulling
herself to the top, one step at a time, she reached the

flat roof and crawled toward the thin lattice that covered a half-open window. Again the sky was cracked by lightning. Thunder roared above her as she kicked against the wooden lattice, breaking away a corner wide enough for her to crawl through onto a narrow ledge, fourteen inches wide.

Wind screamed through the open window, causing the wooden scaffolding to rock and sway just beyond her reach. The lights of the synagogue candles flickered eerily below her. Rachel looked up at the shadows that danced across the faces of Moses and Aaron on the mural above her. The empty scaffolding hung a mere three feet from where she perched. Forty feet below her the mosaic floor loomed. She gasped and looked up again as fear filled the pit of her stomach. *Only a short jump*, she argued with herself, unwilling to let go of the window frame she clutched behind her. *For Moshe. Life or death*. She reached into her pocket and touched the key, gripping it tightly in her sweaty palm. It slipped from her hand and tumbled from her pocket. "No!" she shouted as it bounced on the ledge and tumbled to the floor far below with a loud clatter.

There was no going back now. The key lay where the long rope dragged the ground below the scaffolding. Rachel pulled her legs beneath her and crouched, taking three deep breaths as she studied the distance between the ledge and the scaffolding. "One!" *God help me*. "Two!" *For Moshe*. "Three!" Resisting the urge to grasp the window frame, Rachel sprang from the ledge, crying out as she felt the emptiness around her. The instant of flight seemed endless until the force of her body hit the wooden platform, sending it swinging wildly, threatening to turn upside down.

She closed her eyes and clutched the ragged boards until her knuckles turned white. Nausea welled up within her as the pendulum slowed and finally hung in a fragile stillness. Her eyes still closed, Rachel groped for the rope by which she had seen men pull themselves up and onto this unstable perch. Inching her way toward the rope that led down to the safety of the ground below, Rachel grasped it tightly with both hands and eased herself over the side. For a long moment she hung suspended high above the floor of the temple. Her hands refused to work, and her legs wound around the rope in desperation. "I can't!" she cried. "I can't!" *Life or death. Moshe. Let yourself down. A bit at a time.* The wind whipped against the rope, sending a wet blast of air beating against her. The rope tore at the wound in her arm as she moved slowly down toward the key. Her shoes dropped off, falling with a loud thud.

Once again lightning cracked and thunder boomed directly above the great Nissan Bek. Eight feet from the floor, she saw in the bright flash her shadow cast against the altar. Clinging to the thin strand, she looked almost like a butterfly with folded wings. Her hands slipped, and with a cry, she fell to the ground. Gasping for breath, she rolled over, her hand reaching out to clutch the key.

"Oh, God," she sobbed in relief. *Hurry, Rachel. He needs you to open the lock. Pikuach Nefesh.*

Barefooted and dripping wet, she picked herself up and ran awkwardly past the altar to the doors that led to the basement and the women's ritual bath beyond. She snatched a lighted candle from the altar. "All is lawful in matters of life or death, Akiva," she whispered, startled by the sound of her own voice.

Finally, pushing the door to the women's mikveh open, she called softly, "Moshe?

Moshe? Moshe? Her echo answered.

"Are you here?"

Here? here? here?

"It is Rachel."

Rachel Rachel Rachel.

"I have come with the key..."

Key key key.

Silence followed the loud drips of water falling from the stained ceiling into the round, stone pool. *I am too late,* she thought, holding the candle high as she searched for a door that Moshe could be behind. There was none. Mossy, dank walls rose up to a domed cavern-like roof that dripped water onto the slick floor below. There were no other windows or doors other than the door she had just come through.

"Moshe?" she cried, dropping to her knees in exhaustion. Her own voice echoed back in mocking reply.

"Can you hear me?"

Hear me? hear me?

Two tall, black Sudanese bodyguards of Haj Amin, chosen for their tremendous size and strength, followed Gerhardt over the rooftops of the Old City. At least a head taller than he, they moved with the grace and stealth of jaguars at the hunt. Gerhardt's maniacal skills were far too precious to the Mufti to let him go alone into danger for the sake of a mere woman. "Get him back to us still useful," he had whispered into the ears of his elite. "And bring the woman to us also."

Quietly they moved through the rain-drenched streets of the Jewish Quarter. There were only two soggy young Jews at the barricade, and they died easily enough, the blood from their slit throats mingling freely with the rain.

Thunder crashed above the heads of Gerhardt and the guards as they descended the steps of the tiny apartment. Lights shone through the slats of the shuttered windows. Gerhardt stepped back as the tallest of the Sudanese guards kicked in the door with ease. The lock shattered the wooden frame, sending long slivers of wood flying across the tiny room.

Gerhardt, his revolver drawn, pressed past the two men, his eyes searching the room for some sign of the woman. He stepped over the body of the dog, nudging him briefly to see if he was alive. There was no response, no movement. Gerhardt cursed the muezzin as he pulled the broken cardboard box from beneath the bed. He threw it angrily against the wall, sending letters flying to the floor.

Then a photograph lying face up on the bed caught his eye. He picked it up and carefully tore the young girl's face away from the others. Slipping the fragment into his shirt pocket, he picked up the note that lay beside it.

My Darling Rachel . . . you are alive . . . fondest love . . . take the key . . . women's mikveh beneath Nissan Bek . . . Wait . . . tonight.

Gerhardt smiled and tossed down the note, then, closing the broken door behind them, the three returned to the street in search of their prey.

31   The Tomb

The weight of the shortwave radio pulled Moshe backward as he searched for a precarious toehold leading up from the ancient sewer.

Luke shined the flashlight down on him from yet another passageway twelve feet higher.

"A bit to your right," he coached as Moshe probed the face of the stones with his fingers. "Yes. There you have it. Come along, lad," he urged. "Only a few steps higher. You can make it. That's it! A few inches beyond your left hand now. Another handhold."

Moshe's head swam with dizziness as he clung to the slick stone. He groped with his left foot for the notch in the rock that led yet another step higher. Luke stretched his arm out toward Moshe to grasp the heavy pack. "Just another few inches, Moshe, m'boy. That's It!" Strong fingers closed around the pack and pulled Moshe forward and up against the force that had held him back. Slowly Moshe crawled over the crown of a broken arch that marked the beginning of yet another passageway.

"It is here Rabbi Lebowitz warned me. The passage was blown up. He wasn't sure . . ."

"Let's get away from the stink a bit farther." Luke pushed ahead. "And then I could use a drink of water." He stooped beneath a low arch and clambered down a soft dirt embankment that led to a shallow valley between two arches that had once served as a causeway. He sat down heavily on a broken marble pillar and shined the light upward to the crown of the next arch where a small opening would take them farther into the bowels of the Old City. Dirty and exhausted, Moshe slid down after him and opened the pack. He rummaged through it quickly, smiling briefly when he found the gas mask David had stashed beneath the canteen.

"A gas mask!" Luke cried. "We could have used that back there!"

"I didn't know it, or I would have." Moshe drank deeply from the fresh cool water and handed the canteen to Luke.

"How much farther, would you say?" Luke asked. Moshe noticed his normally well-waxed moustache drooped unhappily, with bits of dirt clinging to it.

Moshe pulled the maps and charts from his shirt front. "Not far now. Rest a minute more. From this point we need to mark our path." He pulled a stick of blue chalk from his pocket. "Rabbi Lebowitz warned me that the tunnels lead off in several directions. From this point we could find our way back, but there is a honeycomb ahead of us. And the pathway we want has been at least partially destroyed." Moshe repacked the canteen and shouldered the pack once again. Wiping his lips with the back of his hand, he started up the mound of earth toward the narrow opening at the crown of the archway. Luke surged past him, resolutely reaching the entrance into the next chamber before Moshe was even halfway up. Cautiously, Luke began to move the stones that blocked their way until at last a gap was cleared just wide enough for him to squeeze through.

"You'll have to take the pack off," he instructed, easing himself between the stones. "Give it to me."

Light glowed eerily from the other side of the archway as Moshe slipped the pack from his shoulders and shoved it through to Luke. "What's down there?" he called, wriggling headfirst after the bulky cargo.

"There are at least four different tunnels! Incredible!" Luke called up from the floor of a chamber roofed by four vaults. "Get the chalk out." His voice fell to a whisper. "I have the feeling we'll be needing it to mark the way from here on." The awed whisper hissed through the narrow passageways.

Moshe scraped the lump of chalk on the archway in a large X before he slid down beside the tall captain. "We are on our own from this point. One of these four tunnels will be blocked by rubble. Rabbi Lebowitz told me that years ago the Jewish and Arab Council hired a man to seal it off. He blew it up. Blew himself up along with it. Behind the rubble is the entrance to the cavern and the way out."

Luke frowned and scratched his head. "We are assuming that none of the other three tunnels is blocked?" he asked.

Moshe nodded and grinned sheepishly. "Look at it this way. At least we are out of the rain."

"And we are assuming that we can dig through this pile of rubble once we locate it? After an explosion that sealed it half a century ago?"

Moshe shined the beam of light into the darkness of a low-roofed passage. Water seeped from the cracks around the stone blocks, and mud oozed over the toes of his boots. "That is the assumption." He stepped into the tunnel, bending low to avoid the slime that coated the face of the stones above him.

Luke shook his head with a mixture of astonishment and admiration. "I suppose I should give up being surprised at you Jews. After all," he said as he stooped, then followed Moshe, "you do seem to have a reputation for having things opening up for you when you least expect it. The Red Sea, for instance." He chuckled and padded through the muck after Moshe, who wordlessly chased the beam of light along the twisting path.

Rats screeched and scurried away as the two men moved deeper into the bowels of the Old City. Occasionally Moshe reached out and scraped a chalk mark across the stone. The sound of their heavy breath and footsteps traveled ahead of them, resounding back like sinister creatures in the darkness. A full fifteen minutes into their trek, they reached the rank opening of yet another filthy stream of sewage.

"This is not it. Wrong tunnel." Moshe halted

abruptly, shining the light onto the slow moving muck below them.

"Our noses could have told us that." Luke turned and moved quickly back the way they had come.

When they reached the vaulted chamber again, Moshe stared up at the shadows that hung from the ceiling. "We have enough rations for three days. And water. But there is not enough time."

"Quite right." Luke shook a long ribbon of green slime from his jacket sleeve." You know, if I'm not back by morning, they'll say I am AWOL," he quipped. "Suppose in the interest of efficiency we split up? You explore the passage to the right. I'll go along this one." He sniffed appreciatively. "I'm a bit taller than you, so I'll take the way with the higher ceiling. Do you have an extra torch?"

Moshe hesitated only a moment, the shadow of uncertainty clouding his face. Then he rummaged through the pack for another light and broke the chalk in two pieces, handing one to Luke. "I'll leave the pack here. We'll rendezvous in fifteen minutes. Seven and a half minutes down and seven and a half back. That ought to be enough to tell the story."

"Good luck." Luke extended his hand in a warm handshake. "By the way"—he turned and grinned as he stooped to enter his tunnel—"if I'm not back in fifteen minutes . . ." His voice trailed off.

"Yes? If you're not back in fifteen minutes, what?"

"Well, man, if *you're* not back, I'm coming after you! Do the same for me, will you?"

Moshe saluted and moved cautiously into the claustrophobic crawlspace ahead of him. The air seemed heavy with the weight of tons of earth and stones above him. Moshe's breath came hard and fast as he crept through the suffocating burrow.

This passage was drier than the last, but the stone floor was caked with rat feces, and the stench was almost unbearable. Fifty feet into the tunnel he remembered the gas mask and struggled back out to the chamber where the pack lay. A dim light bobbed away down Luke's maze, and Moshe breathed a prayer of thankfulness once again for the stubborn presence of the good captain.

Beneath the coils of rope, Moshe found the gas mask. Slipping it over his head, he turned to resume his journey when suddenly an ominous rumble shook the earth beneath him. The rumble dissolved into a terrible roar resounding from the walls as dust filled the chamber. "Luke!" shouted Moshe as he stumbled and fell, clutching the pack to him. The sound of his voice set off yet another threatening groan beneath the dome.

Seconds ticked by like hours until the din subsided. Moshe cautiously picked himself up and shouldered the pack. Dust blocked the beam of light as he frantically peered into the passage Luke had taken. He dropped to his knees and inched his way along the ground, grateful for the bulky mask that covered his face, enabling him to breathe in spite of the thick fog of dust that blocked his vision.

"Luke!" His voice was small and strangled behind the mask. "Luke! Can you hear me?" The sides of the passage seemed to press against him. Rocks and gravel cut through the knees of his trousers. "Luke!" he cried in desperation, the stones around him echoing the harshness of his voice.

Ten feet ahead the dust began to clear like the swirl of a whirlpool. A large black hole gaped and yawned open in a chasm before him. "Luke!" he cried again. *Luke! Luke! Luke! Luke!* the stones called back. Small pebbles slid away into a pit so deep he could not hear them when they crashed to the bottom.

Moshe tore the mask from his face. "Luke!" he cried again. Again the stones protested.

"Moshe," came a whispered reply. "Shut up. The whole earth is apt to swallow us!"

"Where are you?" Moshe cried, shining the light around the rim of the chasm.

"Here. Hanging to the edge. Hurry."

Moshe directed the light to where Luke's fingers clung with white-knuckled intensity to the lip of the jagged opening opposite where Moshe knelt. He could barely see the back of Luke's head as he hung from the precipice.

"Get the rope!" Luke gasped. "Don't come too near. I told you things have a way of opening up . . ." He cried out as a clod of earth rained on him. "Dear Lord! It's deep!"

"Hang on! I'm coming!" Moshe snatched the coil of rope from the pack and secured one end to a huge stone at his right. Then he looped the rope and made a half hitch at the end. "I'll throw you the rope. Loop it around your wrist."

"Not too close. I passed over this once. Found the entrance to the cavern, the one the rabbi told you about. I was coming back for you, and the ground just slid away! Moshe! Remember the scrolls! The shells . . . I can't hold on!"

"Yes, you can!" Moshe lay down on his stomach and slid forward to the edge of the deep shaft. Twenty feet below, in the glow of Luke's dim flashlight, he could see yet another tunnel. The old rabbi's warning came back to him. *Beware the cisterns . . . ancient aqueducts . . . It is a warren . . . a honeycomb where death waits patiently for your mistakes.*

"I can't . . ."

"Here it comes," Moshe replied, working hard to keep the edge of panic from his own voice. Gently he tossed the loop until it caught and hung loosely over Luke's hands. "Now take it! Let go and grab the rope! It will hold you."

Willing his muscles to move, Luke lifted his index finger, then gripped the ledge again. "I'm a dead man, old chap."

"Catch the loop! It will hold."

Suddenly shifting rock and sand drowned Moshe's voice. With a cry, Luke fell away and disappeared into the mouth of the abyss. Moshe scrambled back, clutching the light as the rope was torn from his grasp. "Luke!"

Luke! Luke! Luke! Luke! The tunnels mocked his agony as a cloud of dust rose from the hole like vapor from the mouth of hell itself. Moshe coughed and covered his face against the gritty fog that filled the tunnel, making it impossible to see or move. An eternity of seconds passed before Moshe dared move forward to the dark and empty hole where Luke had disappeared. He directed the light downward where dust still swirled and gravel slid away grain by grain, like his hope. As the beam cut through the darkness at the bottom of the shaft, Moshe saw Luke's face, the color of the dust that had swallowed him. His lifeless hand clutched the end of the rope.

Moshe's shoulders sagged beneath the weight of loss. Unmoving, he gazed downward, hoping for some sign of life; the flutter of an eyelid, a sigh or a groan. Then he slipped back away from the edge, groping for the pack that carried the shortwave and one last coil of rope. Frantically he searched the tunnel behind him. "It's got to be here!" he cried. "Where is it?" His voice set off yet another low threat from the roof of the tunnel. He glanced up, then scrambled once again to the edge of the shaft. Shining the light downward, he scrutinized the rubble around Luke's still body. There, covered with the dust of the shaft, was the pack, resting beneath the head of the captain as though he had lain down to sleep.

"I will be back, my friend," he whispered. "Guard it well for me, eh?" Then he raised his voice. "This was a good man, God. Faithful guardian of your ancient words. Treat him well. He had a great love for your people Israel. Omaine." Moshe wiped his eyes, then backed away slowly as he searched the tunnel ahead for a way around the chasm. A narrow ledge of rock remained, and he cautiously tested it before he put his full weight on the stone. His back tight against the wall, he eased himself toward the center of the ledge that skirted the pit. The leather heels of his boots scraped against the stones. *I will say to the Lord, he is my refuge and my fortress. You are my God in whom I will trust.* His toes seemed to jut out over the ledge into the oblivion of the darkness where Luke had fallen. *Surely He will deliver me from the snare of the fowler. I am yours, my Lord. Your servant. Hold me with your hands.*

Every outcropping felt like hands waiting to push him into destruction. *I will not be afraid of the terror by night nor the arrow that flies by day nor the pestilence that walks in darkness nor the destruction that kills at noonday. And remember Rachel, my own sweet Rachel, Lord. Walk with her, keep her safe. If it means my life, God, help her live to know your love.* Pebbles fell away, spinning a long time in the blackness before they hit bottom. *A thousand shall fall at thy side, and ten thousand at thy right hand; but it shall not come nigh thee.*

Inch by inch Moshe crept along the narrow ledge that stretched a full fifteen feet around the yawning grave. A final three feet beyond where he balanced, the jagged edge of solid pathway waited. "Only a bit more," he said aloud, surprised at the deep echo of his own voice. A low rumble shook the tunnel around him, and the ledge began to slide. Without thinking he tossed the light ahead and leaped after it just as the stones dropped away beneath him. Taking only an instant to regain his breath, he crawled the final ten yards of the tunnel like a man crawling on thin ice. *Distribute your weight across the ground,* he told himself as he scurried toward a small opening above a heap of fallen stones. There at the base of the rubble lay the explanation for the weakness of the tunnel floor. Staring back at Moshe lay the grinning skull of the Turk who had died in the explosion that sealed the tunnel over fifty years before.

Moshe marveled at Grandfather's accurate description. *He was a madman of a Turk.* The hollow eyes and three missing front teeth did indeed have a look of insanity. A bony arm reached out toward Moshe, its fingers spread against the dirt. The tarnished silver ring crowned by a tiny skull that encircled the dead man's thumb glinted eerily at Moshe. He turned his eyes from the ghostly sentinel and scrambled past him up the heap of rubble to the opening that led to the great cavern below—then to mikveh and *Rachel*!

As he pulled himself through the opening, his flashlight barely pierced the darkness of the enormous hall. Everything was as the old rabbi had described. *Its height is well over thirty feet from the floor to the roof. It is all hewn stone; when you come to it, you will know that you are near.* High and insistent, like the whine of the wind, he heard his name float above him among the vaults of the roof.

"Moshhhhhheeee! Moshhhhhhhe!"

The cold grip of fear twisted his heart for an instant as the unearthly voice rose, then swirled away. "This is not the cavern Josephus wrote about," he said aloud, attempting to reason away the dread. "This must be the old Nea Church of the Crusaders."

"Moshhhhhhhhhe! Moshhhhhhhh . . ." the whine faded.

Moshe shuddered like a man who had stumbled unknowingly into a crypt. Then he brushed the dust off and picked his way across the rubble of the ancient ruin until he stood beneath a high stone archway. *Just beyond is a long stone pillar that spans a deep chasm. It must have been a well. I dropped a torch once and watched as it fell and finally the light went out.*

Moshe shone the light from the broken mosaic floor to the large pillar poised precariously over a pit twenty feet across. Grandfather's directions had been perfectly accurate up to this point, and Moshe did not pause to look into the depths of its darkness.

"Moshhhhheeeee!" The sound was louder now. *What is it? That is no ghost,* he decided. He mounted the slippery pillar and balanced for a moment, shining the beam on the narrow green surface.

"Like balancing on a log," he said aloud.

Placing each step carefully, he moved with the precision of a man walking a wire over Niagara Falls. Sweat trickled down his back in spite of the coldness of the air. "Maybe it would be safer to sit down," he murmured.

Now safely across, Moshe directed the beam of light up a steep slope of loose stone and rubble to the crown of an archway. *There is a dangerous climb you must make, and you will find yourself at the top of an archway marked by a cross.* The large cross marked it clearly. *Do not climb up to the right of the archway. The earth will slide away beneath you.* Moshe studied the heap that loomed before him, picking what seemed to be the safest route. *Just beneath the cross you will see a small opening. It will be difficult for you to pass through, but from there you will crawl until you come to the ladder. This will take you finally to the grate.*

"Thank you, Rebbe Lebowitz." Moshe grinned and wiped his brow. Then he whispered, "To Rachel."

———

Rachel held her hands out to the warmth of the flickering candle and, for what seemed like the hundredth time, remembered the words of the note. She fingered the key and shuddered in the cold of the room. Her breath rose in a vapor and her thoughts in a prayer for Moshe. He was trying to reach her, although she did not understand how, she believed that if he still lived, he was trying to come to her side.

Tears came freely as she thought of the love he held for her in spite of her past and the condemnation of others. It was a love she had not expected, did not deserve, and yet it was real. *Remember you are loved.* If his strong arms never held her, if his eyes never looked into hers, at least she would have those words to keep the rest of her life.

She bowed her head and hugged her knees to her. *I am happy just to know he loved me. And he is coming. I just know he is coming for me tonight!*

Above her the dome of the mikveh seemed to tremble with the force of the wind and the thunder. And beyond the room, the hall of the synagogue was shaken by a fierce and insistent crash against the outer doors. Again and again Rachel heard a sound as though someone were trying to break down the doors of the temple itself. She raised her head, her eyes suddenly filling with relief and joy.

"Moshe!" she cried, jumping to her feet and clutching the key to her. "He has come for me!" She started toward the door of the mikveh.

Then urgent and gentle, she heard the voice of Moshe behind her call her name. "Rachel? Are you there?" The whisper seemed stronger than the final crash against the outer doors that filled the temple hall with the sound of curses and angry voices.

"Moshe? Where are you?"

"Here, Rachel. Behind the grate. The key! You must hurry!" he urged.

Her eyes frantically searched the dark shadows, finally seeing the grid of the grate in a gloomy corner of the room. "Moshe?" she asked one more time as she rushed to the dim beam of light that glowed from the tunnel beyond. His fingers reached through the grid to touch her as she wept and knelt, fumbling to find the lock and insert the key.

Across the room the rattle of the door latch caused Rachel to look away in panic. "The rabbis have come for me!" she cried.

"Open the lock!" Moshe urged her once again. "Quickly, love."

At last the key turned with a grating noise and Moshe forced the rusty hinges open. He clambered from the tunnel, wrapping his arms around her and holding her like he would never let her go.

"Oh, Moshe!" she cried. "Oh, you came, just as you promised."

"Never again will we be apart, my love. Never."

The door of the mikveh flew open with a crash as Moshe held her close in his arms. Two huge black men rushed into the room, followed by Gerhardt, whose eyes fell instantly on Rachel. In a flash Rachel recognized the man who had pursued her through her worst nightmares. She screamed and clung to Moshe.

"The tunnel!" Moshe shouted as Gerhardt cocked his revolver and aimed, pulling off a shot that ricocheted off the rusty grate and blocked their way of escape.

"Halt!" Gerhardt's voice was thick with German accent.

Moshe froze in his tracks and pulled Rachel behind him protectively as he faced this unexpected adversary. He did not speak as he stared defiantly into Gerhardt's sneering face.

"That's right, Juden. Do not move, vermin," Gerhardt threatened as he aimed the barrel of his gun point blank into Moshe's stomach. "Or you are instantly a dead man."

"Let the girl go," Moshe said in an even voice. "She's of no use to you."

Gerhardt laughed suddenly. "The girl? No use to me?" He said incredulously. "No use?"

"You're one of the Mufti's men. I've seen your face before. I'm the one you are after here, not the girl. She is not a political."

"Why, Mr. Sachar, Moshe Sachar, do you think I have come here for *political* reasons?" His face was an animated reflection of madness. "I have come to the Jewish Quarter to pay a social call. Like you, eh? Like any young officer in the service of his country." He raised his voice and called to Rachel who stood completely shielded by Moshe's frame. "Surely you remember, girl! All the handsome young officers—strong and tall in the service of the Führer? Strong hungry bodies, every one of them. Seeking some relief from the endless chore of killing. And I was among them. What pleasure you gave us! We spoke often of the Jewish whore when we were in the barracks and the canteen after."

Rachel groaned audibly and sagged heavily against Moshe's back as he stiffened at Gerhardt's words. "No!"

310

Moshe shouted, suddenly realizing that he was dealing with a madman. "Let her go. She is going to be my wife. She is not the woman you say she is."

Gerhardt chuckled and spoke over Moshe. "You see, whore, I have carried you captive in my mind. I have not forgotten. It is the will of Allah that I have found you. I killed for you. You are mine by right of combat. You are for *me*!" He stepped forward toward Moshe, who pulled Rachel tighter against his back. Her tears dampened his jacket as terror flooded her and her shame was recounted before Moshe.

Gerhardt motioned with the barrel of his gun. "The girl. Let me see her face, please," he asked as though buying a horse.

"Don't move, Rachel," Moshe whispered.

"Yes, girl. Yes, whore, *move*! Or this man will die so that I can see you, eh? I have killed for you before. I will kill again."

Rachel attempted to step back from Moshe. "Don't do it!" he commanded her.

"Come into the light now or I drop your protector where he stands. This time I have a gun. I need not use my hands as I did before."

Rachel tore herself free from Moshe's iron grip and stepped forward and away from him. "Rachel!" he shouted, reaching for her. He was stopped by the dull black barrel of a gun against the side of his face as Gerhardt lurched forward.

"She would not like you so much with half a head, Juden!" Gerhardt slammed the gun butt against Moshe's head, knocking him to the ground.

Rachel cried out and rushed toward him as Gerhardt stepped between them and grabbed her tightly by the throat. His lips curved in a snarl as he held her face in the light, then shoved her back against a pillar. He laughed again, looking down at Moshe, who was rubbing his cheek and shaking his head in an attempt to clear the effects of the blow. "Your wife, eh, Juden? Poor fellow. I am sorry to tell you she has been unfaithful to you!"

"Stop!" Rachel cried out. Then she covered her face with her hands and sobbed quietly. "Please stop."

"Oh yes. She has been tragically faithless. The finest whore in the Führer's service. After all, what man wouldn't rather kill for her than for the Fatherland?"

Moshe's eyes burned with fury as he glared at the raving psychopath before him. "Leave her alone," his voice low and menacing.

"You see," Gerhardt said, turning to the guards. "He is aroused by such talk! Even this righteous Jew is captive of his lust for this woman." The guards grinned in lewd agreement. "Come here," he crooned to Rachel. "So that my men can appreciate you as well."

Anger flashed across Rachel's face as she lifted her chin defiantly and wiped her tears.

"Rachel, don't!"

"You are becoming a bother, Jew! One more word and I will kill you. Then I will have her anyway."

Terrified for Moshe's safety, Rachel stepped forward toward Gerhardt. His eyes devoured her.

"Rachel!" Moshe shouted. "Go no farther!"

"Yes, whore. Farther." Then Gerhardt turned to the black guards that flanked him. "She is beautiful, no?"

"The good commander Gerhardt has a fine eye for a woman," agreed the largest of the two bodyguards as his eyes narrowed and his mouth spread in a lecherous grin.

"You like her?" Gerhardt reached out and touched her throat with the barrel of his gun. "Perhaps when I tire of her I will share, eh?"

Unable to contain his fury, Moshe gave a strangled cry of rage and jumped toward Gerhardt.

"Get him!" shouted Gerhardt; the bodyguards lunged forward and tackled Moshe. He fought against their massive strength, matching blow for blow.

"Run, Rachel!" he shouted.

"Moshe!" She cried as he fell beneath them. His elbows were pulled back in a hammerlock and he cried with the pain in his newly healed arm.

"I told you to come to me!" Gerhardt screamed at Rachel. He raised his fist and struck her hard against the cheek. Still Moshe fought against the hold of the enraged giants who brought him, finally, to his knees.

"Please do not hurt him!" she begged softly. "Please."

"And what will you do for me, a great captain of the Mufti, if I let my enemy go free?"

"Anything. I will do anything you wish. Only do not harm him," she sobbed.

"Don't!" Moshe gasped. "He intends to kill me anyway."

Gerhardt jerked his head and the largest of the guards slapped Moshe across the face. Grabbing Rachel by her hair, Gerhardt lifted her up, pulling her tight against him, his breath hot on her face. "You see, whore. This is the end of your love notes, eh?" he sneered. "He cannot help you escape the brothel. This is the end of him."

"No!" she cried.

"Unless, of course, you do exactly as I say. Then perhaps I will be merciful." He jerked her hair harder still and nodded to the largest of the Sudanese, who instantly kicked Moshe in the stomach.

"Please!" she begged as he doubled over. "Yes! I will do anything!"

Still Gerhardt held her, twisting her face around until she could clearly see Moshe as he fell beneath a fist slammed hard in the back near the kidneys. "Now they only play with him. Soon I will give the order; if it is my will, he will die. Like a cockroach beneath my boot. Of course, if you can convince me otherwise . . ."

Moshe choked and fought to regain his breath, struggling to remain conscious. "Rachel!" he pleaded.

"I will do whatever you ask! Only please, do not hurt him!"

Gerhardt leered at her. "Anything?"

313

She nodded wearily, then looked past him. Beyond the door of the mikveh, the hall of the synagogue flashed with the eerie light of the angry heavens. Thunder boomed and shook the walls and the windows as Gerhardt still grasping Rachel, touched his gun to the top button of her blouse.

"Then we shall start here," he announced.

Rachel broke for an instant; then, putting her hand to her face, she brushed away the tears that trickled down her cheeks. She moved to obey.

"No, Rachel!" Moshe struggled against his captors. "Run!"

Rachel remained rooted where she stood, her eyes now intent on the dancing lights in the temple. A familiar numbness crept over her, the resignation of emotionless submission to the inevitable. She absently fingered the button, then unbuttoned it.

Gerhardt laughed. "Very good," he rasped out. "Now unbutton the rest and remove the blouse."

Slowly, her trembling fingers moved to obey. Her gaze never left the great hall even when Moshe cried out in anguish for her. She dropped the garment to the floor, her pale, slender shoulders stooped in grief and resignation at the ritual she had performed so many times before. Her plain cotton camisole covered her. Gerhardt's cruel smile faded and he growled impatiently, then lunged to tear the delicate fabric from her.

Like an enraged lion, Moshe lashed out against the guards. "Rachel!" he cried. "Run!"

Rachel struck Gerhardt hard in the face as he clutched at her, wrestling her to the floor. Moshe's cries drove her to fight against her attacker with new energy as he tore at her clothes.

"NO!" she screamed as his brute strength overpowered her and he pinned her arms against the cold stones.

Gerhardt laughed again. "She fights!" he mocked. "See how this little Jewess fights for her honor! Well, this should make it all the more interesting."

"Let her go!" Moshe shouted.

Cruel laughter answered as Gerhardt tried to kiss her.

"Please!" she begged, her desperate resolve vanishing into tears. "Please, God. God, help me!" she sobbed softly.

"God?" asked Gerhardt, amused. "The ears of heaven were shut to you long ago."

Suddenly the thunder of the storm roared again and the great hall of the synagogue was filled with the sound of other voices and the slap of running feet.

"Where is she?" cried a young voice.

"Help me!" Rachel screamed, her voice cut off by Gerhardt's hand.

"Rachel!" boomed the voice of Ehud as he ran across the hall toward the open door.

Gerhardt jumped to his feet and dashed to the heavy door of the mikveh. "Let the Jew go!" he shouted to his companions. With a final boot to Moshe's stomach, they abandoned him and rushed to Gerhardt's aid. Slamming the door and sliding the bolts shut, they dragged heavy wooden benches against it as the thump of shoulders threatened the hinges. Gerhardt cocked his revolver and fired three times through the door. A sharp cry echoed from outside as Gerhardt issued the warning, "We have the woman here. If you fire she will die first!"

He turned back to where Rachel had fallen. "Gone!" whispered the smaller Sudanese. "Through that opening!"

Cursing, Gerhardt rushed around the pool toward the grate just as Moshe locked it behind him and pulled Rachel down a low-roofed shaft toward the stumps of a worm-eaten ladder. Behind them another gunshot rang out as Gerhardt blasted away the lock and the larger bodyguard tore the grate from its hinges.

"Hurry! Down the ladder!" Moshe whispered as the sound of scrambling feet entered the tunnel behind them. Quickly, he gave her his jacket, but still she shivered from her ordeal.

Darkness encircled Rachel as Moshe stepped onto the rotten rungs ahead of her and guided her feet. Too frightened to speak, she followed, grateful for her narrow escape and for the adrenal energy stimulated by her fear.

"Watch out!" Gerhardt's voice echoed after them. "Give me the light! Give it to me!" he shrieked.

As they climbed downward into the oppressive blackness of the hole, Rachel glanced up to the top of the ladder. A dim light moved closer to the opening from the tunnel. Poised above the rungs of the ladder she glimpsed the silhouettes of three crouched creatures, rustling after them like trolls in an evil cave from a childhood story she had once heard.

She hesitated an instant as a shudder coursed through her. Moshe's gentle tugging guided her foot onto the next rung down. Rachel gulped, then followed in silence as Gerhardt raged in fury at the warriors who studied the decrepit top rung with concern. A full fifty steps downward Moshe guided her, pressing himself against the back of her legs as he protected her from tumbling to a depth she could only imagine in the darkness.

A faint beam of light struggled down from above as Gerhardt tried to see the bottom of the ladder and its condition. Moshe leaned hard against Rachel, pushing her beneath the shadows of the rungs. She did not dare to breathe as the feeble beam brushed inches from her head.

"They have fallen, I tell you!" protested the thick voice of a bodyguard.

"Ha! This Jew has escaped with a woman on his back because you are cowards! Cowards! You will follow now or your own bones will lie at the bottom of this pit!"

A tense moment of silence followed. The ladder groaned as the weight of the first guard stepped down.

Moshe tapped Rachel lightly and began his slow descent once again. Tears of panic filled her eyes. *The cattle cars. Do not think of their blackness, their closeness. Remember the blue sky by the river where you used to picnic with Mama. Do not cry out. Will your hands and legs to move. Command your eyes to close against the blackness.*

"Schnell, Juden!" Gerhardt screamed above them. "You will not escape!"

Rachel's heart beat faster at the cry. *Schnell, Juden! They rammed the old with the butts of their guns. The young they trampled underfoot. And those who ran . . .* The memory caused her hands to clutch the splintered wood of the ladder. Moshe pulled her skirt and then her foot when she still did not move. The terror within was greater than the terror that descended above her. *Machine guns in guard towers. Dead bodies frozen in mine fields and against coils of barbed wire. Those captured alive hung for days in the courtyard. We cannot escape.*

"Run and you will die!" Gerhardt's voice exploded into her thoughts. "You cannot run so far that I will not find you."

Desperate to get her moving and daring at last to whisper, Moshe simply said, "Come, Rachel. Come with me." His voice was urgent but kind.

Rachel shook herself to reality, glancing up at the heavy boots that threatened to crush her one final time. Breathing deeply, she stepped to the next rung.

At last they touched ground. Gerhardt and his men still struggled forty feet above them. Every few feet, rungs moaned and broke and the shaft was filled with dust of centuries and shouts of fear. Moshe pulled Rachel into the small tunnel, only high enough to allow them to pass through on all fours.

"The darkness," Rachel whispered.

"I know the way," Moshe answered, reaching back to take her hand. He did not dare use the light in the oblivion of this unnatural night. Only the faintest glimmer would lead Gerhardt to them.

Ever downward they groped in the darkness, moving as quickly as they could in the awkward confines of the tunnel. Rachel desperately stayed as close behind Moshe as possible, strangely convinced that somehow she had gone blind and he was leading her through a brightly lit pathway. *Surely he can see something in this black grave.* Twice she bumped into the tunnel wall, and the second time Moshe unknowingly grasped the wound on her arm, it caused her to cry out. Then the shouts of Gerhardt and his men quickened and pursued them as Moshe rammed ahead.

"We will find you, Juden! You cannot escape us!" Voices seemed to encircle Rachel.

At last he whispered urgently, "Here! Duck your head!" Feeling the smooth stones of an archway above her, she passed Moshe and ducked through it, forcing herself through a tiny opening. Moshe followed, then pulled her to her feet. He pressed the cold metal cylinder of a flashlight from his belt into her hand. "Take it." He turned her away from him. "From here you must go on alone."

"Please, no!"

There was no time for argument. "There is a heap of rubble in front of you. Climb down and stay in the center. That alone is safe. There is a pillar. It crosses a chasm, and then you must find a place to hide. Inside the cavern—it is huge. Hide. Turn out the light. No matter what you hear, do not turn the light on again. If anything happens to me, do not move. Do not cry out! Ehud and the others will surely come. They will find you!"

"Please!" she begged softly.

Moshe switched on the light and searched her face with a look that said more than words. *I love you always. I wish we had time. I love you.* "Now *go!*" He pushed her toward the path that led to the pillar.

Sliding downward, she turned to see Moshe poised and ready to spring when Gerhardt and his lackeys emerged through the arch. Her heart longed for his eyes to meet hers, but he did not look up; instead, he watched the archway intently. She shone the light ahead of her over fallen stones, the broken remains of an ancient grandeur that had once sparkled in the sun. The voice of Gerhardt grew stronger in the tunnel.

"A light!" came the triumphant cry. "There is a light ahead!"

Her heart jumped to her throat and she slid quickly down to the bottom of the rubble, skinning her knees. But she felt no pain and ran the final twenty-five feet to where the broken pillar lay across the gulf of blackness. *No matter how deep it is,* she thought, climbing onto the slick green surface. *A hundred feet or a thousand, you will die if you fall.* She straddled the pillar and scooted toward the other side. At last she stood on the opposite side of the chasm. She turned and winked out her light as the glow from Gerhardt's lantern bobbed nearer the archway opening where Moshe waited for the first of Gerhardt's men to climb out into his ambush.

Hide! he had told her. But she could not move from the spot where she watched. She had to know. Had to see what would become of Moshe. Where was her hope if he were killed, and what kind of life could even Ehud rescue her for if there was no Moshe in it? Suddenly the small, helpless face of baby Tikvah filled her mind. The trusting, innocent hand that encircled her thumb; the soft, contented sighs when Rachel sang to her. *You must live!* her heart cried out. *No matter what happens, you must live!*

She turned away and quickly groped her way ahead as Moshe had instructed her. Soon she felt the archway opening into the huge dome of a rubble-strewn cavern. The air felt cold, as though she had entered the remains of some great banquet hall in an ancient castle. *Hide where?* She flicked on the light. The ceiling stretched up thirty feet and the width of the cavern seemed endless in the shadows. Enormous stone blocks littered the floor. Cluttered archways filled with debris marked where once doors had opened into the streets of the Holy City. Rachel circled around and around in panic.

Dear God, show me where to hide! she prayed silently. Then a small alcove seemed to beckon. Half hidden behind the broken capitals of an ancient pillar, its obscure darkness all at once seemed to be the only safe place inside the vast cavern. She ran to it and shrank down in a crevice between the wall and the pillar, then switched off the light and listened as the shouts and cries beyond the chasm filled her with dread for Moshe.

Waiting until the second of the bodyguards crawled through the narrow opening, Moshe leaped with the force of a lion from a cliff. The guard tumbled down the loose rocks to the left of the pathway, pulling Moshe with him to the very edge of the pit.

Not waiting to see the outcome of their struggle, Gerhardt stared across the gulf to where Rachel's light had flickered, then gone out.

"She has gone ahead!" he cried victoriously. "This way! Across the pillar." He paused for a moment to watch as the larger of the Sudanese grasped Moshe by the throat and shoved him nearer the brink of the abyss. "Kill him!" he shouted. Then he grasped the second guard by the arm and pulled him toward the rubble slide and the pillar. "She runs this direction! Hurry, fool!"

They both slid down and Gerhardt shoved the guard ahead of him onto the surface of the slippery bridge. Gerhardt was a man trained in the ways of a Nazi Commando. The obstacle was nothing to him, and he moved across it with the confidence of a man unafraid of death. But his companion was less steady, less self-assured, and only Gerhardt's curses spurred him on. The guard glanced back nervously to where his compatriot struggled with Moshe, pushing him nearer to his death.

"Never mind him!" Gerhardt shrieked. "The girl! We want the girl!" In his fury, he shoved the guard so hard his foot slipped from the edge of the pillar. Screaming in despair, he fell to his knees on the unstable bridge. The lamp tumbled from his grasp and spun away, falling until the light was seen no more. Enraged, Gerhardt kicked out at the helpless guard, sending him to spin after the light to the bottom of the shaft.

Undaunted by the falling guard's cries, Gerhardt perched on the pillar and pulled a gold cigarette lighter from his pocket. He opened it and lit it, holding the tiny flame high above him as he completed walking the span. "Finish the Jew!" he yelled back as Moshe was shoved nearer the edge of the black hole. "Then follow me! She has gone this way!"

The weight of the Sudanese moved Moshe's head and shoulders over the brink of the pit. The cries of the falling guard filled his ears as he fought against his massive adversary. Light flickered, then blinked out as Gerhardt passed into the cavern in pursuit of Rachel. Suddenly there was nothing left of the earth but the small hard patch of stone beneath Moshe's back and legs. Repeatedly he tried to kick his legs up and encircle the heavy body of the giant who held him. Their sweat mingled as they fought to live and fought to kill.

A shrill scream pierced the darkness behind Gerhardt as he stood in the entrance of the cavern. "He is dead!" Gerhardt called to Rachel as the resounding cry faded. *Dead dead dead!* Gerhardt's cruel words returned to batter Rachel. "Come out and you will live!" *Live live live live!* beat themselves into her brain. "Your lover has died, I say! He lies at the bottom of the pit!" *Pit pit pit pit!* "Come out! This is useless!" *Useless useless useless!*

Stifling a sob, Rachel covered her ears and hugged the cold stone next to her. *Remember Tikvah! But Moshe is dead! Why live if he is gone? O, Moshe!* Her heart screamed in a whisper.

Gerhardt's boots crunched on the gravel as he walked deliberately across the floor of the cavern to its center.

"You see, woman," Gerhardt crooned, pausing to flick his lighter when the flame died. "There is no one to help you!" *Help you help you!* "No more hope! Come out!" *Come out come out come out!*

His shadow loomed high among the vaults and passed over the hidden alcove where Rachel, not daring to breathe, crouched. Rachel let out an involuntary gasp and drew back from the entrance.

Suddenly the alcove behind her was filled with the scurry and shrieks of fleeing rats who tumbled from the darkness and swarmed over and around Rachel. Involuntarily Rachel gasped out as she beat them away from her.

Gerhardt threw his head back and laughed as the creatures emerged and fanned out across the heaps of rubble. He aimed his lighter and the revolver at the crown of the arch above Rachel's head and squeezed the trigger. The blast seemed to shake the stones of the arch and fragments of gravel rained down on her head and shoulders. Gerhardt laughed again and a thousand echoes assaulted her. "Of course." His voice was low and menacing as he closed in on his quarry. "You are in the alcove, eh?"

Fear and rage gripping her like a vice, she shouted, "You and your kind are animals!" Her defiant voice filled the chamber. "I can die now." *Die now die now die now*, the echo sobbed. "But you will never have me alive!" *Alive alive alive!* "Never again!" *Again again again!*

Like a predator in the forest, Gerhardt raised his head as the last whisper faded away. His eyes bored through the shadows. "You cannot hide, woman!" His words cut into her heart. "You will live." *Live live live.* "As before!" *Before before before!* "For the pleasure of an officer—for *my* pleasure!" *Pleasure pleasure pleasure.*

Rachel covered her face with her hands and leaned heavily against the stones as his footsteps sounded nearer and nearer. Suddenly, from the grim blackness behind her, large, sticky hands reached out and encircled her face and mouth, stifling her scream as she was pulled backward against a sinewy body.

"Shhh," whispered a barely audible voice. "Don't speak. It's *me*, Miss Lubetkin. Luke Thomas." As quickly as he had appeared, Luke released her and slid back into the shadows. Gerhardt's footsteps closed nearer and nearer, now a mere ten feet away, moving deliberately behind the stone where she huddled. His revolver was drawn, cocked and ready. The lighter flickered in a hand held high above his head. As he stepped into the alcove, Rachel could see his face contorted with the diabolical satisfaction that he had indeed triumphed. She stared steadily back into his eyes, her own face a mask of determination. He smiled and stopped a mere three feet from where she huddled. Rage glinted in his eyes. "But you have been trouble. Perhaps more trouble than you are worth. That remains to be seen. Come out, whore."

Rachel remained wedged between the stones. "I said come out!" He lunged in her direction. Weak and still stunned from his fall, Luke sprang from the darkness, throwing the weight of his body full force against him. The light spun from Gerhardt's hand and the revolver clattered to the stones.

"Run, Rachel!" cried Luke. "Run!" he yelled as he and Gerhardt fell to the floor.

Rachel pulled Moshe's flashlight from her waistband and switched it on, turning its beam on the duel like a spotlight on center stage. Gerhardt sat astride the captain pummeling his face. Futilely Rachel searched for the revolver, her last hope. Filled with new resolve, she grasped a large stone in her hands and, dropping the light, crashed the weapon down hard on the back of Gerhardt's head.

He gave a garbled cry, then, leaving the unconscious captain, he turned on her; his murderous rage reawakened. Rachel grabbed her flashlight and fled in terror toward the archway that led to the pillar and the chasm. If there was no hope, no breath of hope, she resolved to die with Moshe.

Faster she ran, her eyes intent on the archway. His

heavy feet slapped after her; his curses echoed around her. *Only a few more yards and I am safe forever. Only a moment and no one will be able to hurt me ever again. Tikvah! Moshe! Gone forever! I will not be taken again!*

Then the pillar loomed before her, and another voice pierced the twilight. "Leave her alone!" Moshe cried as he leaped from the pillar and charged Gerhardt, toppling him where he stood. Over and over they rolled across the ground as fists crashed against hard flesh and bone.

"Moshe!" Rachel cried, still too frightened to really believe he was not dead. "Oh, Moshe!"

Moshe straddled Gerhardt's chest, pinning him to the floor. Grasping his hair in his hands, Moshe smashed the brutal murderer's head against the stones. Finally Gerhardt lay still.

Breathless from his effort, Moshe sat up, unwilling to move until he knew there was no more fight in the monster beneath him.

"Are you all right?" he asked at last.

"Yes," Rachel said in a small voice. "I think so."

"Moshe, old chap!" a groggy voice called across the cavern. "Sorry I wasn't of more help, old man."

Moshe closed his eyes in joyous disbelief at the sound of Luke's voice. "A voice from the grave," he whispered. Then he raised his voice and called jovially. "I could have used you back there! Fell over the edge and hung there till I could manage to pull myself up. The other fellow wasn't so lucky."

"When I came to, you were quite gone," Luke explained. "I picked up the pack. Fortunately there was another torch. Then I stumbled down another tunnel at the bottom of the shaft. Came out right there." He pointed, "behind where Miss Lubetkin was hiding."

Suddenly shaky, Rachel collapsed to the floor and held her head in her hands. "Oh, Moshe!" she cried. "I can't believe it's really you!"

He stood and moved slowly toward her. Taking her hand, he lifted her easily, enfolding her in his arms. "You are not dreaming, my love. I am here."

32   Resurrection

Dawn paled the sky, outlining the guards on the roof protecting the quarter as Moshe sat on the steps outside Leah and Shimon's apartment and listened to Ehud.

"And so when those black-hearted black coats came to take the baby, I threw them down the stairs! Yes! These very stairs where we are sitting now. And some of the women who have known Rachel became very angry at these rabbis and they came to see what they might do to help such a good and kindhearted daughter of Zion as your Rachel. But Rachel was not here, so Shoshanna Cohen stayed with the baby, and I went then to the apartment of Rachel's grandfather. I found the door broken and the inside torn to pieces and that jackal of a dog lying there like one who is dead. Then I found the note. Dov came to me then with news of the two dead guards. Poor boys. They had little chance. So I gathered the others and we came to the synagogue. From up the street I heard what sounded like a gunshot, but others thought it was a crack of thunder." Ehud paused for a breath. "We did not come in time to be of much help."

"Enough though," Moshe rubbed his chin and frowned thoughtfully up at the clear pastel sky. "You drew their attention away long enough for us to get away. God guided you, Ehud. And us."

"Omaine!" Ehud exclaimed. "And Captain Thomas as well, I think. I never believed I might have good to speak of a Gentile, but oy! this man is a *gonster macher*, nu? I am glad he is on our side."

"He must be back in the New City by now." Moshe gazed toward the wall. "God bless him. He'll have a time explaining the condition of his face to the C.O. I'm sure his nose was broken at the very least. And his eyes! Almost swollen shut."

"You are no beauty queen yourself," Ehud noted, scanning Moshe's bruised face. "Those Arabs! Gerhardt especially, nu?" He lowered his voice and put his fingers to his lips as a sign against the evil eye. "A *dybbuk* dwells in his flesh! An evil spirit! Else how could he escape once you knocked him out and bashed his head?"

"I helped Rachel and Luke across the chasm ..." Moshe shook his head angrily. "Then I took a rope from Luke's pack and went back to bind Gerhardt until we could come back to fetch him, but he was gone. I came off the end of the pillar and he had vanished."

"You see! A *dybbuk*! Our men have searched and searched but—"

"He won't come out of that maze alive, Ehud. I had a map, and we almost didn't make it," he said grimly. "Dov and Elihu and Vultch have blown up the pillar, and the passage is closed, at any rate. We will keep Rachel here. If I am not with her, then someone will have to stay here as bodyguard."

"*Someone*!" Ehud exploded. "Can it be anyone but me?"

Moshe studied him for a moment through his half-closed eye. "No, my friend. If love and sheer strength mean anything—"

"Indeed!" boomed Ehud. "When Rachel fainted, it was I who carried her here, nu? With you following after like a pup! I will help you, my friend. Never fear." He gazed silently up at the door. "It is taking a long time. I hope all is well with her, poor child. She has been through so much, nu?"

Moshe nodded and exhaled slowly at the thought of how very alone Rachel must have felt through her ordeal. For the first time since they had arrived at the apartment, Ehud sat in silence beside Moshe. Finally, as long morning shadows melted into the bright gleam of sunlight on the Old City stones, Ehud tugged his beard and said quietly, "I told her that you loved her."

Moshe raised his eyebrows and stared at the damp cobblestones below them. "And what did she say?"

"She would not hear it. Could not believe it."

"I should have told here myself. I never should have let her come here alone. I was almost too late. Almost."

"But you were not. She is safe now." Ehud thumped Moshe on the back. "And if she had not come, where would little Tikvah be, eh? Crammed into a corner of the orphans' home. Rachel loves that little one as if she were her own. That is something old Akiva never thought about. Upon my soul, he is nothing but a blind beggar crying, *I see! I see!* He sees nothing but what makes him look better in his own eyes."

Moshe smiled at Ehud's staunch defense of Rachel and her right to keep the child. "I was wrong, Ehud. God did not leave her alone here. You have been a good friend. To her. To me, I thank you."

Embarrassed, Ehud's weather-creased face flushed a bit and he shifted on the steps, then stared at his hands. "It wasn't just me, you know. We . . . all of us are a bit in love with her. She is an easy person to love, eh? Only it is such a shame she does not know that about herself. She thinks her life is of no value. It does not take a wise man to know this about her." He looked sideways at Moshe, whose brow was furrowed with a frown.

"No value," Moshe said in quiet astonishment. "And I love her as though there were no one else on this earth. How can I tell her, Ehud? How can I even begin?"

"Well," Ehud scratched his beard thoughtfully. "You are here. Maybe that is enough, eh?"

The apartment door opened and Shoshanna poked her wizened face out into the cold morning air. "She will see you now, Moshe." Ehud jumped up and started up the steps. "Not you! She will see Moshe Sachar alone, please!"

Moshe bounded up the steps two at a time, then hesitated on the top step and tried to straighten his disheveled, unwashed hair before he entered.

"Oy! Such a smell!" proclaimed Shoshanna as he stepped around her and stood in the center of the room. "Don't touch the baby!" she commanded.

Lying beneath a blue down comforter, Rachel looked pale but remarkably well in spite of her ordeal. Tikvah slept peacefully beside her, with Rachel's long-sleeved arm cradled around her and her index finger tucked inside the baby's tiny fist. Rachel seemed suddenly shy at the sight of Moshe. Releasing Tikvah's hand, she tugged the comforter higher around her chin and looked down at the baby while Moshe stood self-consciously searching for the right words to say.

"I'll take that meshuggener of a seaman some coffee," said Shoshanna, slipping out the door with a steaming cup in her hand.

The door clicked shut behind her, leaving Moshe and Rachel alone. Still Moshe hesitated, though the sight of Rachel made him want to wrap his arms around her, lay his face against hers, and drink in the sweet fragrance of her skin. He shrugged. "I am glad to see you awake."

"I am glad to see you alive," she answered, allowing her eyes to meet his at last. Quickly she looked away, afraid of the depth of emotion his gaze returned to her.

"Rachel, I—" he began, stepping forward, then stopping again.

"This is my baby," Rachel said quickly, straightening the blankets around Tikvah. "Did Ehud tell you about her? And about Leah? Surely he did. He tells everyone everything he knows." She glanced up again, and this time the unmistakable yearning in his eyes held her. She fought for words as a tender warmth filled her and her cheeks flushed red. "She is a beautiful baby. You see? Come closer."

Still Moshe hesitated. "I know I probably must—"

"What is it, Moshe?" she asked, uncertainty filling her face. She looked away, afraid that he would tell her that the words he had written had all been a mistake, that what she had seen in his eyes was only a delusion.

"I probably . . . Shoshanna said that I . . . smell badly." He rubbed his hand through his hair in an attempt to comb it again. "I washed my hands and face but I'm afraid I . . ."

Rachel laughed and held her arms out to him, the shyness suddenly vanishing. "Oh, Moshe!" she cried. "I thought I was dreaming. But you have really come. It's really you!"

Moshe rushed to her side, knelt beside the bed and buried his face in the nape of her soft neck. "My love," he whispered. "My only sweet Rachel."

She cradled his head in her arms, hot tears of relief flowing down her cheeks at the sincerity of his love and her own unworthiness. "I don't deserve your love, Moshe, I don't. You are too good. You know what I am, what I have done, and still you care for me. It is not proper for you to love me, and though I know I should not love you either, and that a woman like me can never love, still I cannot help myself. I cannot help but love you and wish never to be apart from you!"

Moshe raised his eyes and touched her cheek softly. "I feel all your pain, my love! *All!* And if I could I would bear it for you! When first I loved you, Rachel, I thought then that I knew a little bit how much God must love His bride, Israel. She has been through so much, been misused and hated, and still God has sent his Holy One to rescue and redeem her. To die for her. And so, God has knit my heart to yours, and I would die before I would let anyone harm you ever again. Do you believe that, my love?"

"I hear your words. I know that you are here and that you risked your life for my sake. But I do not understand how you can love me." Her face clouded and she turned away from him. "When I look into the mirror, I see only pieces of a person. Only fragments of what I should have been."

Moshe gently placed his fingers beneath her chin and looked straight into her vivid blue eyes. "I want you to look at me, Love, and tell me what you see."

Rachel frowned and searched his face, finally looking deeply into the warmth of his rich brown eyes. A soft smile played on her lips. "When I look into your eyes, Moshe, I see myself," she said in quiet wonder and delight.

"And in this mirror, you are beautiful and whole. I love you, Rachel. I love you," he repeated simply. "Love is the only mirror we must use to judge ourselves and others. And I will tell you this from my deepest heart: your life and happiness are worth the world to me—worth more than my own life. If I, who am only a man, can love you so very much, when you look into the mirror of God's love, Rachel, you will see hope and joy and mercy. You will see how very much He cares for you and values you as His own dear daughter."

Rachel lowered her eyes to her hands, struggling again with the agony of her past. "I wish I could believe that," she said flatly. "Surely you have heard the judgment of the rabbis against me. I am an outcast among my own people."

"Rachel, the people of the quarter have risen up with one voice in their support of you!"

"Yes?"

"Akiva and his band remind me of another story. It is a true story that happened when Jesus walked these very streets so long ago. There was a woman who had sinned and the elders had taken her outside the city to stone her; to put her to death, as the law demanded. These elders hated Jesus, though our people loved Him and followed Him. And so when a crowd came around, the elders asked the Great Rabbi whether He approved of the execution, nu?"

Rachel nodded, her face intense as she thought of the night before when she had fallen to the floor of the synagogue before the rabbis. "He was a righteous man. Did He condemn her?"

Moshe took Rachel's hand in his own. "He knelt and wrote some things in the dirt. I think maybe He was

330

writing down the sins of the men who stood with stones in their hands."

"And then what did He do?"

"He looked up at them and said, '*If you have no sin in your life, then go ahead, you throw the first stone at this woman.*'"

Rachel laughed and squeezed Moshe's hand. "What a clever man He was!"

"He was the only one among them who had no sin, Rachel. He was the only one who could have thrown the stone. So when the men hung their heads in shame and went away, leaving her alone with Him, He stretched out His hand and lifted her up from the dust. And His eyes were her mirror."

"And what did the Rabbi say to her?"

Moshe paused and grinned at the childlike expression on Rachel's face. "You like this story, eh?"

"Yes, Moshe! Please, tell me the rest!"

"Then Jesus asked her, '*Woman, what man accuses you?*' And she answered Him, '*No man accuses me, Lord.*' You see, she realized that the one who stood before her was the Messiah and that He alone could accuse her. But instead, He said, '*Neither do I condemn you. What is done is over with. Go on now, live a new life and sin no more.*'"

Rachel clapped her hands together and sat back against the pillow. "Oh, Moshe! Then this is the one Leah wanted me to tell Tikvah about! How wonderful to have known such a man as this! If only I could have had Him with me at the synagogue last night!"

"He was there with you, my love. His eyes are a mirror of mercy and compassion even now. And He longs for every one of His children to see Him and know Him."

Epilogue

The call of the old muezzin resounded through the city streets beckoning the faithful to morning prayer. Prayer rugs spread out on the damp pavement as men and women faced the east and bowed their foreheads low against the ground.

Far above them, the persistent hum of a tiny plane rattled across the sky toward the Jewish Quarter and the Square Tiferet Yerusalayim.

Moshe shielded his eyes against the glare of the sunny winter sky, and jogged quickly to the center of the courtyard. "David!" He grinned broadly as the nose of the little Piper Cub appeared over the golden Dome of the Rock where thousands now bowed in prayer, irritated, no doubt at the noisy metal insect that buzzed above them.

The wings of the little plane dipped in salute as it passed over, and Moshe stood up on a bench and waved wildly. Then it banked and made a slow turn back toward the square. Suddenly the door of the plane popped open and a large canvas bag was pitched out, floating down gently at the end of a bright blue-and-white parachute. Three times more he passed over the square, which quickly filled with children and curious citizens.

Moshe removed a large envelope from the first parachute. The outside was marked by a big red heart. He laughed at a hastily drawn caricature of the Jihad Moquades in prayer, their faces to the ground and their backsides pointing up toward the little plane and the parachute. The caption read:

The Mufti taught his guys to pray before every

meal—especially if it's kosher food! Tonight on both sides of the wall we raise our glasses to Life! L'Chaim!

Same time, same place tomorrow! David and Ellie.

P.S. I told you we could do it!

If you would like to contact the authors,
you may write to them at the following address:

Bodie and Brock Thoene
P.O. Box 542
Glenbrook, NV 89413